LIVING WITH EARL

BY

TOM LAMBERT

ISBN-13: 978-1502708311

This is a work of fiction. All characters, locations, and events described in this novel are fictitious or are used fictitiously.

Tom Lambert is a semi-retired cabinetmaker and proud father of three grown sons.

This is his debut novel, which places him side by side with Mark Twain (or a convincing impersonator) so they can play pool, laugh, or grumble about politics.

Lambert currently lives in Bowling Green, Ohio, with his wife Beth, a friendly dog, and three rescue cats.

He is in the process of writing a sequel.

Email: livingwithearl@gmail.com

Tom Lambert

To my mother,

And Miss Elizabeth Gelvin

Tom Lambert

Prologue

I have inherited a houseguest. Not a typical houseguest. Not an Army buddy that I haven't seen in 45 years who was "just passin' through". Not a long-lost relative who came for a weekend and never left. Not an obscure school chum looking to renew old ties. Not someone who is destitute and needs a place to stay for a few days. Not an alien from space who dropped into my backyard to observe an earthling before returning to the mother ship. These would be ordinary houseguests, but this visitor is far from any I could ever have imagined.

I call him "Earl", (which I will explain at some point later), but he insists that he's Mark Twain. He dresses exactly like the pictures I have seen of Twain in his sixties. His typical uniform is a white suit with vest, white shirt, a cravat-style tie, and black shoes. A white Panama hat completes his ensemble. For added authenticity, he most times has a cheroot cigar held tightly in the corner of his mouth.

After careful examination, I am convinced that he poses no threat to anyone by living so persuasively inside of the occasionally charming, but always captivating, character of Mark Twain. When he first arrived I suspiciously speculated on possible motives for becoming someone whom I suspected was far removed from his own persona. After sitting, eating, laughing, and talking with him for hours on end I am certain he is harmless. Regardless of his intentions, he is unwavering in his personification of Mark Twain, and he avoids any explanation as to how Twain might have ended up here in the twenty-first century. For the moment, I have stopped any observable investigation about his true identity or motives even though my curiosity to know "everything" is lying in wait.

Faux News

In the living room after dinner I mistakenly turned on the wrong TV news channel, (I use the term "News" very loosely). Earl was sitting in the large, black leather chair with the local newspaper in his lap keenly watching.

…"After closely reviewing the birth certificate that stated that President Obama **was** born in Hawaii we here at Fox News still have doubts about whether he was actually born in the United States. We will continue to monitor this issue and report any further developments," so said the stuffed-shirt anchor in front of the tacky studio set, which looked more like the public access channel on "Wayne's World" from 'Saturday Night Live' than that of a professional network news organization.

While obviously pondering the blubbering, overly tanned talking head on Fox News spouting his ignorant bias, Earl bites down on an unlit cigar. After several mock puffs, (it's been mandated that he not smoke in the house), he looks off through the imagined thick white cloud and says:

"Get your facts first, and then you can distort them as much as you please."
~Mark Twain~

Right is sometimes wrong

Earl and I were discussing political parties and how some in America are pretty snobbish in how they view the rest of the world's races and cultures. At the end of our conversation and with a loud exasperated exhale Earl said:

"Travel is fatal to prejudice, bigotry and narrow-mindedness, and many of our people need it sorely on these accounts. Broad, wholesome, charitable views of men and things cannot be acquired by vegetating in one little corner of the earth all of one's lifetime." ~Mark Twain~

Senseless

We are having morning coffee in the living room today. The cats have found a ray of light and are sprawled on the floor soaking up its warmth. Earl and I are reading the local newspaper, he the front section and I the second. There is silence except for the intermittent sound of a spoon rattling on a saucer or the slow turn of a page. Behind the open paper there is an occasional sigh or grunt from Earl's obvious incredulity by the news of the day.

He lowered the paper onto his lap and exasperatingly asks, "Are all people crazy Tom, or just the ones in this part of the country? There seems to be a lot of shooting going on in Toledo between people who don't even know each other. People that have never even had words between each other...good or bad are now shooting each other."

"I am reading here where a boy (a good student) was riding his bicycle home after work when some other boys rode up in a car and shot and killed him. It wasn't a fight that escalated; it was an execution of an innocent person who most likely was the only one involved who was trying to better himself. These crimes are so meaningless. Black kids are killing each other and for what, territory wars? It seems to me that they all ought to be working together to make their neighborhoods more unified, and a better and safer place to live. One gang member will shoot someone and then that victim's friends will go into the other's neighborhood and shoot someone. Where does it stop? What a waste of young people who already have a tough enough row to hoe. I just cannot understand how kids can work up so much anger and direct it at total strangers."

Earl raised his paper and after a long sigh he slowly started reading again. I sat quietly without a worthy response; frequently similar stories provoke deep empathy in me, but never any valuable solutions. I was envisioning someone's promising son lying in the street dead because some thug wanted to prove something. After a several-second pause Earl said very matter-of-factly:

"Truth is stranger than fiction, but it is because Fiction is obliged to stick to possibilities; Truth isn't." ~Mark Twain~

Great Advice, useless, but Great.

Last night I shared with Earl how losing a great job that I enjoyed and that paid well and then trying to find any job just in order to live is degrading, though humbling. To be over 60 and be looking for work in a limited job market is a scary thing.

Of course, since Samuel Clemens was self-employed for most of his life, Earl had many things to say about working for others, e.g. "Editors are like slave masters, but they don't use the same size whip; "they can take all of your time, but none of your mind"; or my least favorite, "Jobs are like riverboats...if you miss one, another will be along soon."

In my state of quiet anxiety there was only one tidbit that he offered that didn't annoy me, actually made sense, and gave me hope:

"Courage is resistance to fear, mastery of fear - not absence of fear." ~MT~

Recognizing Futility

The swearing quickly subsided this morning after seeing yet another snowfall, but with our ire and dislike already at the forefront, we sidestepped one obvious frustration and engaged each other in another, politics.

We both had much to say about the inability of Congress to accomplish anything other than to prove that none of them is capable of truly representing us. Our frustration about the elected leadership in Washington was analogous to the control we have over the weather.

I have found that if I ever want to see the veins in Earl's forehead protrude I just need to say the word 'Washington'.

He immediately got up from his chair. Grabbing his lapel with his left hand, and looking towards the living room curtains as if addressing an audience filled room he said loudly:

"Sometimes I wonder whether the world is being run by smart people who are putting us on or by imbeciles who really mean it." ~MT~

Smarter with Age

Yesterday, for some reason, I spent a good portion of my time fondly talking about my three sons. I told Earl of the many things we'd done together when they were kids and how our individual relationships have changed as they've become grown men.

When they were kids I guided them through many pitfalls of life that one would think cemented me into their hearts forever, but they never seemed to grasp that at the time. Today they respect me for my sincere counsel and occasional wise advice. Earl took a long draw on his cigar and as the last stream of smoke left him he said,

"When I was a boy of fourteen, my father was so ignorant I could hardly stand to have the old man around. But when I got to be twenty-one, I was astonished at how much he had learned in seven years." ~MT~

The Guest's Guest

I got up this morning to get ready for work and nearly tripped over a trail of clothes from the front door leading to Earl's bedroom, and they were not all gentlemen's apparel. Picking them up piece by piece and working my way towards Earl's door I could smell the cigar smoke and the unmistakable odor of Howard's Club H emanating from the garments.

As I reached down to pick up a rather frilly pair of undies, Earl quietly opened his door to see me stooped over with a pile of incriminating evidence in my hand. He was standing in the dimly lit doorway with a sheet wrapped around him. The faint light from the hall discreetly revealed a shadowy nude figure lying face down and fast asleep on his bed.

He glanced down at the pile of clothes, and then he looked up with a wry smile. His mustache and hair looked as if they had seen some serious 'wrestling,' Out of the smell of bourbon-soaked cigar smoke wafting from his breath and lady's perfume emanating from the clothes in my hands, he raised his eyebrows and looked nervously left and right, then, as if he was worried that he might be overheard by non-existent bystanders, he whispered the words:

"A sin takes on new and real terrors when there seems a chance that it is going to be found out." ~MT~

Earl reached up to smooth his disheveled hair and I mistook that as an invitation for mutual celebration, and I gave him a hard high five. I laid the pile of clothes inside his room on the floor and as I closed his bedroom door, Earl was still standing there staring at his hand.

A 600 Pound Gorilla in the room

All day yesterday, Earl and I made small talk about everything but the fact that he brought a woman home from a downtown 'saloon'. After talking about

the weather, sports, and our possible dinner menu,   Earl finally said. "I sense that you are upset with me."

I explained I wasn't angry, but it is my house and he could have been a little more respectful by eliminating the trail of clothing. I added that, as a passionate man myself; I totally understood that urgency often supersedes courtesy.

I told him that I understood that within an hour of going into almost any bar, he is 'holding court' with his entertaining stories and opinions. There is a never ending flow of free drinks from admiring folks who find him charming. Recalling my first meeting with him, I added that I know he immediately attracts people's attention wherever he goes. Mark Twain is hard to miss.

I asked him if the lady was someone he found instantly interesting and if there was some magic between them that a relationship might be built on. Peering deep into his steaming coffee and without looking up he said:

"The phases of the womanly nature are infinite in their variety. Take any type of woman, and you will find in her something to respect, something to admire, something to love." ~MT~

From this I gathered Earl was emulating a 'rock-star' of his day and the young lady would not be seen again.

A Nice Shade of Crimson

After I cleaned the house yesterday Earl could not find his cigars. At least a dozen times he went to the chair-side table only to stop, bend over, and blankly stare at where they once were. Finally after several trips to the vacant table, he asked me where I put them.

I told him, "They were right on that table when I finished dusting".

"Well they obviously aren't there now are they", he said sternly while walking away muttering about when I clean he can't find anything....on and on.

A half hour later he walked out of his bedroom and into the kitchen carrying his box of cigars under his arm and wearing a very sheepish grin he said:

"Man is the only animal that blushes. Or needs to." ~MT~

A Rude Surprise

I was reading the obituaries in the paper and saw that a dear old gentleman acquaintance, (only a few years older than myself), had passed away quite suddenly. That surprised me, because even at his age he was very active. He had worked hard his whole life, recently retired with some financial comfort having been very prudent with his savings his whole life, and looked forward to his leisure years.

He exercised regularly and was concerned with keeping fit. The last time I saw him he beamed like a young boy. He finally had everything aligned to fully enjoy his unencumbered golden years.

Earl had just walked into the sunny room when I read the name aloud and commented on my surprise at his unexpected passing. Pulling up his chair to share the warmth of the bright sunbeam with two of the sleeping cats, he slowly lowered himself down into the seat of the rocking chair and said:

"Life should begin with age and its privileges and accumulations and at the end with youth and its capacity to splendidly enjoy such advantages.... It's an epitome of life. The first half of it consists of the capacity to enjoy without the chance. The last half consists of the chance without the capacity." ~MT~

At the Speed of Light

Expanding on one of my earlier assessments of facebook; I shared with Earl that sometimes what is said -- even by those you might assume are close friends-- has to be disregarded to preserve tranquility in your life.

The innocent gist of people's comments can routinely be confused and twisted into hateful phrases. The printed page does not allow for facial expressions or inflection of voices that usually affects meaning. Just as misleading can be an inadvertent mistake in punctuation. It is startling how quickly people get it so totally 'wrong' and proceed to spread the word.

[13]

Earl was sitting in the rocking chair attempting to put on his socks. He was bent forward stretching to reach his toes with the open end of the sock and without looking up he said in a strained voice short of air:

"It takes your enemy and your friend, working together, to hurt you to the heart; the one to slander you and the other to get the news to you." ~MT~

Impossible to Comb-out

Earl and I were having a discussion about integrity this morning over our morning coffee. He is of the opinion that being good is equal to feeling good.

I said that when I knowingly do something that I feel is wrong, it festers and gnaws at me relentlessly until I can rectify it and gain relief. Going against my own better judgment sometimes causes physical discomfort, ruins my day, and makes comfortable sleep nearly impossible.

Earl shared that there have been a couple of times he, too, had experienced the same effects by ignoring his natural instincts. Thinking quietly for a moment he leaned forward and reached for the strawberry jam with his left hand. With a knife poised in his right hand, he said,

"An uneasy conscience is a hair in the mouth." ~MT~

A Life Sentence

A very good friend of mine, (Jana S.), who, like me is a friend of Bill W., is celebrating 25 years of continuous sobriety today. While Earl would never forgo spirituous beverages, he can appreciate and respect others who must abstain from the one thing that nearly destroyed their lives.

He seemed convincingly puzzled by the concept that alcohol addiction never goes away completely – that even after you stop drinking – the addiction lurks patiently, waiting for you to start again.

When I asked him if my brief and basic explanation made it clearer to him, he looked up at me with his best affectionate grin and said:

"You can straighten a worm, but the crook is in him and only waiting." ~MT~

[14]

The Compliment

I was frying eggs and bacon, and making toast for Earl's breakfast. He watched me intently as I turned the bacon to get it just the way he likes it. When it was finished I took it from the skillet and put it on a plate covered with paper towel to soak up the excess grease. I cracked one of his two eggs into a bowl and then poured the single egg carefully into the grease covered skillet and then repeated the process with the second egg.

He asked me why I didn't just crack them both right into the skillet and save time and not end up with a dirty bowl. I explained that if you had a rotten egg then you would know before it hit the frying pan or contaminated the other egg. Still watching me closely he said that it was typical of my character to be thorough in what I do and that he appreciated it since it was HIS breakfast I was being so careful with.

I turned my attention from the sizzling eggs and savory smell of freshly cooked bacon and said, "Why thank-you Earl, that was a very nice thing to say." Rolling his unlit cigar in his lips with his right hand he removed it long enough to say:

"It is a talent by itself to pay compliments gracefully and to have them ring true. It's an art in itself." ~MT~

Is low Intellect a requirement?

I was reading MSN this morning on my computer that a retiring Congressman from Virginia said he thought congressmen are underpaid at $174,000.00 per year. That they work very hard to keep the biggest entity in the world afloat.

First of all it is a good thing he is retiring, as I don't think he would have a remote chance of re-election after spewing such nonsense to reporters. It was also fortuitous that he didn't make his remarks on the steps of the Capitol to an organized press gathering or an audience possibly armed with rotting fruit. Judging by their unproductive record for the last two years, members of Congress should have to give some of their salary back, give up their sovereign style healthcare, sign up for Obamacare, and face termination for their malingering.

[15]

I was on a roll, and continued by saying that Warren Buffet has the right idea about how we ought to handle our elected representatives, they already make more than triple what the average American makes, and how they hardly spend any of their own money on living expenses as the taxpayers picks up the tab one way or another.

Earl was sitting quietly in the rocking chair with Leon curled up in his lap while lightly petting the comfortable sleeping black and white kitty and patiently listening to me rant. I went on about honesty and politicians and how the two are never embodied in the same person. After about ten minutes I paused to gather more ammunition for my assault when Earl slowly said:

"One of the striking differences between a cat and a lie is that a cat has only nine lives." ~MT~

Prosecutorial Equality

Reading the Sunday papers from around the country, Earl stopped on two adjacent stories on the second page of The New York Times. One story depicts a homeless man who grabbed a five dollar bill from a lady's hand while she was paying for a sidewalk hot-dog in downtown Manhattan He gave the police quite a chase before being slammed to a subway platform, handcuffed, and taken to jail awaiting arraignment.

The other story was the sort that has become too typical: a trusted investment banker bilked millions of dollars from family, friends, and retirees in a scam that only he and his inner circle made money from. The article explained how he was caught, made bail after a half-hour in custody, and was awaiting trial in his mid-Manhattan Fifth Avenue penthouse. Investigations into his dealings revealed large campaign contributions to both political parties, and his pretrial hearing is set for weeks from now.

After reading both of those stories aloud Earl sat there silent for a few minutes. Then very quietly he looked over the top of the paper and said:

"Nothing incites money-crimes like great poverty or great wealth." ~MT~

He knows enough to be annoyed

I was reading about John Wayne recently and was sharing with Earl at some length what an icon he was in his heyday on the silver screen. How John Ford directed many of Wayne's films and I named several of the actors who played opposite his bigger-than-life characters through the decades of his career, who became stars in their own right playing the character roles that supported "The Duke".

Earl was politely nodding occasionally, not really taken with the subject of Hollywood and the technology that *should* exceed the grasp of a man of his supposed generation. Even though he might have seen a John Wayne film at some point, he held firm to his expression of ambivalent innocence.

I told him of one actress that I always found to be particularly memorable in those old films with John Wayne. Oh, what a beauty Maureen O'Hara -- large eyes, alabaster skin, and long wavy auburn hair. I went on to name several movies they had done together and their unlikely attraction to each other in every one. He the rough and tumble cowboy; she the schoolmarm or some other proper lady of the town.

Earl got up from his chair, put the folded Times on the end table and walking away I heard him mutter in an annoyed tone:

"When red-headed people are above a certain social grade, their hair is auburn."
~MT~

Much to Do

The weather should not play such an important part in how a person feels, but after this year's winter, the prospect of a day warm enough to be outside without a winter jacket is more than just a little uplifting.

Watching the weather forecast last night I was actually excited about which things I want to tackle this weekend. I remind myself that with Earl here, I can possibly enlist his help in some of the smaller things such as painting, yard work, or, at the very least, driving the mower. Knowing that I won't be doing them alone makes the tasks seem even more rewarding.

[17]

At breakfast I enthusiastically suggested that We eagerly start on the lawn first: rake the flower beds, trim back the Palmas grass, pick up the dead branches the angry winter winds had blown from the trees, and -- to finish the day -- remove the chunks of asphalt that piled up on the right-of-way grass when a giant pothole developed in the street.

As I spoke about all that *we* could accomplish on such a fine day, the higher the newspaper covering Earl's face seemed to climb. I asked him if he was listening and he replied slowly with a "yep". I went on to explain that spring brings with it the responsibility to correct the ravages of a severe winter on my humble property.

I started getting out some old jeans, a t-shirt that is still 'cool' but well worn, and my neglected, lonely work boots. Earl spent more time than usual in the bathroom he then puttered around in the kitchen opening every cupboard, and finally retired to the living room chair, as if he was searching for something very important in the book opened in his lap. Finally, I asked him point blank if he was going to help me outside on such a lovely day. Still staring at his disguised important distraction and without looking up to observe my eventual disbelief he said:

"Diligence is a good thing, but taking things easy is much more......restful." ~MT~

A Few Minutes a Day

As our Sunday ritual unwound Earl and I are relishing the nice change in the weather, sitting on the front porch, and talking about the bold newspaper headlines we both find terribly intriguing or bothersome.

Not knowing for sure how long he has been living in this century, I shared with him the disturbing reality of school violence, there are periods when it appears that school officials, police, and parents have a handle on the problem, and the violence subsides for a time. Then here it is again: front-page news of a teen-age boy going on a rampage against his classmates -- this time with a knife.

I explained that when I was in school, I was bullied for a short time and a tough friend of mine forced me to confront my tormentors and take a stand. It changed everything for me. However, not every kid perpetrating these school attacks was a target for bullies. What has changed over the years to breed such anger and such vicious behavior? Back when I grew up, the serial killers who pathologically planned and carried out several murders didn't kill as many people in their lifetime as one troubled teen with a gun does today in less than an hour.

"As I see it, today's kids are connected to electronic gadgets all of their waking hours keeping them socially quarantined. They aren't running around outside playing in the dirt, racing around on bicycles, swimming in a pond, or playing pickup baseball on some vacant lot. They have become solitary. They are locked into their own world of games that are frequently based on killing something to succeed and become a "winner." Some of their music promotes violence against authority and degrades women. Socially, they are without clear direction. In many cases both parents must work to make ends meet, which means they have less time to nurture their children. Parents are becoming more and more like mere sperm and egg donors rather than engaged fathers and mothers developing a loving environment for kids to grow. Many parents today were 'latch-key kids' themselves. Left to their own minds for ideas kids will do whatever they can come up with," I finished -- frustrated with the hopelessness that faces some parents.

Earl was attentively listening. He turned to me with a soft-eyed look that I rarely see behind his sometimes brash or sarcastic expressions and said:

"We lavish gifts upon them; but the most precious gift--our personal association, which means so much to them--we give grudgingly." ~MT~

The Ballerina

Before getting dressed this morning I decided to take care of something I had planned on doing all weekend. I had assembled a pile of books, CDs, some clothes, and a couple of magazines that I was going to carry upstairs where they would be out of sight and I wouldn't have to deal with them right away. The pile was resting against the upstairs door – a huge stack of stuff I thought I could squeeze together enough to get them up the stairs – sort of like putting dirty dishes in the oven when unexpected company arrives. I had added things to the stack several times so things were in no particular order. That was no concern as I could easily hold them tight enough until I ascended to a handy hiding spot.

Earl was coming out of the kitchen as I picked up this insecurely arranged

[19]

stack of unsorted chaos and I asked him to please open the door for me. As he opened the door, two cats bounded up the stairs in front of me before I could even take the first step. Holding the two foot irregularly stacked pile with one hand on the bottom and the other squeezing it tightly from the top, I carefully started up the stairs.

About halfway up I felt the CDs, which were in the center of the pile, start to slip out. I tilted my hands to one side and squeezed even harder trying to keep everything together. The CDs squirted out of the stack like a wet bar of soap with one hitting directly on my big toenail on my right foot. (Did I mention I was barefoot?) The cats, frightened by the falling CDs ran down between my legs with the last one digging his back claws into my only remaining healthy foot. To finish off this vaudevillian pratfall, the odd assortment of items continued to slip out in all directions. As I was juggling what was left, my throbbing feet slipped on a glossy Land's End catalog. I fell to my knees landing on several open magazines, uncontrollably lofting the few remaining items into the air, and slid to the bottom of the stairs my chin bouncing on each carpeted step. I landed with clothes and magazines raining all around me.

At the bottom of the stairs, lying in the pile of clutter, I reached up to grasp the handrail and painfully pulled myself to my feet. As I slowly turned around, there was Earl bent at the waist, holding one hand over his mouth, making hissing sounds to unsuccessfully keep his laughter silent and the other hand supporting his belly. Needless-to-say, the scene was much more entertaining to Earl than it was to me!

He pulled his hand away from his mouth just long enough to utter these few words -- before a huge exploding laugh enveloped his whole body:

"Against the assault of laughter nothing can stand." ~MT~

In the Eye of the Beholder

After supper last night we were sitting inside again and looking out at the unusual April snow. The conversation centered on a comment I'd received at my new job at the hospital about what age I appear to be. I acknowledged that I know that anyone assessing someone else's age isn't going to say, "You look much older than that," but frequently I encounter people who think I am in my late 40s or early 50s. Of course, I agree politely; in my mind I am still a young man and couldn't possibly be almost 68 years old.

Earl has said frequently that your face should show your experiences...the miles. If I had Twain's 'miles' I might agree, I thought. If one wants to buy some so-called anti-aging cream or opt for flattering surgery they should do whatever makes them feel good. He actually agrees with me about taking steps to make you feel the happiest, although the options of cosmetic surgery or Botox injections are apparently unknown to the person of Samuel Clemens.

"Twenty-four years ago I was strangely handsome. If one looks closely the remains of it are still visible through the rifts of time," he said. I stared intently at his profile for a few seconds trying to think of him 24 years younger and truly strained to imagine him as handsome. What I saw was a deeply furrowed face and forehead, hooded eyes bracketed by deep crow's feet, drooping mouth slightly clenched, swirls of white hair sticking out here and there, and a silvery-white mustache covering his entire upper lip and hiding most of the lower. Nothing in his distinctive age and presence remotely resembles anything I can imagine other than an older Mark Twain. With an expression only Earl could brandish so naturally, he said:

"I urge upon you this...which I think is wisdom...if you find you can't make seventy by any but an uncomfortable road, don't you go." ~MT~

Choose Your Weapons Wisely

Having shown and demonstrated the proper use of nail clippers too frequently I find Earl in various places trimming his fingernails to the quick.

This has happened so often I have repeatedly questioned his need to preen his fingers so often. I thought I had the answer a few weeks ago when he pulled the clippers out of his pocket right after getting dressed in the morning three days in a row. Ah ha, I thought, it is his morning ritual. But no, he was at it again later the same day. I did instruct him to use a newspaper in his lap to catch his off-falls, and he hasn't forgotten to do that as far as I have seen. There is nothing more annoying and gross than to step on someone else's nail clippings and have them stick to your foot....yuck!

In any case, he loves to get the clippers out of his pocket, swivel the lever around, swing it to the open position, push them down a few times just to make sure they are working properly, and then restart the process beginning with the pinkie finger on his left hand, At various times of the day or night I will hear the metallic 'click' from somewhere in the house. Knowing that he is serenely occupied makes me smile; it's also a good indicator that it may be a good time to seek him out for pleasant conversation as his mind is obviously idle. Chances are he hasn't had too much to drink if he's tending to his "manicure." Drinking and nail clipping do not mix; were he to try that, I imagine there would be blood.

It was my day off, and I approached Earl as he was sitting with his knees together on the sofa with a newspaper on his lap. "At it again I see," I said. "Yep, you got to keep the tiger's paws groomed...makes him safer to pet", he answered without looking up.

As I carefully sat down at the other end of the couch, Earl screamed, "Oh shit...goddamn..shit...son-of-a-bitch!!" as he jumped up stomping one foot several times causing everything in the room to rattle and vibrate.

"Are you alright...what happened?" I asked. "Alright? I just cut into the side of my damn finger with this infernal weapon is what happened...holy-shit that hurts.... dammit anyhow. Whoever invented this bastard contraption should be beaten with a fucking horsewhip until the son-of-a-bitch-is bleeding like my poor goddamned finger," he said shaking his injured finger and putting it into his mouth. My jaw gaped open in complete surprise to hear such an outburst and see such an angry display. I've seen Earl vividly angry, but never heard such a prolific stream of profanity.

Removing his injured digit from his mouth with the same irritating sucking sound of a child with a lollypop, he looked at me with one eyebrow raised and said:

"The idea that no gentleman ever swears is all wrong; he can swear and still be a gentleman if he does it in a nice and benevolent and affectionate way." ~MT~

I was glad he explained that. For a moment I thought he was just a short-tempered imbecile with a limited vocabulary who was unable to use a simple grooming tool.

Breakneck Speed

Some people, as they grow older want everything to slow down. Days seem shorter and the seasons appear to run into each other much faster than current memories can sometimes substantiate. A few older people seem to drive and walk more slowly – taking their time to perhaps savor every precious minute of life, or at least be extra cautious as to not rush the inevitable. They may sleep fewer hours, yet they relish the sunrise, which symbolizes another day of living. They may see the end much more clearly than is comfortable and perhaps have concluded that there's no hurry to get anywhere...ever.

"Things have a habit of appearing at their own pace without the constant push of a hurried society. Why should we fly through every day; what's the rush? Why possibly miss a moment that might make the difference between a good day and a great day? " I said, wishfully hoping that by saying it out loud, I could slow the uncontrolled pace of my own life.

I was sharing this theory with Earl at the end of another great day as he sat watching the bright moonrise, holding a burning fresh cigar, (sporting a Band-Aid on his right pinkie) and drinking his after-dinner bourbon. In his typical manner of getting to the point quicker than I ever can, and without taking his eyes off of the neon white moon now resting about a foot off of the horizon, he said reverently:

"What is human life? The first third is a good time; the rest is slowly remembering about it." ~MT~

Gesundteit

One of the cats jumped up on the kitchen counter and knocked a plastic bottle of Ajax dish soap onto the floor. The bottom of the bottle split open and the cat was covered with soap. After trailing his orange footprints under the kitchen table, I finally cornered him, wrapped him in a towel, and took him into the bathroom.

If you know anything about American shorthair cats, you know they hate water. The minute I turned on the water in the bathtub my once loving and nuzzling kitty turned into a ball of fishhooks. Holding the very unhappy and growling cat down on the floor I checked the water temperature with one hand and then with the cat still wrapped tightly in the towel I gently lowered him into the warm water. As I slowly uncovered him, he calmed down a little and I began to carefully shampoo him using the orange-scented soap that covered his body like crude oil on a sea bird.

[23]

I was being very careful not to make much noise with the water and was calmly and quietly talking, as I gently washed him. Everything was going better than I expected, until Earl -- who was standing against the wall by the tub, offering no help of course -- sneezed loudly. Looking for an escape from Earl's cannon-like report, the cat broke free from my grasp, leaped out of the once-calming water, and tried to climb the sides of the tub. His soaked and scared body went from one end to the other, jumping as high as he could frantically searching for an exit. Suddenly he seemed to realize that the only way out of the torturous liquid was past me. In an instant, he leaped out of the water spread-eagled, soaking me and slashing my right arm in the process. He sprinted out of my reach and around the corner into the computer room.

Predictably, he found the safe haven of his litter box, which sits just outside the bathroom and jumped right in. The fact that he was still half-covered with sticky soap was no longer such a big deal. I tried to calm my wide-eyed, petrified friend while reaching out to him slowly, all the while quietly repeating, "Don't sit down! Don't sit down...oh please don't sit down!" Of course, he sat down! Now I was holding a soaking wet cat partially covered with clumping litter.

During this whole ordeal Earl stood and watched calmly, and made no move to help corral or catch the furry bullet. The bottom half of the cat now resembled the top of an ice cream drumstick with the litter coating him like crushed peanuts. I finally got him wrapped back into a dry bath towel with some soothing words and some gentle petting. I walked back into the bath cradling his squirming and shivering body like a baby. I quietly did my best to reassure him he was safe, and eventually got him back into the water. I looked over my shoulder at Earl who was now standing in the doorway and motioned my head to toward the living room urging him to go away. He understood and disappeared. About an hour later, my clean smelling friend was dry enough to turn loose. He instantly disappeared, traumatized but citrusy fresh.

Still in my soaked clothes, I walked into the living room and stood staring at Earl sitting on the couch with a book open in his lap. As I stood in front of him with my hands on my hips – and displaying the three jagged red gashes from my wrist to my elbow – he knew I was not just presenting my pending lion-wrestling badge. I was pissed-off!

He looked, flashed a boyish grin, and said:

"By trying, we can easily learn to endure adversity. Another man's I mean."
~MT~

[24]

I stared at Mark Twain, (or whomever that sarcasm came from), with my most earnest and furious expression. The person sitting in front of me quickly looked away in total submission.

One for the File

Reminiscing over the events of the week by their level of importance is something I do regularly. It is called, "…continuing to take personal inventory and promptly admitting when you're wrong." Reviewing the things that have happened is my way of trying to improve on my behavior, particularly any outbursts of anger or my ability to assume a quick tongue or to judge someone else too harshly.

Having a historical relic under my roof, I cannot possibly avoid regarding his behavior as well. Not so much as to judge him, but to understand how things from long ago might have been seen and reacted to. Earl, while not really Samuel Clemens, ostensibly embodies many authentic characteristics of a man from that place in time. Watching his reactions to modern day circumstances could maybe provide me with a better inclination to the temperament of a man from Twain's era. His response or lack thereof to things he or I have done has been very interesting to record. The perceived differences of men supposedly born 130 years apart are sometimes non-existent; at other times stark opposites. Whether it is because of personality differences or the divide of more than a century of male evolution I will never know for sure.

Thinking back to his incident with the nail clippers I asked Earl, (who was sitting in the leather chair relaxing with a bourbon and a freshly laundered kitty in his lap), what he thought about the way he handled putting a small nick in his finger during his newly discovered and overzealous nail maintenance program.

In typical Earl fashion he paused for what seemed to be many minutes, flashed me with that same glance of cleverness I have seen so many times before -- the look that usually means my question will not be clearly answered to my approval but will certainly satisfy his, and said:

"It takes me a long time to lose my temper, but once lost I could not find it with a dog." ~MT~

How Did That Happen?

Every once in a while I carefully approach Earl in conversation about Twain's writings. Given my fascination with the writer's, style I am irresistibly bound to ask him many questions as if he were, indeed, the famous writer. Being around someone legendary is like seeing someone you don't know wearing a cast on their arm. You just have to ask what happened, does it hurt, and how long must they wear it.

While I was washing up the few dishes last night after a Chinese take-out dinner – with Earl comfortably sitting at the table, but wishing he could enjoy his after-dinner smoke in the house, I asked him what was the motivation for Huckleberry Finn. Sitting there, anticipating his favorite after-dinner pastime with his right leg crossed over the left, his left elbow on the table edge, and pulling the unlit cigar from his lips with his right hand, he answered that the story was supposed to be something light that the child in each of us might vicariously enjoy.

I asked rapid fire how long it took to write, where was he living when he wrote it, and how old was he when he wrote it. He answered evasively and in a terse tone, reminded me again that the story was supposed to be light and all of those questions I asked were meaningless. While staring at me sternly as any indignant writer would, he said:

"Persons attempting to find a motive in this narrative will be prosecuted; persons attempting to find a moral in it will be banished; persons attempting to find a plot in it will be shot." ~MT~

I silently went back to rinsing the plates, wishing he were a complete stranger with his wrist in a curious sling.

Hearst is Rolling

I have been thinking lately about the future of newspapers, that is conventional fold-up-trash-inside newspapers. Last night I was sharing my concerns with Earl about their slow decline.

It'll be tough getting used to if they ever completely disappear. Even though they have become smaller and smaller they still hold some charm of days gone by. The way they used to reach readers with so many advertisements of all kinds of products and services made them very thick, heavy, and not to mention the distinctive smell experienced every time one opened their pages.

[26]

On the weekends they still resemble what once was a seller's first line of advertising with all of the flyers and ads. Before television advertising, pictures in print media were cutting edge. While the Internet certainly affords a low-cost way of reaching so many very fast it has little personality. There is nothing that equals getting interested in an news article only to discover that it is continued on some unrelated page and then swiftly turning the pages with great anticipation trying to find it.

Whether or not newspapers are still the most effective way of reaching people with the news, there is a lot to be said for continuing to have them. The best introduction to responsibility for a child is a newspaper route. Where will columns with by-lines be without print media? The closest thing in my time to a column-style presentation on electronic media was Andy Rooney. And he's gone, too.

Earl listened intently looking right at me, which he never does, saying nothing, and rarely blinking. I could tell that he was also bothered about the prospect of losing an American institution; after-all the newspaper was the Internet of Sam Clemens time. He used to contribute regularly to newspapers back in his day. He reads many of them cover-to-cover with long comments about the content or lack of content in each. He was, I imagined on the verge of a Chernobyl-style meltdown considering their likely inevitable disappearance, judging by the distraught look on his face.

I returned his stare knowing that at any moment he could be on his feet pacing and cursing the demise of the noble and great creation of newspapers. Instead, a long pause ensued. That was also somewhat normal considering the gravity of the topic and finally he stood up, picked up his overflowing ashtray and the small amount of remaining bourbon in his glass, turned to walk into the kitchen and, to my complete amazement, he simply said with a sad sigh of resignation:

"It is the little conveniences that make the real comfort of life." ~MT~

NORAD Visits the Kitchen

Watching Earl encounter, adapt, or reject modern day appliances or electronics has been very entertaining at times. His supposed wonder at some things and ambivalence to others is not always predictable. The computer, which I thought he might feel that he should hang garlic on, hasn't been that big a deal to him; he must have come across them somewhere in his travels.

The things that have really caught his attention are cell phones, satellite television, Netflix, and the DVD player. There are others that he stumbles upon every day that he hasn't made much ado about, but each time another thing presents itself for examination I watch with curiosity to see if he is familiar with it or is supposedly seeing it for the first time. It reminds me of watching a baby find a rattle and its surprise when it discovers the toy makes noise. Sometimes they are so startled that it scares them, and at other times they just ignore it for a time until they figure it out.

The other night while I was sitting at the kitchen table dicing onions for spaghetti sauce, Earl was at the sink puttering when I heard a familiar sound of silverware against the stainless steel sink. That followed with the distinctive thud of it continuing into the garbage disposal. Before I could warn him, Earl reached for what he thought was the light switch to see down into the abyss. The swirling/ grinding fork caused him to step back just in time as the culinary tool morphed into a guided missile and came flying out of the launch tube and stuck into the ceiling.

By now I am next to Earl and calmly reached across him to turn the disposal off. I smiled at him and explained the situation and the danger of flipping that switch when there is anything down inside but unwanted garbage. I also went into some detail as to its exact use to avert him trying to get rid of unwanted newspapers, cigar butts, or broken glass by means of this specific-use apparatus. As he pulled the kitchen chair over to the sink to try and grab the gnawed end of the fork hanging from the ceiling he said with a scowl:

"I would rather have my ignorance than another man's knowledge, because I have got so much more of it." ~MT~

A Noteworthy Reflection

While we were having our morning coffee yesterday Earl seemed more reflective and appreciative than usual. He was talking about how warm he was all winter, (due to my central heat), and that there was always something wholesome for him to eat, unlike some of the other places he has stayed during his travels.

Once Twain's character fully emerged; Earl elaborated about when he was a boy in the 1840s and the way things were back then in terms to keeping warm and having plenty of food. Since refrigeration wasn't invented yet, leftovers were limited because they wouldn't keep, except during the cold months. He said in today's world he appreciates the possibility of being able to go to the refrigerator and sometimes thoroughly enjoy a previous meal again and again.

I sat patiently listening to what amounted to more of an oratory than a recollection.

He shared what it was like to travel to faraway places, the exhaustive preparations taken to leave, and sometimes weeks to arrive. How the mail took weeks, whereas today we can get print messages instantly on the "pocket phone" we carry everywhere. We talked about how people are killing the health of the planet, but it still is so beautiful in spite of our efforts to lay waste to it in our greed for wealth.

Between his convincing portrayal and theatrical style he seemed honestly moved by the hospitality and comfort he has found here in his adopted 'future'. While we talked about the value of today's conveniences, Earl said that being embraced by people's kindness and affection is timeless and feels exactly the same in all three centuries *he* has lived in.

There are many things Twain hasn't seen in so long and his heart yearns for them. The mighty Mississippi with the riverboats churning themselves to all the grand port cities along its banks, the large speaking engagements throughout America and Europe, and his grand home in Hartford, Connecticut.

Looking directly into my gaze he surprised me with a sentiment I felt came from beneath his performance.

"Grief can take care of itself; but to get the full value of joy you must have somebody to divide it with." ~MT~

Our European Lunch

About a month ago while out shopping I asked Earl if he was ready for some lunch. He said he was hungry and since I was approaching a Wendy's I suggested we eat there. He thought we were taking a real chance eating in a place that was so gaudy looking from the outside. I was skeptical of his professed ignorance of Wendy's, but proceeded to assure 'Earl' that while the food might be different from what he ate in the 1880s, he might really like it.

I didn't want to possibly scare 'Mark Twain' so we went inside to eat rather than attempt the drive-through with the talking box. As we stood in line he asked me if the food was German and French. Confused I told him no, it was probably the most American food we might ever eat. (Pointing up at the menu board) "Then why are so many of these sandwiches named Hamburg and those yellow sticks called French fries?" he asked. I was in the midst of trying to explain when it became our turn to order.

Standing at the counter and partially bent over looking closely at a tray of food of the increasingly annoyed lady in front of us who was trying to get around him he said to the girl behind the counter, "Do you have anything that is safe to eat?" She just laughed and looked at me for my order. I ordered for both of us, so as to not hold up the line for an hour while Earl asked as many questions as Twain himself might have about what each thing was and where in Europe did it originate.

We got our food and went to sit in a booth by the window to hopefully enjoy our lunch in a warm sunbeam streaming through the glass. Even though I assumed he knew all about fast food long before now I patiently played-along and explained the whole ground-beef conundrum, and how it really isn't ham, when Earl took his first bite. He looked like I must have looked when I first discovered chocolate. His face lit up and before swallowing his first bite he took a bigger second one filling his mouth. "Watevir yew cawl dis itz incwedibal", he said with his eyes wide and exaggeratedly chewed like he hadn't eaten in weeks. Then the discovery of the French fries, which were obviously another surprise he allegedly wasn't prepared for. I doubted it, but maybe this really was his first hamburg. The people at a table close by were staring as he pushed several fries into his mouth with his right hand while still holding his burger missing the two huge bites in his left. "Dis is willy guud fuud!", he said spitting a piece of French fry onto my glasses. 'Yes it is and I am glad that you are enjoying it', I said as I wiped the greasy speck from my glasses with the corner of my shirt.

We ate in silence except for the occasional garbled theatrical outburst repeating how happy he was with his "fuud". As we were about to leave I went back to the counter which was now empty, (either because lunch was over or the word of Earl's rude eating habits had quickly spread through town), and I bought him a Frosty. Handing it to him with a spoon and a napkin as we got into the car he looked at me while pulling the spoon from his mouth and with deer-sized eyes and said:

"The exercise of an extraordinary gift is the supremest pleasure in life." ~MT~

We now eat at Wendy's at least twice a week, but without the over-the-top 'I've-never-been-here-before' outbursts.

Marketing 101

While at the University library recently, Earl and I decided to take a nice walk through the center of campus to the Student Union for a cup of coffee. Watching Earl examine things is a major part of my enjoyment. His imagined or contrived discovery of things that I take for granted is frequently surprising and sometimes refreshing. When he is totally immersed into the Character of Mark Twain it is hard to stay annoyed with his 'acting', which often requires me to patiently explain the obvious.

A good example of his amazement of ordinary things is concrete sidewalks. In Twain's day, sidewalks were usually dirt or in better-quality areas, planked wood. His surprise that this material is used so routinely today seemed quasi-genuine so I shared what I know about it. I told him that concrete has been used in several forms for centuries, but not used as widespread until modern times due to mechanization which lowered the cost. Around the turn of the century, milled sandstone was used for most sidewalks, (in our town at least), but has been replaced in today's world with concrete. It is now easy to manufacture and is relatively cheap. He nodded as if truly interested and then glanced at me with a satisfied smile as if to say "thank you."

We continued our walk between the buildings as many students smiled and said hello to Earl. In his ivory colored suit and tie, he always draws a lot of attention. It is obvious that he is unusual and college students embrace unusual.

When we finally got our coffee and found some seats in the center of the Union Earl asked me if our military had reinvented itself. Confused, I asked him what he meant by that. He said that he saw a shirt on a student that said "Old Navy" and wondered what the "new" Navy was like. I explained to him that Old Navy is a clothing store and that is just their brand logo.

While we were sitting there I discreetly pointed out that there were many people there wearing clothing with brand names displayed prominently on them. An Adidas t-shirt, Levis, 'Pink' sweat pants, American Eagle, Abercrombie and Fitch, Under Armour, and many more examples surrounded us on all sides.

[31]

After looking all around the room his focus came back to me and he said, "So just to be clear, these students pay for these clothes and wear them as free advertisements for the manufactures?" I smiled and said, "Yes".

"So the manufacturers have somehow convinced them to **buy** these things and wear them like billboards for **free**?" he said with his eyes widening and his voice going up an octave. I told him it has been the custom for many years to wear what you like and proclaim your brand loyalty to the world at the same time.

Suddenly I could tell that this seemingly new uncovered reality was completely more astounding to him than the widespread use of concrete. He shrugged, smirked, and as he slowly picked up his coffee to take the first sip he looked at a boy wearing a Nike t-shirt and said:

"Many a small thing has been made large by advertising" ~MT~

An Exercise in Humility

I was telling Earl that I was very impressed in his writings with his ability to casually point out the obvious to people who seem in too big a hurry to notice the world around them. To make the ordinary extraordinary was a real gift.

We recently watched a George Carlin video, which in some way reminds me of Mark Twain's approach to social examination. Earl appeared lost a bit in the content, but was very interested in George's keen eye for observation and his animated delivery. I told Earl that Samuel Clemens' ability to pick things out of plain sight and make them seem like you are seeing them for the first time is very enjoyable and was sure that Mark Twain's approach to observation had acutely influenced Carlin.

Earl mentioned that he has always been able to see what most cannot and turn it into a witty and loquacious commentary. He said that during his day there were few writers who could truly grasp the apparent literary value of their environment to the point that people would line up to buy their books or hear them speak.

He went on to say that most people of his day would rather listen to him for ten minutes than spend a week reading any other author of that time....he knew *he* would. I smiled at him and said mockingly," Earl why don't you tell me how you REALLY feel about your talent?" He stopped for a moment and with I-just-took-the-last-cookie-out-of-the-cookie-jar grin, and said:

"I was born modest, but it didn't last" ~MT 1909~

The Kenny Rogers' Lesson

While sitting in the living room after a fine meal and Earl settling in with lubricating bourbon, he proceeded to tell me a story. While taking a riverboat from New Orleans up to Memphis about two years before the start of the Civil War, he decided to play some cards the first evening out on the river.

He watched a game for a time and asked if he might join. It looked to be friendly and the stakes were within his means so he drew up a chair between a banker-looking fellow and a dandy wearing a gold and green brocade vest. He said that he played about an hour before noticing that the fancy dressed dude was regularly raking in every third pot like clockwork.

He thought about saying something, but in those days if you suspected someone of cheating you better have the means to back it up regardless of the stakes. As the evening went on and other players came and went, Earl started to win occasionally, but he never went beyond merely looking at his cards on the hands he knew the card sharp had a design to win, and then quickly folded.

As the hour grew late the gambler started winning almost every hand and Earl found himself increasingly eager to point out his suspicions. After folding his cards on a particular hand he closely watched the betting. Even closer he watched the fancy dude dealing the draw cards. The gambler was wise to Earl's scrutiny and casually opened his coat with his forearm revealing a pearl handled revolver wedged accessibly behind a suspender and behind it by his side was a very large knife tucked into his waistband. Earl looked at the gambler's advertisement of arms and looked up to catch the piercing glare of the man literally holding all the cards. Earl looked at his meager stack of chips and counted them...he was down $ 18.00, which in Twain's day was a lot of money. Again he looked over to the man, the chips he had swindled out of Earl and the innocents, and his weapons at the ready. Earl paused for several seconds, until I eagerly asked, "So what did you do?"

Picking up his bourbon and after swallowing a large gulp he looked at me and said:

[33]

"There are several good protections against temptation but the surest is cowardice." ~MT~

The Return Trip

Earl and I were running lots of errands around town yesterday. We went to buy lawn fertilizer, a bolt from the hardware store, shopped for some shoes for him, stopped to see my insurance agent, went to the bank, shopped at Aldi's for a couple of sale items, and ended up at Wal-Mart, (Earl's favorite place to spend some time acutely watching people).

I was very quick to get in and out of every place, well as quick as you can when you have a man with you that looks at every single thing like he has never seen it before, which in some cases is probably true. Standing in the checkout line at Wal-Mart and removing the remaining bills out of my bank envelope, I realized that something was not right. The amount of money was wrong.

I stood there, looking upward towards the ceiling and mentally adding up all that we had spent and came to the realization that I had fifty dollars too much money somehow. As a lady in a scooter moved forward to put her groceries on the conveyor I slowly moved forward also almost reluctantly as if I wasn't sure I was supposed to be there. After double-checking the figures in my head and looking over the receipts in my hand I realized that the girl at the bank had given me too much money.

As I started to empty my cart part of me deep inside started to smile. This day was turning out much better than I had planned. As I put the bags into my cart, I tugged on Earl's coat, (who was now standing with his back to me talking to three college girls buying hair products, chips, and beer), and told him I was leaving.

Pushing the cart to the exit, I tried to whistle and smile at the same time, which only caused me to laugh at such a futile exercise. When I swept my foot under the tailgate and it magically opened, Earl showed up to help load the groceries. "What are you so cheery about"? He asked. I explained that I gotten back $50 more money from the bank than I was supposed to.

Getting into the car I heard myself say, "The way banks overcharge you overdraft fees, ATM fees, mortgage interest, and everything else you pay a fee for, it's only right that I keep this extra fifty. I mean somewhere along the line they have gone into my account to get more cash out of me for this or that so this is just a little payback for all of their greed."

While sitting there with the car in reverse and my foot on the brake I paused as my ethics abruptly returned. "What if that poor girl at the window has to make it up out of her own pay? What if they make her stay late trying to find the error? I mean we all make mistakes and she, while not the most pleasant, doesn't deserve to get in trouble for something anyone of us could do in her place Earl, I cannot keep this money I am going back to return it right now."

"If I had found it blowing along the street and had no idea who it belonged to I would enjoy spending it, but not like this...this isn't right." I said ignoring that I had ice cream sitting in a hot car. As I headed back toward the bank Earl, who up to this point had nothing to say about me discovering the error and who was most likely still thinking about the three giggling girls in the store judging by the silly grin on his face said:

"A conscience takes up more room than all the rest of a person's insides." ~MT~

He was right of course, but sometimes doing the right thing fills a body with a smile.

An Immoveable Object

I got up today at 5:15 and found Earl already sitting in the living room reading. He usually doesn't get out of bed until much later so I asked him what he was reading so early in the morning that couldn't wait until his customary rising time of nine o'clock. He said he has been really bothered by the way our Congress has treated so many issues that he thinks fundamentally help all Americans in the long run.

He was reading a commentary that addressed the minimum wage issue. He went on to say that not only the minimum wage bill, but the women's equal rights legislation, and the continuous barrage of repeal attempts on Obama-Care just bewilder him.

"Doesn't the whole country benefit if the poor, all women, and all the people who need healthcare get better treatment?" he queried. I said that even though I agree with everything he mentioned it hits businesses, (and subsequently investors); in the purse and that is the problem.

[35]

I went on to say that another great example of frustration about the lack of concern for human life by those who live to have more money is GM's refusal to fix/ replace the ignition switches when they were first revealed to be defective. Their reasoning that it might add a small cost to each car is inexplicable. After several tragic deaths they are now recalling millions of cars, which will ultimately cost more than the switch replacement would have when first discovered. Money sometimes governs the depth of caring I said. It is cheaper to pay out a wrongful death claim once in a while, than to initiate a recall to fix the problem.

Everything we do as a country today seems to be about money and/ or power, which of course have become synonymous. Earl nodded and went on to say that obviously it has been that way for many years because he witnessed the same in his day. He went on to say that people who were poor were treated as if they were expendable, with little regard for health and safety. And women..."we well know how long it took for them to even acquire the vote let alone consider paying them equal wages for equal work," he said in an exhausted tone.

He slowly got up from the leather chair and dropped the paper into the dimple where he had been sitting, ostensibly to save his spot. As he turned I could see his brow furrowed and his face twisted in disapproval and he said:

"Loyalty to petrified opinions never yet broke a chain or freed a human soul. ~MT~

Aw Nuts!

After work yesterday Earl and I went to the hardware store to return a bolt that was the wrong size. We went to the desk in the back of the store and after several minutes of patiently waiting, the man behind the counter rudely asked, "Whadaya want?" He was busy fussing with some papers when we walked in, and as customers, we were obviously interrupting him.

I explained that I purchased the wrong size bolt earlier in the week and was there to return it and get the correct one. "You *do* have your receipt don't you?" he asked brusquely. I explained that since it was only about $ .40 that I didn't think I even picked up my receipt when I paid. He said with a raised eyebrow that people frequently steal things and return them for cash. I explained that driving all the way across town to return a stolen bolt to get 40 cents hadn't occurred to me. Now that he mentioned it, I thought, I might consider switching from my day job to a life of crime in this newly discovered lucrative field of: "bolts for cash."

I was getting increasingly annoyed with his tenor and tone so I said I would just give him the bolt...free of charge and start all over. "Why would you just give me this bolt if you actually paid for it?" he said shifting his weight to his other foot and again raising a suspicious eyebrow.

I wanted to say that it was worth the 40 cents just to get on with my life, but instead I said in my best pleading voice, "Can I just get the right size bolt that I need so I can get out of your hair?" So he snaps right back with, "You obviously don't know what size you need" I told him I would know it when I see it, but I know that the first one that I bought, (or perhaps stole, I said under my breath), is the wrong size. He slowly pulled out a pair of dial calipers and at a glacial pace measured the diameter of the bolt. I am more than annoyed now and can feel myself getting angry. "I'll just go up there and pick up what I need and bring it back here and pay for it?"

So, Earl who was completely bored at this point with the entire conversation and certainly with this clerk who was offensively unhappy with his job followed me into the front of the store. Within ten seconds I had the right bolt with the price of $ .42 written in ink on the provided plastic bag.

When we got back to the register we were again greeted by Mr. Friendly with his hands on his hips asking, "Are you sure this is the right size?" I said I was, but if it wasn't I would be back for round two of our enchanting chat. He took the bag and with his chest puffed up under his red vest he rang up the sale explaining that there was *no way* he could give me credit for the other bolt without a receipt because it would be impossible to know whether I ever really paid for it. "People would have boxes of bolts in their garages that were never paid for if I start to let that happen." *Yammer- yammer- yammer.*

As I was leaving with the correct bolt and the sometimes essential iron-clad receipt in my hand he called out to me, "Hey you forgot your other bolt!" I stopped, turned, and then stopping myself from saying something really rude I settled for: "You can keep it for all of your trouble."

In the car I was so mad that my face was hot and I was wondering why returning that first bolt was so important to go through all of that. I should have just thrown it away had I known the fuss it would cause. Looking at Earl sitting emotionless in the passenger seat staring at me I snapped at him, "What?" He calmly said:

"If the desire to kill and the opportunity to kill came always together, who would escape hanging?" ~MT~

The Interview

Earl was in a rather talkative mood the other night and told me a few stories of when he was growing up in Missouri. Each of his recollections could easily be another popular Twain book taking us along a path of schemes and laughter.

He also told me of his time living in the "big house" in Connecticut and how he loved to play pool in his study on the second floor. He told me of a particular time a man came to interview him for a magazine article and they shot pool. They played for hours in silence, Earl's one non-negotiable rule. To Earl's great delight, the man lost every game.

After 3 ½ hours, as Earl was putting his cue in the rack, the innocent casualty of the rout asked if he could now start the interview. Earl looked him sternly in the eye and said, "That was the interview; write whatever you heard here." The young man pleaded for some time to ask the questions he had painstakingly prepared in advance. "You can quote me on everything I said", exclaimed Earl.

Escorting the exasperated man out of his house, he broke into laughter once the heavy front door latched pausing to light a fresh cigar.

I asked him if that episode actually happened that way. I explained that I didn't mean to sound like I didn't believe him. It was just that much of his story telling is spoken in such an entertaining style that it sounds like he's quoting from something he's writing or a piece by someone else he had enjoyed reading. I am amazed by his memory for detail and his intrinsic ability to paint convincing images. To be in the company of someone who claims to have done so much and supposedly remembers it all is mesmerizing.

Earl looked at me with his usual slight smile on one side of his mouth (the other side held the omnipresent cigar), paused briefly and said:

"It isn't so astonishing, the number of things that I can remember, as the number of things I can remember that aren't so." ~MT~

Maybe Next Year

I was standing in front of the bathroom mirror wearing only my striped boxer shorts seeing the round belly I have apparently developed overnight. As I was so engrossed in this confusing anomaly, was unaware that that the bathroom door was wide-open, until, of course, Earl materialized. He was almost past the bathroom door, when he caught sight of me from the corner of his eye. He did a double-take, took a couple steps backwards so he could clearly see me holding my belly like a cantaloupe. "What **are** you doing?" he asked, I told him I was confused: this protuberance suddenly appeared and I need to remove it.

"You have had a bit of a belly the whole time I have known you;" he remarked to my surprise and added, "I have thought it might be getting bigger". I answered, that with my fast-paced, continuous walking at work, I was surprised that it hadn't simply vanished before it was noticed.

Knowing that many men have such a "thing" was of little comfort to me since I have worn size 32 pants for 45 years. I reached down, grabbed the offending blob of flesh, and pulled it up while sucking in my breath. This was both awkward and painful. "I am just going to have to figure out what is causing it and work at getting back to my fighting weight," I said with resignation.

Then I got a bright idea that would make losing weight fun. As I had noticed that Earl also had a prominent protrusion, I said. "How about the two of us start watching what we eat then go to the community center and get some structured exercise?"

Earl turned to align his entire self within my view and gave me a wide-eyed glare. He had that same look of determination in his eyes and the deep wrinkles in his face that he had the day he couldn't find his cigars after looking for an hour. I knew his response would be anything but an enthusiastic endorsement of my proposal.

"I have never taken any exercise, except sleeping and resting, and I never intend to take any. Exercise is loathsome. And it cannot be any benefit when you are tired; and I am always tired." ~MT~

I looked at him, then his belly, back at my own stomach and with his words fresh in my mind I said to myself. "This man is smart beyond belief"

[39]

The Best Government Money Can Buy

Again politics became the evening subject between Earl and me. The immorality of government is the greatest trigger of Earl's frustration.

He has shared that, in his time, there were a few louts who went to Congress to make good connections and achieve great wealth. But, he said, the majority were just plain people who cared about their country and its citizens.

"In today's Washington for one Congressman to judge another on his honesty is like having one skunk saying another smells bad". He said with a sneer.

I replied, "Everyone seems to be on track for a great job when he leaves office. Many I go on to be lobbyists in the very Congress they just vacated. And, they become very, very rich doing it."

Earl appeared confused by the term 'lobbyist' so I asked him to imagine a manufacturer who needs to have a bill passed in order for him to make more money. He can't get anywhere with anyone in a position of power. He then hires a lobbyist. The lobbyist, who has connections or knows of some scandal in the legislator's past, is usually able to find a listening ear. I explained that another downside to this system is that often gifts are exchanged to ensure that a particular piece of legislation not only makes it to the floor, but is passed.

"Some lobbyists are more powerful than the congressmen themselves. If they reveal all they know about illegal gifts for favorable legislation, they could ruin many political careers," I said.

I continued, "It used to be that you selected a party to endorse out of respect for their ideals, not out of mere dislike for the opposing party. Today, it has become the norm to turn on the evening news, only to see a microphone tree in front of a stately Roman column and a "talking head" defaming a colleague for dishonesty. By its very nature, politics is contentious. But isn't there a point when working for the greater good should become everyone's focus?"

Earl listened respectfully to my rant, which was now focused on my disappointment in the inept Congressman from my own district. I explained that he has toed the party line his entire time in office; He routinely picks every Democrat apart not because their ideas are faulty, but because his party tells him to. His way to congress was assured because his father was a respected

Republican Congressman from this district for many years, plus the fact that there hasn't been a Democratic congressman elected from this district since 1933. This representative was so arrogant of victory; he didn't appear for a scheduled debate. In my opinion, that was a practical move. His mumblings are barely comprehensibly. The only thing he has done since his election victory is to parrot the party line, criticize the opposition, while he offers absolutely nothing of substance of his own.

Earl had loaded a pipe, which he opts for time to time, and waited to light it as if waiting for a break in his thoughts. As my tirade finally stopped, he looked down, struck the match on the underside of the porch chair, and put it to the tobacco. He puffed and puffed until a cloud surrounded him. Blowing out a billow of smoke, he stared off blankly and said in a rather tired tone:

"One mustn't criticize other people on grounds where he can't stand perpendicular himself." ~MT~

A great ethical principle that has escaped all of Washington, I thought.

Buena Vista

I was fixing breakfast this morning for Earl. As I cooked, my friendly and always hungry black cat Lalo was going in and out of my legs with obvious anticipation of some sort of treat.

While his anticipation was probably less than the cat's, Earl was sitting at the table reading the newspaper while waiting for breakfast. As I sat the plate on the table and turned to get Earl's coffee, Lalo jumped up onto a chair, peered over the table's edge, and stared at the steaming plate.

I gave Earl his usual huge cup of coffee. As I turned back to the stove, he was folding his newspaper and reaching for his napkin. Lalo seized the moment and jumped on the table directly across from Earl. As Lalo turned to check for my reaction, the only non-black mark on him – a large pink spot under his tail – was two feet from Earl's plate, Before Lalo could move, Earl, (with both hands full of silverware), and staring straight ahead said:

"Nothing helps scenery like bacon and eggs." ~MT~

All in a Day's Work

While listening to Earl's tales, I can safely assume they are filled with poetic license just as Twain did in his writing. Some of Earl's stories put him in two different places or eras at one time, so I know they didn't really happen. I rarely point this out. Regardless of the truth, the content is so extraordinarily fascinating.

Last night was a good example. We sat in lawn chairs in the back yard in the unusually warm late afternoon. For once there were no bugs to spoil the serenity.

Earl was relating exciting stories of his Missouri days and how Samuel Clemens assumed the name "Mark Twain." Apparently, it was a common riverboat term used then to measure the depth of the river.

The particularly unbelievable story involved him piloting a boat that ran aground on a sandbar. He related how he took a one-inch line (rope), looped it over his shoulder, swam to the bank, and tied it to a team of waiting mules that pulled the boat free. Having seen lines used on boats I knew the weight would have dragged him under before he could swim a mere ten feet.

He went on to say that after reaching shore, he hooked the rope to the team, swam back to the boat, and directed it to shore. The Mississippi is not a little stream easily navigated by even the best of swimmers. I really wanted to believe him, but I was incredulous. He couldn't have made it both ways in the best of conditions and certainly not while dragging a half-ton bowline on the first segment.

I told him with a smile that I doubted his story and chided him to "come clean." Earl has a "tell" when he isn't being exactly forthright. He twirled his cigar, pursed his lips to hide an emerging grin, looked at me, leaned back, pulled the cigar from his mouth, and said:

"It is often the case that a man who can't tell a good lie thinks he is the best judge of one." ~MT~

Mountain from Molehill

At 6 am, while I was dressing for work, I heard the unmistakable sound of glass breaking. As I rushed to find the source, I found Earl on his knees on the bathroom floor, picking up shards of a water glass that normally sits on the bathroom sink holding his toothbrush. There was glass everywhere on the ceramic tile floor. I rolled a flashlight across the floor to help spot all the pieces as we carefully gathered them up.

Suddenly Earl yelped and pulled his hand close to his face. He was squeezing his left hand; blood was running down his arm and starting to drip off his elbow. I carefully stepped over some remaining pieces of glass and turned on the cold water. Earl reluctantly put his hand under the running water, winced a bit, and settled down enough that I could look at his wound. There was a clean slice in the side of his index finger about an inch long, but deep enough I knew he would need a stitch or two. He was scared standing there watching his blood swirl around in the water and go down the drain. I covered the cut with a gauze pad and secured it with tape. After wrapping his hand in a towel, I hurriedly finished getting ready for work and swept up the remaining pieces of the offending glass.

As we neared the emergency entrance, Earl asked if the hospital was inside the huge building in front of us. As we walked from the car I explained that the whole building **is** the hospital and that there are many advanced things there that were never even a notion in his day. I briefly told him of some of the machines that could diagnose illnesses and prolong life.

Because the hospital is also where I work, I stopped by my supervisor's office to explain that I had a bit of an emergency with my houseguest. My boss said that they were shorthanded so please get back there as soon as I could. I took Earl down the hall towards Emergency with him slowing to look all around. He marveled at the automatic doors, highly polished floors, attendants pushing carts down long hallways, friendly people everywhere greeting both of us. He was overwhelmed.

We reached the ER and I quickly explained that after a few simple stitches, he should be ready to go back home in about an hour. The triage secretary nearly fell to the floor when he told her his birth date. After I explained with a wink about how he believes he was born in 1835, I left Earl with my credit card; assuring him it would work just like money and cover the charges for his treatment. I reassured him that he was in great hands -- and added that the care would be thorough and entertaining. I told him he would discover many new things. The secretary agreed to page me when he was finished so I could arrange his trip back to my house. I went off to work my shift which I knew would be very busy.

After two hours, I had not heard a thing. I headed toward the ER to find out why things were taking so long. I suddenly saw the back of Earl's head disappear into the LAB. He was being pushed in a wheelchair. I approached the LAB window and asked what was going on. Of course, I was asked if I was related to the patient. I answered that he was a visiting houseguest from the "past" and I was as close to a relative as he has. I was instantly admonished for asking after a patient, and reminded that as a hospital employee, I should know about patient confidentiality. Annoyed, but understanding, I went back to work. I knew I would eventually be notified and I could simply ask Earl in person for the details.

Before I took my morning break I thought I would swing by the ER to see if I could get some clue as to what was happening. As I approached, doors beeped and opened, and out rolled Earl lying flat on a gurney. He was being pushed across the hall to the CT scan. He smiled broadly and gave me a wave before disappearing through the closing doors. Totally confused, I walked back to the cafeteria wondering how in the world that small cut on his finger could have prompted such extensive testing.

At 2 pm, I finally got the call that Earl was ready to go home. I explained to my supervisor that this was a situation I **had** to take care of immediately and walked to the ER. Earl was sitting in a wheel chair in the waiting area holding a stack of papers and chatting with a lovely and smiling nurse. His upper finger was wrapped neatly in a white bandage with a little string wrapped in a loop around his wrist. "All good", he said holding it up for the world to see. After calling for a cab to take him home, I dismissed the nurse, and she disappeared after giving smiling Earl a warm hug. I anxiously turned to him and asked about all the testing, what was wrong with him.

Smiling broadly again, (as if he had stopped since arriving), he revealed that my telling him about procedures and machines that could prolong life, he figured he would have some "treatments," since he was already there. Once he got started, it was easy to keep the tests coming by just adding more symptoms to the receptive, concerned nurses and doctors. From what I've come know about Earl, I knew this diversion was no more than a casual 'walk in the park'.

I wheeled him to the waiting taxi. I was thinking about the huge credit-card charges I would be facing, I stood on the curb looking like the RCA Victor dog with my head cocked sideways trying to digest the whole ordeal. As the cab pulled away Earl turned towards me, gave me a big smile, and through the open window said,

"It is easier to stay out than to get out." ~MT~

Mother's Day 2014

Established long ago, perhaps when I was away in the Army, I spend time reflecting on my mother on Mother's Day. It isn't anything I have to force myself to do, it just always happens. This time, I was sharing it with Earl. I told him of her becoming a bride at age 17 and a mother at 18. And that her life had been hard in many ways. I felt she had a harder row to hoe than most mothers, but knew the complete details wouldn't be that meaningful to Earl. Still, I wanted to share my fond thoughts with him, so I gave him the pared-down version.

"Being a widow at 31 with four children ages 4 – 12, she had only modest skills to supply us with basic needs. Taking a basic bookkeeping course at the local university, she was able to get an office job where she eked out a meager living to keep us clothed, fed, and provide a home to live in.

"As kids we didn't have much, but always more than she had. As all good mothers she provided for us first and put her own wants and needs second. She wasn't quick to judge or offer authoritative opinions just to remind us of who was the boss. Her rules and her recommendations always came from her love and concern for us. She was more comfortable showing us love by providing for us rather than physical emotion, but that changed as times got easier for her. She became more sentimental and loving with age.

"After we all were gone from home she went on to provide for herself in a way that surprised all of us. She was self-sufficient until just before her death. Somehow women, (while looked upon as the weaker sex), frequently rise to the needs of their children in a way that should make any man envious of such strength and character. My mother was the strongest person I have ever known, and she did it in such an underplayed and demure manner. To this day I look back with amazement" I concluded looking off into the distance as if seeing her smiling back at me.

Earl was quietly sitting there in the leather chair very respectfully listening to my every word while finishing his morning coffee. I went on to say that seeing my mother work every 4th of July on the billing statements for Hamblin's Dry Cleaners, while the rest of us went to enjoy the fireworks, still sticks in my mind. It was just one of the many sacrifices she routinely made to provide for us by putting herself last.

Turning to Earl, I asked rhetorically, "How many men would pick up the pieces so thoroughly like she did and make a secure life for their kids?" Earl who had not said a word or tried to the whole time I was talking looked at me warmly and said softly:

[45]

"No civilization can be perfect until exact equality between man and woman is included." ~MT~

That Sums it Up

Winding up one long conversation with Earl about current affairs it ended with his customary "last word."

I asked why he also felt the need to put an exclamation point behind everything I said. I wondered if that was because I never wrap everything up when I speak. He asked if I was referring to questions, which obviously need a response. I explained that it was more a general thing that he always seemed to need to add a witty or judicious titbit to whatever we had just finished discussing. He thought for a moment and said:

"I cannot keep from talking, even at the risk of being instructive."   ~MT~

My Laurel to His Hardy

As I pulled into my driveway yesterday I discovered that my old work van, (which I am not sure why I still have since I never drive it), had a flat tire. After changing into my jeans I went out to pump it up. After filing the tire, I could hear a hissing coming from the valve stem. Annoyed, I set out to change the tire.

Earl brought a lawn chair from the garage and sat down under the maple tree to watch. I asked if he knew what the jack was and, to my surprise, he did. He sat quietly smoking his cigar while I pried off the hubcap and began loosening the lug nuts.

"Back in your day you would find only one nut when changing a wheel", I said. Earl waited a moment to allow my bait to hang in the silence before running with it, "Yes sir some things never change," he said with a self-satisfied laugh. I smirked and continued with the remaining lug nuts. I picked up his cheap imitation of a thrown gauntlet, smiled at him and said that his comment had cobwebs draping from it, and I could see it coming from a mile away. Even a desperate novice in the art of artistic slander would've grabbed that straight line and fired back such a cheap old-fashioned shot.

"I **am** surprised", I said, "that someone of your creative stature couldn't come up with something a bit more inspired." While I lifted the tire off of the studs and leaned it against the van Earl quickly added from his shady, supervisory spot behind me.

"You may be right, but...

"The only way to classify the majestic ages of some of my jokes is by geologic periods." ~MT~

It Was Obvious, but Still Surprising

Earl told me of a time he happened into a Catholic Cathedral drawn by the beauty of the huge stained-glass windows. When he entered, he heard singing from a practicing choir he couldn't see. From the back of the stately church, he could see an ornately decorated alter with many candles flickering across the entire front of the church in small red-glass cups. He stood there silent for a moment, not wanting to spoil the mood, when he noticed an appealing piece of furniture off to the right side of the foyer. It was a beautifully carved walnut closet with a door in the center and two smaller openings on each side covered with gold-trimmed, red velvet curtains. The door was open and inside was a very comfortable looking over-stuffed chair also with red covering trimmed in gold.

Earl said that he thought he could inconspicuously sit in there being appropriately quiet and still hear the wonderful music filling the marble columned building.

He walked over to the open door of the closet, stepped in and sat down. He no sooner got comfortable when he saw a lady entering the cathedral through the huge thick door. Not wanting to be obvious to people who actually had business there, he quietly pulled the door shut.

As he sat there quietly, he heard her footsteps on the marble floor coming increasingly closer to his hideaway. With the instantly recognizable whoosh of a curtain, he heard someone rustling about in the area to his right. He sat there motionless for what seemed to be an eternity when suddenly he heard a slight tapping on the wall. He looked up and saw a small sliding panel directly where the sound was coming from. He slowly slid it open a crack and squinting he could see that the woman who entered was knelling on the other side of a wooden screen. "How may I help you", he asked quietly. "Forgive me Father for I have sinned," she said.

Earl froze for a second and hesitantly asked, "Oh really, what kind of sin are you referring to?"

She went on to say that she had seen her neighbor naked and could not pull herself from her window while he finished getting ready for bed. There was another silence, and then the woman said, "Father?" "Uh yes", said Earl. "What should I do to ask for God's forgiveness?" She nervously asked.

Earl thought for a moment and then said, "Get yourself a big glass of bourbon --maybe even two -- and drink it right down", he said. "Really?" She said in a failed exasperated attempt to whisper her surprise.

"It always helps me to forget seeing things I want but cannot have", he said. She let out a loud sigh and ran out of the little closet. Earl sat there for a couple of moments when suddenly the door opened and there stood a priest with his mouth hanging open and his hands firmly planted on his hips. "I was just giving some advice to a distraught woman who wandered in off the street.... good day sir," he said as he brushed by the clergyman who was frozen in disbelief. I looked towards Earl; I couldn't say anything other than, "really?"

"I like a good story well told. That is the reason I am sometimes forced to tell them myself." ~MT~

My Vanity Saved

Last evening Earl and I decided to watch 'Braveheart' on Netflix. I paused it at the opening credits and I asked if he would like some popcorn. He declined, saying that he had it before and it was without enough taste to justify all the chewing. I was on my way to get myself something so I asked if there was anything else I could get for him while I was up. He said no, that he might get a snack later.

I went into the kitchen, also decided against popcorn; I quickly grabbed a package of fig bars and a small glass of milk. On my way back to the living room I stopped in the computer room and quietly opened the cabinet door above my desk to break off a piece of a chocolate bar that I keep concealed for just such an occasion. I slipped my hand inside the secure hiding place and feeling the wrapper I pulled it out. It was empty. As I looked down at a few crumbs of what once held 5.29 ounces of fine European chocolate, I tried to recall the last time I had eaten any. I could only account for eating one quarter of what was missing.

"Are we watching this fable or should I open a book?" boomed a voice from the living room. "I am coming, just give me a minute". I put the wrapper back into the cabinet and closed the door slowly still trying to remember if I could have actually eaten it. That is something that I face more frequently now than in years past. Sometimes, I have to strain to remember if something actually happened. Still standing in front of my desk where a crime may have occurred I

[48]

turned over rocks in my memory to determine if I might have been the guilty party.

I rejoined Earl and sat back on the couch with my cookies and milk, feeling confused and disappointed. I hit "play" but as soon as the movie ratcheted forward, I paused it again. "Do you know what happened to the chocolate I had in the computer cabinet?" I asked glancing over at my impatient friend

"You mean the cabinet right by your computer?" Earl replied. I said, "Yes, that one – the one that **used** to have my chocolate in it!" Earl asked if I might have taken a sleep aid that causes a person to do things that he can't recall -- gotten up and eaten three-fourths of a bar of chocolate and simply didn't remember. "Maybe one of the cats got into it," he added, "they are pesky like that."

As I tried to imagine a cat swinging open that cabinet door,...(*wait a second*), I suddenly realized that Earl had said, "Three-quarters of a bar of chocolate."

"Earl, how did you know that three-quarters of a bar is the exact amount of chocolate that is missing?" I asked sternly.

After a pause in our true-life saga Earl turned and said, "The other day when you were standing in front of the mirror wondering how your belly grew so quickly got the compassionate part of me thinking. How might I lessen my good friend Tom's concern and return him to his usual quietude? So while looking for...ah...ah... um something to read, I stumbled purely by accident upon this unfriendly cache of potentially deadly stomach fat disguised as sumptuous chocolate. Over the next several days I was able to save my good friend much anxiety and possibly even his LIFE!"

I sat there in disbelief for several minutes holding a boring fig Newton that I suddenly had no interest in.

"So you were doing me a **favor** by eating my chocolate? You were sacrificing your own health for **mine**?" I asked sarcastically. Earl again turned to face me with his most earnest, failed attempt at sincerity and said:

"I make it a point to do something every day that I don't want to do. This is the golden rule for acquiring the habit of doing my duty without pain." ~MT~

"One Moment Please"

One of the most entertaining things is observing Earl using the telephone. When I'm around at least, he talks extra loud, and occasionally pulls it from his ear to look at it like it's a sea shell with the ocean sound inside. No one calls for him here, but he enjoys calling places to hear recordings for time and temperature or just the automated answering menus from any number he dials. I rarely answer the house phone – I rely mostly on my cell -- and the calls that come there are usually from telemarketers, Earl loves to talk to them. They usually hang up long before he does. I cannot leave my iPhone 4S out for any length of time before Earl is asking 'Suri' all kinds of questions. He said he thinks she likes him even though she won't say so directly. The telephone is obviously something that Mark Twain himself would certainly be familiar with, but Earl plays Twain's ignorance and curiosity to the hilt.

The other day he took a call from someone who was telling him that he had inherited millions of dollars from an anonymous lady in England. Of course I could only hear one side of the conversation, but I could tell that the person on the other end was getting more than they expected when Earl started grilling them on the history of the English monarchy in his best British accent. He was rather convincing when he started listing all the lords and ladies of the late 1800s and asking several questions about each as if he was administering a test to the poor person on the other end.

"Surely you know of Disraeli, he is more current you know, you must know of him being a solid Englishman yourself", he queried. "Old man, you must really polish up your knowledge of the historical leadership and the aristocracy if you are going to talk about it with any authority. One must know the leaders who command them and their complete lineage. Don't you agree good man?" he said with a Cockney drawl. Earl went on to ask the caller all about London and the pubs, hotels, and sights he vividly remembered when he lived there years ago. With each question, he admonished the caller for not knowing enough about the very place he was supposedly calling from.

I can only assume that the gentleman on the other end said he had another call coming in as I heard Earl say: "...by all means take your call good sir and do not hesitate to ring me back forthwith and we can continue our rousing conversation on English history and I can also tell you where you might send that suitcase full of English pounds most generously given to me by a total stranger, better yet how about giving me your number and I can ring you again later after lunch and we can talk for the whole afternoon," he said holding one lapel of his make-believe hounds-tooth jacket. I thought for a moment that I saw a monocle, (complete with satin ribbon), appear squeezed tightly over his left eye as he held the phone saying loudly, "Hello.... HELLO?", before he reluctantly returned the receiver to its cradle.

I looked at him with a friendly grin. He returned the smile and still fixed in the thick accent he said:

"Earn a character first if you can. And if you can't, assume one." ~MT~

A Gasp is worth a Thousand Words

One day a week ago Earl volunteered to take Cali out for her morning ritual as I went to retrieve the mail that had been delivered very late the evening before. We were still in our robes. My robe is a thick maroon and navy paisley print. It is knee length and has a heavy belt. Earl's is a very short, lightweight red-and-yellow; Japanese style that overlaps in the front and barely covers anything. The reason I detail the looks of these will be revealed, so-to-speak, in a moment.

As I was waiting to cross the street to the mailbox a car carrying three elderly ladies turned into the driveway behind me. My driveway is a popular turn-around so I just smiled toward the car and continued across the street. It was very windy and my robe started to blow open. I held it down with one hand as I opened the mailbox and pulled out a few envelopes and flyers. As I was walking back to the house I noticed the car full of ladies had stopped and one door was open. As I approached my front door I met Earl being pulled from the back yard by Cali, now excited to get into the house for her breakfast.

The three of us stood there for a moment while Earl reached for the screen door handle with his free hand. Just as he was slowly opening it against the wind the impatient dog lunged towards the open door. Earl bumped my hand, and all the mail fell on the ground at our feet. Feeling responsible, he reached down to pick up the swirling pieces of mail. I heard a muffled voice from behind me and turned to see all three ladies standing outside of their car clutching a stack of somewhat familiar "Watchtower" pamphlets. The Jehovah's Witnesses have occasionally left their literature in my door while I quietly hid in the house. At that precise moment, the ladies' expressions all changed instantly from happy little "Have you heard the good news today?" smiles to various degrees of distress and revulsion. I turned around to see Earl bent over with his flimsy robe blown up onto his back revealing all that he deems sacred hanging there in the brilliant Saturday sun looking as if he was smuggling some rouge-colored part of a turkey. Of course, being the restrained sort of guy that I am, I started laughing hysterically and pointing at the shocking display. Earl, who was totally focused on stomping on the blowing envelopes, asked me what was so funny. As I was attempting to tell him, the ladies hastily got back into their car and were backing up before I could squeeze a single word through my fit of laughter.

[51]

With their engine screaming loudly, the driver slammed the car into gear with a noisy squeal, and disappeared down the street leaving only their shock and exhaust. Finally I was able to quiet myself enough to tell Earl the cause of my insane laughter. He stood up, reached around with the hand holding the leash and pushed his robe down. He handed me the crumpled wad of foot-printed mail as I continued to laugh and point towards the street and then to him.

A small crooked smile appeared on his face as he finally forced open the storm door and with the dog still pulling him, stepped onto the porch. As he reached for the house door he paused for a second.

"Everyone is a moon, and has a dark side which he never shows to anyone". ~MT~

"Moon indeed", I thought, "moon indeed," laughing out loud.

Lost?

This morning before work I was frantically looking for my keys. I stood in one spot looking down as if expecting them to magically appear, and straining to remember where they might be. As I pondered, my hand checked the pants pocket at least five more times. As I checked the kitchen counter, my hand went back into my pocket. Could I have really missed a big ball of keys the first twenty times I looked for them. As I resigned myself to the fact that the keys were lost, I suddenly flashed on George Carlin's comment, "Things aren't lost...they know right where they are... I am the one that is lost from **them**."

Coming out of the bathroom, Earl asked what I was doing. As I explained my dilemma, I glanced at my watch and realized I'd better find them quickly or I'd be late for work.

"Where did you see them last?" asked Earl. I told him that I had them when I came home from work yesterday, again checking my pocket. Earl said that I needed to retrace my steps, which I annoyingly explained I had already done a dozen times "I gotta find them soon or I'm going to be late", I said.

I decided to look in the car, (which makes no sense because I used them to unlock the house), because I sometimes leave them in the console. As I yanked open the front door, I heard a familiar sound and there were my keys dangling from the lock. Earl was standing behind me as I pulled them out of the door and put them into my hungry front pocket. I hastily gathered up my lunch, put on my hat and stepped onto the porch. As I opened the storm door to step outside, a voice from over my shoulder said,

".... In order to make a man covet a thing, it is only necessary to make the thing difficult to attain." ~MT~

"No kidding Earl...really?" I muttered.

Crushed Ego

I was working in the wood shop today on a project for a friend and realizing how much I miss the elaborate procedures in making something from such a taken-for-granted material like wood. I was using American Black Walnut harvested from here in Wood County Ohio. The tree has a very interesting story behind it that I should share at some point, but today I was concentrating on selecting just the perfect grain for the anniversary box that a young man and I are making for his wedding.

While standing on a ladder I took the dusty boards off a wall rack I had not touched in five years. As I pulled up this piece and that looking for exactly the right color and grain, I felt a bit like I was looking through an old photo album. Each uncovered piece looked like an old friend I had temporarily forgotten, but was happy to see again. I pulled several boards down, leaned them against the wall, and came back down the ladder. As I brushed my hand across their dusty surface and examined them, I found three of the seven that were the exact color and character that I wanted. I put the others back on the rack mentally promising them that they too would eventually have their metamorphic chance.

I adjusted the planer to a one-half inch thickness turned it and the dust collector on, and waited for them to both reach their high pitched whir at top speeds. Each board fed into the planer emerged from the other end with an even more distinctive and spectacular color. It was a return to the days when each time I flipped the switch on that machine and experienced a lovely piece of wood emerging from the other side, it felt like seeing a wonderful Christmas present that a moment before had been hidden in paper.

I measured and cut to size the pieces of walnut, and then precisely cut box joints in each piece to interlock the sides to the ends. An hour later, after gluing the pieces together and squaring the box – but while the glue was still tacky, I sanded the outside of the box. This method uses the sanding dust to fill any small gaps in the joints by mixing with the tacky glue that has oozed out of the joint. Earl had entered about an hour into my procedure and was entertaining himself on a stool next to my assembly bench playing with a strong magnet, a screwdriver, and some screws much as you would expect a young boy to do. Just as I had the box all sanded I took my finger, licked it, and ran it across the side of the box. The grain instantly danced into view almost three-dimensional and it looked incredible.   Holding the box above me I said, "You know something Earl, you are living with a true craftsman with a great eye for quality and detail."

When I looked over to see his expression, I lost my grip and the box fell to the concrete floor with a noise more disturbing than hearing the echoing sound of long fingernails slowly raking a blackboard. I squatted down and reached for it as carefully as I would retrieve a baby bird that had toppled from its nest. One side was cracked and one corner was mashed in such a way that there was nothing left to do except sigh, cry, and call the coroner.

Earl sat there motionless with a magnet holding about a dozen two-inch screws. Standing up I cradled the box in both hands not quite ready to accept its death. As I looked around for suitable resting place, Earl finally spoke:

"Human pride is not worthwhile; there is always something lying in wait to take the wind out of it." ~MT~

Reverence Revealed

Armed Forces Day came and went with little official attention. There was a short mention of the day at the end of the evening news, but other than that brief snippet it was not as newsworthy like its big brother coming up; Memorial Day.

Earl has mentioned, (in character of course), that he served briefly in the Civil War. I suspect that 'his' loyal feelings to America runs deeper than Twain's strong hold on his personal expression, thusly the day did not escape Earl's genuine patriotic notice.

After dinner I was trying to decide what to watch on TV when he earnestly asked me how I viewed the United States during the Viet Nam War. I explained that, in a much less obvious way I suspected it was somewhat like the climate during the Civil War. The country was divided. Fathers and sons disagreed about the strategic deployment of our troops, the ultimate cause we were fighting for, and the overall unachievable goal dictated by Washington. I described how the young people rebelled against the possibility of being sent to their deaths defending a country that did not want our help. How almost an entire generation walked away from all that their parents held dear or at least familiar and set a course on finding a peace tempered with the warmth of love not napalm.

I expressed somewhat apologetically that the attitude of the '60s wasn't about devaluing the gravity of WWII, or the grave sacrifices Americans made to prevent Germany and Japan's world domination, but this was a different era and the mindset to just blow up some faceless enemy or send more American bodies like stacks of cordwood was unacceptable. I added that I loved my country back then as much as I love it now, but policies were so wrong during Viet Nam that I was ashamed of my government. All of America was angrily weary of watching the never-ending stream of flag-draped coffins solemnly unloaded from airplanes each evening on the national news.

Memorial Day has a special meaning to all Americans who have lost loved ones, and many will go to a cemetery and decorate graves with flowers and tears. To the thousands of Americans who have died tragic deaths away from their families in foreign lands, it has a special meaning. To those of us who respectfully consider the benefits of their service, our feelings run even deeper. I added that I was not proud that I served during Viet Nam, but I am proud that I served.

Earl was very quiet while I spoke, knowing Mark Twain's feelings on war and freedom I knew if **he** had anything to add he would. Most people who have served during times of great tragedy and death don't care to talk about it casually. There was great veneration from each of us during our conversation on the eve of a weekend filled with barbecues, boating, and sobering trips to thousands of cemeteries to hold in the highest regard all those we've lost, but especially to remember our fallen soldiers.

As I picked up the paper and turned to the TV section, Earl was staring blankly as if he was perhaps looking into **his** own past. After what seemed to be a long silence he quietly spoke:

"We are called a nation of inventors. And we are. We could still claim that title and wear its loftiest honors if we had stopped with the first thing we ever invented--which was human liberty." ~MT~

An Equitable Resolution

Earl was talking to me about the power of gossip -- how it can hurt or ruin a person without the perpetrator ever facing the victim. "It is the equivalent to adult bullying," he said. "It amounts to pushing people around with half-truths and falsehoods in order to make an insecure, scared rodent of a person look better."

He recalled a time when an editor spread some nasty rumors about him -- implying his drinking had become a huge problem for his family, that his

[55]

finances were immeasurably affected, and that, most likely, he was about to give up writing altogether because his stories were so putrid and slipshod.

I asked him how he dealt with such a mean-spirited man. Not acknowledging my question directly, he related the editor's own troubles with alcohol -- and his gambling which led to his pilfering money from the coffers of the newspaper with which he was entrusted. Earl detailed one occasion when the editor took one of Twain's short stories, changed a few words, and submitted it to a magazine as his own.

The rumors surrounding Twain hurt him although he always tried to act as if they was just more fodder for humor. Having been lied to throughout his life, spurred him to write about truth and lying more than any other subjects. Politics was a close second, but just, "the other side of the same coin," he said. While Earl certainly loved to embellish the truth – or take with poetic license, as he might have put it -- he never said anything about anyone to deliberately injure them in a lasting way or make them look as foolish in the same hurtful manner that his editor had done. Earl said he felt sorry for that man that he had become so shallow, he lived his life vicariously through people he envied, but wanted to see fail so his own life would shine a little brighter.

I asked again how he confronted the editor and what he did about the nasty lies. Again, Earl continued on as if he hadn't heard me. He related details of the man's deeds and the hurt they caused. He was specific about how the newspaper couldn't pay the master printer and a couple of writers because the editor had a bad run of luck at the poker table in saloons that would no longer hold his markers.

He recounted a time when the editor got into a vigorous dispute with a woman at a brothel and handed her a wad of embezzled newspaper cash to keep his visits quiet. He went on to tell that this editor, while falling-down drunk went to the printer's house very late one night and woke the man from his sleep. He demanded that the printer's wife make him something to eat, after which he fell asleep with his head on their kitchen table.

After several minutes of following the sordid path of this scoundrel's escapades I asked again, this time louder and with more urgency. "So, what did you do about the way he treated **you**?"

Earl twirled his cigar in his mouth for a moment, took a long draw, and in his usual pre-luminous manner, emitted such a huge cloud of smoke that the cats ran to the other end of the porch. Still looking away from me, which he always did when he anticipated disbelief," he said:

"If a person offends you and you are in doubt as to whether it was intentional or not, do not resort to extreme measures. Simply watch your chance and hit him with a brick." ~MT~

Rainbows and Singing Birds

When asked about his early teenage years Earl had much to say. He was a tall, slim, awkward-looking boy with a long neck and feared that no girl would ever have him. He did odd jobs to make a little money and once ironically painted a fence, (by himself), to earn enough to buy a book he wanted.

In his travels around Hannibal, Missouri looking -- for a yard to rake or a tree to cut -- he met few other kids at the stately homes where he inquired about work. Mostly he met girls, because the carefree boys his age were off playing ball, swimming, or fishing during the summer. Earl wasn't a shy boy although he was a bit self-conscious and he made friends if others gave him enough time to talk. His gift of expression opened many doors for him, especially among wealthy people who were willing to pay him for things their own children wouldn't do.

One day while knocking on a handsome mahogany door of a grand two-story home, he mentally prepared his sales pitch. He would tell the lady of the house that such a lovely home should never have such a pitiful, poorly shaped tree displayed so prominently. Armed with his pruning shears, he waited for the door to open. He tugged at his shirt, licked his lips, and pushed his curly hair to one side. The door opened and standing before him was the most gorgeous girl he had ever seen. She had carbon-black hair pulled into pony tails on each side of her head, each tied neatly with red ribbon bows. Her bright green eyes caught the late morning sun and left him nearly speechless. He has no memory of anything else about her-- just her angelic face and hair. He stood there frozen for a moment trying to remember why he had knocked on her door in the first place. Had a divine power directed him to this one door all the doors in the world? As he stood there, probably with his mouth open, she asked how she might help him. "You can just pinch me to make sure I am really here," he thought to himself.

"I just thought maybe I could....uh....you know....maybe...use these on you, (holding up the shears) ...not on you...you're perfect......I mean on your tree......out there........in your yard...you know the yard....that tree (pointing again)", he said stumbling over his every word.

[57]

She giggled while shifting her weight and smiling a smile that he was certain made the birds sing louder and created several rainbows that arched across Hannibal at that very moment. "Gosh, she's beautiful," he thought. There was no mistake; she was looking at him not as a boy looking to earn a few cents, but as a handsome prince who had come to rescue her from her boring summer days in the castle. She had been waiting for him her entire life. Destiny was being fulfilled. She was smiling that smile that every boy waits to find. She liked **him.**

As he stood there nailed to one spot on the porch, the girl's mother appeared and quickly ushered her back into the house. Struggling to see around this large protecting hen's apron as the lovely girl disappeared into the darkened foyer, he realized that all he would be taking with him was that blinding memory when she first opened the door and the sinking feeling in the pit of his stomach.

"We have a gardener who comes tomorrow; if it needs to be trimmed, he'll do it. Run along now," she said in her best my-daughter-isn't-interested-in-a-boy-like-you voice.

Earl stepped off the porch nearly tripping over his feet as he looked back over his shoulder. Dejected, he scuffed along the bare dirt street, abandoning the idea of making any money, and slowly headed back to his lonely house.

As I sat there recounting my own youth and reflecting on the first time I experienced an unparalleled view of feminine beauty, of a girl who actually looked back at me with genuine interest. I asked him if he ever got over her.

Sitting in the leather chair with his after dinner bourbon he looked off with a fond smile as if he was seeing her looking at him again at that very moment and said:

"You can't reason with your heart; it has its own laws and thumps about things which the intellect scorns." ~MT~

The Bigger Picture

The modern appliances of the 21st century have sometimes supposedly confused Earl. If you remember the incident with the garbage disposal or the riding lawnmower, you know how his confusion and curiosity can be downright dangerous. As it turns out, the most confusing thing, he deals with daily is the television. I have a remote for the satellite, a second one for the DVD player and yet another for the TV, the technology is a challenge when something out of the ordinary occurs. A striking example is when a cat steps on one of the rarely used remote buttons.

At first he wouldn't try to watch anything unless I was here to set it up for him. As he acclimated and watched me closely, he's gotten good at turning things on just enough to surf channels and find something interesting to watch.... usually the History Channel. Coming home from work one evening, I could hear the TV as I came through the door. Glancing towards the living room I could see Earl's white hair above the back of the leather chair and could smell cigar smoke. I heard the program faintly and figured out that it was one of the many unsolved mystery shows – the ones that could be told in 15 minutes, but by rehashing and showing things repeatedly can be stretched into an hour. I called to him, asked him how his day went and would he please put out his cigar "Pretty good so far...and you?" he responded, sounding a bit annoyed. I told him that it was another busy day and my feet were tired. I said I couldn't wait to get out of my scrubs, and into some jeans, and relax with an ice-cold drink.

From the living room I heard him say that he liked TV better when we watched together, as he got so much more out of it. I smiled thinking how nice it is that he is comfortable here – that he has not only gotten used to my company, but also enjoys me. What a great thing to hear when you walk in the door that the occupants of your home actually enjoy having you there. How different it is from the time when the boys all lived at home, when my coming in the door was merely an untimely interruption of their fun.

I changed clothes, got my Pepsi and walked into the living room just as the forensics expert was testifying about blood spatter. As I plopped into my usual seat and looked up, I saw that Earl had the satellite menu on the screen of the 42" TV and the show he was watching was limited to a 3-inch by 3-inch square in the upper right corner.

"How long have you been watching like this?" I asked. "All day," he answered, "That's why I like watching with you......the pictures are so much bigger when you are here to fix it." Suddenly my presence didn't mean so much. Like having a plumber show up at your house and you are all smiles, not because you want him to stay for dinner, but because you know he'll fix what's wrong and soon be gone out of your mind and your house.

"So, when you watch TV when I am not here you always watch it like this?" I asked. "Yep...always", he answered. Nervously, I imagined those menu images burning into the screen and ruining the TV. "Why haven't you said anything about this long before now?" I asked. Earl, thinking silently, and anxious to get back to the show, answered quickly,

"To lead a life of undiscovered sin. That is true joy." ~MT~

May 24, 2014

I drove into Oak Grove Cemetery to see if someone might have put some flowers on a good friend's grave. I was only 15 when he died and his death has always been troublesome for me. The mere mention of the month of May brings three things instantly to mind; the 17th, the date he drowned, the 27th , which is my birthday, and Memorial Day when with proper reverence I visit my lost family and friends.

As I suspected, no one had been there as there were no flowers. I knelt down and pulled some grass from around the marker while I thought about all the good times he and I had in the few years we knew each other. Standing back up and looking around, I saw all the flags waving over the many graves of the veterans from all of the wars. The amount of flags in just this small cemetery in this one little town in Ohio gave me a solemn pause to vividly imagine one huge burial ground on a flat plain where every fallen veteran from all of the thousands of American towns were buried together. My imagination could envision a picture like those taken at night above a brightly lit city expanding to the horizon and beyond, but Instead of sparkling lights at night all you could see in all directions were small American flags waving in the bright sunlight. The sheer amount of the little red, white, and blue banners could cause one to weep without shame.

Looking across the cemetery, at all the flags waving on this beautiful Ohio day in May suddenly made me feel very small. I could not shake the thought of all the sacrificed veterans being together in one place -- their staggering numbers extending as far as I could imagine. I again looked out over the flags and thoughtfully remembering my friend, I walked back to my car. As I opened the door I took one last look over my shoulder at the sea of red, white, and blue and was struck by this thought. All of the veterans from every war who fought for me, (in some cases even before I was born), **are** all in one place together. They are in my heart and thoughts – and isn't that the point of Memorial Day?

Teary-eyed but smiling, I drove away knowing that I while I may seem small, I'm big enough and important enough that people before me gave up their life so I can be free to do something as fundamental as driving wherever I want to honor anyone I choose..

When I returned home Earl, who didn't care to join me, was sitting on the porch enjoying the lovely day. I joined him and shared with him my emotional observations at the cemetery.

He sat quietly for a moment as if he had no comment, but then very solemnly he said:

"Honor is a harder master than the law. It cannot compromise for less than one hundred cents on the dollar, and its debts are never outlawed." ~MT~

Hearing something different in his voice I was drawn to glance at him. I was amazed to see a small tear slowly flowing down his cheek.

Safety First?

Earl and I were doing some needed cleaning yesterday. I assigned him to a basic task that wouldn't take so long that he'd lose patience. All he had to do was wash three window screens out back while I scrubbed the screened porch in preparation for scraping and painting.

The entire neighborhood was abuzz with mowing, painting, and planting. Everyone was generally enjoying the day outside working on things that needed done. I was also in that spirit when I suddenly heard a chain saw. "Holy Crap," I thought, I threw my brush into the bucket, splashing suds everywhere, and ran towards the back of the house.

I found Earl sitting on the back steps smoking a cigar. One screen leaned against the garage and two others were waiting to be washed sitting on the concrete, and the chainsaw noise was thankfully coming from somewhere else. Whew! That was close. Earl looked at me with a slight smile as though I had seen a ghost, "Why are you so pale?"

Before I could answer, I turned to see my neighbor standing on an extension ladder about 25 feet off the ground with a chainsaw stretching to his right to cut a large branch over his head.

As I started across the backyard toward him; he saw me, stopped cutting, and turned off the saw. Resting at the chest high fence, I asked what he was doing; He explained that several limbs from the huge Red Oak tree were hanging over his patio. He wanted to cut them back before a storm could topple them onto his furniture, grill, and possibly some guests.

I muttered an inaudible expletive and said politely, "You do know that working with a chainsaw on a ladder is breaking the number one cardinal rule?" His look turned from "welcome neighbor" to "get the hell back to your own house." And he replied, "Well maybe, but since I don't own a bucket truck, this is what I have to work with. How do you think early Americans had to do things before lift trucks were invented?"

As I debated explaining that early Americans didn't have chainsaws either, he reached down and gave a fast tug and the saw came back to life. He held the running saw with both hands, precariously leaning on the ladder, and stretched towards the offending branch. "I can't watch...he is hopeless." I thought as I turned back to the land of common sense.

I was about ten steps away from my garage from over my shoulder I heard the branch crack. I turned just in time to see it leave the tree about the same time the chainsaw hit the ground. The end of the 20 foot limb, and the diameter of a basketball, first hit the steel grill turning it into a shiny "V", the very large attached branches morphed the new patio furniture into a modern lawn sculptures, and the sawed end fell on the ladder, narrowly missing its newly designated "rider", and propelled him into a freshly planted flowerbed. My feet felt the thud. I jumped over the fence and rushed to his aid. He was okay but very embarrassed. I tried to help him out of the tangled mess of furniture and small branches, but he said he could do it on his own. Even though I knew that kind of thinking didn't work so well for him moments before, I stepped back. I wanted to say, "I told you so," but instead my sarcasm took over and I quipped, "You now have enough wood to make some rustic lawn furniture."

I didn't wait for a thank-you for my assistance and advice. When I came back up through the yard, Earl was standing with his hands on his hips and a huge smile on his face he said:

"The trouble ain't that there is too many fools, but that the lightning ain't distributed right." ~MT~

Reptiles and Amphibians

Sitting on the freshly painted porch yesterday and thoroughly enjoying the most perfect day we've had this year, Earl and I were having iced tea and admiring our efforts. I asked if he was up to helping me paint the outside of the whole house over the summer, a little at a time. He said he would help about as much as he did with the porch, which meant he might wash three screens. "We might have to rethink painting and hold out for siding until I can afford it", I said.

"That's probably a better idea anyhow," he answered, "preparing to paint is really strenuous work for a man of my age and experience". I pondered his comment long enough to try to envision Earl engaged in anything remotely strenuous.

I broke the quite by mentioning that as it was Memorial Day weekend, I was thinking more about my mother than usual and for some reason about all the things that I said or did that made her laugh. Some of what I did was only funny years later. Had she caught me at the time, she would have beaten the tar out of me.

Earl recalled a time when his mother was baking many pies and had all of them sitting on the kitchen table almost ready for the oven. When she was called away to answer the door, Earl sneaked in, took a pie from the group. With his knife, slit the top edge, and put a frog inside the pie. He had been carrying the medium-sized creature in his pocket off and on for more than a day. He pinched the slit shut rendering his operation nearly invisible. He then hid around the corner as his mother made her way back to the kitchen.

She returned to poking each pie with her fork making vent holes in pretty designs on the top of each one. The third pie she poked was Earl's "special one" and something stopped the fork. She stuck it in again, this time a little harder. This time, when the fork hit the frog, the top of the pie started moving like a cat under a carpet. She gasped and jumped back about the same time that the frog broke through the crust and leaped onto the floor, hopping away covered in cherries and looking for cover. "Sam!!" she screamed. By the time her scream reached him, Earl was long gone out through a dining room window and into the neighbor's back yard.

I had to wonder if that had really happened to young Sam Clemens or was it just another of Earl's fables. Whatever, it brought back a similar trick I pulled on my mother.

My mother didn't particularly like one of my childhood friends; she said we should stay apart, as together, we always spelled trouble. Said friend had brought a baby alligator from Florida. It barely fit, but we got it into a cigar box, held the lid tightly closed, and approached my mother. She was sitting in a favorite armed rocking chair darning socks. Mom really didn't like rocking, but preferred the fit of the chair when she was sewing as she could rest her arms easily. It had a prominent place in the opposite corner from the TV.

I walked over and stood silently in front of her. My pal wisely chose a spot near the door, assuming we would likely have to make a fast exit. Mom looked up and asked what I had in the box. I told her it was a gift for her.

(Here I must interject a side note: Mom was terrified of anything without fur. She was so terrified of reptiles she would leave the room if a snake appeared on Wild Kingdom.)

As I knelt down to set the box on the floor, she leaned forward saying, "How nice." As soon as I released the lid when the box touched the floor, it sprung open and the alligator jumped onto the edge, opened its mouth, and stared right at Mom. She jumped straight up without touching either arm of the chair and suddenly she was standing on the seat of the chair as it rocked wildly back and forth as she tried to keep her balance. I was almost rolling on the floor when I realized that wasn't such a funny joke. I wrangled the reptile back into the box and ran. As we disappeared into the summer sun, I could hear my mother's threats echoing from the living room.

I remember that story like it was yesterday and that every time I reminded my mother about it, she would feign anger, making a squeamish face and shudder as if the creature were still at her feet. Earl and I were still laughing loudly when he said:

"What, sir, would people of the earth be without woman? They would be scarce, sir, mighty scarce." ~MT~

I sure do miss my mother's laugh.

Half Full

After a nice long weekend graced with lovely weather, I was contemplating another birthday without fanfare or celebration.

I was telling Earl I prefer not to draw attention to the fact that I am getting older. Energy, gravity, and the ability to rise from a chair slowly while sounding like a bowl of breakfast cereal is evidence enough that I am not the man I used to be. Do not get me wrong, I love the fact that I am able to get up every morning, work a full day, and can still do most everything I once did, albeit slower.

I thanked Earl for proving that no matter how old you are, keeping your mind sharp will encourage your physical self to tag along. I added that his ability to make everything interesting makes what comes next in my life exciting. Isn't the best part of being young the ability to find wonder in things around you? Every year I seem to discover a new bird, as if it was just created. I don't often take the time to allow myself to witness the fullness of the world around me.

"If it takes a geographical journey to see something new then you aren't seeing your world for what it really is. New things aren't magically appearing; you're just noticing or finding them for the first time. Just knowing that there is so much to learn and experience that I haven't yet imagined gives rise to excitement about what tomorrow might bring. Optimism helps foster discovery," I said, surprised by my philosophical insight.

I hadn't thought Earl was even listening – as he was reading the *Times Picayune,* which a friend sends him from New Orleans. He lowered the paper just enough to peer over the top of the page and said,

[64]

"The man who is a pessimist before 48 knows too much; if he is an optimist after it, he knows too little." ~MT~

One Point of View

After an especially full day; worked my usual work shift, took a pair of violins to be appraised (found they're worthless), attended a meeting, picked up some snacks at the grocery, gobbled down a makeshift supper, and ran off to another meeting. When I finally got home in the evening, I flopped into a chair on the porch. I sat there sinking into the familiar cushion and enjoying the smell of fresh paint and clean fragrance of the spring air. Earl joined me, and handed me a welcome glass of iced tea.

I recounted the events of my busy day, after which he asked, "As birthdays go, how did this one rank?"

"Oh yeah", I said "And it was my birthday too and it was pretty good. It was a tough day at work, but all in all it was a very nice birthday for sure.

"I got some meaningful well wishes from people I care about from all over the country. I could not believe how many birthday notes I received on facebook. Almost 90 greetings this year compared to only a few last year". I said, "I assume that was probably because of the writing I post every day that has gained some additional attention.

"I have no idea what you are talking about", Earl said looking confused. "You know, that little thing I write each morning about my life......on facebook....you know....the Internet?" I added.

"I have never read anything you have written for that facebook thing and I try my hardest to stay away from that confounded Internet," he said tersely.

I went on to say that there are people who actually look forward to seeing what happened in my life the day before and have become fans of the 'characters' in those stories. I also mentioned that having a daily outlet for self expression was giving me something to look forward to each morning. Getting out of bed is not only easier, I look forward to it. Having people say how much they enjoyed reading my little morning entries -- and wishing they could write something like that themselves -- gave me a very good feeling that added worth and purpose to my day. Earl sat there with his hand cupped under a very long ash of his smoldering cigar, staring at the sun that was disappearing below the trees across the road, and said:

[65]

"Man will do many things to get himself loved, he will do all things to get himself envied." ~MT~

Not 25?

Earl was sitting quietly on the porch this morning when I asked if I could vent to him a bit. He said he didn't mind and, as always, he indulged me by listening or at least pretending to listen.

So I decided on the long version; Tuesday at work I was asked to pick up some large totes full of wax that were very heavy, and transport them to a storage area for proper disposal. One of the more difficult things about getting older is accepting that one's physical ability gradually diminishes. So as I looked at these 24" x 24" x 28" heavy containers, my ego said, "You have lifted heavier things in your life; just get them on the cart and get on with your day." I wrestled them onto the cart and took them away. When I got to the storage area I learned I had to stack them three high. I managed that with some serious straining.

I felt normal when I went back to work – and my day with other tasks was considerably less strenuous. I left work feeling fine. Until I got up for work, I had no clue that those 100 pound totes had any effect on me. Earl was nodding a little at this point, but I didn't want to shake him so I continued, but louder. As the day progressed yesterday, it became 'painfully' obvious that something was not completely okay with my back. By lunch time I was okay to sit, but when I got to my feet I couldn't straighten up completely. Trying to walk upright almost took my breath away. I did get through the whole day even though it involved more lifting and storing freight. I went to the doctor after work and then came home to lie on an ice pack. "That's why I wasn't sitting on the porch last night after supper Earl," I said very loudly. "Zzzzzzzzzzzzzzzz", was the only response. "So, that is the reason I am home today -- waiting to see the doctor again at 3:15," I said.

"EARL!" I shouted."

Earl gave a start, yawned, and with his eyes slowly opening gazed at me. "What?"

"Don't you have an opinion about what I just said, something witty or profound?", I said, loud enough to penetrate his fog

Stretching his eyes wide as if he had been paying close attention he said: "Well of course I do. I... Uh..... have been thinking carefully about.......your every word and uh......this is what I have to say about that."

"Do your duty today and repent tomorrow" ~MT~

(It's uncanny that when Earl isn't actually listening he can still snag an appropriate Twain quote to end a conversation).

I should have been Wearing Boots

After seeing the doctor yesterday I was supposed to pick Earl up at the library promptly at 4 pm. He wasn't there when I pulled in to the lot, so I sat in the car to wait. Every time the door opened I looked to see if Earl was coming out, and before the tinted door shut, I strained to see if there was anyone else coming down the exit hall.

After fifteen minutes I was getting anxious. Sitting in the car was irritating to my sore back. I found a spot that looked like six and a half miles from the door and parked. As I painfully swung my legs out the door I wished for a handicap placard for my mirror – something I've never wanted and dread owning. As I slowly stood up, I realized I must look every bit my age, and that my shuffling to the door was just further proof that time marches on even if I can't keep up.

At the front door I reached for the handle and thought of how ironic that my back was injured on my birthday. "Now," I thought, perhaps I will get the message to only do what I can do today -- not what I used to do. I slowly walked down the long hallway and asked the smiling young lady at the checkout counter if she had seen a man who looked like Mark Twain around the library. She told me that he was around the corner at a large round table with a group of high-school students. Earl noticed me as I approached and motioned me to a chair. It was too painful to sit and get up again, so I just stood there loaning my weight to the back of a chair. Sitting at the table were seven teenagers with their eyes fixed on Earl anticipating his next word. He was quietly telling his enthusiastic listeners about the time he was a policeman working in Chicago and catching cattle rustlers at the Chicago Stockyards. After he acknowledged me with a raised eyebrow and a small smile, he related a time when two men were running away. He lassoed them with a 10 foot loop that pulled them to the ground, and rendered them motionless.

For a moment I thought I might have inherited Will Rogers instead of Samuel Clemens. Without a break or enough time to allow the students to swallow this latest yarn, he launched into a tale of how he captured ten men with nothing but a wooden pitchfork and forced them to parade, single file, off to jail.

When he paused for breath, I cleared my throat and Earl looked toward Me. "Well friends," he said, "My ride is here to fetch me home, so we'll have to continue this another time." There were a couple "aw c'mons" and a sigh or two, but they each stood, gathered up their unopened school books, and slowly walked away saying their good-byes to "Mr. Twain".

As we reached the car and were headed home, I asked him why he told such outrageous stories to a group of seemingly nice kids who would have been just as happy to hear true stories of Twain's travels. As is sometimes his custom, when being criticized or questioned, he looked straight ahead while answering:

"There are 869 different forms of lying, but only one of them has been squarely forbidden. Thou shalt not bear false witness against thy neighbor." ~MT~

Rural Palaeontologists

While Earl and I were out driving, I drove through the City Park where the 7th Annual Alicia's Voice free concert will be presented later in the month. He said he liked music and would probably attend. We drove around the park twice and he asked if I had always lived in Bowling Green. As I turned south onto Maple Street, I told him that I lived in New York City for a year, California a couple different times for short periods, but mostly Bowling Green. "Oh yeah, I almost forgot," I said "I lived in Weston, Ohio for a few years when the boys were small. He asked if it was a big town, and I explained, that it was basically a small farm community, with nothing much more than a grain elevator, a few churches, and a couple of small businesses. As we were already on Sand Ridge Road, and Weston is only a few minutes away on the same road, I suggested we take a drive over there.

Taking that drive – which I used to drive at least twice a day for five years -- brought back many memories, of the turns, dips, and sometimes scary blind curves. We got to Weston and I showed him the two places where we lived back then; the two-bedroom apartment on Taylor Street where we lived when Daniel was born, and then the house on Russ Street we rented when Christopher and Seth were born.

We were near the carry-out that sells great soft-serve ice cream so I suggested we stop for a treat before heading home. He agreed. As we entered the store the lady behind the counter was telling a young man that he needed to be wearing a shirt and shoes to get served. He was putting up what he thought was a great argument, "Oh yeah: he said. "Well my shoes and my shirt ain't buying the ice cream, lady. I am," he said loudly as he threw a crumpled wad of bills on the counter. The lady looked away from him and said to Earl, "May I get you guys something?" The boy just stood there huffing and puffing as we made our selections. Earl ordered a large chocolate cone and I requested my traditional favorite, a tin roof.

Finally the boy left angrily and Earl and I sat down at one of the two tables where none of the chairs matched. We hadn't been sitting there very long when the door with the bell on it swung open loudly sounding like a old fashioned telephone ringing. "Now will you serve me?", bellowed the same disgruntled customer. He stood before her wearing a wearing a flowered pillowcase with head and armholes cut into it. The pillowcase "shirt" pulled his arms so tightly together that he looked like a Tyrannosaurs Rex with his little arms pushed out in front of him. I elbowed Earl to look down. Our "Beau Brummell" had a piece of cardboard on each foot with duct tape wound over the top and around his ankle that made him look like a Roman soldier. Had my ice cream been thinner, it surely would have been squirting out my nose. I reached for my phone to take a picture but couldn't stifle my laughter and take a picture at the same time. Without any expression, the server asked him what he wanted. He pointed to Earl's large cone and said, "Give me what that old dude is having."

She pulled a cone from the shiny chrome dispenser and started swirling a thick ribbon of ice cream around and around into it. Earl and I waited for her to stop at the 6 inch size. Instead she kept piling it higher and higher until it was about a foot tall with a sideways lean. She put his change in his boy-sized hands at the ends of those little bitty arms crammed together in the pillowcase. "That's more better lady", he said victoriously as he walked out the door.

As soon as the door closed, we saw him cock his head – and with those little T-Rex arms, he pulled the ice cream up to his wide open mouth. Just as the tip of his tongue touched the ice cream it fell out of the cone onto the stone parking lot. That in itself was funny, but seeing him throw an absolute fit with those arms crammed together while he was spinning around in his cardboard sandals and swearing was worth a trip to Weston any day.

As we headed home, we saw our prehistoric pal riding a banana-seat bike with easy rider handle bars trying to steer with his arms crowded into the now unnecessary pillowcase. After we passed him, Earl looked at me and said through a sufficient smile."

"Damn these human beings; if I had invented them I would go hide my head in a bag." ~MT~

Awww...

In the checkout line at the grocery, the lady in front of us had a small infant in a carrier tethered to the cart handle. I was pretty sure she was a first-time mom. As she advanced up to the clerk, she moved to the front of the cart to unload her many items. The baby was directly facing Earl and me only a few feet away. We couldn't help but notice the little guy; he was wearing a blue outfit with a red airplane on the front partly hidden by his suspenders. The airplane had a bright smiley face with the propeller on its nose and its wings curled up looking like little hands. As soon as the check-out clerk got a peek at him, she squealed and women magically appeared and descended on him like pigeons to popcorn. The oohs and aahs were coming from all around us and the checkout line came to a full stop. Followed by rapid-fire questions: "How old is he?" "Is he your first?" "Does he sleep through the night?"

The new mother only answered, we are so happy!" The crowd disappeared as fast as it had formed, leaving no evidence of their presence other than a broad smile on the little young mother. Earl and I looked at each other as if to say, "what in the hell was that?" The proud young lady was putting her bags into her cart when Earl and I both noticed that the cute little boy had spit up some foreign substance all over Arnie the Airplane. At the same moment, we both detected the unavoidable stench emanating from the opposite end of this cute little cherub. The woman pushed the cart, the child, and the overpowering smell toward the door.

"A baby is an inestimable blessing and bother" ~MT~

Robbing Peter...

Earl was interested that I now collect Social Security. He knew from the news that Congress wants to take money from the fund for this or that. But, he acted confused about where the money actually belongs. I explained exactly -- as if I was talking to someone from another century -- how it came about, how all working Americans pay into the fund, and how it has accrued interest over the years from many prudent investments. I went on to say that if the system is going broke it's because Congress has borrowed almost a trillion dollars from it (the worker's money), too many times to fund wars, reduce the national debt, etc.

After some discussion Earl said, "how can people call it an entitlement when the people who are drawing this money out at retirement are the ones who paid the money in all of their working lives?' I told him that I was just has confused by that as anyone. I said it reminded me of someone who has a cookie and another person comes along, sees the cookie, and eats it. When asked about who took the cookie, the culprit says, "It was just sitting there. Nobody was using it so I took it." Later, when the person whose cookie was taken asks for it back, he is accused of wanting a handout – a "free" cookie.

Earl thought for a minute and laughingly said that if Twain was eligible for Social Security it would amount to nearly $25,000 a month. His comment caused me to wonder if Earl – whoever he is – is not entitled to draw Social Security. Perhaps he is collecting it, and it is in a bank account somewhere.

I explained that if the system goes bust it would be because the government is either using it for some unintended purpose or people hoodwink the system by drawing from it dishonestly. I added that I would rather see *Twain* get his hands on some of it than any member of the government.

Earl, laid his evening paper aside, pulled a fresh cigar from his breast pocket, and held it in his mouth for a couple of minutes before swirling it around to get it moistened. He struck a match on the wicker chair and lit the cigar with three long puffs. As the cloud disappeared through the screen, he blew out a small stream of smoke and said:

"It could probably be shown by facts and figures that there is no distinctly native-American criminal class except congress." ~MT~

Faster than a Cobra

Spending time with Earl has taught me many things. Miss nothing. Observe the world around you and see the many stories left to be told. Look to everything as a possible subject even if you have to distort it some to make you smile. You can twist your memories to mean whatever the telling of them renders them most impressive or entertaining.

When I was young, I liked to lie on my back in the cool summer grass and imagine the clouds as living things drifting off to places far away; magical places with names I invented to make them feel more real. Sometimes, it seemed that they looked back at me and urged me to come along with them. Every shape was open to my interpretation and imagination to change into whatever excited me the most at that moment. There were scores of times during my youth when a cloud ride fit perfectly into my schedule.

I thought my ability to start a fabrication sometimes with a single word was a talent only I possessed. I could make up anything on the spot. If no one else believed my tales, I was always entertained by my creative skill; I was easily convinced that my story could be true, just because it was said aloud. I wasn't pathological about fabricating a tall tale, but I did feel that my stories were just as believable as real life happenings. "It could have happened…it could've," I thought. I remembered a summer day long ago when I found a couple of odd-looking bugs in a rusty red Radio-Flyer wagon at my cousin's house, kitty-corner from where I lived on Ada Avenue. They were about a half-inch long, had segmented pointed tails and squat legs on both sides of their bodies. After very close, (but not too close) examination I immediately named these newly discovered creatures "Kookadikles". My mind took the word "crocodile" and made it into a frightening insect. In my best whispered voice, I warned the assembled and cautious group of younger cousins of the incredible danger of this bug – how with lightning-fast speed, it could leap onto your throat and kill you with its outrageously painful bite. I added that if you killed a Kookadikle or made one angry by staring at it that others would hunt you down wherever you sleep -- even in your parent's bed. My story scared the youngest children so much that they ran screaming into the house, crying for their mother. Needless to say, my aunt scolded me later for my sadistic but creative yarn.

It's odd that I've never seen one of those bugs again. Still, the memory is vivid. My cousins and I still laugh about it 60 years later.

I read this account to Earl as he set aside Ayn Rand's "Atlas Shrugged." His mouth curled into an affectionate smile as he said:

"A truth is not hard to kill…. a lie told well is immortal." ~MT~

America's Greatest Pastime

I took Earl to a minor league baseball game recently. After we settled into our seats, we l had about 45 minutes before the first pitch so we jokingly talked about the people in the stands and made up stories about them.

I started by saying that the family a few rows in front of us would not stay past the fourth inning because the little boy would get so restless or sick they would have to leave. The youth had a pennant, a hat with a propeller, a big ice cream cone, a sack of peanuts, and the game wasn't close to starting. Setting between him and his mother was a huge plastic pan of nachos and melted imitation cheese, which we agreed most certainly would disastrously end-up on someone.

Earl noticed a woman seated alone in heels and a formal looking dress dripping in cheap costume jewelry and sunglasses almost as big as her face. She had a very long electronic cigarette attached to a jeweled chain hung around her neck and occasionally would exhale a thin cloud through her glossy red lips. Earl asked why he couldn't smoke his cigars if she was going to smoke. I tried to explain the 'e-cigarette' thing, but of course he didn't want to hear my explanation and assumed it was a purely a gender issue. He said that he doubted whether she would last as long as the family seated in the same row, because she most likely had a date with a casting couch somewhere.

There were several other colorful people there and, if the truth were told, Earl certainly was one of them. By anyone's standard, I, too, was a unique-looking fan. I was wearing my Eric Clapton 2004 Tour t-shirt and my HK firearms ball cap – probably more appropriate for a concert than a ball game.

Earl went to find a place to smoke. I sat there, loving the blue sky, the few pale puffy clouds, the smell of popcorn wafting through the grandstands, and the teams warming up in their clean white uniforms contrasted against the bright green grass. Earl returned just as the first inning was underway.

The first batter popped up to the shortstop on the first pitch. The second player took so much time digging a hole for his feet, stepping in and out of the batter's box, knocking dirt from his cleats, and adjusting his helmet, I thought he was going to really pound one. He struck out in three pitches, all of them low and outside. The next guy got to first only to be picked off by the pitcher on a careless 20-foot lead off to second.

As the home team ran to the dugout the little boy I was periodically keeping an eye on knocked the nachos off the seat, making a puddle of fake cheese in a yellow circle about the size of a small sombrero narrowly missing the man sitting in front of him. Of course, he put his feet right in it. His mother was trying unsuccessfully to clean it off with those postage-stamp-sized napkins just as the lady in the fancy dress decided to get up and go somewhere. As she approached the family, -- which were engrossed in getting Jr. cleaned up, she became increasingly annoyed by having to wait to get through. She was so focused on the exit and the end of the aisle; she didn't bother to look down and see the yellow pool in front of her. Before Mama could herd her ham-fisted offspring out of the way, the starlet's took a step right into the center of that cheesy goo. She slipped as if in an exaggerated movie pratfall, slapping several people with her flailing arms on her way down and knocking the hat off the man who moments before was narrowly missed by the falling mélange of cheese. She landed with her bottom squarely in the center of the cheese. Before she was even back on her feet, the whole family disappeared as fast as a cloud of e-cigarette vapor. All of the fans in that area immediately started applauding, and one man yelled, "9.5...you nailed the landing". She hurriedly got out of the row. The back of her dress was covered in the yellow mystery sauce and broken pieces of nachos and cheap ballpark napkins fell behind her as she ascended each step.

[73]

For the life of me, I can't remember any details about the game except for 'starlet and the family', that the home team won, and, of course, what Earl had to say about it.

"Some civilized women would lose half their charm without dress; and some would lose it all." ~MT~

Lucky to be Alive

Lately I seem to have a deeper appreciation of my youth. Until I hit 50, I hadn't heard of "fiber." I certainly hadn't thought about maintenance visits to a chiropractor, and shoes naturally became comfortable as you broke them in. When I was young, if I woke up feeling poorly, I knew I was sick. Now, I have to be up for a while and wait to see if that feeling subsides, before I can come to an accurate conclusion as to my condition. Why is this becoming so clear all of a sudden? Seeing my reflection in the mirror yesterday (leaning forward with a five-degree bend in my spine) I was struck by how I now struggle with things I couldn't have imagined just a short time ago. Earl and I were recalling our childhoods and commenting on the things we did then that would seriously injure or kill someone if tried today. I told him of how my friends and I repeatedly attempted to jump off garage roofs, using blankets, sheets, and umbrellas as parachutes, hoping we would slowly drift to the ground. We were never successful and always fell to earth like stones. We Toppled out of trees, fell off bicycles, (**without helmets**), and tumbled downstairs while running too fast. By each of our accounts, black-and-blue bruises and cuts lasted only about three days in the 1850s and 72 hours in the 1950's.

Earl's descriptions of fishing and swimming seemed so much simpler than the same things I remember in my youth. Back then, fishing consisted of a strong stick with a line and hook tied to it. When I mentioned a tackle box, rod and reel, he laughed and said "Those contraptions were for people who wanted to look good, play with the equipment, but not catch fish. If you could sit still for a half hour you could catch fish using pieces of corn for bait."

For him swimming was the same way: no towel or suit. All you needed was a spot that wasn't too muddy, slimy, or shallow. You merely dived in avoiding logs and rocks. He talked of sword fighting with fence pickets and even when you actually hit someone, there were never bad injuries, maybe a mashed finger or two.

He told how he once knocked on a grumpy neighbor's door very late at night and in his haste not to get caught; he fell off the porch and broke his wrist, which had to be wrapped tightly for a month. His point was clear: No matter what he did as a child did not have any lasting effect on his current physical condition.

There is no reversing aging but embracing it feels a bit like surrender. At some point we all have to acknowledge our physical limitations. If we continue to try the things that – at age 25 might have been routinely easy – we will most likely suffer injuries.

At his age, Earl has little sympathy for my ignorant stubbornness to accept my physical limitations.

"So what is your secret to keeping fit?" I asked, adding sarcastically, "besides totally avoiding physical work, that is?" Without any hesitation he quickly answered:

"The only way to keep your health is to eat what you don't want, drink what you don't like, and do what you'd druther not." ~MT~

It's All in Your Head

As the weather has warmed, it's become almost a ritual that we sit on the porch after dinner. The aromas of spring are wonderfully comforting after the interminable gray winter. Take a pleasant climate, combine it with a witty old sage, and you have a recipe for contentment. I sat quietly savoring the gentle sounds of evening, the setting sun, and my comfortable chair. Earl was smoking his after-dinner cigar adding his own particular smell to the evening air. After about a half-hour of pure silence, he said that as long as his mind was comfortable, that all places seemed perfect.

"So environment starts in your mind?" I asked.

"To a degree I guess everything around you is subject to how you think you feel at that moment. If you are in a grumpy mood most likely you will miss the singing bird or the beautiful sunrise", he answered.

I thought for a moment and agreeing with his logic I went on to ask. "So if you were standing at the Louvre looking at the Mona Lisa and you were in a bad mood she might look ugly to you?" I asked, assuming I had completely grasped his logic.

"Well Tom, I have been to the Louvre and I have seen the Mona Lisa and she **was** ugly, and I was in a perfectly great mood inside and out", he said, smiling slightly.

Knowing I had made a huge leap from mental comfort to personal taste, I tried to back up my meaning by asking, "Have you ever found yourself at a

[75]

place where everything felt bad and you could attribute it to your poor outlook at that moment?"

Earl sat there silently rubbing his chin for what seemed like a long time. Finally, while turning to face me so as to see my expression he said:

"I once visited Congress while it was in session!" ~Earl~

Better the Second Time

While my back is mending, I have a lot of free time. Earl and I sometimes have several small conversations during the day instead of our customary after-dinner chat. Yesterday I was sitting on the porch in one of the wicker chairs with several pillows propped awkwardly in an attempt to find a comfortable sitting position.

Earl came out onto the porch, laughed, and commented that if I only had a muscular servant with a large fan on a pole, I would look like a sultan. Not being able to imagine myself as a sultan, I pulled and yanked at the myriad of colorful supports to find a position that – at least momentarily – felt better.

Earl pulled up a chair close to mine. And set down two large glasses if iced tea on the table between us. I thanked him as he positioned himself into his chair and reached into his coat for a cigar and match. The sky was robin-egg blue and only the tops of the trees were moving on this otherwise still afternoon. It is quiet on and Ridge Road until around 3:30 in the afternoon when people start returning from work. The street is usually busy for a few hours before resuming to its comfortable, rural feel as evening sets in.

After getting his cigar roaring and a taking a long sip of tea, Earl asked, "Did I ever tell you about the time I was piloting a steamboat on the Mississippi and ran it aground?" He must have intended his query to be rhetorical as he ignored my interjection that I had heard this story, and quickly launched into the retelling.

"I ran aground on a hidden sandbar right in the middle of the river. I stripped down to my waist and swam under the boat to see what the problem was and how bad it was stuck. Then I swam to the shore pulling a long line and hitched it to a team of 6 horses. I swam back out to the boat and using a large gaff under the flat keel, -- while holding my breath for at least five minutes -- and levering as hard as I could, I was able to free the boat from the sandbar. The horses helped a little, too."

I looked at him in total amazement as he twirled his cigar in his mouth. "Seriously...Seriously Earl? You really did that?" I asked in disbelief."Yes sir, one of the most impressive things I have ever done in all my life," he said cocking his head, blowing out a small cloud of smoke, and taking full command of the moment.

"So, you have run a steamboat aground? How many times did you do that in your piloting career?" I asked.

He answered quickly, "Once was enough, one learns how to sense those sandbars after the first time. I learned very fast how to avoid them.

I pondered this a for a few seconds before I said, "I remember a story like that you told me a few weeks ago, but in that story there was a pair of mules on the shore instead of 6 horses, and you were in the wheelhouse steering the boat off the sandbar not under it holding your breath for five minutes." I waited a moment, giving him time to further embellish a way out, and added, "either you are mistaken about how many times you ran a steamboat aground or your facts are more fabrications than truth".

Earl sat silently looking straight ahead as if searching for a good answer hanging out there in the still of the evening. The only sound piercing the pause was of a Cardinal calling to his mate from the spruce tree in the front yard.

After several minutes Earl took his cigar from his mouth, and with a sly grin, said:

"Yes, even I am dishonest. Not in many ways, but in some. Forty-one, I think."
~MT~

Whipped and Beaten

Earl and I were on our way back from shopping in Toledo when I tried to call a good friend of mine whom I hadn't heard from in several weeks. The call went directly to voicemail, which couldn't accept any more messages. His house wasn't that far out of our way so I asked Earl if it was okay with him to make a quick stop to see if he is okay. Earl said it was fine with him so I made the turn and headed to his house.

When we arrived, I saw his riding lawnmower in the driveway. There were grass-stained tire tracks leading up to where it was parked and the yard was freshly mowed and manicured. Both his car and his wife's were in the garage and the front door was standing open behind the full-view storm door, so I knew they were home.

[77]

I left Earl in the car with the air conditioning running walked to the door, and quietly knocked. His wife came to the door wearing a huge purple Hawaiian print frock that almost reached the floor. She opened the storm door just a crack as one would for unwanted salesmen and said in a very businesslike tone, "Hi Tom, John is very busy!" There was no, 'hey how are you Tom; long time no see" -- not even a small smile to fake a welcoming front?

"I was just stopping to see if something was...", I cut my answer short when I saw John come into the room and walked up and all but disappear behind his robust wife who might have been wearing a drapery stolen from a huge hotel window in Honolulu.

"How are you doing Tom?" he said with a broad smile looking around his wife's shoulder like a curious child who is being blocked from something forbidden.

"Doing pretty good John," I answered. Just thought maybe there was something wrong since I haven't heard from you in so long. I left several messages for you and never heard anything. Just thought I'd check and see if you were sick", I answered timidly.

John's wife, Harriet had added her hands to her hips, which made all but John's head, disappear. "He's been fine, just too busy to be playing around", she said without a hint of warmth.

John squeezed himself in front of her almost pushing his face against the glass of the door. "Come on in and let's visit for a minute," he said.

I explained that I had Earl with me and didn't want to intrude. I added that I just wanted to check on him and should be on my way. He would have none of that, told me to fetch Earl, and at least come in for a cool drink. Upon hearing his apparently objectionable invitation, Harriet raised her hands and then left the room with a loud sigh. I went to shut off the car and fetch Earl. We were going in for just a minute.

We walked through the house and out onto a patio that looks out over a lovely area with two Blue Spruce trees, a couple Cedar hand-made bird feeders, and a great little waterfall John assembled by stacking flat river rocks. The waterfall poured quietly into a miniature pool complete with a few tasteful water plants in the kidney shaped pond and the entire areas was landscaped with hostas, day lilies, and ground ivy. Everything was arranged with great care and taste, and it looked very restful.

Next t to the house, someone had stuck an array of plastic flowers into the dirt. Many were exotics, of the type that wouldn't grow here naturally, and therefore looked even more out of place. The gaudy arrangement really detracted from the otherwise tasteful backyard. John noticed me looking at the flowers and said quietly," That was my wife's idea." I didn't say anything but could sense Earl also raising his eyebrows in response.

"So why are you not taking my calls. Did I do something to make you mad that I don't remember", I said with a smile. John handed Earl and me each a glass of lemonade that he poured from the sweating pitcher most likely left there while he mowed. He said that Harriet took his cell phone because she was annoyed with the amount of calls he was getting and had turned it off – adding that he certainly wasn't mad and that he was sorry I hadn't gotten through.

I knew that Harriet was a bit of a shrew, but until now it had only been slightly annoying for his friends. I asked if he had been out on the golf course since the weather has been so nice. He said sadly that he hadn't had the time with all the chores that she had planned for him to do. I told him the yard looked great. And noting that it was finished, I asked him to go with Earl and me for an ice cream. He politely begged off saying that Harriet wanted him to iron the bed sheets so he didn't dare leave today. With a sad look, he said, "maybe some other time".

Earl, who had been sitting quietly, suddenly blurted out, "I gather she wears the pants in your family?"

John quickly launched into a long spiel about how Harriet was the salt of the earth with what she used to do to keep up such a big house. He said that since she had gotten so big she had become grumpy because she couldn't lose weight. He said that most of the time – well, some of the time -- she's very nice and asked us not to judge her too harshly by her brusque and emotionally efficient greeting.

He clearly loves her, and as evidenced by the scene at the front door, literally gets lost in her shadow. "She just has so much that she wants to do. And since she is physically unable to do it herself, she needs me to stay 'focused' on getting it all done", he said almost apologetically. He added, "I do love her so even if sometimes she is a bit bossy."

After a few minutes Earl and I looked at each other, quickly finished our drink simultaneously, and stood up.

John vacantly looked at me and said, "You're leaving already?"

"Yeah we gotta get going home and you need to get to your ironing," I said a bit sarcastically, wishing he would man-up and escape with us.

As he slowly led us back through the house, Harriet came to the kitchen doorway blocking all the light from behind her except for a faint space around her head like an undeserved halo. She was holding a plate with a huge wedge of cake in one hand and a Diet Coke in the other – presumably to offset the calories in the cake -- and said curtly, "You know, John you got to get over to Kroger's before all of the good strawberries are picked over."

John answered sorrowfully, "Yes honey, I know," as he let us out the front door toward the driveway and freedom. He stood at the door and waved pitifully while looking me directly in the eye. Like a passenger from the Titanic stranded alone in the cold water as the last full lifeboat drifted into the darkness, he disappeared into the house.

As I backed up faster than usual, not wanting to become a fellow casualty, Earl said succinctly:

"Heroine: girl who is perfectly charming to live with,...in a book." ~MT~

Recollection

I went into my shop over the weekend even though I wasn't physical recovered enough to work there yet. The place was in total disarray. Things had been strewn around haphazardly for lack of clear storage space. It resembled a shop of someone who died long ago; no one could possibly have worked in it with so much stuff piled on and around the many machines.

Tool boxes are stacked on each other, covered in dust. I felt sad know that many loyal and trustworthy tools hadn't seen daylight for more than three years. In the right light, I could see cobwebs reaching across areas that were once well travelled during a busy day of creation and construction. Adding to the disorder was evidence that a squirrel had been trapped in there and tried frantically to get out at each window. Things on each adjacent shelf was knocked on to the floor and the window frames had been gnawed in his feverish attempt to get out.

Easing myself onto a stool and looking around the cluttered room I saw pieces of wood that I fondly remembered using for one project or another. Fixtures I made to accomplish a task that otherwise would have been impossible or sometimes dangerous sit idle waiting for another chance at useful employment.

I noticed the photo book peeking out from under a saw blade and a magazine, in which I used to document past and current shop projects. I picked it up and started looking through it. The first pictures were of a spice cabinet I made back in 1975 using very basic wood tools in a spare bedroom of a house on Third Street. The book documented some neat things I made. Over time, I had not kept the book up to date, taking fewer and fewer pictures. I always meant to ask my customers if I might return to photograph their custom-made items for my book. Sadly, I never got around to it.

While the shop had not been as profitable as I had hoped, it allowed me to live out my dream of having my own woodworking business. It afforded me the freedom to drop whatever I was doing to help one of my sons when they needed me. Having the shop right at my house, I felt like I was close enough to keep an eye on them after school – and help ward off the problems "latch-key kids" seem to have. I am finding out years later that sometimes only a few feet away from me things went on in the house that I never had a clue about. I must remember that they were all Lambert boys and trouble was an invention they each discovered in much the same way as I did…, with a smile.

I sat there feeling a bit melancholy looking at everything around the room. It looked more like a storage area than the functioning shop where I once created challenging items for joyful [happy, satisfied] customers. The things I made that are scattered about the world stand in testimony to what I once accomplished and are tangible evidence of my life. Now, focused on today, I thought about the fact that I have a job with people I enjoy, good health, and a regular income. Also, I'm happy to have this shop full of tools and vibrant memories. It could be a vital shop again should I clear the debris, remove the musty-attic atmosphere, and get back to work.

I walked to the door, flipped all three light switches at once and as the room went back to a dry dark storage place I thought of a Mark Twain quote that unfortunately fit both his life and my story perfectly.

"My axiom is, to succeed in business: avoid my example." ~MT~

A Painful Game

Today after returning from Physical Therapy I gingerly adjusted some porch pillows and sat down to enjoy the fresh air of a beautiful mid-morning day.

The landscapers in the neighbor's yard across the street were removing some ugly bushes, and preparing to plant newer healthier versions of the same variety. I watched two of them as they dug, pulled, and eventually removed the most stubborn one. They laid it up on the sand and wiped their foreheads, almost in unison.

A friend had stopped earlier and graciously brought me a quart of fresh strawberries. They were sitting on the little table in front of me minding their own business, looking perfectly delicious. The cats were snoozing on the porch carpet, except for one who was very curious about the container of luscious berries posing for me in the white wooden crate.

Having already shooed him away a couple times, my attention strayed. All of a sudden, he knocked a half dozen of the berries to the floor and was batting them around – with no respect for the future I had planned for them. I gently pushed him away from one with my foot and he simply turned to another. Since bending is difficult in my current condition, recovering the berries quickly was futile. As I managed to get to a few, he knocked others further away/ His resolve was stronger than my ability.

Earl had been watching this spectacle and was visibly entertained to see an agile cat playing keep-away from a slow-moving, injured old man on his hands and knees' cursing his usual favorite creature.

Earl took the box from me, retrieved the few berries beyond my reach and put them back in their proper place. "Having a little trouble there Tom?" he asked with a soft smile. I quickly explained that I was in no mood or condition to play strawberry hockey with a sinister cat. Earl sat there looking at the cat, which by now was sitting on the screen ledge, licking one paw as if signifying he had won the game.

We all sat quietly for a while, when I suddenly laughed loudly thinking what I must have looked like to Earl, while I slowly fumbled for the loose berries like someone searching the floor for a contact lens.

The cat had indeed, been victorious and I likened his preening himself in front of me to a feline wide-receiver spiking the football. I looked at Earl and said that regardless of their trouble, I cannot imagine a house without a cat. Having four cats is quadruple the good life.

Earl looked over at the offender still cleaning himself after making a fool of me and said:

"When a man loves cats, I am his friend and comrade, without further introduction". ~MT~

Was That John Carradine?

The screened-in porch is an "L" shape. The long side of the "L" is parallel to the street, about 20 feet away. On this same side is a large window that provides a great vantage point for the cats to see onto the porch from the confines of the house.

The porch has two large armchairs, a loveseat, a small low table, and a rocking chair at the very end. They are beige painted wicker with comfortable floral cushions. There are two small marble pedestal tables and two small subtle wind chimes hang from the white ceiling at each end of the porch. The brown carpet softens your steps and the sound. It is a very restful spot that I use almost daily even into late fall, when I need a coat to be comfortable in the brisk air.

It was raining lightly this morning when I made it out to the porch with my coffee. I hadn't heard Earl stir so figured he was still in bed. I thought of yesterday's incident with the strawberries and the cat, and I felt my face gently widen into an amused smile.

Just as I turned the corner I heard, "You're a little early this morning". Knowing who it was didn't alleviate the surprise in my voice when I answered, "What are you doing out here?" As if there would need to be a reason for Earl's presence in the place where he spends at least a third of every day. "Just enjoying the quiet and the smell of this fresh rain," he said, tilting his head back and breathing very deeply in an exaggerate manner. "It does smell nice and God only knows we need the rain," I replied.

I had no sooner got the words: "God only knows" prophetically out of my mouth, when a car pulled into the driveway and stopped. As I strained to see the driver through the rain-covered tinted windows, a man wearing a suit got out followed by an umbrella that opened automatically with switchblade speed. He walked around the front of the dark sedan with his head tilted forward and the umbrella covering his face. As he reached the storm door, he lowered his umbrella enough to knock. At that, I saw he was wearing a clerical collar. "May I help you?" I said, slowly rising from my chair". I am looking for Mr. Tom Lambert", he said.

I looked at Earl. He had a puzzled look on his face that I felt I must also have on mine. "That'd be me," I said opening the door to let him get in out of the rain. As he stepped onto the porch I asked him why he was looking for me. He said that he heard I was providing the sound system for the upcoming Alicia's Voice Concert in the City Park. Further, he asked if I might provide a P.A. system for a tent revival he was having in July.

I explained that I've been off work nursing a strained back and that, because the sound equipment is very heavy, I probably wouldn't be able to help him. I invited him to sit and offered him a cup of coffee or iced tea. "Oh no, caffeine is the Devil's blood itself", he said sternly. I discreetly raised an eyebrow and glanced over at Earl who looked as if he was cornered on his end of the porch.

I politely asked what size of P.A. he would need so, thinking I might point him to someone who would have such gear. I asked, "How many singers will you be having and will there be a keyboard of some sort?" "Oh no," he said emphatically, "music is the thunder of Hades itself!" "Hmmmm okay then, well I can give you a name of someone who might be able to help you out", I said quickly. I stood up and walked back into the house to get a pen and paper.

As I was returning, I heard Earl say, "Can I offer you a fine Cheroot?" I walked back onto the porch just in time to see Earl retracting his hand holding two fresh cigars. The other man held up both hands in protest. "There will be plenty of time for us sinners to smoke in the fires of hell", he said with a voice loud enough to be heard in any large tent with or without a P.A. Earl was leaning back increasingly as if the volume of the evangelist was blowing him off of his feet. With a few fast steps he fell back into his chair.

I quickly wrote down the name of a guy who has lots of sound gear, thinking as I was scribbling that I'd better call him immediately after "Mr. Fire and Brimstone" leaves and apologize for the referral. The man folded the paper, thanked me, stepped back into the rain, and vanished down the street just as quickly as he appeared.

With a wide-eyed expression I looked at Earl and promised that from now on I would be careful before saying "God" out loud. He laughed and added:

"I haven't a particle of confidence in a man who has no redeeming petty vices."~MT~

The Third Wright Brother

Earl is very curious about my shop and recently we spent a couple hours there playing "show and tell." He would ask me what a particular machine or tool was for and I would explain or show him the proper procedure to operate it. Sometimes I would show him a sample of what it produced.

He showed some aptitude for woodworking. When I handed him a tool, he grasped it like it had been in his hand for years. You can tell a lot about one's possible ability when you see him pick up pliers, screwdrivers, handsaws, etc.

After our extended session, he hung around to look at things further. He poked about in the large boxes of wood scraps that I've been saving for years, thinking one day I'd use them for a project. Occasionally, Earl pulled out a sample, held it on edge in both hands, and sighted down the board in an experienced fashion. It appeared that he was looking for something of a specific straightness. He put it back in the bin. I didn't say a word, but I was wondering what was going on behind his one open eye as it looked down the edge of the wood like an archer sighting his prey. What did he have in mind to make? Of course, I always remind myself that I'm dealing with a highly intelligent man – but my watchful eye is always part of my catastrophe-prevention strategy. As I was dozing off in a comfortable chair, I heard loud cursing. This is a sure sign that nothing good is happening. Earl doesn't curse when the neighbor brings freshly baked cookies or when the newspapers arrive on time. He usually starts off slow and then gains momentum, as his wheel of profanity gains speed and pitch. Nine times out of 10 it's because he has done something stupid -- not because the malicious universe has played a dirty trick on him.

As I tentative eased up from chair, Earl came running out of the shop, his cursing getting louder with each step. He had a board about 1½-feet long stuck to each hand. The boards banged against the door frame as he flailed his way out of the shop and onto the driveway.

"What in the world?" I said out loud even though he couldn't hear me over his gruff rant. "A little help here DAMMIT!!!!" he yelled. The sight of him with boards stuck to each hand flapping wildly brought to mind an humorous vision. I recalled little black and white video snippets shot during the days of experimental flight; they ran clickty-clack through my mind complete with the flickering light. I conjured men running downhill wearing multi-layered wings, jumping off a cliff and crashing in a heap below. I saw a man with rockets strapped to his back falling down with people throwing snow on the back of his pants to put out the fire. I even envisioned a man on top of a barn, flapping wooden arm/wings and falling flat on his face in the dirt below. The amusing mental movie lasted just a few seconds before I turned my attention back to the reality of Earl's dilemma.

"What happened here"? I asked, still smiling at the image of Earl soaring above my house like an Eagle with his makeshift wings. "That damned glue you got in there.... how the hell can you use that stuff?" he said trying to bite at the board stuck to his right hand."Wait a minute. Did you try using that big bottle of super glue?" I asked as I pulled the board away from his open mouth.

"Well." He said, "If you're asking if it's super glue I guess even a blind man can see it is SUPER glue", he said shaking both arms wildly. As I ducked away from his flapping "wing," I explained that super glue isn't what one uses for large projects. As I walked him back into the shop -- his arms outstretched like an exaggerated sleepwalker, he told me he was trying to make a birdhouse for Purple Martins. ("They eat lots of mosquitoes you know").

[85]

I thought better of asking him about his design or at what point he was in his construction I merely focused on squeezing out the de-bonding agent between his right hand and the pine board. It was 20 minutes before it loosened it enough that the board could be removed. I then turned my attention to his other "wing." As I worked to 'free' him, I was subconsciously re-assessing Earl's natural woodworking ability. Earl quietly watched my careful application of this miracle substance to his left hand, tilting his head to see exactly where each drop was going so he might strain to release it as I went. After several minutes he spoke:

"The proverb says that Providence protects children and idiots. This is really true. I know because I have just tested it." ~MT~

Father's Day

Looking over my shoulder this morning Earl examined my Facebook posting of a picture of my three sons, (no relation to the TV show of the same name from the '60s). He commented that Father's Day seems to be a big deal judging by all of the nice comments and the people who approved enough to click "like."

With tongue-in-cheek I explained that outraged fathers all across America lobbied stubbornly to get their own day after the big fuss was made over Mother's Day. "Really, like they locked arms and marched in Washington or something?" He asked knowing full-well I was joking. I smiled and said no, and that I didn't know the exact year of when it actually became a holiday. I added that Father's Day most likely came about in the same way that it is celebrated, without much fanfare. I think it's cool that there is a day when your children come around to wish you well even if it is only in between 'important' things they are doing. I don't think fathers want a lot of hoopla; just knowing they are appreciated as fathers and that they have hopefully contributed favorably to the future of the planet by providing responsible offspring -- is enough of a gift.

As all three boys were fresh in my mind as we moved to the front porch so Earl could smoke. I shared some of the times each of my sons did something memorable that either shook me to my core or made me laugh out loud.

We settled into our chairs basking in the bright, cool air, and listening to the sounds of lawnmowers on this busy Saturday. I told him about my eldest son when he was about three. He got separated from his mother in a large grocery store. While she frantically searched up and down every aisle, he casually walked up to the office area of the store and asked the clerk, "Can you page my mother? I think she's lost?"

My middle son who had a lesson in first grade about the dangers of smoking came into my shop after school announcing that some of the chemicals in my cigarettes are poison and could kill me. I dismissed his concern by saying that I didn't smoke enough to worry about or cause him any real concern. The following day, he got off the bus, made a bee line into the shop, and said, "Just so I understand, you want to die?"

I then launched into the story of how we almost lost our third and youngest son in some unusually violent waters at Marblehead Lighthouse when he was about seven. I decided against it because the length of the story and the emotions it evokes wasn't something I wanted to chronicle at that moment. It always brings tears, but ends in such a positive way that it deserved at least an abbreviated version, though it's not as thought-provoking or amusing as the previous two tales. I told Earl in broad detail how the rest of our family and several bystanders helped to rescue him, his oldest brother, and their mother from certain tragedy in the waves crashing against the rocks. I also mentioned that my middle son who was only three years older than his youngest brother in distress, was key in quickly coming up with the plan that eventually pulled them all safely from imminent danger. Earl looked at me and tearfully said, "That is such a touching story, and they all are lovely stories and they all are great boys".

I ended my trip down memory lane by telling how we enthusiastically 'encouraged' them into wearing a wrinkly purple suit and white four-fingered gloves dressed as the "California Raisin" for Halloween. They laugh at the pictures now, but recall how mortified they were to each take a turn at showing up at school wearing that outfit. My oldest son says, "We looked like a big purple turd." Thank God that was only during the early grade school years. Otherwise, they would have been permanently scarred and most certainly would have ignored Father's Day; and Mother's Day would have came and went with no word or mention. Earl laughed at the image of all three young boys dressed up at various Halloween celebrations looking like a dried grape.

While they have all weathered some embarrassing father moments, they seem to sincerely like and respect their Dad I said gratefully.

Earl, who was sitting in the wicker rocking chair drinking a glass of freshly brewed iced tea, appeared to be thoroughly entertained by my telling of my sons' exploits. He turned to me -- with his signature smile evident by the rising of his moustache at each end -- and said:

"It is a wise child that knows its own father, and an unusual one who unreservedly approves of him." ~MT~

A Great Lake

Earl was invited to go up to the lake for a couple of days with some student friends he met at BGSU before he and I were acquainted. I explained to him I didn't feel at all left out, because water and its supposed pleasure has not been of interest to me since losing a friend to its depths when I was a young man.

While I will miss him, his absence will be neutralized by my anticipation of his adventurous stories when he returns.

It was after Noon, a week later, when Earl finally emerged from his room. His hair, which is never really in place, was unusually messy. He was wearing the Japanese robe I found for him at Goodwill, which he had cinched at the waist with a brown dress belt. I guess he must have lost the matching cloth belt that was attached before he left. He passed me, while I sat at the computer typing, and shuffled into the kitchen..

"There is some different coffee if you are interested. It is the new breakfast blend from Green Mountain", I said looking after him. "I don't care what mountain it comes from; I just need a hot cup of java," he mumbled. "Whatever", I said to myself and went back to typing. Minutes later Earl emerged from the kitchen with a steaming cup in one hand and two pieces of toast in the other. As he got to the front door he looked down and raised both hands as if he just discovered he only has two and they both are holding something -- or to choose which he should he drop to be able to open the door. Seeing his dilemma I quickly got up and opened the door to the porch.

He thanked me and walked out and as he slowly settled into his seat my curiosity got the best of me and I followed behind. I sat down in my pillow-covered chair next to him. We were separated only by the small table that held his coffee and an ashtray awaiting the inevitable morning cigar. He sat in total silence, slowly eating his toast and taking quiet sips of coffee between each bite.

"So, did you have a good time up at the lake?" I asked. He explained that he thought the lake would be smaller, but felt foolish thinking that, considering that it **is** one of the **great** Lakes. I laughed and said that anytime I cannot see land on the other side of a lake, it is a great lake to me.

"Perhaps," he said, but Lake Erie is indeed a Great Lake and lives up to being in the group judging by the amount of fun one can have along its coast." He went on to say that he heard lots of odd music, stayed up to see the sun rise several times, and had many different alcoholic drinks in the last week. He added that he didn't understand how people who live there could take it for a whole summer; he thought he might lie down and die after only a few days.

I told him that most of the people he saw there were probably not residents but folks who were just kicking up their heels for a couple of days with the same enthusiasm as he and his friends. I also said that there isn't any reason to over indulge if you don't feel like it's the right thing to do. There is no Island law that says you have to drink constantly.

"Oh, it **was** exactly what I was supposed to do," he replied. "And the people were so charming, you certainly couldn't say no to their hospitality" I gave up making a case for moderation and turned away knowing that, as always, his rationalizations would win out over my logic.

"I see you have a souvenir from Cedar Point. Did you go there, too?" I asked."Oh yes, there were some people I met who had a boat at Put-in-Bay who took me over there with them," he said excitedly. "I got in free because we convinced the girl at the ticket booth that I was Mark Twain and was appearing there as an attraction later that night," he added laughing.

"We had a big time there, but some of those contraptions that people climb onto there are absolutely insane," he said.

I asked him what he thought of the Gatekeeper coaster. "Once you get your mind used to the fact that thousands of people have done it before you -- and lived through it -- your fear hides its head. It's a real thrill."

"You mean **you** actually rode that ride?" I said in disbelief.

"I did, but you couldn't get me on some of that scary stuff", he said, finally lighting his first cigar.

I was staring at him like he was Lazarus and decided I needed time to process the picture of this white-haired old man wearing an Ivory suit and a green Cedar Point visor riding Gatekeeper. As I slowly got up out of my chair I was thinking about those little poles that say "If you are this tall you can ride", and thought there ought to be a measurement for determining common sense before allowing old and fragile people to board some of the crazier rides. What park owner would want an old guy who died from a heart attack carried off of a roller coaster in front of hundreds of kids waiting to ride it?

"Well I think you were nuts for riding some of that stuff, but as long as you lived through it and had fun I guess it was a good week for you," I said as I headed back to the computer.

Earl looked at me with his little boy smile and said:

"Of course, no man is entirely in his right mind at any time." ~MT~

Style

As is my summer custom, I was sitting on the porch after dinner last night. I was particularly enjoying the clean scent of the freshly scrubbed ions left by the on-and-off showers of the day. I was tempted to hyperventilate so I could fill my nostrils and lungs again and again with the enticing and calming aroma before it disappears. It was peaceful outside although a bit muggy. The porch screens prevented any bugs from interrupting an almost perfect end to what had been a soggy, gray day.

Earl came out with a squat glass of bourbon and sat downwind from me, engaging in his own adopted ritual of an after-dinner drink and cigar.

We both sat there quietly for a few minutes; the only sound that pierced the silence was the scratch-swoosh of a wooden match being dragged across the underside of Earl's wicker chair. Out of the corner of my eye, I saw the first big cloud of cigar smoke grow larger and then thinner until it disappeared through the screen. He puffed a couple of times, blew out a slow cone-shaped stream of smoke that he savored completely, and reached for his glass on the table between us.

After a while, Earl asked me if I still had Thursdays off now even though I'm working in another department. I said that I did and that there were some things that I needed to get done this Thursday, because I'll be working the weekend. He asked if I had my writing done for what I planned to read at my 50th Class Reunion. I explained with a smile that I had some basic notes, but I would probably leave it appropriately for the last minute just as I always had with "school work". He laughed a little and said, "I know what you mean. I used to do the same thing." We resumed sitting quietly and I began to think about what I must get done on that single day off.

"I know one thing I have to do". I said, as if he would really want to know. "I have to take my new suit downtown to be altered. The pants hang on the ground; I'll look like a teenage boy wearing his father's suit to the prom if I don't get them fixed. I don't know if I should get cuffs or not."

"Well I have never seen a suit without cuffs on a full grown man, but that means nothing. Today's fashions are a complete mystery to me. Pants dragging on the ground and hanging off a boy's backside doesn't even seem to turn a head 'cept mine," he answered in presumably authentic Twain fashion.

I ignored his tempting bait hanging low like ripe fruit and chose not to comment further on the ridiculous style that makes old white men crazy. I went on to say that I haven't had a new suit in years and not one in a light color since I was a boy. Had I been inspired to buy a new suit before now, it would only have been a dark pinstripe. There is something about this class reunion that has me excited enough to look forward to dressing up in a completely new and cheerful ensemble. I am enthusiastic about standing before my class one last time and reading the composition I've written just for them.

Earl sat there twirling the end of his mustache with his right forefinger and thumb, which usually indicates an impending profundity. After a lingering pause, still looking straight ahead, he pulled one of his aphorisms from an obscure corner of his mind and uttered:

"However, we must put up without clothes as they are--they have their reason for existing. They are on us to expose us--to advertise what we wear them to conceal. They are a sign; a sign of insecurity; a sign of repressed vanity; a pretense that we despise gorgeous colors and the graces of harmony and form; and we put them on to propagate that lie and back it up." ~MT~

I looked back at him expecting something further to tie his comment to mine. He continued to look silently into the evening, apparently indicating there wasn't anything more to say.

He took a deep draw from his cigar, and pushed another large cloud of smoke into the heavy evening air without another word. After what seemed to be a long time I finally said, "Well okay then", I said, putting a period at the end of that odd conversation.

I slowly stood up from my chair and without another sound from either of us I went into the house figuratively scratching my head and reviewing what I said to trigger such a philosophical response.

A Touching Scene

Earl walked the two miles from my house to the hospital and decided to have lunch with me. While I enjoy him so much and truly regard his company as one of the many good things in my life, I'm not real comfortable with him being at my workplace. His odd appearance just begs the same questions again and again. "Who was that man; why is he dressed like that; is he in a traveling theater group; why does he live with you; is he your brother?" etc.

He found a seat in the outpatient surgery waiting room 30 feet from the Welcome Area where I was seated and opened a *Redbook* magazine, which caused me to do a double-take. I looked around at the other people scattered around the big room. In such an eclectic collection of people, Earl really didn't look that strange. There was a guy wearing a Detroit Tigers t-shirt, long denim shorts that first looked like pants that were too short, and brown leather sandals with tire-tread soles. A very large lady several feet away, wearing pink shorts, a man's white ribbed undershirt, and flip-flops was sitting on a scooter. She was breathing so hard I wondered at first if she should be in Emergency. Another woman, dressed in yellow shorts, yellow blouse, yellow tennis shoes, and a big yellow bow in her hair was accompanied by two small children -- one dressed in red, the other in blue. The kids were down on their knees focused on open coloring books facing the seats in front of them and being very quiet. Among all those very "colorful" people, Earl fit right in.

The one puzzling thing about this scene was that everyone waiting there was waiting for a patient in surgery and no doubt knew in advance the date and time of the procedure. In Emergency you typically find people who were unprepared in any fashion to be there. Sometimes they are wearing slippers, pajamas, curlers in their hair, etc. In outpatient surgery, however, one might think that visitors would have taken the time to dress differently than a college student on laundry day.

When we went to lunch we sat down in the cafeteria facing the line of people slowly sliding their trays toward the cash register. Most of the patrons were obviously hospital employees, except for an older couple that we both noticed immediately. They were moving slowly, looking at everything displayed, as they probably had never been there before. The thing that caught our eye almost simultaneously was that they were holding hands. I looked closely as they slid their tray along trying to see if their connection was merely to stabilize each other. They were quite advanced in years to be sure but they seemed to be holding hands not out of fear of falling or being separated from each other, but because they just enjoyed holding on to one another.

Earl turned to me and said, "That is something you don't see enough of". I agreed and smiled at the couple as they shuffled by to find a seat behind us. As we finished our lunch and got up to leave, I noticed the couple was sitting side by side. Earl who saw them too, smiled, leaned over, and whispered to me:

"No woman or man really knows what perfect love is until they have been married at least a quarter of a century ~MT~

A Clear View

When I went into the kitchen to make my coffee this morning, Earl was bent over the kitchen table with a section of paper towel laid out in front of him "Why are you up so early....what are you doing?" I asked. Not breaking his concentration or raising his head, he replied, "My glasses came apart last night while I was reading and I am trying to replace this very small screw that holds the lens in."

Looking over his shoulder I saw that he had a single-edge razor blade in his right hand attempting to turn the screw with the corner of the blade while squeezing the frames together with his left hand to keep the lens from falling out.

"Let me get something for you", I said while I opened the designated "junk drawer" behind him. In the very front of a drawer that has everything from incomplete decks of playing cards; dried-up super glue, and odd-looking pieces of replacement parts for things long forgotten, were my mini-screwdrivers. I took the smallest flat blade screwdriver and handed it to him while reaching around his left side to take over holding the lens tightly in the frame. He quickly got the threads started and holding the driver with his forefinger on top as it was designed he instantly tightened the screw. "I wish I had known you had such a thing; I have been messing with this for about an hour," he said thankfully.

I went on to prepare my coffee and bagel for my breakfast. I moved around the kitchen -- taking my vitamins, getting the butter and knife out -- as I waited for the toaster. I noticed Earl was holding his glasses flat with the lenses in his open mouth and breathing on them in preparation for cleaning.

Once again, I intervened, "Hang on a second; I got just what you need". I returned moments later with a small spray bottle and a micro-fiber, lens cleaning cloth. I carefully took his glasses from his hands and sprayed both sides and wiped them dry. In less than ten seconds they were spotless.

"Why thank you Tom", he said as he put them on his nose, pulling the wires behind each ear. He tilted his head up toward the light, and I saw a smile leak from beneath his silver mustache as he added, "That is **so** much better."

I went back to buttering my bagel and poured coffee into my favorite cup. I sat the steaming brew in front of Earl who was now wadding up the paper towel. He looked up and said, "Thank you" with a grin. I went back to the toaster and brought him the bagel, too. "That was **your** breakfast." he said.

"I'll make more for myself.... sit....enjoy", I said as I patted him on the shoulder.

As I prepared another coffee and bagel, I was aware that he was looking at me. I looked back at him as he said,

"If a man has just merciful and kindly instincts he would be a gentleman, for he would need nothing else in the world." ~MT~

Rising Above

After I finished mowing the yard in the sticky Bowling Green summer heat I settled into my porch chair slowly sipping ice water before embracing the shock of the air-conditioned house.

Earl came out and took his usual seat. He must have seen me through the front window or heard the mower stop and figured I would be where I always am after the grass' weekly manicure.

He was holding a copy of *US* magazine, which surprised me, but then he reads everything he can find so I should not have been surprised. He hadn't had the cover open for a full minute when he looked at me and asked, "What is a movie star?" I sat there for a moment thinking how I might accurately answer.

"There are two different types of Movie Stars my friend. There are those who are marginal actors and crave the spotlight only for the sake of stardom, money, and fame. The other type has become famous simply because they are just so good at what they do," I said.

"I have heard you refer to people in ordinary life as 'movie stars', what you mean when you call them that?" he asked. I took a moment to think of people I might have called that and said: "Some people exude star quality in their everyday lives. They may have had a tough way growing up, a bad marriage, lost a spouse, or had jobs that did not show their true talent or passion, or maybe they endured circumstances that made things more difficult for them than most other people. The point is that, no matter what their background, they have risen above their problems to become more. When there is a shortage of money, they do their best to manage with what they have. Maybe they were not educated but became voracious readers. Generally speaking, they carry themselves in a way that shows their spunk and spirit. A "movie star" of this type has to have style and grace above all else for me to hang that title on them, and oh.... a commitment to be more than their past dictates", I added. "My mother was a movie star. My sister is a movie star. If the people I meet and see have those ambitious qualities, they, too, are movie stars."

"So it has nothing to do with actually being in films?" he queried.

"In this case," I answered, "that title is an honorary one setting them above many others who never reach beyond their circumstances. Sometimes the real heroes of life do not get the credit they deserve. Some of the most attractive, brightest, and brave people do not get noticed because they don't seek the public spotlight. In my eyes they are all 'movie stars' in the purest sense of the word."

He continued to absently turn the pages of the magazine while he looked through the porch screen and beyond. I assumed that what I said might have struck a chord with him, and I was hoping that I hadn't lost him by taking a term that could be unfamiliar to Twain and turning it into something ambiguously bewildering.

He sat very still, which possibly meant in his mind he was running through a library looking for a place to store the dual meaning of my endearing term. After about ten minutes as I was about to go back into the house, he turned to me and said:

"It is better to deserve honors and not have them than to have them and not deserve them." ~MT~

Spare the Rod

Earl and I went to Wal-Mart yesterday to pick-up a few things. He'd rather go there than watch a comedy on Netflix. He pulled a cart from the long row at the entrance and I looked down hoping I had the only cart in the store with a broken front wheel that would wobble, pull me to one side, and make noise the whole time I was shopping. I have learned that if you set your heart on having a defective cart more times than not you will get a perfectly good one.. (Oh crap, we got a perfectly good one again!), I thought as I looked down with a satisfied smile at the four wheels tracking and rolling quiet and straight as we walked into the store.

"Good afternoon young men, welcome to Wal-Mart enjoy your shopping experience," boomed the greeter who only lacked a straw hat and bamboo cane to be taken for a genuine circus barker. "Experience" was the only word in his greeting that would likely be accurate.

I have to usher Earl along every few feet like a cat in a seafood store. His head is on a Linda Blair swivel as we snail through the aisles.

Since he knows I can take pictures with my phone, he frequently gives me an elbow and says, "There's a good one for you." He doesn't quite get it that you can't just whip out your phone, and snap a picture when you're standing three feet from someone who is apparently dressed for "Let's Make a Deal." -- Especially after some old guy in a white suit has loudly blurted "There's a good one for you", that causes a big fellow named "Bubba," (it's tattooed on his forearm), to turn around flashing a sinister grin at you with his one good tooth.

We picked up all of the groceries that we needed and headed to the opposite end of the store to buy cat litter. We took a main aisle that leads through both men's and women's clothing, electronics, jewelry, house wares, and sporting goods.

As we were about to turn into the pet-supplies aisle, we came upon a woman and a small boy by an end cap filled with toys. The little boy, about three, had obviously touched some bright colored toy on a low shelf in front of him while the woman, (probably a grandmother), was looking at things far above him. She had him by one arm and was slapping his bottom, "I told you (slap slap) not to touch, (slap slap) **anything** (slap slap) while we are in here (slap slap)," she said with a severe tone.

Several other shoppers caught her action and stopped their carts to observe her obvious anger. A few seconds later she slapped his bare arm and hand a few more times saying, "I have told you a thousand times you don't touch anything...you hear me??...**anything**..." she shrieked, adding another very hard slap to the top of his head, accented with yet another "**Anything.**"

Earl turned to me and said, "Someone ought to grab her and give her fat ass a few whacks." I looked at him extending my hand like a maître d as if to say, "Step this way."

Earl casually walked up, and stopping directly behind her, gave her three very loud slaps across her three-sizes-too-small shorts, as he said, "How many times (slap) do I have to tell you (slap) not to beat a child (slap)?" The woman reached back trying unsuccessfully to cover any portion of her largeness. With her mouth wide-open she screamed, "What the hell do you think you're doing?" She no sooner got that out of her mouth when very loud applause broke out all around us. One girl captured the entire incident on video, which will likely make the lady an instant YouTube sensation.

The woman hastily rushed away almost dragging the little boy with the glowing red arm while the clapping continued punctuated by a couple whistles from the approving crowd. Earl took a couple low theatrical bows, and we went on our way to the pet aisle.

Earl was grinning and had his thumbs tucked into his vest in cocky theatrical style. As I pushed the rare, perfectly tracking cart toward the checkout aisle, Earl turned and said:

"To be vested with enormous authority is a fine thing; but to have the on looking world consent to it is finer." ~MT~

Delayed Beauty

At last, my back felt normal enough that I could plant the drooping impatiens I had received for my birthday more than a month ago. I got out the trowel, --a birthday gift from long ago -- I was being extra careful about how I was bending as I took the salmon-colored South American weeds one flat at a time to the front yard. I was looking at the stacked pieces of limestone circling the trunk of the maple tree and recalling fondly how my son Chris and I hauled those stones from a backyard abandoned flower bed in his Radio-Flyer wagon nearly 20 ago. As the stones are not mortared together, they occasionally need to be re-stacked from the ever-shifting dirt and the occasional errors of cars backing from the driveway. They need it again now, but I thought better of tackling that chore in my current condition. The majestic maple will have to be satisfied with some pretty flowers. The rearrangement of her stone necklace will have to wait, hopefully, until next year.

As I stood there trying to figure out how to position myself most effectively without any discomfort, I heard over my shoulder the latching of the porch door. There was Earl carrying a glass in one hand, a folded aluminum lawn chair in the other, and, of course, he had a cigar clenched in his teeth. He walked past me, sat his chair where he could see up and down the street but that also gave him a vantage point for watching with sympathy my physical, albeit slow, labor.

I pointed at the flowers overflowing from their flimsy black plastic trays and asked, "What do you think?" He nodded and with verifiable historical accuracy he said, "In my day we didn't have any exotic flowers like those, but they really are pleasing to the eye with their dark green leaves and small little pink blossoms."

I dug a hole about three inches in diameter, (the size of the trowel), and perhaps four inches deep. With my left hand I grasped the stems where they met the dirt, and wiggled them a bit as I pushed up the thin bottom with my right forefinger at the same time releasing their root-bound squares from their would-be plastic tombs. The little white arteries snaking around the smooth square sides of the dirt about to be buried forever looked like a road map of a very congested city somewhere.

I put the newly freed plant into its more spacious home and repeatedly pushed the freshly excavated dirt tightly around its base. Earl looked at me and said, "It looks like you are performing that CPR maneuver." I laughed as I thought that doing compressions on flowers as I plant them was rather appropriate considering the possible outcome, and that to passing motorists, it might seem like I was doing exactly that.

After I had planted the eight inch plants, I reached below the blossoms about four inches above the dirt and pinched them off leaving just the little green stalks and an occasional low bud or two. As I threw the blossoms aside, Earl asked loudly, "What is that you do? You dig a hole, plant a pretty flower, then rip the pretty blossom right off?" I explained that doing that insures you will eventually have bushy plants with more flowers instead of tall spindly ones that droop over in the rain or wind. I went on to say that you must endure a couple of weeks with very little evidence of growth, but once they start to come on they will grow to be a foot and a half tall with plentiful blossoms.

I continued around the tree, losing sight of Earl for 15 fifteen minutes but very aware of his presence by the aroma of cigar smoke coming from either side of the majestic Maple. I ended where I started having exactly the right number of plants. I slowly stood up and stretched what felt like a stiff, kinky wire where my spine was supposed to be. "Well that'll look great in a couple of weeks," I said as I gathered up all the little plant boxes and plant tops strewn outside the rocks on the grass.

"So, what do you think of that?" I asked Earl who was staring at pile of blossoms waiting to be thrown out.

"I am impressed at your efficiency, your thoroughness, your commitment to make things pretty even while your back is hurting. And, you did it all in less than an hour", he said.

That was such a nice thing to say, considering he was taking into consideration he was obviously still skeptical that there would be anything around the tree other than resuscitated green sticks poking out of the ground.

As I finished cleaning up, Earl folded his lawn chair and walked toward the porch. Suddenly he stopped, turned back to me, and said:

"Do right and you will be conspicuous". ~MT~

"You too, could have been conspicuous and given me a hand," I thought to myself as I watched Earl sit down in a cushioned wicker chair with a sigh.

A bird in the Hand

Earl was walking up the driveway as I came out of the house. "Where were you?" I asked.

"I took a short walk down around Tanglewood Lane to see what's back there, he answered. I've never bothered to venture that far, but there are some very nice houses on big wooded lots." I commenced to tell him of my brief opportunity to

[98]

be part of developing that area, but things between the eventual owner and me did not work out. He basically wanted me to do most of the legwork, provide half of the money, and receive only a third of the proceeds.

Earl stepped onto the porch and sat down across from me crossing his legs in a manner that indicated he was readying himself for a very long story. I recounted it as one of those "what if" stories – the kind that makes you think how things might have turned out if the deal had gone the way we had agreed to when we became partners. Earl said that investing and going into business were things that never went well for him, no matter how great the deal or how hard he tried.

He said that we are each a sum total of our experiences and if I had done things differently, where or who might I be now? I briefly thought about that and agreed that being right here in this moment is actually pretty good. I had a cabinet business for over 30 years and I was able to craft lovely things that will survive me to become living testimonies of my love affair with wood. The thought that the items big and small that left my shop heading to someone's home and to make someone else's life happier made me smile despite my penitent mood.

Once my mind shifted from the pain of what did not happen to what actually occurred, I easily slipped into a grateful frame of mind. That launched me into telling him about a couple particularly challenging projects that were very rewarding in the end

I told about making the cherry raised-panel counter front for Chuck Boss' law office in Maumee. How I strapped it onto the ladder rack of my small Nissan pickup using two sixteen foot two-by-fours. The section was one continuous piece and measured 177¼ inches long. He was amazed that I remembered that measurement after 25 years. I told him given the trouble to make and transport it; I wouldn't ever forget it as long as I live.

As I spoke my face must have been glowing; I could feel a smile stretching at my cheeks with each detail of that beautiful project. "You're right, Earl. Where would I be today if I had jumped into land speculation with an attorney?" I said curbing my enthusiasm and slowly returning to earth.

"You might have gone totally broke and never had your cabinet shop. You might have had to go prostitute yourself for someone who could have cared little about how you feel about wood or what your talents were, he said (pausing to light a cigar), and simply doing whatever you were told just to make a wage."

As I sat there thinking about the common sense Earl brought to bear I realized I had done exactly what I was supposed to do. Becoming wealthy wasn't part of the plan for me. I found my wealth in experience and memories; more money would have been nice, but certainly couldn't have given me that.

I am aware of the troubles that Samuel Clemens went through in his business life, but I had to ask Earl the question; "So, after all that you went through with your investments and inventions, what wisdom did you take away from those experiments?" Earl found an appropriate expression, twirled his cigar while building my interest, and then said,

"There are two times in a man's life when he should not speculate: when he can't afford it, and when he can." ~MT~

America's Birthday

Earl wasn't up to attending the city fireworks last night. That was alright with me; I was tired and the thought of dealing with traffic overruled my desire to go. We sat on the porch – him reading by a small light and me listening to the explosions in the distance and imagining the colors. They must have been impressive, because several different times when I thought I was hearing the grand finale, the loud booms began again.

The whole process of pyrotechnics intrigues the boy in every man. Perhaps it goes back to our caveman days when men were in charge of fire. My fascination with fireworks and the many experiments I have tried with them swirled in my mind as I remembered trying to invent new ways to use and propel them and generally just enjoy their explosive, and sometimes destructive effects.

Earl said that fireworks were a great excitement for him as a young boy, too. He told of putting them under tin cans, running away quickly, and watching them fly into the air. He also told of a time that 'he' threw some firecrackers into the street scaring a horse pulling a carriage. He got a good licking for causing the horse to bolt with two very frightened passengers aboard even though there were no apparent lasting injuries to man or beast.

I Said, "We would take M-80s and shoot them high up into the air with sling shots. To us, the explosions sounded just like the big four-inch shells the pros use."

His eyes widened and he leaned up on the edge of his seat. "Damn I wish I'd have thought of that," he said smiling, "You don't have any of those things around now do you?" I told him I always have firecrackers, but those larger fun things have been outlawed for years. He sat back with a sigh, "Yep, he said. "A person finds something that is truly a lot of fun and the government regulates it away. The same with dynamite, anymore you have to have a really good reason to buy it." I looked at him and raised a curious eyebrow, he didn't elaborate.

I told him about the movie "Jackass" that has a lot of shenanigans with fireworks. The only one that came to mind quickly was of a 20-something guy who obviously had way too much to drink. When he combined his inebriated state with his obvious mental deficiency, he thought that sitting down naked, pulling his feet up to his head, putting the stick from a rocket firmly in his butt, and launching it from there was actually a pretty good idea. The possible effects of 2 feet of blasting fire shooting out of the back of the six-inch rocket only a few inches from his flesh apparently didn't occur to him when he lit the fuse. It didn't take long for the reality of the fiery detonation to get his attention. The next scene showed his laughing friends pouring water on his blistered and hairless undercarriage.

Earl was almost rolling on the floor with laughter and it was hard for me to get the whole story out what with my own out of control laughing. "Now there is a picture I would love to see", he said still roaring.

As the night air started to grow cold and we concluded our laughing, Earl re-opened his book, smiled, and added:

"Statistics show that we lose more fools on this day than in all the other days of the year put together. This proves, by the number left in stock, that one Fourth of July per year is now inadequate, the country has grown so." ~MT~

A Level of Security

Having the day off, I slept in this morning. Even though I was up by 8:15, I would most likely beat Earl out of bed. I assume he reads late every night; I can usually see the light under his door no matter when I get up during the night.

In the kitchen I started my ritual. I turned on the coffee machine, took my handful of pills, cut a bagel and set it in the toaster, and took the dog out. Coming back into the dry house from the cool dampness of the dew-soaked morning, a stirring in the bathroom indicated that Earl was vertical and preparing for another day in the 21st century.

The door opened and he emerged asking; "Is there coffee made?" I told him that the machine was ready he just needed to pick out a coffee and push the button. As I poured the dog food, Earl was putting a K cup of Green Mountain French roast into the machine. As he closed the lid and it began to whir, he turned and asked if I was making bagels. I said, "I could," and proceeded to get another from the fridge for myself. I readied another coffee for me as I pushed the toaster lever down to make Earl's bagel.

Earl was waiting patiently leaning against the counter in his robe with his thin white legs sticking out like two Popsicle sticks. He was wearing very old slippers from Goodwill that he just had to have because they showed "character", and probably once belonged to someone great, or at least interesting.

I buttered his bagel and put it on a napkin and as he leaned over to pick it up, I could smell the lingering cigar odor on his clothes. I thought, "I'll have to scrub and paint that room once he leaves." He knows he's not supposed to smoke in his room, I'd have to ask him to leave for him to stop smoking in there completely, and that was something I was not prepared to do. I imagined him, like a teenage boy stealing a smoke, trying to blow the proof out the window and then, spraying air freshener around the room unsuccessfully trying to hide the smell.

We both left the kitchen about the same time and headed to the porch. Our movements sometimes almost look choreographed the way we move around each other and into our usual seats. "What are you doing today", he asked. I explained that I was going shooting at the range in the morning, and after that I would try to complete some tasks around the house that will not aggravate my ailing back.

Earl and I have had conversations about carrying guns. We wish people didn't feel the need to arm themselves, but we agree that there seems to be a growing need to protect ourselves.

I said that the idea of the only people carrying guns is the police and the criminals scare me. There was a time when only a few criminals had guns and the police were much more effective in stopping violent crimes. Today, though, most of the criminals have guns. Frequently the police and the thugs are far apart and defenseless people are the ones in the middle. It reminds me of the way predator wolves separate mothers from their babies so the other wolves can kill the helpless young. While the protectors are in one place, the defenseless victims are being attacked in another. It's a sad development, but as my son said when he got his permit, "I never plan on shooting another person, but I'll not let them easily take my life because they have a gun and I don't."

Earl said that after reading much about it he certainly likes the idea that when he and I go out that we aren't two vulnerable old guys with signs on our backs that say: "easy pickings." He added, "I hope you never have to use your gun, but I rather have one with us and not use it than to need it and not have it."

I drained my coffee and went into the house to get dressed. When I came back with my range bag, I related, "I had a state trooper tell me that when he stops a vehicle late at night, runs a check on the license plate through the system before approaching the car or truck, and the retrieved information reveals that the owner of the car has a concealed-carry permit, he feels much safer walking up to that car."

I paused and added, "A car that is registered to legal permit holder, if the permit holder is, indeed, the one driving, it probably indicates he or she was responsible enough to legally obtain a concealed weapon permit. The cop will still take precautions to make sure that if there is a weapon in the car that both he and the driver behave appropriately. Also, he is reasonably assured that the driver knows how to properly react to the officer's request so everyone remains safe."

"And another thing, I continued, "The criminals certainly don't have permits. They just put a gun in their waistband and off they go. More people need to realize that the individuals who legally carry firearms are rarely the ones who go crazy with weapons. The anti-gun people need to see the faces of the people who carry guns. The radical wing of the NRA does not represent me or most of the people I know who have permits. There are many liberals who, just like everyone else, want to live in peace and safety, and many have taken the steps to arm themselves responsibly. They aren't looking for trouble, but are simply prepared for it."

"Since this is the day after the celebration of our independence from tyranny, it is worth mentioning that not all who fought for that freedom enjoyed carrying a weapon or loved violence. They just wanted to live free, without threats of oppression. Today is no different in terms of wanting to be properly prepared for threats to our lives whether at home or on our streets."

By this point in my monolog, my bag and I had made it out to the driveway. Still, I continued my point.

"In my desire to outlive an attack I have been trained and disciplined not to be a threat to anyone other than an attacker. If people think that being a victim is better than protecting themselves and their family they certainly have that right. But, knowing I am allowed by law to possess the means to protect myself and those around me -- and then to ignore that option -- would prevent me from sleeping at night."

"Everyone should make his/her own decisions as to what feels comfortable and secure when it comes to self-defense. But no one should criticize me for my responsible choices. I feel a lot better knowing that I will not have to possibly lay

[103]

helplessly wounded or dying waiting for the police to show up. I am allowed to protect myself immediately. That's it in a nutshell. That's all" I said.

Earl listened respectfully and occasionally nodded. When my impassioned speech finally gave him a sliver of opportunity, he injected:

"Policemen are queer animals and have remarkably nice notions as to the great law of self-preservation. I doubt if the man is now living that even caught one at a riot. To find "a needle in a haystack" is a much easier matter than to scare up one of these gentry when he is wanted." ~MT~

I flashed an affable smile, assuming that he was agreeing with me. However, after such an indicting commentary I couldn't be 100—percent sure.

As I placed my things in the car and settled in the driver's seat to focus on what needed to come next, my fervor and heart rate both calmed, allowing me to safely back from the driveway.

If you're Nice I Will like You

I couldn't sleep last night for more than a couple of hours at a time, (the back again), so I got up around three o'clock and took something to help me rest. It worked so well that my eyes didn't unlock until 9:45. The day had begun without me...again.

I came out of the bathroom unhurried and into a very still world. There was only the sound of an occasional car driving by as I readied myself for the day with my usual small breakfast. Once I finished my bagel I took the remainder of my morning coffee to the porch. Walking gingerly around the wicker furniture to my spot, I passed Earl who was already in his favorite chair reading the Sunday paper. The table between us was covered with many 'used' sections hanging over its edges. A large black cat was curled up on his lap purring loudly. The discarded and ignored advertisements were strewn around Earl's chair on the floor.

"Good morning my friend", he said while lowering the paper just enough to look at me politely.

"Good morning to you too", I said while slowly settling myself into the pillow lined chair. "What are your plans for today?" I asked pretty much knowing his answer. Since Sunday is the designated day of rest Earl will take his full

[104]

allotment. There was a short pause and then he spoke, chuckling, "I think I'll do today what I did yesterday and the day before that. Matter of fact, Tom, I am going to keep doing that very thing every day until I get it perfectly right".

As to my day, I replied, here were several things I could do, but most of them involved bending which was not an appealing thing on today's menu. He suggested that I just relax and enjoy the race at Daytona on TV. This was one day when doing nothing was a first-rate guiltless idea, and I thanked him for it. I decided it was time to get dressed even if I was simply going to move from the porch chair to a place on the couch.

I stood up, carefully supporting myself on the chair. I gingerly squatted down to retrieve my empty cup, rose slowly, and looked at Earl as I headed back into the house. It was heartwarming to see him and his cozy pal enjoying each other on a quiet Sunday morning.

Earl dropped his paper to the floor. He was petting the black cat, which was lying with his head upside down resting on Earl's legs, his front paws bent in a mock begging position. His chest was heaving slowly as he purred the morning away with his most continuous "friend."

Earl, without turning and while gently holding one of the trusting cat's back feet said with a tender smile:

"I simply can't resist a cat, particularly a purring one. They are the cleanest, cunningest, and most intelligent things I know, outside of the girl you love, of course." ~MT~

He and I do not agree on everything, but we are in a perfect coalition about the importance of cats. Earl has been thoroughly adopted by Lalo to the point -- except for feeding time -- I am almost completely ignored.

Ships Passing

I was out of pain medication and needed razor cleaner and was headed out for the drugstore, when Earl asked if he might go along; said he hadn't been out to "see the sights" in a while.I opted for Walgreens because they're the only drug store in town that stocks my electric razor cleaner. We got into the car, which took more time than usual, because of my aching back and started off through the gray threat of a possible afternoon shower. Driving along in my normally smooth-riding newer car, I felt every bump in the road as if the tires were over-inflated or the shocks worn out. I knew the road had not deteriorated over night and my tires or shocks were not the problem – my sensitive spine had become my body's seismograph. The ride felt like at a least a 6.5 on the Richter scale!

We pulled into the parking lot and Earl got out of the car first. Walking around to the other side he said, "Give me your hand old man." I looked up at him, giving him instead an annoyed frown, waved him off and answered back, "Don't you dare." He turned away, shrugged, and headed towards the door five steps ahead of me sporting a small grin.

Once inside the store, I felt lost. I swear they hire people to arbitrarily move stuff around about every three months. Perhaps someone making a six-figure salary has some logarithm that tracks each person's movements around the store and compares those to their average purchase. Selling has become more and more like herding cattle I thought as I looked up at the signs above each aisle. Spying **Headache medications** (the aisle between beef jerky and toilet paper), and set out to search through the hundreds of bottles of pain medication for one that hopefully would say, "For Tom's Back." I picked up what appeared to be a quart sized jug of Aleve, (immediately forgetting my razor cleaner), and headed directly to the checkout counter, which was very busy, and the line was moving way too slowly. Earl had not moved since we entered the store; he was standing at the magazine and book rack thumbing through a Hollywood gossip magazine. He looked up, saw me standing in line, quickly grabbed a recent issue of US, and slid in behind me in line. Seeing his selection, I smiled.

As we waited, Earl's attention was caught by a solitary shopper at the end of a long aisle. She was reading the contents of a small white tube in her hands.

"Just look at her," he said in an energized whisper. "Isn't she a perfect picture of loveliness?" I looked and saw that she was undeniably attractive, but through my discomfort I couldn't appreciate his fuss. Noting my expression, he went further, "Like you said the other day about people in ordinary life being movie stars, well she is certainly one in my opinion, and my opinion is always aligned with non-negotiable and unqualified truth". With his hands on his hips he was modeling an authority he thought I would heed.

I glanced at her again and raising an eyebrow at him I said, "That isn't at all what I was saying Earl". As we moved a couple steps nearer to the register, he convincingly tried to make his case with a detailed and salient description. He assumed after hearing his persuasive parade of adjectives I certainly would have no choice but to agree that she indeed definitely fit perfectly into my measure of everyday movie stars.

"She has perfectly styled highlighted hair, her skin is exquisitely tanned over her few character wrinkles brought on by lots of smiling and a few sad experiences no doubt; she is shapely without being buxom; her clothes are bold but tastefully chosen; her eyes are dark pools of compassion -- maybe a bit mysterious like Angelina Jolie or Ann Hathaway; and she carries herself not with any arrogance but with confidence and style," he answered with his eyes wide in anticipation of my agreement. By now he was staring and nearly pointing at her. I pulled his hand down, and tugged at his arm moving him along next to me in the line. I asked him with genuine curiosity, "You can see all of that from here?" ...(Ann Hathaway looks mysterious?? I thought.)

Suddenly, Earl's "movie star" came out of the aisle and moved to the line directly behind him.

Unable to contain himself, he turned around, made a low bow, and said, "Good day milady," and began a predictable flirtatious conversation, which I quickly tuned-out. He was still talking playfully when I finished paying for my industrial-sized jug of painkiller.

I steadied myself on the counter waiting for Earl to pay for his magazine from his handful of change, all the while keeping his eyes intently on his newly crowned 'movie star', and chatting up a storm. It was taking him forever to sort through his coins. It was obvious he didn't want to leave. I caught her glance and she smiled politely. She had perfectly straight, white teeth and her smile lit up her face. Since my goal of getting my pain reliever was complete I had time to take a more objective look at her. She was very appealing and I may have been hasty in short- changing Earl's keenness, In fact, I thought, he had made some valid observations about her pleasant appearance, and I now found her much prettier, but he clearly had missed my point about what makes an everyday person a "movie star".

We got into the car and several feet away the 'mysterious' lady got into a shiny black sedan. He waved towards her, but she didn't see. He turned to me, and said, "Tom, we just witnessed a movie star shopping in a drug store!"

"Really?" I said. "I can see that she's very attractive but your gushing is not entirely warranted; my point about movie stars wasn't simply about beauty."

"To each his own I guess", he said turning away. "But understand, you're the one who started the whole movie star thing and she is an unconditionally perfect illustration of what you described the other night."

"The sultans in the middle-east would give up all of their wives for just a glimpse of such perfection. The scent of wild Jasmine in the evening air would wilt from the aroma of her remarkable locks. -- Did you get a whiff of her hair? -- She didn't actually walk to her car, Tom, she just floated lightly like she was walking on air." I backed out of the parking space without any response hoping my silence might quiet his infatuation and mystification.

As I turned onto Main Street a black car pulled up next to me. I glanced over to discover Earl's "movie star" at the wheel. He saw her; stared across me and waved frantically, obviously hoping she would look his way. She didn't. The light changed and she turned left as we drove straight but with Earl's yearning gaze following her car until it disappeared from view.

Our ride home was quiet except for the slow and suitable country song that seeped like syrup from the radio about a man whose true love had just left him. When we arrived home, Earl opened his door; and as he got out, he grabbed a lapel, looked right at me, and in his best semi-authentic Missouri drawl, he said:

"It is not best that we should all think alike; it is difference of opinion that makes horse races." ~MT~

I carefully extricated myself from the car and for a split second entertained the idea of giving Mr. Twain a snappy retort of my own, but then thought it was better to simply let Earl have his moment. After all, she actually did have 'star' quality, even if it wasn't precisely the kind I was referring to.

Where do we start?

As the evening grew darker and the air remained stiflingly hot and thick, Earl and I sat on the porch talking about the troubles in the world: weather, wars, and violence that is plaguing America and so many places around the globe.

"Why are Americans so angry these days?" Earl asked. Can't they see they still have such a better life than people everywhere else in the world? Why must people fight each other...kill each other over what? In Chicago, a tough-guy shot at a group of people because one of them removed the shooter's drink that was sitting on the roof of their parked care. No angry exchange, he just pulled out a gun and started shooting. There is so much anger in the world. What we need are more Christmases and parades. People are in a better temperament during both of those."

I sat there thinking that, again, Earl had made a point many have made countless times before. I asked, "How can we integrate that feeling of brotherly love into everyday living without looking weak or becoming a victim? Gandhi was able to convince a whole nation that violence was a futile exercise. How do we get back to living as a community instead of secluding ourselves in walled-off houses to keep the world out? Like the days when we talked to our next-door neighbors while hanging out our laundry. Summer picnics were a routine way for many people to visit with each other and "interacting" was a way of life as well as a word. What can we do to live like that again?"

Earl quickly said, "We can never go back, not collectively anyhow." Maybe if the people who are bothered by it just change their own little part of their world it might become contagious. If two people are arguing and yelling at each other - - and one of them stops and begins to talk softly it isn't long before the other will do the same. Maybe that would work here. In any case we must change what bothers us about others in ourselves first. Otherwise, we have no credibility. No reason to change if everyone is doing the same thing. Weird becomes normal if you have enough people acting weird. I don't see real change happening anytime soon." His voice quieted, and he added. "It surely will get worse before there is any measure of improvement."

I replied by asking, "So how does one start the process of change? How can we each become more connected and also better people?"

Earl rose from his chair, and in an exasperated tone said:

"Keep away from people who try to belittle your ambitions. Small people always do that, but the great make you feel that you, too, can become great". ~MT~

He walked into the house leaving only a feeling of frustration to keep me company.

Gone Too Soon

I was reading the obituaries in the newspaper and saw three people I knew had died -- two of them younger than me. Losing people in your life, whether close or merely familiar is sobering. I contemplate my own mortality at those times. I review the life of someone I once talked to, laughed with, or waved at in passing.

It's easy to forget how temporary our time on earth is, when the only people we see dying are strangers. I momentarily feel badly when I read that someone that I didn't know was killed or died unexpectedly, but when it's someone I knew, it carries great weight and provokes prolonged thought and recollection.

I was sharing those feelings with Earl as we had a cup of tea after dinner in our usual chairs on the porch. As the day faded and the sun grew dim, I expressed my particular sorrow for a man I had worked with at Lowes who bravely fought but recently lost his battle against cancer. Part of my grief was caused by the fact that we hadn't gotten along well together and had exchanged inhospitable words on more than one occasion. I said I thought there was an obvious lesson in this experience. Earl said that we can't pattern our personality or reaction to people based on knowing they will die one day. I agreed, but said that I regretted being contentious with him before I found out he was going through such a hard time. When we react to people we rarely know what kind of struggle they might be facing.

"He wouldn't want you to soft pedal your words just to mollycoddle him," Earl said. "If he was as strong a man as you say, he would not want that kind of response from you."

I nodded and said, "I know that, but still I feel badly that in the midst of his fight to survive, I was so unbending." I added that I felt even worse because he had beaten the disease twice, and the third time was just too much for him to overcome. He never got to enjoy all he had worked for. We sat there quietly for a long time. I knew by the way he was slowly turning his cigar that he was working through a thought. Just as I began to think he wasn't going to say anything meaningful or profound, out of the stillness and with a small quake in his voice he said:

"Death, the refuge, the solace, the best and kindliest and most prized friend and benefactor of the erring, the forsaken, the old, and weary, and broken of heart, whose burdens be heavy upon them, and who would lie down and be at rest."

~MT~

(At some point in Earl's life he also apparently had faced the pain and unfairness of an untimely death as he summoned what Samuel Clemens himself had written sometime after the devastating loss of two of his children).

Interesting

Yesterday after work Earl and I were watching "Justified" on Netflix. Out of the blue he asked if I would show him how to use the computer. I asked him very pointed questions to find out what he really was looking to do as I could see the potential for problems if given free reign. He said he wanted to find things of interest from his era. I said after dinner I would give him a crash course on how to navigate the Internet so he could find what he's looking for without causing problems for my ancient computer.

We had a great dinner of pork loin grilled on a wet Cedar board, freshly made potato salad, baked beans, celery, carrots, and homemade sweet pickles. Rounding out the meal was some wonderful pineapple-blueberry-pecan bread that a good friend from work had sent home with me for the two of us to enjoy.

After I finished clearing the table, I joined Earl on the porch, where he was enjoying his customary smoke. We sat there talking about how wonderful the pork turned out and how we should cook out more often, possibly all-year-round. Earl was anxiously puffing faster than usual. I knew he was eager to get started on his computer adventure.

"Do you realize that in the last 20 years, more things have been invented than in all of history up to that point?" I asked. "Really?" he said, giving me a look of disbelief. If in fact he was a legitimate transplant from the19th century, he wouldn't be able to comprehend that men had walked on the moon nearly half a century ago. "The computers that we all have today are at least 20 times faster and much more effective than the computer that launched astronauts into space. And that computer was as large as a house I said. Rising from his chair he said, "Then let us proceed to the eighth wonder of the world".

I showed him how to connect to the Internet, find Google, and how to open several windows at a time if he wanted to search for things in detail. The mouse was the hardest thing for him to get the feel for so I went to "settings" and adjusted the speed so he could follow the cursor more easily. "You mean to say that this black box right here in your house is connected to all the information in all of the libraries all over the world?" He said looking up as if in complete disbelief. Assuming that he certainly had at least some peripheral contact with computers in his travels I simply played along.

"Yes sir it is, I answered. "Well not like sensitive sites that are encrypted for national security or personal privacy, but otherwise, yes. If you want to look up things about.... ah... let's say, Mark Twain for instance just type Mark Twain in that white box there at the top of the screen. Awkwardly taking his cursor to the search bar with one finger he slowly typed in "Mark Twain." "Now what?" He asked. "Press the enter key.... there by the shift key or over here on the right corner," I said while pointing at the keys.

I watched him for another few minutes then went off to throw some clothes into the washer feeling secure he could read about 'himself' or other writers he might Google until I returned.

While I was getting the washer started I opened the dryer to find things that needed folded so I went ahead and did that while I was there. The wire hangers that are always in a tangle caught my eye and I straightened them out too, since I was in the area. Getting ready to leave the laundry room, I opened the dryer again and decided to empty the filter. As I carried the squares of lint from the filter into the kitchen to throw away, I glanced into the computer room and noticed that Earl had his face amusingly close to the screen. After disposing of the lint, I noticed that the water dish on the floor for the pets was nearly empty so I took it to the sink to rinse and re-fill.

The total time away from Earl couldn't have been more than ten minutes when suddenly I heard his commanding voice from the computer room, "What is your credit card number?" I quickly walked back to him asking, "what do you need **that** for?"

"This place asked for it and in order for me to keep looking I have to give them a credit card number, he said matter-of-factly. I looked up at the screen to see several young girls in various poses, some with their tongues out, others holding their hands over their bare breasts, and some with their bottoms stuck into the air. "Meet young women in your area": said a banner across the screen. I grabbed the mouse from his hand closed down each open window until I arrived back to the first one we had found together....'Mark Twain'. "There you go, Earl. Stay here or ask me again how to find something. How did you get to that site with naked women in the first place? What did you type in that search box?" I asked with my voice a bit louder than usual.

"I just typed "pretty girls," and all of these boxes with pictures of lovely ladies without many clothes started showing up all over the screen". He said ruefully, giving me a hangdog grin.

"I told you how to search and I assumed that you were looking for things that would interest a man of your age and...." (I heard my own words and voice trail off as I realized that indeed he had found something that interested him).

[112]

Gathering myself I said, "Well I showed you exactly how to research acceptable subjects and particular people so from now on that is what you should do, okay?

Do exactly what I showed you so we don't end up with all kinds of stuff we shouldn't have on here". While strongly emphasizing my need for him to fully understand, I placed one hand lightly on his shoulder. He sat there staring blindly at the Mark Twain website for a minute looking somewhat disappointed and then said.

"Against a diseased imagination, demonstration goes for nothing." ~MT~

I was still smiling when I returned to the laundry room.

Smoke and Mirrors

In the news there continues to be contentious debate between congress and the president over a myriad of issues. This adversarial relationship, (while it's not particularly new), has taken on a vulgar and schoolboy tone that makes one feel a bit ashamed of all of those involved. Earl has mentioned his disgust for the behavior more than I have, possibly because he has studied history more extensively and has a deeply educated opinion about past relationships between the executive and legislative branches of government.

I mentioned that each side has merit in their arguments, but what I can't understand is how can the overly spray-tanned orange-skinned congressional leader from Ohio simply forget the things that happened when his party occupied the White House not so long ago.

"They are all a bunch of accomplished and creative liars", said Earl as he poured himself an after-dinner bourbon. "They all memorize what they want to remember. It doesn't make any difference if it was just yesterday that their party was making the same mistakes, or abusing the authority of the office of President. All either putrid party can see is their own faults in the other."

"It makes one question the wisdom of voting Americans when you see who they have elected to look out for their interests while in Washington," I added. "We are like mindless sheep when voting. We just follow blindly along with this party or that, and all of us are being collectively led off of a cliff by intentional empty promises.

"There is such a din of white noise coming from Washington in the form of rhetoric and partisan saber-rattling that it makes thinking about the real issues almost impossible regardless of which side of the aisle you might choose to join."

Earl sat there holding his glass while looking at the quickly sinking sun. Drawing his glass to his mouth he strained a large sip through his mustache and curled his bottom lip up over it to clean off the Kentucky-born nectar held in the coarse white hair like paint in a paint brush. Then, he said profoundly,

"Noise proves nothing. Often a hen who has merely laid an egg cackles as if she had laid an asteroid." ~MT~

Hiding in Plain Sight

Earl was in the kitchen when I got up this morning. He was hanging on the refrigerator door like a drunk leaning on a lamppost. His head was most of the way inside, and the yellow light brightened his squinting face. "What **are** you doing?" I asked. "I am **trying** to find the bread", he answered with annoyance.

I reached around him and picked up the loaf of bread that was lying on the shelf 10 inches from his face. "It's right here, in front of you", I said handing it to him. "If it had been a snake it would have bitten you."

"I cannot find my glasses and even though I really don't need them for anything but reading, I am used to wearing them when I look for things", he said as if trying to convince me that his glasses were merely a hood ornament for his nose that offered no useful aid except for the printed page.

"I have looked everywhere for them and have come to the conclusion that one of the cats must have taken them off of my nightstand and hid them from me," he accused. I instantly had a vision of Lalo, the big black cat, walking through the house with Earl's silver, wire-rimmed glasses balanced on his shiny nose. I laughed a little and asked, "Where were you right before bed?" He thought for a minute and said that he had been reading in the living room, (most likely sitting in the big leather chair). "So you have looked everywhere for them and haven't found them?" Slowly turning toward the sound of my voice, he answered sarcastically, "No Tom, I found them; I was just having so much fun that I kept looking for them even **after** they were found."

I walked out of the kitchen knowing I was only making him more angry and frustrated. I looked all around the living room, nothing. I checked the porch; no sign of his glasses. Lalo followed me into his bedroom to search and I grinned as I turned to make sure he was not really wearing them as imagined. I walked back into the kitchen as Earl was balancing his saucer of toast on the top of his coffee cup and reaching for the light switch with his other hand.

"I have looked everywhere for them Earl," I said. I have no idea where you might have left them, but rest assured that they will be in the last place you look!"

"Well thanks, Tom, for pointing out the observable. When you find them in the LAST place you looked, the search would be over, right? If you found them in the first place that you looked that would also be the last place wouldn't it?" He said again becoming more annoyed with my feeble attempt to lighten his frustration. I decided to shut up and allow him to deal with the situation he created. I was making it worse by trying to humor him. At this point I wished that one of the cats would turn the corner wearing his glasses and give him a loud raspberry followed by, 'Na na na na...naaaa.. na!'

As he reached the kitchen doorway he stopped and turned halfway around. Looking blindly towards the wall, he said:

"They are as unlocatable as a cricket's noise; and where one thinks that that is, is always the very place where it isn't. ~MT~

His glasses were eventually found on the top shelf of the refrigerator.

Hold My Beer

The morning air was heavily with humidity. If you ran fast enough it might actually soak through your clothes. The heat left over from the uncomfortable night was increasing from the blazing mid-morning sun. It was shaping up to be a day best spent in front of a fan.

Earl was not up yet as I returned from the grocery and carried the bags into the kitchen. Bagels, milk, crackers, yogurt, carrots, celery, and of course cat litter. The herd of cats descended to sniff every bag as if there might have been a 700-pound Blue Fin Tuna hidden in the bottom. By the time I reached the last bag and put the crackers into the cupboard, the cats scattered as quickly as they had arrived – as if one had whispered, "false alarm." I put the re-usable bags away and made myself a rare second cup of coffee.

I took my cup of French roast to the porch and settled into the damp cushion of the wicker chair. Normally I don't drink hot beverages in the heat. I know people who do and it confuses me, but this time I had a plan of my own. I was going to sit in the hot, close morning air and drink my steaming coffee. Then, I was going to go back into the house and sit down in front of the fan. I imagined my eventual great sigh of relief as the cool air lightly brushed away the reality of the weather only 10 ten feet away.

I finished my coffee and went back inside. The window air-conditioners had been on most of the night and, though they were turned off now the air in the house was thinner to breathe and certainly much cooler than outside. I moved the floor fan from the kitchen doorway and turned it to face my computer chair. The computer room is painted green – a shade of green that was very popular a few years ago in everything from shutters and siding to painted furniture. With the shades drawn and the curtains closed, the color seemed to make the room feel cooler. Sitting down, I prepared myself for a day of writing, until, that is, I run out of ideas, get bored, or the room becomes too hot to concentrate.

The bathroom door opened and Earl came out completely dressed, which isn't always the case when we first meet in the morning."I didn't know you were up already," I said with surprise.

"Yep, been up for hours, couldn't sleep," he said as he walked behind my chair toward the kitchen. I asked him why he couldn't sleep and he answered that it was, 'just too damn hot'. I have tried to explain to him that since he has no air conditioner in his room he should open his door so he can benefit from some of the cool air from the next room. He has repeatedly declined, as he knows the no-smoking-in-his-room rule means to make a feigned attempt at compliance he must keep the windows open and the door shut. He has his priorities, I thought, as I turned back to the computer to reconnect with my thoughts.

I spoke out to Earl as he moved about suspiciously in the kitchen, "Have you ever thought of what you will say as your last words, assuming there is time for you to speak to someone at the very end"? He came to face me in the doorway with a clump of grapes in his hand and leaned heavily against the jamb as if he was contemplating a long conversation. "Why do you ask?" he said, while popping a grape into his mouth. "I am just curious if you have ever thought about that," I said. "I am writing my eulogy today and it just naturally made me think of what I might say at the end, assuming I have an opportunity to say anything, and of course there would have to be someone there to listen."

"Well I hope it isn't, 'Oh no, a train!' he said, laughing so hard he had to put his hand in front of his mouth to keep from spitting chewed grapes at me. I laughed at that too, instantly bringing to mind the line from "Jackass," 'Hey watch this', which must be the last words of many foolish people attempting dangerous things. Or, as I suspect, "Oh shit," which is the common phrase last heard on the voice recorders of the recovered black boxes from plane crashes.

After Earl gathered himself, he stood there unblinking and serious as if peering into the future and finally said:

"A distinguished man should be particular about his last words as he is about his last breath. He should write them out on a slip of paper and take the judgment of his friends on them. He should never leave such a thing to the last hour of his life, and trust to an intellectual spurt at the last moment to enable him to say something smart with his last gasp and launch into eternity with grandeur.... There is hardly a case on record where a man came to his last moment unprepared and said a good thing---hardly the case where a man trusted to that last moment and did not make a solemn botch of it and go out of the world feeling absurd."   ~MT 1869~

There was little to add to that, and he disappeared back into the kitchen.

Busy?

I was already on the porch when Earl, (who had eaten in his room), came out to smoke and enjoy the setting sun. It had been another hot and muggy day, but was starting to cool off as the quiet darkness approached. He politely positioned himself downwind from me and fired up his cigar. We sat there peacefully, each holding a cat in our laps. The big black kitty in Earl's lap will sit there very contented until Earl eventually blows a small puff of rancid cigar smoke at him with a devilish laugh. The cat leaves for a time but then comes back and the ritual will begin again until one of them tires of it and moves on to something else. They adore each other.

After a long silence, I as usual, spoke first, asking "What did you do today?"

"Today was a busy day, he said. "I read most of the morning, got up and ate around 9:30, had a smoke on the porch, went back into my room and read until about 2:00, had a late lunch, read a bit more before dropping off for a nap, woke up and had another smoke or two, fixed myself a snack, read for another couple

[117]

hours finishing that Steven King book you recommended, and here we are now." After finishing this laundry list, he looked at me with a well-satisfied look that indicated that the affairs of his day were accomplished and in perfect time. I sat there thinking about my day and how the two might compare.

I had mowed the grass, put new string on the trimmer, trimmed, blew the debris off of the driveway, found a pair of lawn shears that needed a new bolt and repaired them, sharpened them, fixed lunch, went downtown to pay a bill, trimmed a couple of low limbs from the Mulberry tree, cut up the branches for disposal, vacuumed the porch carpet, and then sat down at the computer and wrote for three hours before dinner.

"So today was a **busy** day for you?" I asked -- as if our efforts were a contest. Oblivious to my bait he simply said, "Yes." I sat there hoping he would ask me about the level of activity of my day so I could illustrate what **busy** really looks like. To my disappointment, he didn't ask. After a few minutes, he took the cigar from his mouth, blew a small stream of smoke toward the sleeping cat (which caused the predictable sneeze and the fast exit from Earl's lap), smiled and said:

"To be busy is a man's only happiness---and I am---otherwise I should die." ~MT 1868~

Making Friends Wherever He Goes

I was working in the yard standing at the edge where it meets the street. Since there is no curb it is vague as to where the street really stops and my yard starts. There is the grass and then a few inches of loose stone and then the actual pavement. Frequently people will drive by with their tires right up against the grass, which they certainly wouldn't do if there was an actual curb.

A lady walking her dog stepped into the yard to avoid an oncoming car. She had the leash in one hand and a plastic bag crumpled in the other. We caught each other's glance and she said, "Beautiful day today, isn't it?" "It sure is," I answered cheerfully. "I'll take 11 months of this and then a bit of cold or a light snow for Christmas".

I carefully reached towards her large dog and petted it lightly on its silky black head. She said, "I have never walked this far down Sand Ridge before. It must be very nice to live out here." I nodded in agreement, but said I wished that the people driving out this way would be a more careful at the curve about 200 yards from my house. "Twice since I have lived here "Life Flight" has landed down there for really serious accidents", I added. "Too many have missed that curve completely".

"There are some very interesting houses along here," she said looking down the street. We talked briefly about our lives; discovered that we both have children and what they are doing now. She told me that hers are much older and live out of state. She spoke of her grandchildren and their ages and what they are doing. I explained that all of my boys are single and still live in Bowling Green, which suits me just fine because I love having them close by. As we stood there sharing pleasant sketches of our lives, Earl spotted us and came out to join the conversation. As he walked up, the dog at that exact moment opted to relieve himself. As the dog bunched its legs together in that comical fashion it proceeded to deposit its 'gift' onto the grass. Earl watched intently. When the dog finished and scratched the grass like a cat in a litter box. Earl looked up at the nice lady and said, "I sure hope you are going to pick up that stinking pile of poo."

"Well I intend...," she began before Earl cut her off saying, "I'll bet it's your dog that leaves those foul-smelling lawn bombs out here every night. He now had his hands on his hips and gaining momentum as he continued, "Do you have any idea what a mess it is to try to clean dog poop off your shoes or out of the tires on a riding mower?" The lady looked at me as if to say: Call this guy off, please!' As I was about to speak, Earl spouted off again, "You know Tom has a dog. How would you like it if he brought her down to your yard and let her crap all over **your** grass?"

"Sir," she said, "I never have..." Again Earl interrupted and pointed to the dog sitting quietly by her side, "Tell that to Tom when he is out here with a stick and the garden hose picking that animal's crap out of his tractor's tires." The lady looked at me with a half smile/ half sneer, picked up the dog's remnants with the bag she was carrying, tugged on the leash, and before I could say a word they both quickly walked away.

Earl looked at me and said, "I am glad I came out here when I did. Otherwise, she'd be back with that mutt night after night." I felt my face twist into a scowl reflecting my anger, and I informed him that she had never been past here before with her dog and that he had just scolded a innocent soul, with whom I was having a very enjoyable conversation.

He stood there looking very surprised and somewhat embarrassed. As he started to say something, I brushed by him and headed for the garage. I was ten steps past him when, from over my shoulder, he bellowed in his best defiant tone,

"Ah, well, I am a great and sublime fool. But then I am God's fool, and all His works must be contemplated with respect." ~MT 1877~

Lost

I was sitting in front of the computer with my chin in my hands and looking at the screen. I was poised to write my speech for my class reunion. Recalling the many memories, (good or bad), from back then has caused such a flood of thoughts that I am drowning in possibilities.

Earl walked by and asked me what I was doing and I told him how I was blocked. He said that I should divide my thoughts into what I would like to say and what I would like to hear, and then take half of each. Confusing me even further with more options, I continued to stare blankly at the empty page that was waiting patiently for me to populate it with some wit and wisdom. While words never escape me -- to the contrary, I can go on for hours talking about almost anything -- I am stuck trying to write a 12-minute speech that should be meaningful and/or entertaining to most everyone.

Maybe, I should start with a joke, I thought. Many good speeches do, and joking was very typical of me back in school. I thought perhaps I should focus on the qualities that separated me from my fellow classmates. Maybe that's not a good idea, as it might appear that I'm preaching. What if I compare myself to them – the ways we are similar that brings us together 50 years later? But would that be putting me in a place where I don't belong? Clearly, this little speech was not going to be so easy after all. I interrupted my busy question-and-answer session to make a cup of coffee, hoping a jolt of hot caffeine might trigger some better ideas.

Earl was sitting at the kitchen table with his coffee, as it was an unseasonably chilly morning so sitting on the porch in our robes appealed to neither of us. I made my coffee and pulled up a chair across from him. He sat there looking somewhat incomplete without a cigar and clearly not as comfortable as he would have been if one was either in his mouth or close enough to easily reach.

"I have so much information at hand and trying to sift through what I could say to get to what I should say is making me dizzy." He cautioned that having too much is like having too little. "Remember," he said, "Nobody there will be thinking of all the things you should have said or could have said. They will be thinking only of what you are saying at that very moment," he said thoughtfully. While I was mulling over his bit of profundity he added:

"I made the great discovery that when the tank runs dry you've only to leave it alone and it will fill up again in time, while you are asleep--also while you are at work at other things and are quite unaware that this unconscious and profitable cerebration is going on." ~MT 1907~

It seemed that Twain's observation had indeed accurately occurred while I slept, as the next morning I awoke surprised by a refreshed outlook on what my classmates would eventually hear. I began to write like the turning of a windmill.

"The Majestic Vice"

Having lived with Earl for over three months, I have begun to wonder what his plans are for the future. I am as just as fond of him as I probably would be if he were Mark Twain himself. But, just how long can he maintain his life living in Twain's character -- his clothes, his mannerisms, which I assume are precise 19th century reproductions, his habit of reading everything he sees, and, of course, his incessant smoking.

Later, I took the dog for a walk. As I returned -- before I could even see the dim light of the porch, I got a whiff of cigar smoke. Even though, I'd been a smoker for many years I never could quite stomach cigars. No matter the cost or quality they always seemed to bear the smell of a cross between horse manure and burning tires, and they tasted even worse. Earl enjoys them, or says he does, but I think I should remind him that Mr. Twain also enjoyed a pipe. Maybe he will take up that more pleasantly fragrant habit, and give my neighborhood a break from the rank odor he refers to as "the majestic vice".

As I unhooked the leash letting the dog into the house for a drink I slumped down onto the love seat facing Earl. I tried not to stare, but it's hard not to fixate on Earl. His almost white hair and big sprawling mustache draw your attention as if they were blinking, neon lights. The ever-present cigar in his mouth, awaiting its occasional removal, and finally for Old Faithful to spout a stream of smoke is impossible to ignore or predict.

He looked odd sitting there, so out of place and time, yet I somehow admire his simple life: the commitment to Twain, his daily ritual of reading whatever satisfies him, and his ability to enjoy smoking. I almost wished I smoked again just to see if I could duplicate his manipulation of smoke and his distinctive moves to un-ash his cigar in such an effective yet seemingly unconscious manner.

He looked up from the newspaper he was reading, turned a page, and said "Back from your walk I see,"

"Yeah," I answered. "The dog was thirsty and I was tired so we came back a little early", I answered.

He pauses and then raised the paper hiding all but the side of his face. A cloud of exhaled smoke hit the fold in the newspaper and traveled straight up before turning into wispy swirls that drifted toward the screen and disappeared. I sat watching him and remembering my days of smoking -- recalling how much I thought I loved it. It was a ritual I enjoyed -- lighting a cigarette, holding it in a unique way, flicking the ashes off, drawing it to my mouth, sucking the smoke in deeply, and feeling it fill my lungs as if it was liquid, and various ways of expelling the nicotine harvested smoke into the air, and watching it magically melt into nothing.

As I romanced my own love affair with smoking I also, almost instantly, remembered the morning hack, the foul breath that would send any woman reeling away from my kiss, and the small burns on the front of my t-shirts, sweaters, and car seats. I shuddered and thought of how glad I was that I no longer indulge in such a filthy and dangerous habit.

I asked Earl how long he had been a smoker. He exhaled a huge cloud of smoke that I was sure would reach me with its choking stench. At that last moment, it politely drifted back towards him as if planned and out through the screen.

He lowered his paper, took his cigar from his mouth just long enough to say:

"I have been a smoker since my ninth year--a private one during the first two years, but a public one after that--that is to say, after my father's death." ~MT 1906~

The Bronze Star for Bravery

Last night Earl and I were watching a movie on Netflix, "Out of the Furnace", with Christian Bale. It wasn't a horrible movie, but like several other uneventful time-killing movies, I will soon forget it. Then, a year or two from now, I'll start to watch it again before remembering why I had forgotten it in the first place.

We were about 15 minutes into the movie when one of the cats came running into the living room, turned quickly to run back into the foyer and jumped about wildly. He repeated this three times before either of us realized he was chasing a bat that was flying close to the ceiling. I have had a few encounters with bats in my life and I wasn't terribly shaken by this sudden appearance, although I admit have it flying around my living room was a bit disconcerting. As I got up to figure out how to best remove this scared creature from the house, he flew onto the screened-in porch. I shut the door to the house, turned on the porch light, found my very bright Surefire flashlight, grabbed a broom from the laundry room, and walked out the back door and around to the door of the porch. I opened the door and slid the little silver disc up to the plunger to hold the door wide open.

The bat was flying from screen to screen trying to find his way out when I entered the porch. He fell to the floor behind the wicker love seat probably pretty tired and dizzy from banging into everything. So much for perfect radar, I thought. Maybe the screen was giving him a false reading of open air and easy freedom. I slowly moved the love seat out a little to find him back there motionless. Suddenly, he was airborne again flying back and forth thrusting himself desperately into the screens.

Earl, who had escaped my attention momentarily, suddenly appeared between the curtains of the large window facing onto the porch. He was wearing a football helmet! Seeing Earl in a football helmet and white suit instantly brought the image of Jack Nicholson in 'Easy Rider' to mind. I grinned at Earl as I caught his glance through the window. He was holding a string mop. Had I not been on a mission to find the killer vampire bat that would, according to legend, get tangled in my hair—if I had any--, and gnaw on my neck until I was dead, I would have stopped to take his picture. Facebook would have loved to see a photo of Earl with white hair curling out the bottom of a football helmet and through the ear holes. His eyes were wider than I've ever seen them and the look on his face was of complete terror even though he was on the opposite side of the glass from the rabid fangs. He could have joined me in my quest to usher the culprit outside, but instead he took a tactical position of defense right inside the front door – in case the crafty bat turned the door handle and let himself in to feast on Earl rather than the thousands of mosquitoes outside.

I went in search of a box that I could use to trap the flying nuisance that had Earl fearing for his hair, his blood, and ultimately his life. When I got back, I couldn't find "Bella Lugosi," (I had named him on my way back to the house), anywhere. I poked around in the cushions and carefully turned the furniture upside down. There was neither bat nor even a silky, black cape to indicate an escape. I opened the front door and motioned Earl to come out. He stood there holding the mop across his body like a Roman centurion refusing to flinch. "I'm stayin' right here in case he gets by you," he said while quickly pushing the door shut with a loud bang. I put the box and broom away and came back in through the back -- not wanting to risk being mistaken for a vampire and getting a mop slapped across my face by the "guardian" of the front door.

I casually walked in and issued an: "all clear". Earl started taking off the football helmet slowly as if he was exhausted after four quarters playing defense in a championship game.

"Whew, I'm glad we got that taken care of", he said as he ran his right hand through his compressed hair.

"We?" I asked.

"With us working together, he didn't have a chance," he said smiling at me like a fellow Navy Seal might after a tough but successful mission.

I scratched my head and sarcastically responded, "Your actions *were* certainly amazing Earl". He looked at me in complete seriousness and said:

"A brave man does not create his bravery. He is entitled to no personal credit for possessing it. It is born to him. ~MT 1906~

The Assault

When I took the dog out I could almost touch the rare stillness of a totally silent Sunday morning. For several minutes there was no evidence of any other living thing on the planet except for the sound of my hurried swooshing through the dew-soaked grass saturating the toes of my shoes. When I stopped walking, I heard nothing beyond my own heartbeat.

[124]

As soon as I'd acknowledged the golden silence, it disappeared. Just seconds before, there wasn't even the subtle buzz of a bee; now I heard cars passing loudly. Birds were suddenly in choir from every direction when they were in silent conversation only seconds before. The stillness was repeatedly broken by exaggerated sounds as if started on cue. As I walked back to the house I met Earl standing on the porch, holding his coffee, and looking down the street. "Good morning to you," he said as I opened the door and stepped onto the porch.

"How are you this morning?" I asked walking over to my empty chair. He said that he slept well, but would have slept longer had not Leon (the black and white kitty),   awakened him by stroking his face with a paw as if to say 'it's time for breakfast'.

"I told you not to let the cats into your room," I said. "They do that to me every morning when the alarm goes off. On mornings when I want to sleep in, they assume I must have forgotten to set the alarm and wake me up with their soft but annoying caresses," I said.

Earl sat in his usual spot and opened the Sunday New York Times. He started to read quietly to himself with the paper opened like a white tent around him -- indicating that routine conversation was no longer part of his morning plans. I turned my attention to the view across the street and the grass that was brightening from dark green to almost yellow as a cloud drifted west making way for the golden light to streak across the neighbor's yard. We sat there in the relative calm that was broken only by the occasional car possibly speeding to help the occupants claim the last seat in church.

I suddenly noticed that in the very corner of one screen, there was a fly just innocently walking about slowly doing what flies do...looking for something to eat. It is curious when a fly stays in one area too long; that usually means there must be something foul or worth eating that is keeping his attention. They are such filthy creatures, drawn to all that is disgusting, diseased, or dead. When they walk around on food one is about to eat, it's repulsive to think they probably were just recently standing on something foul.

Just then the fly left the screen and dived into Earl's shrouded world. Earl started slapping at it with both hands, while trying to hold on to the paper. The buzzing stopped; he shook the paper back into the original position except for a few added wrinkles, gave a sigh and started reading again. Within 30 seconds, the buzzing started again. Earl dropped his grip on one side of the paper, stood up, and started swatting at the fly with his free hand. The fly appeared to be making a game of it, staying a foot in front of Earl's slashing hand. "Damn flies!" he said still swinging at the elusive intruder that seemed to be enjoying Earl's torment.

After a few seconds the buzzing stopped and Earl, assuming his tormentor had lost interest, settled back into his chair to resume his reading uninterrupted. A few seconds later the buzzing was back again, but with a vengeance and urgency not witnessed since the Red Baron roamed the skies of Europe with complete freedom.

"I'm gonna kill that multi-eyed bastard if it's the last thing I do," Earl said jumping from his chair and balling the paper into an unreadable wad. He slapped, swung, swatted, and even kicked until the fly ran into the screen just out of Earl's reach. If I had super human hearing I might have heard the fly say, "Uh Oh!" right before Earl pushed him through the screen like meat through a sausage grinder. "Okay my little annoying friend; try buzzing now", he said with the same bluster as a champion dancing in the center of the ring with both fists in the air. He glanced down at the unreadable, torn clump of papers with the small greasy spot of victory and simply dropped them to the floor. As he was about to step back into the house, he looked at me and, in a exasperated tone, said:

"Nothing is made in vain, but the fly came near it". ~MT 1903~

Finally, I thought, a quote that not only fit the event, but was perfectly timed.

The Mirror does not Lie

Over time I have noticed that Earl doesn't do much in terms of maintaining his personal appearance. But then, as he rarely goes out, he probably sees little reason to get 'gussied up'. I don't mean that that he isn't clean, because he surely is, actually almost to a fault. He certainly has embraced the shower. And, now that he loves it more than a tub bath, he stays in there humming or singing until the water is no longer warm. (He sometimes compares it to sex, but says that a good shower lasts a lot longer and is certainly a lot less strenuous).

I can only imagine what bathing was like during Twain's early years before indoor plumbing became the rage. It would have had been a huge hassle to bathe everyday even if one had hired help. Water would have to be heated on a cook stove, poured into a tub of sorts, and sometimes several people would use it before it was finally thrown out. Each one, of course, hoped to be the first one in while the water was still hot and clean. (Recent research has shown that bathing too often is very bad for the skin. That is no surprise to me; I made that discovery when I was about 10 and for years did my best to convince my skeptical mother of that fact).

Earl went into the bathroom as I finished getting ready for work. A few minutes later he came out with his hair sticking up in the front and matted down in the back. His "bed head" is one of the most pronounced I have ever seen on any human being. It was difficult not to point and giggle the first few times I saw it. But I acclimated quietly, because he is blindly unaware and that mentioning it directly would certainly be rude, unnecessary, and mean-spirited. So, of course on this day, I had to say; "Hey Earl, I like what you've done with your hair."

"Oh, this?" he asked; Reaching up with both hands and patting the sides of his head softly as to not disturb a strand. "I work very hard on this look and I think I wear it better than anyone". I laughed and agreed that he indisputably does. "If you have noticed I don't care much about my presentation unless there is a woman about and then you will have to pry me from the bathroom mirror," he said (again theatrically primping his disheveled coif).

"I have always been a strikingly handsome man and sometimes I purposely try not to accentuate that, so that other men may have a chance to dance or talk with the pretty ladies. I have never been anything but the fine-looking man you see before you. Never unattractive or ugly," he said as he put one foot forward, arched backwards, and put both thumbs behind his lapels.

"Ugly! I was never ugly in my life! Forty years ago I was not as good looking. A looking glass then lasted me three months. Now I can wear it out in two days." ~MT 1906~

Growing Evidence

I was home yesterday nursing another bout of 'vertical syndrome': i.e. it hurts to stand up straight. I got little done all morning except exchange ice packs from the freezer every hour or so. I have not had that much sleep in one day since I was an infant, and, I found that consequence of my condition most comforting.

Later in the afternoon when I could move around without grabbing furniture so tightly that I made fingerprints in the varnish, I sat on the porch with Earl. He was sorting through some pictures in a gray flat envelope that he keeps under his bed. There looked to be letters and some very old pictures of Mark Twain. At first glance I thought it was odd that he would have so many pictures of him, but then it immediately made sense that most of the pictures were in fact of Earl taken at various times 'in character'. There was one authentic picture of Twain posing like Napoleon with his hand jammed into his jacket between the buttons and standing so straight that he was almost leaning backwards. Earl handed it to me and we both laughed.

There were also pictures peeking out from under others that were faded and in color. They were not of Twain and I asked Earl about them. He shuffled them under others and said, "Those are just some earlier pictures of me before my 'transformation'." In respect, I didn't press further with questions that would not be welcomed. The more he sifted through them, the more the colored ones appeared from underneath as if they wanted to be discovered or needed sunlight. Earl was staring at a picture of a group of people posing by a small stern-wheeler with a caption on the back that said "Cincinnati, Ohio, 1881."

I spotted a picture in the corner of the box that was mostly uncovered with an image that looked like Earl, although much younger. He was grasping the shoulder of a woman who had her arm around his waist. Judging by their hair-styles, clothes, furniture and familiar fading, the picture appeared to have been taken in the 1960s or '70s. Guided only by the love I saw on their faces, I assumed that Earl had a girlfriend of maybe even a wife at some time in his life. I resisted the temptation to ask, postponing what I would eventually ask – and turned my attention to the picture he was holding.

He turned the picture toward me. There were several people in the picture and of course Mark Twain/Earl was in the very center holding his lapel with one hand and a carved white Meerschaum pipe in his other. Laughing, I said that all the people looked like they were boarding a ship to Devil's Island or heading to the gallows. He explained that the photographer took so many pictures on that blisteringly hot day at the insistence of the wife of a wealthy publisher who was paying for the Memphis-to-Cincinnati river cruise, which made getting a genuine smile at that point out of the question.

Traveling with Mark Twain in his period of extreme popularity would warrant several pictures, of course, but this unusually sour one looked capable of curdling vinegar. I pointed out that Earl's facial knot was particularly more convincing than the expressions of the other unhappy guests and asked if perhaps someone was standing on his big toe. He laughed and said:

[128]

"No photograph ever was good, yet, of anybody...If a man tries to look merely serious when he sits for his picture, the photograph makes him as solemn as an owl; if he smiles, the photograph smirks repulsively; if he tries to look pleasant, the photograph looks silly, if he makes the fatal mistake of attempting to seem pensive, the camera will surely write him down an ass. The sun never looks through the photographic instrument that it does not print a lie." ~MT 1866~

The Master's Voice

I was sitting at the computer putting the finishing touches on my speech for my class reunion on Saturday night. In times past, I would have had it written weeks ahead of time and read it over so many times that I could almost recite it. Lately, though, with so many things happening all at once, I put it off to the last moment -- just as I would have for any school assignment so many years ago. With that in mind it seemed more than appropriate that I wasn't fully prepared far in advance.

I recalled that the only speech that came easily to me in Speech Class was the one meant to entertain. The toughest was "informative," mainly because that one required research and was much trickier to ad-lib. This speech, however, was to be the last of its type. I thought that even though it may not be as polished as those I've given before, the content should have some enduring effect. Almost everything I write is from the heart, so I expect the listener will remember what I said, if not by the exact words at least by the emotion behind them.

Writing this speech caused me to pause and recall many of my high school days. I never liked the structure of school. It was a bother with little reward. Despite my frustrated mother's cajoling and school reprimands, the desire for better grades never found its way into me. I wanted the friendships, the laughs, and the intrigue of possibly being caught for a clever prank or stunt. School work got in the way of all the fun things I could imagine while sitting in class and staring out the window.

However, Speech was one of my favorite classes and I was able to get good grades, (C's), from Mrs. Renz. My unabashed showmanship and ability to make things up on the spot excited me. Speech and Industrial Arts were the two classes I enjoyed the most – no doubt because both encouraged the use of my best tool -- my imagination.

I'll never forget what Mrs. Renz said so many years ago, "What you say and

[129]

what people hear are two different things". That has come in handy through the years when trying to figure out an angry reaction when I clearly meant something other than what people apparently heard. As I turned back to my writing I realized, in this instance, that quote came in very handy. I was thankful at that moment that I retained one useful thing from my days in school besides my supernatural ability to anticipate the exact moment of the dismissal bell.

I was sitting there staring and reminiscing about those long-ago times when Earl walked in and asked, "How are you making out, Tom?" "I'm doing pretty well; I just need a better transition between these two paragraphs so it doesn't sound so disjointed", I answered. Focusing on the flashing cursor at the end of the last paragraph, he said, "They are too separate to just add the word 'furthermore.' Maybe you need to add another paragraph between them so that you can allude to the next topic without slapping the listener with a brand new subject?" He then disappeared into the kitchen. Moments later, he was back.

"The best and most telling speech is not the actual impromptu one, but the counterfeit of it...that speech is most worth listening to which has been carefully prepared in private and tried on a plaster cast, or an empty chair, or any other appreciative object that will keep quiet, until the speaker has got his matter and his delivery limbered up so that they will seem impromptu to an audience." ~MT 1885~

Maybe there is Hope

I finally finished writing my speech and left a printed copy on my desk. Earl evidently came by sometime during the night and read it. He went further to leave comments in the margin in red. I felt like I was back in school, but this time grateful when I found the 'graded' version this morning.

His comments were mostly favorable and I was surprised to find very little criticism in any of the six pages. I was just finishing his notes when he came through the computer room heading off for his morning smoke on the porch.

"Thank you for looking this over for me," I said. "I was going to ask you to proof it for me later. I especially liked your final comment that you wished you had written it and would be the one who would have the privilege of reading it to the class", I said.

From over his shoulder I could see a subtle smile spout, and as he reached for the doorknob he said: "Always remember...

"An author values a compliment even when it comes from a source of doubtful competency." ~MT~

As Good as it Gets

The day of great anticipation has arrived. The full festivities for our class reunion are tonight. All of the preparations will be evidenced at 6:00 pm by an excited gathering of old acquaintances some of whom haven't seen each other in decades.

I was sitting at the computer doing a last minute edit to my speech when I looked at the clock and realized that I needed to be loading things up soon to be there in time for the decorating and set-up. I was printing the finished draft when Earl came in the front door and asked. "It's all written and complete?"

"I think so," I answered tentatively "I just hope that what I am trying to convey comes across in the way I mean it."

Earl stood there in the doorway of the computer room – and before he headed for the kitchen -- he stopped behind my chair, laid a hand firmly on my left shoulder, and said:

"People can always talk well when they are talking what they feel. This is the secret of eloquence." ~MT 1869~

A Long Exhale

Arriving home very late after the class reunion I took off my suit and went to sit on the porch to decompress in the still, wet hot July air. I thought back over all the preparations for the evening and assessed how it was received from the people who had traveled half-way around the world to revisit their launching pad. I was well pleased with our efforts in making this an evening one our classmates would not soon forget.

Reliving my speech I thought of so many things I could have said or might have said differently. To my surprise, I gleaned more from my own words even though I was hearing them for the 100th time. Perhaps the difference was that this time my thoughts echoed in a place where the intended audience was facing me just a few feet away. While I spoke the room was eerily silent; when just moments before I started reading we couldn't get the group's attention for an important announcement. Once I had their full attention and felt the full resonance of the silence it added weight and consideration to my words.

Points were made, some tears were shed, and all who listened received the message. The message was a simple one. Now that we have spent almost an entire lifetime sometimes dabbling in things with little lasting merit, maybe now is the time for us to look beyond the shallows and reach for something with a deeper meaning.

I think my final words packaged my intended feelings perfectly: "So as we all go forward from here I propose that we adopt a NEW class slogan marking the 50th anniversary of our graduation. One that gracefully transitions us together into the next chapter of our lives and with a new unified meaning."..."We are great, there's much more to do, you are me and I am you."

I thought of Earl sleeping soundly in the house and wondered what profound epilog he/Twain might have given the end of the evening. I came up with this seemingly credible notion:

"The person providing good insight generally isn't looking for a reward if he can be the first to benefit from it." ~TL 2014~

Turn the Page

The sun has set on the last official class reunion. Most people are back home and reflecting on their weekend with old friends in the town some left so many years ago. There were many people I never had time to talk to which saddened me, but there was so much to do in such a short time. The main thing was it was a success, with much reflection and many laughs. I was humbled to have been part of a committee that at a distant point in my life wouldn't have considered me for any role, and certainly not entrusted me to deliver an address to the entire gathering.

I was sitting at the kitchen table Monday afternoon when Earl came in, brewed himself a cup of coffee and pulled out a chair to join me.

He sat down and asked, "Are you feeling somewhat relieved now that it's all over?" I smiled and told him that I was very glad that people had such a good time; that the atmosphere was filled with laughing and smiles. Knowing I had a hand in that made all of the work seem insignificant. Earl said that from what he saw, there was much to be proud of. I told him that our committee has always put together great events and to be included in its success was truly a great feeling. I told him most of what I could remember from the night, and I went into some detail about one particular person who sought me out at the Sunday morning brunch specifically to tell me how impressed she was with my prepared words. Judy was always a very pleasant girl in school who never looked disheveled or mussed. She is the kind of person who quietly turns heads when she enters a room. No flamboyance about her whatsoever, but she exudes a distinctive style and poise.

She came over to me, softly laid her hand on my arm, and said gently, "I just want you to know how much I appreciated hearing your words last night. I wish we could all have heard those 50 years ago. Thank you for finally saying what needed to be said and with such deep emotion. You are a good man, Tom. I wished I had known you better back then; we would certainly have been great friends." She gave me a nice hug and walked back to her table.

I looked down at my breakfast and felt a tear welling up. I had, indeed, accomplished exactly what I had intended. At least one person "got it." That one person was someone I always respected and receiving such a validating comment from her was heartwarming. Earl sat there listening politely, and then with a warm smile he said,

"The happy phrasing of a compliment is one of the rarest of human gifts, and the happy delivery of it another. ~MT 1907~

Only Missing the Ears and Tail

Yesterday after work I was sitting on the porch enjoying the summer's best day yet. Warm sun, cooler air, and very little breeze brought a peaceful calm rarely felt on the sometimes busy thoroughfare into town at that time of day. Even the tops of the trees were perfectly still. The neighborhood was unusually quiet, no lawn mowers or barking dogs to ruin the silence. I rarely get such quiet for any extended time. Even though I was hungry and needed to start cooking supper, I couldn't drag myself away from the relaxing stillness.

After nearly 45 minutes of sublime tranquility, Earl joined me. He had an unlit

[133]

cigar in one hand and the New Orleans Times Picayune in the other. I assumed he also sensed the uncommon serenity, because he moved to his chair without the slightest rustle of his paper. We sat there adding to the library-like mood, not saying a word. Suddenly, after only a few minutes, he pierced the quiet by asking in a normal volume, "Have you gotten the mail yet?"

I quickly turned to him with what must have been a surprised scowl as he crouched slightly and in a low whisper while pointing toward the mailbox, "Is the mail still out there?"

I said nothing and shrugged my shoulders as if to say, "It isn't important enough to spoil this perfect atmosphere," And turned away. Again he crushed the quiet, "You want me to go out and get it?"

I quickly turned my head toward him, leaned forward for emphasis, and with my eyes stretched wide open my eyebrows disappearing over my forehead, I mutely waved my hand towards the mailbox with a slow matador pass. Apparently, my motion was prophetic.

Earl got up and walked out toward the street, only stopping long enough to light a kitchen match with his thumbnail and fire up his cheroot. As he opened the mailbox, I could see that there was a lot of mail and magazines.

Earl **never** gets mail, so his urgency to interfere with such peacefulness to retrieve it annoyed me. As he closed the box, I heard a car coming from his left and gaining speed as it whined into the outskirts of town. Earl, who was completely wrapped up in looking through MY mail, stopped in the center of the street with his feet planted firmly on both yellow lines. The car was only a few feet away when the quiet was shattered by an irritating horn blast. As the car whizzed by Earl looked up just in time to give the iron bull a low Matador arm swing with a magazine. Another car quickly appeared from the other direction; approached and passed with Earl waving him by with his other hand filled with mail. Earl had no clue until he looked up from the last piece of mail, as another car from his left came barreling past him, that he had been dangerously close to being hit at least three times. The writer/lecturer turned death-defying bull fighter with his head held high, his chin up, and his back arched as he slowly made his way out of the bull ring back to our quiet porch carrying grocery coupons and a fistful of bills as if they were a gold-brocaded red cape.

I asked him if he knew how lucky he had been. "Who would hit an old man standing in the street while holding the sacred U.S. Mail? Do you know how big of stain I would make on the fender of an automobile?" he said with a laugh. I

[134]

told him that the whole affair was unnecessary and very foolish. He looked down at me before settling back into his chair and said:

"If all the fools in this world should die, lordy God how lonely I should be."
~MT 1885~

The County Fair

Walking through the County Fair with Earl is like having a monkey on a rope. First of all everyone looks, a few whisper, and some smile assuming he is a living exhibit or an advertisement for something within the grounds. Kids follow along behind him at times, and adults sometimes look and stop themselves short of actually pointing. Imagine a man in a cream colored suit with a longer-than-current-style coat, a white shirt, a turn of the century black tie, and a white hat with a black satin band. He does command attention in a sea of baggy shorts and t-shirts that are large enough to be dresses worn by many of the men in the crowd.

We walked along the midway and came upon a group of teen-aged girls who were walking, giggling, covering their mouths while pointing at boys, whispering and then giggling even louder as they passed the boys. They obviously shopped together. Except for colors, they were almost in uniform. Each was wearing sandals or flip flops, tight shorts, (mostly denim with a smart phone in a decorative case precariously sticking out of the back pocket), and cotton tops with small straps. Most had exposed bra straps, usually of a different color showing over their shoulders or drooping down their arm. And they all had expensive-looking sunglasses perched on their heads – even though the sun was bright enough to be wearing them over their eyes. They had Earl mesmerized, as did all of the other girls clumped together in every direction. "Do they ALL go to the same school or something?" he asked as if he was truly from the 19th century and had never seen such a display. I patiently explained that it was just a current fad and by next year they would probably be dressed differently but their actions would be exactly the same. "Some things never seem to change," I said.

Earl bought a large lemonade and he sipped at it as we slowly walked along – frequently stopping to look curiously at something that he obviously thought would fascinate Twain. He openly laughed at the political tents as I ushered him by them quickly to avoid any possibility of heated banter. He appeared more at ease in the animal barns. I suspected, though he didn't say of course, that it was one place that would feel normal to Mark Twain. Animals haven't changed in the way people or trends have. To him, I thought this was a place where appearances were similar to what Twain may have seen many times before, except, of course, for the electric breeze-box fans blowing on the pigs to keep them cool.

We walked the dusty roads through the entire fair and looked at everything. The games of chance caught his attention, and although he didn't wish to play, we stood there for quite some time watching people unsuccessful at taking home a huge teddy bear. He was particularly drawn to the shirtless farm boys trying to ring the bell with the oversized wooden sledge hammer. Some things he found fascinating; others he showed little or no interest. After about two hours of meandering about he said he was ready to go home. The large clusters of people and the noise were getting to him; and his wide-eyed curiosity had been replaced with impatience.

As we walked down a relatively quiet paved path toward the entrance, we paused to look at the farm machinery parked along the fence. We walked around the John Deere equipment and climbed atop a huge combine. With his hands around his face Earl peered into the glass-enclosed cab -- being the best Mark Twain he could possibly be -- he asked, "Is this kind of thing being used by all the farmers instead of large teams of horses"?

I humored his anachronistic question and explained that in today's world, time is everything and without large machinery to harvest we couldn't afford what food would cost. "So even a small farmer would have to use something like this to get his crops out and to market?" He asked, still staring into the cockpit and gaping at the numerous controls, air conditioning vents, radio, and the large GPS screen.

"He either has to own one or pay someone who has one to get his fields emptied during harvest," I answered. He slowly lowered his hands and peered along the side toward the back, which was twenty-five feet away.

We climbed down and walked along the fence towards the gate past more large machines, some I didn't have a clue as to what they was used for. We walked through the large chain-link exit gate and stood there on the dusty concrete waiting for the traffic light to change. After the light had turned green Earl stood motionless looking over his shoulder ostensibly at nothing in particular, causing people to bump and move around us.

Once we finally reached the other side of the street, he turned, grabbed a lapel and looked back again toward the huge combine. Standing on the edge of the street, with his head cocked to one side, he pulled himself up to what he imagined Twain's full height and in a loud voice said:

"Civilization is a limitless multiplication of unnecessary necessaries". ~MT~

Like a good neighbor

The air was cool and tranquil at noon, but the sun was warm on my face as I went across the street to see if there was any mail. I opened the box and found a couple of magazines, an advertisement for pizza, and an insurance bill. I winced. I hate paying for insurance. It is sometimes a shock to open an insurance statement because it always reminds me in a cold but ominous matter-of-fact way that I'm going to die, (like that is ever that far from the mind of a man of my age). Not only that but it's an eye-opening statement of how much someone will get when you do. I mean it isn't like you can ever escape the thought of one day keeling over, but seeing a State Farm envelope every month, drops a good day down a notch or two with a rush of reality.

Remembering Earl's lucky "bull fight" the other day in the center of the road, I carefully walked across the street and back to the porch where he was sitting, still in his slippers and robe. I stepped in, looking down at my nearly empty – and cold – cup of coffee. I reluctantly opened the State Farm bill, and once I saw the amount I am worth dead, my mind struggled to find a loophole in this beneficiary scam that would give ME all of that money now, while I am alive. Knowing that someone else will get it causes me to look over my shoulder a bit suspiciously and taste my food more carefully.

There should be a system --perhaps a lottery – I thought where once a year State Farm randomly pulls out a policy or two and the holder of that policy gets the 'death benefit' amount in one huge lump sum, but leaves the policy in force until his death. That would sure make paying the premiums a more cheerful exercise. At least it would give the person who would be doing the dying a chance to 'live' a little, using that pile of cash now instead of having it go to someone who would buy a new car with it...maybe even a Kia!

I told my idea to Earl. He nodded behind his paper and said, "Life insurance should be sold by a man cloaked in black and carrying a scythe." He then lowered the paper to his lap, covering his bony white knees, and said:

[137]

"There is nothing more beneficent than accident insurance. I have seen an entire family lifted out of poverty and into affluence by the simple boon of a broken leg...I have seen nothing so seraphic as the look that comes into a freshly mutilated man's face when he feels in his vest pocket with his remaining hand and finds his accident ticket all right." ~MT 1874~

(My apologies to cousins Rose Marie Bostleman and Kenny Shroyer)

Life Is But a Stage

Ironically last night I watched a special on PBS about Mark Twain. I gained some insight that certainly will make my time with Earl more fascinating, if that is possible.

Mark Twain's life was certainly no bed of roses. The years when he enjoyed lots of money and opulence were much better than others. Other times, when there was very little money and depressing things happened, he would confine himself to his home for months at a time. During these periods, he did very little writing to possibly ease his deepening despair. He was a complex man, viewed by the world as a strong intellectual. Even though he successfully combined his breezy Missouri story-telling with his Eastern sophistication he yearned to be more. Other than the joyous times he spent with the members of his beloved family -- that he helplessly watched die -- he never found the happiness that he searched his entire life for. After the program was over I walked through the house looking for Earl. I found him on the porch sitting in the dim light reading, while a gentle rain fell outside. His silence seemed appropriate to my mood. Sitting in the stillness, dressed like Mark Twain, he smoked his cigar, sat with one leg crossed over the other, and held a pose that caused me to feel like I was actually in the company of Twain himself. After a few minutes, he asked what I had been watching. I told him that it was a story about a man looking for something his whole life and never really finding it.

"Sounds depressing," he said, turning a page.

"Well," I answered nonchalantly, "Like real life, we all are looking for more than we will ever find I suspect." I wondered if Earl knew all that I just discovered about Mark Twain. I was certain that Earl had done his homework on Mr. Clemens. Otherwise, how could he offer such quick quotes? He surely knew before taking on the role that Twain's was not the happiest life one might choose to assume.

[138]

I sat regarding Earl, and I felt that I was beginning to understand why a man might take on the persona of another. Maybe Earl's life was less of a picnic than Twain's. Perhaps being someone else augmented his own reflection of accomplishments or the lack of them. Earl was certainly content to be a popular writer from the 1800s. He had the look, the boastfulness, and the intellect to pull it off. Still, I wondered, why would a person become someone who wasn't the happiest of people?

With the black and white images of the documentary fresh in my mind and watching Earl sitting in a similar light on my front porch, I concluded that Earl possibly picked Twain to mimic because he admired him as the author and celebrity he wished himself to be. His selection most likely was not influenced by the many tribulations suffered by Twain; he just happened to like him enough to want to be him. Kind of shallow maybe, but for whatever reason Earl left his own life to become someone else. I thought it must be working pretty well for him as he picked only the best parts to mold into his own personality. How great it would be if we could only live through the good times and ignore the bad as if they never happened.

Feeling like I had literally crossed back and forth through two centuries in the past two hours, and thankful that I was able to keep part of each in my mind, I went back into the house.

Looking over at Earl I was struck by a quote I had memorized long ago, that fit Earl, Mark Twain, and the moment perfectly:

"I am only human, although I regret it." ~MT 1907~

A Good Reflection

Recently I was reminiscing about my early days of employment while preparing a speech. I had many jobs during my life but few were as interesting as my first ones. I worked at a bakery when I was 11 years old; imagine a business remaining open today if they hired under-age children. I enjoyed running hamburger and hot dog buns through the slicing machine, and actually got my fill of doughnuts and jelly rolls. I never tired of watching Mrs. Wentz decorate the wedding cakes, and the smell of the bread baking in the huge rotary oven never grew old. All those sights and aromas reminded me of pleasant kitchens filled with happiness and anticipation.

[139]

Warren Bassett hired me at the Hotel Barber Shop in 1961. Warren was a slight man, not very tall, and had a hidden temper that, when spurred, would turn his face bright red. He was the best barber in the shop and when I got my hair cut, I always hoped he'd be the one to do the honors. I was disappointed when I was summoned to anyone else's chair, even though every barber in the room was capable of fashioning my customary crew-cut. Warren's touch was different; always very gentle. And, as it turned out, he was also a great man to work for. He treated me kindly in and out of the chair and gave me great advice when he saw I needed it. He was rigid in his politics and his views were sometimes narrow, but he was always fair to me.

My daily job there was pretty simple; I had to sweep up the hair on the floor periodically while the shop was open depending on how many customers we had, and how deep the hair was. I also was supposed to be available to shine shoes when needed. When the green and red neon sign in the window and the turning barber pole in the glass tube were turned off the shop closed and my final tasks began. I would thoroughly sweep the entire shop, damp mop the green mosaic tile floor, fill the shaving cream dispensers, empty the ashtrays, and neatly arrange the magazines.

I proudly had my own set of keys and every Wednesday when the shop was closed I unlocked the door, tuned the radio to a rock and roll station, cranked up the volume, and set about my weekly chores.

I cleaned the mirrors which lined every wall of the shop with steaming hot ammonia water drying and polishing with white cotton towels. I enjoyed looking into the mirrors at my reflection as I cleaned them. It bounced off the mirror behind me and then in front of me. I seemed to go on forever becoming smaller and green before my image turned into a single unrecognizable spot somewhere deep in the wall of glass.

I cleaned the windows using the same solution, but I was able to use a squeegee to pull the water down the glass. I mopped the floor with scalding hot soapy water rinsing it twice, mixed up a gallon of shaving soap solution for the following week, scoured each washbowl behind the barbers' stations, scrubbed the white porcelain barber chairs -- being careful not to soak the brown leather seats or backs, and polished the antique chrome trimming on the chairs. It usually took me four or five hours and my weekly pay was $3.00.

The shoeshine stand seemed more like a throne than a chair mounted high off the floor. The stand itself was made of white marble with charcoal streaks. It was a two-tiered stand with two polished-brass poles sticking up from the base with angled shoe rests at the top looking like the sole of a shoe reversed and turned upside down. The chair was on the top tier anchored to the base with brass brackets. The chair itself was made of dark-brown oak and was very old. The black leather back and seat inserts were secured with brass, round-headed tacks placed tightly together around the edge resembling small gold coins. The patron had to step up between the brass supports, grab on to the arms of the chair, and step again onto the top platform while turning to sit down. The whole maneuver commanded everyone to look at the figure that was now seated two feet higher than anyone else in the room.

First I would saddle soap the shoes to clean them thoroughly, go through the polishing sequence using my fingers, followed by vigorous brushing, and then the ceremonial snapping of the buffing rag. That final rite brought the leather to a brilliant shine and turned people's attention from the man on the throne to the rhythmic sound of my finale. I think cracking that buffing rag was my debut into advertising.

Each shoeshine cost 15 cents and if I was lucky I might get a dime tip, assuming I got no soap or polish on the customer's socks. I got to keep all the shoeshine money, and on a very good day, which was usually a Saturday, I might make a dollar.

It was a good job in those days, but working there sometimes felt like looking out of the bars of a prison. I could see my friends going in and out of Isaly's ice cream store directly across the street laughing and having a good time, while I sat in the front of the shop watching their fun from behind the barber shop window. I would always sit in one of the 'on deck' cushioned seats with my feet up on the white ceramic ledge and watch the world go happily by as I waited to be summoned to sweep or renew someone's shoes.

I was telling Earl about my early days at the barbershop recounting several things that I found interesting while I worked there. I told him of the attorney who had the Kangaroo leather shoes that I loved to shine because they looked like glass when I was finished. I recounted some of the most colorful people who came in to get their hair cut. Some stories were as vivid as if I were sitting there today – listening to the barber and patron talking and laughing as I stared at the striped Morgan Linen aprons, which had the random dabs of hair on them that looked like patches of paint brush strokes.

"Those days were not lost on me," I said." I still enjoy going to a barber shop even though, unfortunately, the shoe shine stands have been gone for years. As an adult, I would have enjoyed getting a shine and tipping the boy handsomely, so that one day I would be part of *his* childhood memory. Now I'm the man joking with the barber like those old guys did way back when."

Earl sat there only listening and grinning and then said:

"All things change except barbers, the ways of barbers, and the surroundings of barbers. These never change. What one experiences in a barber's shop the first time he enters one is what he always experiences in barber's shops afterward till the end of his days." ~MT 1871~

As I thought about how true those words had become for me, I smiled and opened up the Sentinel-Tribune.

The Digital Age

A couple of times a year I make a point to see my doctor and, even though I like him, I never look forward to my visits. He rarely gives me bad news. If I'm not feeling well, he gives me good counsel and medication. Still, I've had white-coat syndrome my whole life and it doesn't seem to be going anywhere soon.

Since I hadn't been there in a while, the staff asked a million questions that I swore I have answered many times before. But I was pleasant, hoping compliance would expedite a rapid escape. If I ever forget my birth-date I won't be able to buy an aspirin. I felt like a parrot answering the same questions over and over. Perhaps on my next visit, I will try to imitate a talking bird just to see if they are listening to me after the third of fourth time they ask the same question.

After several minutes the doctor knocked softly and opened the door slowly, perhaps thinking I was in the stirrups and came in. We exchanged pleasantries and got right to the lab results and the general examination. He listened to my heart, pushed on my abdomen, looked in my ears and throat with one of those Allen and Welch apparatuses hanging on the wall. He sat down for a minute to review some more details about my general condition and made a recommendation about seeing another doctor for an in-depth look at some symptoms that concerned him. I thought I was finished when he pulled on a purple rubber glove with a loud snap, and produced an ominous looking tube of something from a drawer that I suspected was going to be used with the glove.

He smiled and said, "I could dim the lights and put on some soft music if you like". Well the details of that scene will have to be imagined much like the stirrup image. Let's just say I obeyed his request and it was not what it was 'cracked up' to be. Considering the level of intimacy and compliance, there should have been at least the promise of dinner and a movie. There wasn't.

After I dressed, finished the paperwork, and was leaving the parking lot I thought of the entire experience and of course the last part, which made me sheepishly smile to myself.

Turning onto the street I thought of a quote that Mark Twain wrote that fit this moment and most likely one that Earl would quote to me if I was foolish enough to give him a recent accounting.

"I was born modest; not all over, but in spots; and this was one of the spots". ~MT 1889~

A Place for Lessons

Yesterday while sitting in front of University Hall at BGSU I had one of those moments that nearly overwhelm one's ability to absorb it. Looking around at all the chairs set up for graduation and the hundreds of parents, family, and friends walking around waiting to share the end of a significant chapter in their loved one's life gave me pause to reflect on events that occurred long before we came to this place.

Looking at pictures of my son from the time he was born -- up to and including this day – gives credence to all the time that has actually passed. But my mind couldn't grasp how long ago I had been at the hospital holding him for the first time. Giving him a long hug after the graduation ceremony brought back the exact same emotion I had that first time we touched, but without the curiosity and wonder of how he might fare in this huge and sometimes cold world. He was now not only a man, but one whose efforts has been rewarded and recognized. My wondering about how he might turn out has been replaced with profound relief that his options and opportunities will be many. What more can a father ever expect to witness?

When I returned home from the ceremony, I found Earl sitting in the leather chair in the living room, getting ready to head out to the porch for his first afternoon smoke. "How was it?" he asked.

[143]

"It was very nice and the weather couldn't have been better", I answered. As he headed for the porch, he said, "I want to hear all about it. I got a glass of iced tea and joined him moments later, settling into another perfect summer day.

I started with how ironic it was to sit in that wide expanse of grass in the center of campus where I once played Frisbee by the hour. I recalled how we ran in the shadows of the huge oaks trees that surrounded such a serene and safe place to play. Were we even aware that there was higher learning going on beyond that fringe of trees? This one-time entertainment venue for hippies and activists 40 years ago was now formally staged for academic acknowledgment. That observation caused another smile, but this one triggered by irony. There I was, a man who never benefited from advanced education, had only 'played' on campus, and found myself sitting on that very playground to celebrate my eldest child's accomplishment.

Earl smiled as he turned to me and said, "Children need to learn to play properly, too Tom. Education isn't just about opening books and pouring the contents into your mind. I am sure you taught him lessons he could never have learned anywhere else."

I told him that I appreciated him saying that, but today was not something I could help my son with; he had to do it alone and for reasons only he could explain. He was always the child who had to do it his way regardless of how much guidance I tried to offer. The final outcome would be based on what he came up with no matter how far afield he might go to arrive there.

Earl was obviously lost in thought, because his cigar burned out and he needed to re-light it. As he puffed on it making a balloon-sized cloud in front of his face, he took the cigar from his mouth long enough to say:

"Independence--which is loyalty to one's best self & principles, & this disloyalty to the general idols & fetishes of others" ~MT 1888~

Wanna See some Pictures?

It was a dark, humid, and rainy morning -- perfect for quiet reflection. I was sitting on the porch watching the straight rain make bubbles in the puddles, which theoretically signifies that it will rain all day. As I sat there in the otherwise quiet dim, I was thinking over the weekend and my observations about my oldest son receiving his MFA and with honors. It's hard to focus on such an accomplishment and not gush about it. After all, isn't that one of the rewards you get as a parent, having people indulging you as you boast of your children's achievements?

Once my thoughts returned to other things, I instantly thought about my other two sons and something my mother taught me many years ago. 'You must never give more to one than any of the others,' she counseled. 'You must be equal in your recognition, treatment, and love for each of your children.' I suddenly felt a little guilty like perhaps I did forget the other two for a bit this weekend. But then I thought when any one of them steps into the limelight the other two is always in his shadow. There's no way around it. They each have their talents and each has had times of individual recognition. I sat there and took comfort in knowing that they each recognize how special they are to me and that these moments of significance are shared in turn. They love to tease each other, but there doesn't seem to be much sibling rivalry among them. When one does something that is important to him, the others always rally with their support and well wishes.

I guess I am not an unfair father after-all for dwelling on my oldest son for a day or so. Being a parent isn't as simple as being good or being bad, but being consistent with your affection and just being there when your kids do something that makes them happy and you proud at the same time.

If I didn't single each one out when he achieved something of importance I would be like the little league coach that gives every player a trophy regardless effort. They are smart; they know.

"Embrace your children equally but separately. Never allow them to suppose they are all alike to you. Their only common similarity should be the level on which you love them." ~TL 2014~

I felt good arriving at a place in my appraisal where I might put an appropriate exclamation point, so I got up from my chair and went to get a cup of coffee and knock on Earl's door.

Unequalled

When I heard the news of Robin Williams' death, I was surprised by the depth my grief. I felt very sad, sadder than I can remember feeling over the unexpected deaths of other celebrities. Philip Seymour Hoffman's death was a shock, but

Robin Williams' struck me in a more profound way. His style of odd-ball humor made it easy for me to identify with. At times I've thought my mind raced in a similar way -- not with as much creative power of course, but enough that I could see a tiny bit of his comedic spirit in myself.

Perhaps his creativity troubled him, as that often seems to be the case with brilliantly imaginative performers. Some of the greatest artists of all time were plagued with incredible amounts of creative energy, complicated by secret fears and flaws. Williams' rapid-fire comedy was something you either liked or you didn't, but regardless of one's opinion of his humor, I think most people could appreciate a mind that could improvise at warp speed. An imaginative mind bursting with the unpredictability of a lightning strike had to be such a busy place – at times -- for Robin to comfortably live.

I turned off the TV and sat there in the quiet focused on his incredible movie roles. He brought some amazing characters to life in a more resonant and meaningful way than anyone else I could imagine. I smiled to myself thinking of the attention-grabbing and humorous image of Robin as "Mrs. Doubtfire". And of course one of the greatest monologues ever put on film in "The Dead Poets Society" came immediately to mind. He gave believeable life to so many roles. Several made me laugh out loud, some simply prompted a smile, and through his compelling interpretation others made me think and feel things in ways I never experienced before. Through their natural and persuasive manner, great actors can carry you off against your will to places you never dreamt of being. I trusted him as a person and an actor, and that allowed me to willingly hand him my life for the entire length of a film, and I never once regretted the time I spent with him.

While I sat in the calm Earl came and joined me. He asked what was distressing me and I explained that a great actor had taken his own life, and how troubling it was that he was alone and sad when he died. I added that for a person who brought so much gaiety to his fans, it seems that he wasn't an especially happy man. Earl sat there silently respecting my admiration for the man I mourned. "Why is it that people who are so talented and can make people laugh so easily are sometimes so unhappy?" I asked rhetorically.

Sitting in the uncommon stillness of the living room, I pondered that unanswered question. It seemed to hang in the air as inexplicably as the 'super moon' had hung in the sky the night before.

"His reasons are not something I can ever rationalize," I said. "I can only try to remember him for his warmth and talent and be happy that I was fortunate enough to have witnessed part of his life". Earl got up to leave, paused and said in a soft, tender voice,

"People forget that no man is all humor, just as they fail to remember that every man is a humorist." ~MT 1905~

A Portrait in Black and White

It has been pointed out several times in my life that I am analytical by nature. Sitting with Earl wherever we happen to be often triggers thoughts or conversations that cause me deep contemplation. Even though I know that he obviously is not Mark Twain his archaic persona is convincing enough that I can't help but treat him as if he really is the great writer. Earl brings Twain to life by presenting a forceful portrait of him. On some days it is difficult to tell whether he has traveled into the future or I have taken a trip to the past. It isn't nearly as important to know as it is to just experience the allure of being in the company of an enigmatic man.

Sitting in the big wingback leather chair with his evening bourbon, a folded newspaper in his lap, and a book held open by the thumb of his left hand and his palm supporting the spine. I carefully studied him as if I was going to draw his profile. His hair, which has a mind of its own, was swept back over his ears, but with the cottony bulk puffing out at the sides. On top of his head his white and silver waves spread out and up in no particular direction. No matter how unkempt his hair appears it always looks authentic. If you combed it flat he would lose the look of a disheveled genius that has become part of his recognizable trademark.

The skin where his ear meets his jaw has three distinct lines that gives the appearance that at one time his ear may well have been higher on his head. Maybe it was pulled down by a correcting parent, a frustrated teacher, or an angry editor. He has a subtle jaw and his nose, even with its distinctive hook, fits his face nicely. The focal point of Earl is his sprawling mustache, which much like his hair doesn't have perfect order. However, without its freedom to flourish, he would be just another face in the crowd. The thick white hair hides his mouth almost completely so as to cover the frequent sly smiles or disguise the meaning of his contentious comments.

To me, he is a very distinctive looking man. Partly because of the person he pretends to be and of course the unique look that his features naturally display.

After finishing my detailed and surreptitious assessment I turned back to finish watching Nature on PBS. The Snow Monkeys were pushing an unwanted aggressive juvenile down the mountain and away from the others when Earl, (who I thought wasn't paying any attention), said something that not only fit the image on the screen but my scrutiny of him only moments before:

"In this world one must be like everyone else if he doesn't want to provoke scorn or envy or jealousy." ~MT 1902~

The Tradition Continues

Today is the day I start the yearly tradition of making pickles. My mother and I did this together for so many years that the process since her death seems hollow. The recipe is one that her family had been making before she was born; the tradition lives on today through me, my sister, and a couple of cousins.

I miss those times when she and I would sit at her kitchen table with her recipe box and read over the original recipe every year and find the same humor in the way it was written. 'Five cents worth of stick cinnamon' and other amounts equally as nebulous always made us laugh. Mom had converted that early recipe to one that we could actually measure years ago, but reading the original always made us chuckle.

One would have to know my mother to fully grasp how meticulous she was about recording every detail. She had 3 X 5 index cards listing every detail for each year; the date we got the pickles, (homegrown or purchased and from where), the amount we purchased, the date we started them in the crocks, the exact amount of ingredients, the canning date, the number of jars we ended up with, the total cost, how many jars I took home, and how many she kept. So before we started the procedure for the current year it was her ritual to read completely through the last few cards. "Well in 2001 we got four plastic shopping bags of pickles from Elizabeth, (her sister/my Aunt), and that filled three two-gallon crocks," she would say. (I had the least patience with this part. Going through those old index cards and hearing about something that meant very little to what we were supposed to be doing right then aggravated me. I was there to make pickles, not to rehash every procedure from years past.) What I wouldn't give today to sit in her kitchen and listen to her loving voice read through the carefully recorded notes from our many years together canning that old family recipe. Continuing, she said, "You came over at noon on the 6th and we washed them and put them in the crocks and covered them in cold water to sit overnight."

The custom was the same each and every year. Repeating this ritual alone now is nothing like that experience and can't be recaptured. What remains, however, is the joy I get from giving out the finished pickles to select friends. I treasure knowing it was all due to that special one-on-one time my mother and I shared. Last year I took a dozen jars to a small gathering of my mother's relatives, and each family took a jar home. That is definitely something Mom would have done. It is ironic that some things that irritated me most about her when I was a child I have completely embraced as an adult. Open cupboard doors, chewing with your mouth open, a throw rug with the corner turned up, a large jug or pitcher of anything on the table while you are eating are all things that annoy me in the same way they bothered her.

One year Mom and I each prepared a jar of pickles from the same batch that we planned to enter in the county fair. The only subtle difference was perhaps the way the jar was packed. She won a blue ribbon and I won the red, which confused me because after-all I learned my canning technique from her. We had a good laugh about that every year when she might pick up one of my recently loaded jars and ask me with her cute smile, "Is this Blue Ribbon quality?" When we filled the jars she was slow and meticulous and I was always in more of a production mode. The answer to why she won the blue ribbon is so obvious to me now that I have taken her example and started enjoying the time of doing it right rather than just finishing quickly. Her patience came from being a mother I guess and her natural demeanor was to take things slow and do them right the first time.

Sitting with Earl at the kitchen table preparing to start this year's pickles, I enjoyed telling him some stories of those times when my mother and I canned together. Sharing them with someone new was a good way to relive them; he seemed interested in my reminiscing over an evolving legacy that I hope my children will carry on. Earl shared that his mother, (I had a distinct feeling he wasn't talking about Mrs. Clemens), also enjoyed canning vegetables and soups. He went on to tell me what little he could remember, and said he wished he had spent the same quality of time with his mother as I had with mine. He said he envied me for the time she and I shared together. His comments, and the first smell of pickles filled the kitchen and I smiled at the sense of her presence.

[149]

I busied myself at the sink washing the larger cucumbers that Earl and I were going to slice for dills. The noise of the water interrupted our chat which gave Earl the opportunity to remember more about his mother. After I turned off the water and the room was once again quiet enough to be heard, Earl said in a soft penitent voice, "She would have taken the time with me had I shown an interest, but being anywhere else always seemed to draw me away from home and her." He paused and then added:

"Technically speaking, she had no career; but she had character, and it was a fine and striking and lovable sort" ~MT 1890~

Most people I know could use that Twain quote to aptly describe their own mother. Apparently, motherhood has been the same for centuries.

A 'Friendly' Duel

Recently on a trip into Toledo to pick up a part for my gas grill, Earl and I were talking about billiards, to be more exact, pool. Understanding that I was talking to someone who thinks he's Mark Twain, I thought the likelihood of Earl playing at the caliber of Mark Twain was remote. He did; however, seem to know much about pool. As I drove along we talked about different games and certain matches that were memorable to each of us. He was unusually vague when relating some things that I thought Twain would have excitedly described in great detail, but, *no* matter, pool is still one of my favorite topics of conversation regardless of the other person's depth of knowledge or interest.

On our way back from the barbecue shop I saw a huge sign above a strip mall that said "Pool," and thought we should take a look so I turned into the lot hoping it wasn't a store catering to backyard fun. At the rear of the lot was a large building that had another sign above a long glass front that said, "Johnny's Pool Hall," spelled out in black letters on a green background. The sign was shaped like a pool table complete with pockets and random balls garishly painted around the lettering.

Earl asked what we are doing and I told him that I thought we might look around inside and get something cold to drink. We got out of the car and I opened the back hatch and took out my cue case. Earl's eyes got big and he said, "You have your own cue"? I nodded. "Don't you have your own?" I asked sarcastically. "I had several back in Hartford," Earl answered, "As you know Tom, the two-piece cue is a rather new invention, and while I have had ample opportunity to buy one in my many modern-day travels I still feel more comfortable with a solid piece of wood in my hand. I also think it suits my antique style, don't you?"

I nodded and pushed open the door. We walked into the large foyer allowing our eyes to adjust to the dark interior. As I squinted to focus, I could only make out, faintly, green rectangles with glowing spots above each of them. Suddenly everything became clearer and the room became completely real in depth and familiarity. The sound of a cue ball hitting another ball, presumably sending it toward an awaiting pocket was music to my ears. Somewhere else in the room someone broke a rack with a loud crack and I turned my head hoping to see a nine ball slamming into a pocket off the break. The smell of the place and the lighting removed any sense of unfamiliarity. I had been there hundreds of times, though not in this specific location. The people were shadows moving in and out of the light. I couldn't describe a specific thing about any of them, but each was a potential adversary.

I walked up to the counter and asked for a rack of balls. The man working the counter looked at my case and then at me doubtfully. He then gave a long stare at Earl who was still standing on the large rug by the front door looking out over the expanse of tables.

"Both of you playin," he asked. I said yes and added that I wanted a table near the back of the room. I usually pick the back tables because they get less play and usually are in better condition. All the young showboats want to play on the front tables so everyone coming in can see them and their imagined competence. The disinterested counterman told me table 18 and pointed towards the back where there were three darkened tables. While I stared wondering which table was "18," he flipped a switch from behind the counter and the four lights over a table came to life. I motioned to Earl to follow me through the maze of tables to 'my' table.

It is strange how optimistic I feel when I walk up to a table that is "mine." On a good day, I do truly own it. I sat my case respectfully across the corner of the table resting it on the wooden rails only and unzipped it. I paused to run my hands gently over the clean green cloth like I was smoothing a wrinkle on a freshly made bed. It felt like it was the best table ever and that my admiration was wishfully soothing it to make my day there the best as well. I felt a protective bond with that table, and from that point on, I thought, Earl or no one else better get in the way of the guarded relationship I had immediately established with the stone, wood, and wool that made up "**my friend.**"

[151]

Earl chose a cue from the wall rack and asked what we should play; I told him it was up to him. (After all it was his funeral). Looking back at that day at Johnny's, I see that I appeared to be a bit conceited about my pool skill. But every pool player who takes his game seriously is a ruthless competitor. Confidence is the first tool you must use to be victorious. It builds within you to make difficult shots and can intimidate naive opponents. You must be cordial to every player between shots, but when you are leaning on the green of the battlefield, go for the kill at every opportunity. Each time you walk to the table and aim your shot carefully, do it as if your very life depends on it. I cannot remember the professional player that said it, but his take on the attitude of playing pool was perfectly stated: "Pool is about as friendly as a knife fight." That applies to when you are standing alone at the table looking at your options. You want to keep your opponent in his seat, and only allow him to get to his feet to rack the balls for the next game.

I jointed my cue and racked the balls. Earl broke the rack for eight ball, (my least-favorite game), and made two balls. I could tell by his bridge and stroke that he was no stranger to the game, but he was certainly not the player I've read that Twain would have been in his heyday. In his house in Hartford, Twain had his own table for years and dedicated hours of each week giving 'lessons' to innocent pigeons who would happen by and get sucked into a game with the passionate marksman.

Earl made some nice shots, won a couple of games, and was pleasant enough when he lost -- my test of a player I care to play with more than once. I enjoy sharing the sacrament of pool with one who can accept defeat without whining or losing his temper. We played for about an hour, which was enough for both of us; me from winning most of the time and Earl from losing. We walked back to the front, leaving my green friend as we had found her, alone, quiet, in the dark, and I paid for our time.

As we drove home I asked Earl if he enjoyed playing. He chuckled and said, "I once took a whipping for stealing a pie from a window sill and it was a lot more fun than that." I felt bad that my good friend had to lose, but better him than me I thought.

He added that he always enjoys watching the adversarial "dance" that occurs when two people meet over the green. "The precision one must use to best his opponent should be appreciated no matter which side you are on", he said. That statement alone could easily cement our friendship forever and certainly guarantee that we would play again and again. We didn't play the same, but our attitude about the game was perfectly in tune with one another. To watch someone take a game away from you never feels as good as winning yourself, but your appreciation for a game well played keeps you from being bitter or angry. In my book that is the definition of being a gentleman, and the essence of what makes a real *pool player*.

We were quiet for a while when suddenly Earl loudly said, "DAMN...you really kicked my butt!!" For a moment after hearing that I wondering if I should re-assess my opinion of his good sportsmanship when he erased the notion with a loud laugh and said:

"The game of billiards has destroyed my natural sweet disposition" ~MT 1906~

The Academy Award Goes To

Many years ago, there was a Greyhound Bus stop in Bowling Green named 'Green Gables'. It was located on South Main Street which was also US Route 25. This major thoroughfare cut right through my little town, extending from Canada deep into Florida. The building was painted white with two gables facing the street, (one at each end), and the long fascia boards were painted leaf green. There was a green sign hung on a large pole close to the curb that read "Green Gables" vertically and with the smaller horizontal word "Bus" at the bottom, all in white letters. The sign was red electric neon and at night it became a beacon for travelers to stop and rest before continuing on.

The building had a drive on the south end that circled around and ended on the north side where passengers would get off and on. My mother knew several people who had worked there at one time or another including my Aunt Rose. It was a nice place for people to stop and use the facilities and if they stopped during the day and had little money for restaurant food they could go next door to Sparrow's Market and buy something to eat later on the bus to save some money.

I stopped there frequently during my paper route -- especially in the winter to get warm and sometimes splurge and buy hot chocolate or toast. The details while subtle to some always captivated my attention. The walls were paneled in a comfortable golden knotty pine. The floor was a checkerboard of green and white linoleum tile throughout. The linen-printed, Formica-topped tables sat on heavy black pedestal bases and each was encircled by green, cushioned chrome chairs. On each table sat a chrome napkin dispenser, salt, pepper, a glass sugar shaker with a little flap lid on its chrome top that held, of course, saltine crackers. To complete this 'still-life' was a green, vinyl-backed stitched sleeve with a clear front that protected the menu inside. It had brass corners and stood between the napkin holder and the sugar shaker, flanked by the salt and pepper. It was always the same on every table -- except the one marked: "Drivers Only!" that had ketchup and mustard added to the assemblage.

It was a comfortable place to stop and the food was typical cafeteria quality for the 50's and 60's. My exposure to its ambiance was just inside the front door, where I could get warm enough to face the bitter winter winds outside as I trudged through the last hour of delivering the Toledo Blade. I sometimes resented my customers because, I thought, they probably wouldn't read the stupid paper even though I almost killed myself getting it to them.

I would sit and through the windows watch the passengers get off the darkened bus and wander tentatively into the brightly lit restaurant, looking for a clue as to what to do next. Judging by the urgency of the way they looked around, I could read "Where is the restroom?" written on some of their faces.

I once saw a poorly dressed woman clutching a cardboard box wrapped in string sit down in the furthest corner of the brightly lit restaurant, after getting a cup of hot water from the large urn in the center of the big room. As I watched, she slowly looked around, and then carefully pulled a teabag from the pocket of her threadbare coat.

There were all sorts of people who traveled by bus back then. Air travel was in its infancy and routes were only between major cities. For many people there were only two types of public transportation at the time, either train or bus. Sometimes people would have to take both to get to remote parts of America.

I once saw a well-dressed man in an expensive-looking suit walk in; he had a thin mustache, dark black receding hair, and carried a fur-collar overcoat over his left arm. He looked out of place, contrasted with the casual dress of his fellow travelers. The longer I looked at him, the more I was convinced that he was none other than David Niven, an actor who was very popular at that time in the '50s. As he vacantly walked by me I knew it actually wasn't the famous actor, but the thought of someone renowned coming to my little town excited me to the point of actually convincing myself that it was indeed him. I left to finish my paper route without even buttoning my coat.

"I just saw David Niven at Green Gables," I said to myself as if by saying it again and again would make it so. The agonizing fact of facing another hour in the freezing cold became just as real as what I pathologically repeated as I trudged off through the snow, "I just saw David Niven at Green Gables," I said aloud feeling the arctic cold cut into my throat.

When I finished my route almost an hour later, with my neck and face numb from the cold, I rushed into our house and announced excitedly, "I saw David Niven at the bus station and he talked to me for a long time. He liked me and said that he wished he could stay longer and talk, but he had to be somewhere to make another movie." My mother was in the kitchen fixing supper and simply said, "Uh huh", and went on with her work. "But you don't understand mom....it **was** David Niven right there in Green Gables!" I said loudly. She politely smiled at me and said, "Of course he was", and continued to stir the pot of beef stew.

The rest of the story goes the same way each time I try to convince siblings and friends that David Niven might actually be riding a Greyhound bus through Bowling Green alone on his way to make another movie, and that he took the time to sit with me and talk. Eventually, I gave up trying to find someone to share in that possibility and to become thrilled along with me. As time went on, the fabrication of the famous actor crossing my path faded back into my wishful imagination. I never saw anyone famous in Green Gables again, and eventually, I stopped looking.

If I had conveyed this story to Earl, who was still sound asleep, I'm sure he would have a Twain quote to fit. Instead of disturbing him, I looked one up that I thought he almost certainly would have employed.

"Good little boys must never tell lies when the truth will answer just as well. In fact, real good little boys will never tell lies at all--not at all--except in case of the most urgent necessity." ~MT 1865~

I agreed completely with Twain's outlook on "good little boys" always telling the truth, especially the last part. Boring periods of my youth became "most urgent necessities".

A Good Plan is Painless

Sitting quietly on the porch with Earl this morning I was drawn to another memory of long ago when I was a small boy. As Earl attempted to quietly read several neglected Sunday papers I interrupted his silence and took him perhaps reluctantly on a trip back in time to a blistering summer day in July.

In that recollection, I was sitting on the steps by the sidewalk in front of our house at the corner of Ada Avenue and Prospect Street. There was no one around to play with and I was smashing a roll of caps with a hammer. The only sounds were coming from the television inside the house tuned to a baseball game, an occasional car squeaking to a stop on Prospect, and of course my persistent bang bang with the hammer on the strip of caps. When a car went by I thought of how I wished I was in that car.... going somewhere...doing something with at least the air coming through the windows and cooling me off. Better yet, I wished for a convertible with the top down, cruising all over town and, of course, ending up at the A & W for a frosty mug of root beer.

I peeled more caps off the roll and tried hitting them in rapid fire like a machine gun. I had, maybe, hit eight out of ten when I spotted a lone black ant, which I mashed into a small wet spot. "Gotcha!" I said. 'Nothing to do and nobody around', I thought to myself. Just another boring day that was too hot to do anything but hang around in the shade of the two Maple trees, sit on the cool sandstone sidewalk and smash caps or careless ants that innocently happened by.

I went into the house to get a drink of water. As the water was running to get cold, I noticed a little package sticking out from under the corner if the metal breadbox. I carefully lifted up the corner and pulled out the cellophane package with a stapled paper top that was printed with multi-colored circles and the words "Party Pack." Much to my surprise, it was an unopened package of balloons. I immediately looked around to see if my mother was lurking close by, (she had radar for ears and might have heard me lift the bread box), and quickly slipped them into the back pocket of my jeans. I drank my water so fast some spilled down my chin soaking the front of my white t-shirt. It felt cool against my skin as I raced back out of the house and around to the side furthest from the TV.

As soon as I pulled the package of balloons from my pocket, the devil who was always perched on one of my shoulders, whispered my assignment into my ear, I quietly crept around the side of the house and gently dragged the garden hose toward the back of the house. I was ducking down below the open, screened window, through which the Tigers' game was blaring. I tried to turn the faucet on as quietly as I could. It always squeaked so loud that I stood there waiting for a hit and the yell of the announcer so I could open the valve quickly. Heck of a time for a pitcher to throw so many balls and for a batter to hit so many fouls, I lamented. It felt like an hour before the crowd cheered as someone got a hit and I was able to turn the faucet on. I went quickly back to the business end of the hose, flashing a devilish smile knowing that I had been waiting the whole day to find something fun to do.

I filled one red balloon to about the size of a grapefruit, walked to the curb, seeing nobody around, threw it high in the air, and watched as it hit the street with a loud splat. Within less than a minute the water had disappeared and the only evidence of my prank were nearly invisible pieces of curled-up rubber withering on the hot concrete.

I returned to the hose to fill several more, and was wondering what I was going to do with them....'Hmmmmm,' I thought. Then with the help of the 'friend' on my shoulder a plan came to mind. It required some additional supplies. I went back into the house, quietly sneaked by the TV room, gathered up my WWII canteen and a newspaper delivery bag that once belonged to my brother, and sped out the screen door leaving it to slam carelessly behind me. Thankfully the sufficient excitement of the Yankees/ Tigers game dissuaded my mother from investigating my frequent and suspicious comings and goings. I slung the bag over my head, filled my canteen from the hose, and carefully put the five water-balloons into the bottom of bag.

I nonchalantly came back around the house, looked in all directions and then climbed up into the leafy cover of the Maple tree. I was almost exactly above the Ada Avenue stop sign. I tried unsuccessfully to comfortably position myself for an eventual good target to appear below. The smartest part of my plan was filling the canteen. It was hot even within the leaves of the tree and there was no air moving. I settled in –as best I could -- for what I thought might be a long wait.

After about 15 minutes a car stopped on Prospect, but way too far away to hit with a balloon through all the branches. Other opportunities slipped away -- bicycles on the wrong side of the street or too far away. I needed someone to pull up to the stop sign directly below me. Just as I prayed for it to happen, a beautiful mint-green '56 Ford convertible with green and white interior pulled to stop. The top was down and the target was directly beneath the Norden Bomb Site I imagined I was gazing through. Without hesitation or a thought to possible consequences I dropped all my bombs at once perfectly onto the couple in the front seat -- soaking them and most of the inside of the car. They turned the corner and screeched to a stop. The driver was a tough-looking guy in a sleeveless white t-shirt, He reached me just as I was about to get my second foot on the ground and make my unplanned but hasty escape.

[157]

"You think this is funny? Look at the mess you made, he said as he grabbed me under my arm, practically lifting me off the ground while dragging me over to the car. The lady in the car was dressed nicely. The headscarf she was wearing was now plastered to her head like a wet dishrag, and her skirt held a puddle of water with a broken yellow balloon floating in her lap. I immediately recognized her as my neighbor's sister who was visiting across the street. About that time my mother, (obviously hearing the screeching tires), came out of the house and stood on the porch with her hands on her hips angrily asking what was going on.

Well, the story gets boring and painful after that, but suffice it to say that sitting on the cool sidewalk felt pretty good after my mother finished with me. I'll never forget the behavior adjustment that day, and after that I planned my crimes more carefully, always acutely aware of the consequences of detection.

Without asking for Earl's input, he offered these words for my consideration:

"A genius is not very likely to ever discover himself; neither is he very likely to be discovered by his intimates". ~MT 1907~

A Surprise Appearance

Saturday Earl and I went to Pemberville to pick up more pickles and some other farm-fresh produce. It naively didn't register to either of us why people were starting to line Main Street and why little kids were sitting on the curbs until it was way too late. They were preparing for the Free Fair Parade. We were mired too deeply into the town and the growing crowd to simply turn around so I pulled into one of the few remaining parking spots. I hadn't seen a parade in a long time and Earl seemed excited by the possibility, and it was a cinch nobody would be at the produce stand, so we got out of the car and ventured to the street. There was a large white painted concrete planter not far from the curb that was about three-feet high -- with a small American flag stuck in the dirt. I walked to the front and rested against it. Earl, seeing that it was a good vantage point, followed suit. We stood there looking around when suddenly, off in the distance, we heard a marching band strike up "The Stars and Stripes Forever," causing people to excitedly scurry from one side of the street to the other, where they had placed chairs in advance. Some groups of chairs were strung through with rope apparently 'reserved' for what must be a family's favorite spot.

We could see the band now coming towards us slowly and the music got louder as it echoed through the small valley of the Portage River behind the storefronts. The uniforms were the familiar black with bright orange trim of the Otsego Marching Knights. On the chest was a large orange, keystone-shaped panel lined with silver buttons and a embroidered black and silver knight's

helmet. The members all had orange plumes of feathers on their helmet-style hats and each wore spotless white gloves. I had forgotten how impressive a marching band could be with its look and muscular brass resonance. The band passed us in tightly spaced rows that were straighter than one might expect from high-school students. Just as the tail end of tubas reached us, there was a whistle from somewhere in front. The band stopped marching forward, marched in place directly in front of us, and started the song again. After a few notes I heard two whistles and the band marched forward again continuing down the street. After the band came a couple of convertibles, one with the Pemberville Mayor sitting up on the back automatically waving at everyone and occasionally pointing to someone specific like it was an election year and not one person adult or child could be neglected. Several feet behind, a red Corvette followed carrying a young girl in a billowing blue, prom-style dress with a silver sash that said: "2014 Fair Queen."

Twenty feet behind was a John Deere tractor pulling a flatbed trailer that was covered with green astro-turf. Atop toward the back was a huge white cloverleaf made of chicken wire, and with crepe paper pushed through the openings spelling out "4 H" in green letters. To the front were several small pens made out of wire fencing with baby goats in one, -- lambs in another, and right in the front of the float were four pink piglets. Each group of animal pens was surrounded by kids dressed up in bib overalls and plaid flannel shirts, sitting on bales of hay. They all held a piece of straw in their mouths, look like the standardized picture of the American farmer – a depiction you see everywhere but in real life.

Behind that came a float advertising a realty company with banners on the side that were blowing in the gentle breeze. A teenage girl sat at a desk complete with computer monitor, professionally dressed in a gray suit and wearing oversize black-rimmed glasses. She waved at the crowd with one hand while operating a computer mouse with the other as if she was finding someone in the crowd his first home.

Not far behind came a group of men, dressed in suits and ties, carrying attaché cases and marching stiffly. Occasionally, they stopped to make perfectly choreographed moves in and around each other. They swung their briefcases

[159]

overhead holding them with both hands and then in unison slapped on the side twice with one hand as the other holding the handle brought them back to their sides and ended back in the same rigid position where they had started. I didn't catch their name, but they were refreshingly different than what I've seen before and the crowd loved them.

Following them was a large vintage shiny red fire truck with lots of kids on-board wearing little plastic fireman hats that said, "Junior Fireman." The ones that were not waving threw handfuls of candy towards both curbs, causing the children sitting there to scurry out and gather up as much as they could between the fire truck and the next band that was coming several feet behind.

After about a half hour of silently enjoying the various parade entries, Earl loudly said into my ear, "I want to go to the other side of the street." Before I could reply, he started out across the street between a band and a VFW marching unit. As he reached the center of the street, people on both sides started to applaud. He stopped for a second, took of his white hat, and waved. The applause increased as he stood there, somewhat shocked by the greeting. He looked behind him and saw the VFW guys closing in, he turned toward me and with a shrug and a resigning smile he started walking forward behind the marching band. Some people were standing, clapping, and smiling as he waved his right hand as he held his hat high in the air with his left.

In his long white coat, white pants, and tie he was either Mark Twain himself or perhaps Hal Holbrook accurately portraying the famous writer. Regardless, the appreciative crowd recognized him to be worthy of their attention. Perhaps the most familiar with his appearance were the older folks who applauded loudest once Earl emerged in the bright summer sun and could be plainly seen following the band and in front of the unfurled flags.

I smiled as I watched him disappear down the street completely absorbed in the excitement, the applause, and the music. When the parade ended 15 minutes later, and I was now sitting on the planter, I could see Earl walking toward me, shaking hands with adults and children and smiling broadly. Before reaching me he was stopped by an old man who pumped his hand excitedly while saying, "You sure brought history alive today!" Earl thanked him graciously and walked up to me as I slid off of the planter and dusted off the seat of my jeans.

Walking back to the car; I looked at him, smiled, and shook my head in disbelief. I was surprised by his unsolicited participation but also very happy for his moment of public admiration. I said, "You have made quite an impression on these folks Earl, with your appearance in their parade. According to the crowd you were a sensational hit."

We got into the oven of my car and Earl emptied his bulging pockets of cellophane-wrapped candy. His lap overflowed with his spoils. I started the car and turned the air conditioning on high as he reached for his seat belt. Just as I heard it 'click' he looked up at me with a very satisfied smile and said:

"Public opinion is held in reverence. It settles everything. Some think it the Voice of God." ~MT 1900~

I glanced towards him maybe to find a look that might indicate a measure of humility, but there was nothing to be seen other than my friend Earl popping a piece of candy into his wide smiling mouth.

Drenched in Reality

This morning I decided to go to the Bass Pro Shop and pick up a new pair of moccasin style deck shoes. I wasn't planning on making a production out of going and wasn't going to be gone long so I asked if Earl would like to ride along. He was dressed and ready before I was. He loves going into stores to see the enormous amounts of things for sale and of course the people. Wal-Mart is a standing favorite, but he has never seen Bass Pro and I assumed he'd enjoy that too.

After a slow-moving drive through the construction on the interstate, we finally arrived at the store. It was amazingly busy and we had to park very far from the entrance. It looked like it could rain at any minute, but we opted to leave the umbrella in the car as any self-respecting man would do. The huge front doors with the antler handles stopped Earl in his tracks as he had to inspect them closely. This, of course, caused a backup of people behind us. Once in the store he again stopped dead in his tracks to look up and around; other customers pushed their way past us. "C'mon Earl let's get out of the way of these folks," I said as I grabbed his arm and lightly pulled him toward the turnstiles. "Hello guys, welcome to Bass Pro," said an older man with a sincere smile. Earl wanted to stop and chat with the friendly *boy*, but I gave him another tug. Finally, we were in the store, and away from the hurrying crowd.

The store is large and there are many ways to get lost, so I asked Earl if there was anything he wanted to look at with me before I headed out to the footwear department. He said he would just mosey around looking at this and that. I could see the potential for problems, so I suggested he look around in the huge fishing department while I quickly bought a pair of shoes. I added that after I had what a came for, we could walk around together and see the whole store if he was really interested. Before leaving him, I said, "For now please just stay right in this vicinity. There is much to see and you'll still be looking at fishing stuff once I grab that pair of shoes". Trying to see some sign of comprehension in his darting wide eyes, I added, "DO you promise me that you will be right here when I come back?" He nodded. "I am serious Earl are you going to be right around here?"

"I will not be more than 20 feet from this spot, okay?", he said looking off in the distance annoyed by my insistence. As I walked away I looked back; he was still standing there looking at the first fishing rod in a line of hundreds. "That'll keep him busy," I thought as I headed up the stairs.

I walked into the area where the deck shoes were displayed in a cone on a round table. There was a "**special sale price**" on an orange Day-Glo explosion-shaped sign at the top of the stack. I quickly found my size and tried them on at a nearby stool. I walked down to the mirror to see what they looked like even though I'd never see them again from that angle. However, since the mirror is there, I always feel like there must be an unwritten fashion law that you should do that. They looked great from every side, they fit as well as new shoes can, and the price was perfect. I put my own shoes back on, tucked the box of new ones under my arm and started down to collect Earl.

I scoured the entire fishing department and he was not there. I asked a clerk, who said Earl left immediately after I did -- to where he had no idea. I walked around the first floor looking for his white hat in a sea of camouflage. I wasn't really nervous, but I was concerned that he might walk outside and I would have to spend wasted time looking for him inside the store. I went up the stairs, stopping at a landing where I could get a full view of the lower level, No Earl. I walked the rest of the way to the top by the gun department and again looked all around to no avail. Going to the railing at the far end of the very long firearm counter, I again scoured through the crowd on the first floor. I started asking clerks who were stocking items if they had seen an old man dressed completely in white.

I remembered that I had a picture of Mark Twain on my phone so I pulled that up and showed it to several people. Some remembered seeing him, but didn't know where he went. I went back to the entrance and the friendly man that greeted us when we came in was no longer there. I couldn't rush outside, as I had not paid for my shoes.

I was annoyed, then worried, and then annoyed again. "Damn, he promised," I said to myself. I walked over to the customer service desk and asked the clerk if she had seen him. She asked how old he was and I showed her his picture. She laughed and said that if he was a young kid and still in the store she would have sent me to camping gear, "Kids always end up there for some reason". I looked in that direction and then thought that since so much time had passed that he probably went back to the car.

I waited in the checkout line my head on a constant pivot still trying to spot him. I paid and then walked out the door to the sound of thunder looming right above me. I started to run, but buckets of rain soaked me completely before I was halfway to the car.

Once inside, I realized my run for the car had been foolish at best. Earl didn't have a key to the car, and would never have ventured further than the smoking area by the exit.

I grabbed the umbrella from behind the passenger seat and waited for a break in the downpour. After about fifteen minutes, the rain seemed to let up so I portaged my way around the huge puddles and headed for the door, which was hundreds of feet in front of me. Several people stood under the entrance roof waiting for the rain to stop. I must have said, "Excuse me," 30 times to get to the blocked doors. I was soaked and probably looked very out of place to the cozy dry people who were side-stepping me to avoid getting wet by my soaked clothes. I decided to check the camping department, but no sign of Earl. While I was turning away, I heard a very familiar voice, ".... and there we were, barefoot on the banks of the muddy Mississippi trying to stick frogs with our sharp sticks when all of a sudden...." I threw open the flap on a huge tent and there sat Earl cross-legged with five or six little boys and a couple of dads sitting in a circle mesmerized. "Where have you been?" I said with clenched teeth. "Well we have all been right here having a big time haven't we boys?" Earl answered (They all nodded with big smiles.) I glared at Earl without saying another word and he slowly got to his feet. "Well it seems our time here is over guys. I must help my friend find some dry clothes and get him home safely. Maybe we'll meet again sometime", he said, rubbing his hand through the red hair of one of the boys.

We left quickly without any words. When we reached the parking lot he said, "Seems silly that you are completely wet while carrying an umbrella." I didn't answer as I felt the tips of my ears heating up; I just kept walking rapidly towards the car. When we got in I checked my watch. It had been two hours since we had parked, at least two zip codes from the store entrance.

I looked over at him and talking softly with deliberate slowness as to control my percolating anger, I said, "I want you to think of a very good reason why you broke your promise to me. I DO NOT want an answer until you have come up with something better than a lame apology. Do you understand me, Earl?" He nodded and we headed home.

Other than Eric Clapton's tribute to Robert Johnson playing inconspicuously in the background, the drive home was made without a sound. The volume was low enough that Earl could easily have been heard if he had something of importance he wanted to say.

When we reached the house, and before I had a chance to open the door, Earl turned and said:

"I could never keep a promise. I do not blame myself for this weakness, because the fault must lie in my physical organization. It is likely that such a very liberal amount of space was given to the organ, which enables me to make promises that the organ, which should enable me to keep them, was crowded out. But I grieve not. I like no halfway things. I had rather have one faculty nobly developed than two faculties of mere ordinary capacity." ~MT 1868~

He then looked away and opened the door and got out closing the door behind him. I sat unblinking in the car for an incomprehensible amount of time before I quietly opened the door. I walked slowly to the house still soaked from the rain and with his astonishing words fresh in my mind I left a wet umbrella and a new pair of shoes behind in the car.

The Wire Sanctuary

A porch can be a very interesting part of a house. On a large house, it might simply resemble a covered patio or Lanai. Sometimes, its attachment appears as an afterthought if it is empty of furniture. To an un-informed observer, a very large porch might imply that the owner ran out of money and couldn't afford to finish it as the enclosed room it was designed to be. A porch is part of the house but sometimes, depending on its size, it's like the proverbial neglected, red-headed stepchild of the home. My "L" shaped porch has lap-sided walls covering the bottom third, which ties directly into the siding on the house. The top two-thirds is screen, which closes it off somewhat from the outside -- more like another room. Simply being covered by woven aluminum screening, it allows the weather in but keeps unwanted critters of all varieties out. Having a screened in porch confuses pizza guys as they don't know if they should knock on the screen door or boldly open it to walk up to the main house door. By its design, it is more of a refuge than just an attached porch and affords a great vantage point for doing nothing more than perhaps watching the world on the other side of the woven wire. When you are on the porch, you aren't expected to be thinking hard; you are predestined to simply relax and enjoy. Perhaps something or someone new can more easily unfold and relax under the roof of a welcoming porch.

Frequently the porch becomes a depository for things not wanted in the house. A bag of trash placed there by someone in their stocking feet, a kitchen project gone wrong in a smoking skillet, a throw rug that has a pet's by-product folded in it to be dealt with later, or things left for someone to stop and pick up when you are not at home...."It'll be on the porch,"

I thought back to the many "porch" events in my life. My mother's porch had a long concrete railing, which served as the bar in a western saloon when I was a kid. The neighbor boys and I would use shot glasses and root beer Kool-Aid to help recreate western movie fight scenes on that porch. The only thing missing was a piano playing in the background and of course 'girls'. In high school I sat on that same porch waiting for a ride from friends who had cars.

My first kiss was on a second story porch during a cool spring rainstorm. We were covered with a blanket, and huddled on a porch swing hidden from view. I can remember sitting and talking nervously under that cover about meaningless things to keep the terrifying silence at bay. We were just two kids attracted to each other who had nothing to say that really mattered. So we jabbered, smiled, and rarely looked right at each other. Then suddenly the inevitable happened and we kissed. It could have happened anywhere, but, at that moment, that porch was the most romantic place in the world and everything was absolutely perfect because of it.

The openness but private nature of my current porch is the perfect environment for exploring new things, either alone or with others. When I reach a point when there's nothing left to say or think about, I just smile and embrace the atmosphere, grateful to have a comfortable place to sit and do nothing but enjoy the world going by just a few feet on the other side of the screen.

[165]

Today the porch is the setting for many great conversations with family and friends. In the summer it serves as the informal, pleasant reception room for the house. Without its inviting comfort many talks would never occur. It's fitting that my porch is center stage for most of my "Living with Earl" tales. It suits us both. And best of all for him, he can smoke comfortably while churning out candid observations that otherwise might be muted in the restrictions of a smoke-free house.

Earl told me long ago that sitting outside on the porch and smoking his cigars was a habit he adopted because its informal environment allowed him to feel genuine contentment. He looks forward to his frequent visits there and found consolation in its comfort whether alone or engaged in friendly conversation. He summarized the experience this way:

"When I search myself away down deep, I find this out. Whatever a man feels or thinks or does, there is never any but one reason for it--& that is a selfish one." ~MT 1905~

I let that statement hang for a moment, and then replied, "That might apply to you and your incessant smoking, but for me sharing the space is more enjoyable than merely occupying it." ~TL~

Appreciation

After breakfast I busied myself with the next procedure of the pickling process. After cleaning up the kitchen, I walked out onto the porch to check the temperature on the thermometer and check on what Earl was up to.

As I stepped outside, a rush of sticky air hit my exposed skin like a hot damp rag. The temperature was quickly rising and would probably reach the predicted 92 degrees. Earl was sitting with his legs crossed, wearing his usual long suit coat, and a fresh shirt fully buttoned to his throat. "Aren't you a little hot out here?" I asked. He lowered his paper and said, "Tom, you don't know what hot is until you have lived in Missouri in August". "Well maybe not but this is hot enough for me," I answered. "Do you want something cool to drink?" "A nice glass of iced tea would be great, thank you," he said, and pulled the paper back up to his face.

I went for the ice tea – and placed fresh slices of lemon over the edge of each glass. When I got back to the porch Earl was just finishing wiping his head with his red railroad handkerchief. "It is warm, Tom; I'll give you that." he said tucking his handkerchief into his back pocket. He gratefully reached for the cold glass covered with glistening beads of sweat.

"Have you ever thought of wearing just a t-shirt on these hot days?"I asked smiling to myself at the thought of Earl in a in a white t-shirt with the Nike Swoosh on the front and to top it off, possibly a ball cap.

"If one wants to run around half-naked that is no affair of mine, but for me to engage in such a display would tarnish what little polish I have left," he said with a chuckle.

I sat there quietly, sipping my refreshing tea, while enjoying the now-permanent image of Earl's new appearance in a t-shirt emblazoned in my mind. We sat and drank. I watched the shadows of the low clouds drift across the tennis court in the distance; Earl slowly turned the pages of yesterday's New York Times.

"If you ever change your mind I have lots of them that would fit you. You could have your pick, just ask," I said. "I'll keep that in mind my friend, thank-you," he said from behind his paper.

What was left of the morning passed the same way: an occasional comment, short answers, and independent activities by each of us. By now, it was lunchtime and we were both hungry. I prepared lunch and served it on the porch since the kitchen table was occupied with the canning process. A couple of ham sandwiches, potato salad, sliced tomatoes, and a dish of fresh peaches unquestionably filled our stomachs which could easily promote an afternoon nap.

The porch was becoming even hotter as the sun was now directly overhead so I opted to lower the air temperature by 20 degrees by going inside. Earl chose to stay on the porch to smoke and read. I was alone in the house with the four cats sprawled in various spots, the dog lying on her side in front of the air conditioner, and I was nestled into a pile of pillows and watching the ceiling fan slowly spin.

Just as I crossed my arms which is the usually indication of an imminent siesta, the door opened and Earl came in carrying his empty ice tea glass with a shriveled lemon slice at the bottom. He stood there looking at me expectantly for a minute until I said, "What?" After a lengthy pause, he finally said:

[167]

"I don't remember that I ever defined a gentleman, but it seems to me that if any man has just merciful and kindly instincts he would be a gentleman, for he would need nothing else in the world." ~MT 1906~

After his pronouncement, he nodded directly at me as if to say, "That is you Tom." At least that was how I chose to interpret his remark. I smiled and replied, "Thank you, Earl," and closed my eyes.

A Second Opinion

Today I went to the hospital for a stress test. I hate when your doctor tells you a test is "just as a precaution" and in the next breath adds that if you happen to go into cardiac arrest as a result of the test, you'll be in the right place to receive treatment. How about if he just looks in my ears with that little light, takes my blood pressure, listens a bit with his stethoscope while tapping around on my back and we call it a day?

I took the test and bested the goal of 129 BPM (beats per minute) by reaching 152 BPM. I suspected that all my worry last night was for nothing. However, being neurotic has some rules to follow and I am always most compliant.

I was back at home by 9:30 and, except for where they sanded the spots on my skin to stick the electrodes, I don't feel much different. Relieved that my heart is strong, I literally exhaled a long breath of relief.

Since I hadn't been allowed to eat before the test, (they don't want people throwing up on the treadmill), I made a bagel and toast and sat down on the porch. It was already 75 degrees. I sat there alone for 15 minutes or so before Earl came out, completely dressed for the day. He said hello, took his usual seat left of mine, and asked, "You had that test this morning, didn't you?"

"I did. All the evidence says the world is stuck with me for a while," I said. "Everything looks good, but it will be reviewed by the heart doctor before my follow-up appointment."

"I hate doctors." He said. "They always want to give you bad news......why if it wasn't for bad news they'd be out of business," he said reaching into his breast pocket for a cigar. "I tired of doctors long ago when one told me I needed to cut down on my smoking, that coming from a man who frequented the saloons to all hours of the day and night with a glass of bourbon in one hand and a ten-cent

[168]

cheroot in the other. He told me once that smoking was going to cause my death, so I said I would get a second opinion. I asked my bartender and he didn't see no harm in it, so I kept smoking my thirty cigars a day and never visited that misguided doctor again."

I mentioned that death, while inescapable, should always be looked at as an extremely dim light at the end of a very, very long road. Even though my life is progressing faster than I might wish, I try to be open to the myriad of potentially beneficial things that become available to me. There are healthy things I feel compelled to try -- or at least curiously examine right up until death claims me.

Earl sat there silently for a second twirling his cigar in his lips as he put the last comma in his impending retort and then said:

"Palmists, clairvoyants, seers and other kinds of fortune tellers all tell me that I am going to die, and I have the utmost admiration for their prediction. Perhaps they would convince me a little more of its truth if they told me the date. But I don't care so much about that. It was enough to know, on their authority, I was going to die. I at once went and got insured. ~MT 1907~

Taking Flight

I wonder if the day you stop daydreaming is the day when your mind gives up. Is day you wake up and decide that there's nothing beyond your immediate environment that is interesting enough to ponder in detail, the moment you start to fade away? I do not believe, however, that if you find everything in your life to be fine and wouldn't change or expand anything, that you're ready for the eternal "dirt nap." I am thinking more about one's capacity to think outside of where he is physically and soar through space and time to distant places, without his body moving from his favorite chair.

If I were vacationing on a white beach in the South of France, I might be thinking of another place or even of being another person – and know those could become realities if I let my imagination roam without restraint. Being able to dream and transport one's self anywhere your mind can go is an ageless freedom I never want to lose. Perhaps when someone gets very old and seemingly stares vacantly for hours, he or she is actually daydreaming of different places or other times. Maybe the mind can transport you to enjoyable sanctuaries to help cope with some of the depressing realities of old age. If that is the case, getting old will not be nearly as bad as I have sometimes projected. I never want to lose the ability to imagine something pleasant or have some mythical force magically carry me away to another place, a different time, and allow youthful wonder to put a smile on my face. I want the "conscious" people to look at me and speculate where I might be, like the teachers back in high school used to do.

Living with Earl has been a stimulating exercise in imagination and daydreaming. Being able to almost smell the Mississippi by being in the same room with my convincing friend gives me pleasure. I smile, just knowing that through the inspiring images he triggers, I can travel at will. I can close my eyes and be riding in my car with Mark Twain, or I can sit in front of my computer and see the two of us in Wal-Mart laughing together. For just a few short minutes, I am somewhere else.

Each day Earl's example reminds me that living happily is a fifty/ fifty proposition. Half of the time you must tend to the essential, sometimes boring affairs of everyday living. You must care for yourself with sustenance, protection from the elements and disease, and tend to all the responsibilities that keep your physical being comfortable and safe. The other half of your time must be spent keeping your mind active, alert, and happily engaged. Just taking care of the necessities of living isn't enough to keep your mind healthy. You must return to your childlike marvel frequently and let you imagination take you away. You need to learn new things, to read, to laugh, but most importantly you need to dream while wide awake. Whoever said that immortality is impossible was certainly not a dreamer.

The same year that he died, Mark Twain wrote:

"Everything in a daydream is more deep and strong and sharp and real than is ever its pale imitation in the unreal life which is ours when we go about awake and clothed with our artificial selves in this vague and dull-tinted artificial world." ~MT 1910~

Brace Yourself Michigan

Looking out the window this morning I saw a long, shiny black limousine edge carefully into the driveway. The driver, who was dressed smartly in a black suit and signature chauffeur's hat, got out and opened the rear door. He stood there with one hand behind his back for a few minutes when suddenly Earl walked into view carrying a small worn suitcase with a brown buckled belt holding it closed. He handed the bag to the driver and disappeared into the black leather interior. The driver promptly closed the door, walked behind the car, and quickly placed the dismal looking bag into the trunk.

As they waited for a couple of cars to pass before backing into the street, I walked out on the porch to watch. I was a bit dismayed, but not entirely surprised. I leaned forward as if I could see through the dark tinted windows by being five inches closer. My maneuver didn't make any difference; all I could clearly see was my reflection in the glass. I waved hesitantly, not knowing if Earl could see me or if he was even looking in my direction. Suddenly the window lowered and I could see a squat glass, half-filled with amber liquid in a familiar hand being raised as if to toast me or his departure. Either way I knew that he was off on an adventure. But since he didn't give me the courtesy of a "good-bye," I felt slighted.

When I walked back into the house ushering three of the four cats with my foot I looked over at the 'marble table' as I've always called it, and saw a note.

Tom,

I had a chance to go visit an old friend in Detroit. He offered to fly me up there, but that is for the birds...haha. He is sending a car for me tomorrow morning and I will be spending the long weekend in Grosse Pointe relaxing by the Detroit River and looking out over the green lagoon known as Lake Erie.

I would have mentioned it before, but I was afraid you might take offense that the invitation did not extend to you as well, so I beg your forgiveness and of course your well wishes that my weekend will be lovely. Just remember that for four days you will be sullen and bored and even perhaps a bit suicidal, but have no fear Earl will return to enhance your life on Tuesday assuming my host runs out of twenty year bourbon by then.

Best Regards,

Earl

I read it over, smiled to myself, and then set off to come up with all the things I might do while he would be away. As I walked towards the kitchen a familiar Twain quote flashed into my head as if it had been poised like a runner set in the blocks just waiting for the smoke to leave the barrel:

"And what is any joy without companionship?" ~MT 1869~

Walking into the kitchen and seeing the pile of dishes left for me to clean I smiled even more broadly and said out loud as if the occupant of the limo somewhere on the northbound freeway might faintly hear, "It's going to be really tough, but I'm going to desperately try to enjoy this time alone!"

In Tribute to Earl's Absence

My suggestion for Labor Day weekend is to do something that will benefit everyone who knows me. Find a pool table and play for a few hours – an activity guaranteed to remedy whatever ails you. It will cure hoarseness, insomnia, lethargy, remove warts, and generally just do a body good! That's my plan!

A Random Lament

I was sitting having my morning coffee earlier, (not that early; I slept late), and thinking about how people reflect on their lives. Specifically how I look back on mine.

When I recall my past, I often think about things I wish I had done differently. Some mistakes I made changed the course of my behavior immediately. Others became lessons that helped shape me into the man I am today.

Depending on my mood, I can regard my entire life as a complete waste of time and view it with a mountain of regret. At other times, I see my failures and miscues as steps to learning. I sometimes focus on my negative results, despite the many things I accomplished successfully. Things that seemingly yielded nothing of value become sorrowful misgivings. My attempts to always do the next right thing become elusive during my "the-glass-is-half-empty" periods.

At this point in my life, the most important thing to cherish is having few regrets. There are so many ill-conceived things I have done in my life, and so many bad decisions that netted no tangible or positive results. The only way I can move forward without beating up on myself each morning is to see who I am today. Look deep into what I have become -- not in spite of all that mistakes I made, but because of them. Like it or not, I am the net result of everything I have done. If I could remove all of my mistakes with one sweep of a magic wand, it wouldn't make me a better person.

[172]

To spare me from making myself crazy with "what ifs," I have to distinguish myself as the person I was meant to be, not the person I could have been. I understand that I don't get an automatic pass for doing all those foolish things simply because they helped me grow, but I do need them as proof of who I have become. If I were able to keep only my honorable actions and surgically remove the shortcomings, who would I be?

Without Earl sitting next to me poised to pounce with some meaningful witticism, I am left to search for a Twain quote on my own. I think this one nails it.

"We can't reach old age by another man's road. My habits protect my life, but they would assassinate you." ~MT 1905~

In His Mind

Earl surprised me when he emerged from his room this morning, as I never heard him come home. He was completely dressed including his hat which he respectfully never wears indoors. He was headed for the kitchen and I was ten paces behind him. He heard my steps on the kitchen floor and turned to say, "Well good morning, Tom. Did you have a great weekend"? (I wanted so badly to say that it was kind of nice to have the house to myself but I decided against it).

"Yes I did thank you.... quiet, uneventful, but very nice, I answered. So what kind of excitement did you find in Detroit?"

Earl turned from the sink to face me, grasped both lapels, and said, "There were many people there, lots of kids and dogs running around. It was quite a circus actually, but at night when it became quiet with the absence of children and unruly canines, the good bourbon came out and there was much fun to be had by all who dared to stay up late enough to enjoy it." This last statement was said with a distinctive twinkle in his eye.

"Don't leave me in suspense. What kind of fun are we talking about here?" I asked eagerly. He began to pace back and forth. "Well, there was much drinking as you can imagine, and some odd music from a hired band...Howard called it 'classic rock', (Howard Johnson the host...no relation to the motel person), and some dancing by some pretty girls on the large outside patio that faced the water, he answered. "But the highlight of Saturday night was when I was asked to read some of my most famous works to the many gathered guests. Their anticipation of seeing me standing there at the band's microphone -- while quickly pulling lawn chairs around to face me and the full moon was rising overhead had to be intoxicating for them. Howard handed me a copy of *Huckleberry Finn* to read from. As I thanked them I heard my voice echo across the huge grassy lawn filled with chairs, out past the long dock, and onto the water beyond as I smoothly eased into my favorite passages. It was most exhilarating. I can only imagine that they must have felt like excited school children to hear Mark Twain, himself, read to them," he said with his usual humility. "I read a few chapters, interjecting a bit of commentary here and there, and about an hour later finished to a rousing round of applause followed by lots of handshakes, and a few pleasurable hugs from the prettiest of ladies. It was most enjoyable and the remainder of the weekend was spent eating, drinking, and laughing -- with all things centered around me of course.

I know it was unbelievable fun for them and although exhausting a bit at times for me from all the adulation and such, I would unselfishly go back anytime I am asked to oblige those who adored me so," he said. Pouring himself a cup of coffee while still wearing his hat like an ill-mannered Southern sheriff he pulled a chair from the table.

"So, you were the center of attention?", I asked politely, knowing full well the answer.

"Well of course I was, he said, (while laughing out loud and easing into his chair), the same as when I am almost anywhere." Still laughing he stopped long enough to take a small sip from his steaming cup. After he sat the cup on the table he nonchalantly and with complete seriousness looked directly at me and said:

"I am.... made merely in the image of God, but not otherwise resembling him enough to be mistaken for him by anybody but a very near-sighted person." ~MT 1886~

I looked closely at him to see if a sign of humorous intent had emerged, there was none.

[174]

There's An Idea

I was outside this morning in the rising fog after dropping my car off for service. I noticed the dry grass looked pretty pitiful having been starved for significant rain for over a month. I hadn't mowed since July and the only thing that looked healthy, of course, was the weeds. It is interesting how the lawn fools me every year. The early spring brings everything to a lush Irish green allowing me think this will the year my yard will look like a golf course fairway. Then comes the Dandelions followed by all the other odd looking plants that would look more at home on the ocean floor than in my lawn. It isn't long after that everything looks like a dreadful greenhouse experiment gone bad. The season for growing is coming to an end and the time to start clearing out the leaves is approaching faster than I want.

I walked through the backyard and up the hill toward the shed following a mole run -- another annoying aspect of yard keeping. I walked heel-to-toe hoping to push it down flat enough that the grass might re-root and come back again next year with its usual grand entrance. As I awkwardly snaked along, I saw Earl emerge through the porch door carrying a bag of trash to the curbside container. I thought about taking a picture of him actually doing something to help, but thought better of it. I must remember that he was/ is an invited guest and, while certainly isn't very helpful, his lengthy stay here satisfies my need for good company and provocative conversations. I smiled at the image of Earl holding a bag of trash and walked back to the house.

Earl and I arrived at the porch door at the same moment and I asked him what he was doing. "There was something rotten in the kitchen trash and I decided it needed pitched," he said stepping into the porch. "Thank you for that. I was going to get it myself when I got home...you saved me the trouble," I said stepping up behind him. "You are most welcome Tom. Anytime," he answered.

We both sat down in 'our' porch chairs and I thought of the past weekend spent completely without Earl. I determined that having him here -- no matter how unsettling it can be at times -- is so much better than before he came for dinner and never left. He has caused me to think, to dream, and to laugh so uncontrollably I thought I might pass out. On other occasions, he has forced the art of self control to the point that I've subtly bitten a hole in my cheek to keep from losing my temper. Indulgence has been a good thing for both of us -- his indulgence of my structured hospitality, and my indulgence of his sometimes lack of consideration. He prefers what he believes are more meaningful habits to observing common courtesies I take for granted.

[175]

After a few minutes he spoke up, "Being here with you is a wonderful way to spend my life; you are a good, true, and helpful friend, Tom. You ask very little and put up with so much. How a guest in anyone's home could ask for more from a host I could never know." After a short pause he added, "You certainly could write a book on "Living with Earl." I thought for a moment and nodding I said, "I think I do have enough ideas to put some words into print."

Reflecting on my comments about Earl's household manners, I felt petty and a bit stupid. That reminded me of his often used quote:

"Concerning the difference between man & the jackass. Some observers hold there isn't any. But this wrongs the jackass." ~MT 1899~

The Black Swamp Art's Festival

I just came from downtown where I left Earl for the afternoon to read, drink coffee, and smoke outside at Grounds for Thought. There was much activity preparing for the upcoming Black Swamp Arts Festival. Golf carts were zipping around carrying supplies, traffic barriers were being staged by city workers for placement early tomorrow morning, and there was an impending carnival atmosphere everywhere.

It's a time of reuniting with people that you only see once a year during this event. The entire weekend feels almost as festive as Christmas, but without a strategic or obligatory schedule. You show up downtown, walk around looking at the wonderful art, and enjoy the tempting aromas from the many food vendors in the parking lot behind the Main Street stores. I have a fondness for this temporary reality. For three days, Bowling Green transforms into a place that embraces all styles of art, music, ethnic food, and the various types of people who come to share in this short-term conversion of our typical college town.

I clearly remember the year I was accepted to have a booth in the juried section of the show. Mine was one of four booths in a large white tent, situated on South Main Street, in front of Kaufman's restaurant. It was a great experience to display my wares and talk to the many people who stopped by to browse, examine, and sometimes purchase. I can visualize that booth clearly in my mind like it was yesterday. The Black Walnut entertainment center that covered the back of my portion of the space consisted of three sections bolted together. The client I had built it for generously allowed me to use it throughout the show and then deliver it to him on Sunday when the event concluded.

I made more than 60 distinctly different decorative boxes that I displayed on the glistening glass shelves. The fine piece of furniture was transformed into one of the most elaborate backdrops of all the exhibits.

For the first time, I actually felt like an artist. For the duration of the show, judging by what was exhibited, I thought I looked more at home there than several of the other artists. Some of my items departed from my usual designs and I thought they might have seemed peculiar. But I also thought variation of style and design could be one definition of art. A large red circle on a white canvas couldn't have taken more than a modicum of effort, but some viewers would consider it art. I had strayed far from my usual comfort zone to produce some eye-catching pieces that took considerable time and effort, and I was well pleased.

A fellow exhibitor unabashedly told me that I was not an artist because what I displayed could not be defined per se as "art". Being puzzled as well as insulted I pressed her to explain to me the definition of "art".

She said, "Art is something that is aesthetically pleasing...period! What you make is craft because it has utility and function."

I thought for a moment and then asked, "So, if Renoir used one of his paintings to prop open a door it would no longer be "art"?"

She thought for a second before putting her hands on her hips like an exasperated mother and snapped back, "Tom, you are just trying to be difficult. You know exactly what I am saying and you know I am right."

Knowing I had her reeling, I accused her of being condescending and rude, which she of course quickly denied with righteous indignation. We continued to disagree, but with me feeling like I had completely won not only that skirmish but the entire war against her magnified pretension. The fact that I succeeded by using something so unfamiliar to her kind as logic seemed a bit unfair, but didn't tarnish my victory or stain my conscience in the slightest.

She went on to win 'Best of Show' out of a field of 145 artists. I am certain that in her mind the Blue Ribbon and $ 500 prize chiseled her 'expert opinion' into an imagined grand marble edifice in front of a museum somehwere, and turned my argument into bits of her chisel dust that would be swept up with the remnants of all the other inferiors when the festival closed.

I thought about our exchange again as I scoured Twain for a quote that might fit. I came up with this:

"It vexes me to hear people talk so glibly of feeling," "expression," "tone," and those other easily acquired and inexpensive technicalities of art that makes such fine show in conversations concerning pictures. There is not one man in seventy-five hundred that can tell *what* a pictured face is intended to express."~MT 1869~

Happy Birthday Daniel James Lambert b. 9-5-85

One cannot control what he remembers or what he forgets. Our minds are entirely on their own when those seemingly random selections are made. There have been times while I was engaged in a very specific task that required total focus when some random memory totally unrelated ran through my mind like a subway train on the express tracks. It doesn't linger long enough to be examined closely; it just rushes right through as if taunting me to connect it to what I am doing or to simply distract me. The timing is just as inexplicable as the content.

This morning I was sitting at the computer writing in the quiet of the house when a little message popped up on *facebook* reminding me that today is my oldest son's birthday. I knew that, but seeing it officially in the corner of my screen made me smile to myself and stop what I was doing. It launched me into a series of vivid memories of the day he was born, complete with visions of the colored pictures in the album we made to celebrate the occasion. The focus on my task evaporated and I sat back in the computer chair, clasped my hands behind my head, and let the memory roll like a favorite vintage movie completely from beginning to end.

I saw myself standing in front of the nursery window where the tightly wrapped little babies were lined up like bread dough in little clear loaf pans waiting to expand into real people; I could clearly spot my son. He was the only one that was awake and seemed to be looking all around as if to examine the entire room. I can say unequivocally that his curiosity for all things started almost immediately after his birth. I was happily mesmerized with him; his beauty, his fascination of his surroundings, but I still felt all the uncertainty that a new father should feel. Inwardly I had faith that I would try very hard to be a good dad, but not having a model to go by in my own life caused me to vacillate from complete confidence to terrifying uncertainty.

That entire day was a roller coaster of many emotions and thoughts, but when I left my wife and our new son at the hospital that night I was feeling pleasantly shocked. I was now a father and regardless of anything else that happened from that moment on there was nothing that could erase that heart-swelling fact. I was fortunate enough to experience the exhilaration of fatherhood twice more with two amazing sons, but the feeling of being a first-time father cannot be duplicated.

Not having anyone to share these memories and new insights with, (Earl walked to *Grounds for Thought* again this morning), I sat feeling much like I did on the night Daniel was born. I smiled as I thought about him back then and flashed on a memory from yesterday, when he came by to check mail that had been delivered here for him. The same looks he had as a small child emerges at times in his smile, his pensive mood, and his infectious laugh. I know that his birthday is important to him, but it will never mean as much to him as it does to me. It simply can't! Thanks to Daniel for being the first one on the dance-floor. He certainly made the prospect of having more children not only comfortable and appealing, but inevitable.

Having watched the Daniel 'movie' from beginning to the present, I felt like I hadn't been the best father, but I knew I was the best father I could be. I am still learning how to be better in this role and I suspect that I'll never get it perfectly right. But I'm reassured that all my sons know my efforts to improve will never stop.

"It is a wise child that knows its own father, and an unusual one that unreservedly approves of him" ~MT~

I finished my cruise back to 1985, and went back to reading the facebook posts complete with pictures of kittens and puppies.

All Things Pretty

Today promises to be another gorgeous day for the local art festival. Weather is so important to all of the artists who have come from all over the country, hoping to enjoy brisk sales from the hundreds of people walking up and down the street in hopefully beautiful inviting sunshine.

Earl has spent the last three days meandering around the show and talking to many people, some of whom stop him to ask if he's a 'living exhibit' He, of course, loves the attention. When I watched him from a distance yesterday, he seemed to add new interest to the already enjoyable atmosphere the way a juggler or mime would.

He also obviously enjoyed listening to the music of Bob Manley playing with the Bob Rex Trio, because that is where I first spotted him on Saturday, leaning up against the gray stone wall of the bank atrium conspicuous in his white suit. He was subtlety tapping his toe and occasionally I could see the brim of his hat move to the music as well. I watched him for a little bit, then turned my attention back to the tight but free-flowing jazz echoing in the concrete courtyard. I did nothing to gain his attention, as it was fun to just observe him away from our customary environment and unaware of my surveillance.

I walked into the bright but very welcome coolness of the outside air and headed to my seat on the porch. I knew Earl was sitting around the corner as a puff of smoke preceded my view of him and wafted out in a round cloud then quickly separated into thin wisps before disappearing. Standing in front of my chair I said 'good morning'. He looked up over his paper and said, "It sure is a lovely day isn't it?"

"It sure is and I'm happy for the festival. Except for the Friday evening rain, they've had great weather," I said as the stretching wicker in my chair quieted after I settled into its friendly fit. The Sunday scene on the porch has become such a welcome routine: thick papers strewn around, great coffee, a few cars driving by, and the two of us sitting in the shade of the porch enjoying another morning of the waning summer. Once the weather gets cold and the porch furniture is covered, we will need a new ritual to replace the comfort of this one.

As it approached noon, I got up to get ready to meet a friend at 1:30. Earl asked if I was heading uptown I nodded and offered him a ride. We agreed to be ready in an hour and I left my cozy nest to get the day's affairs moving. As I showered I thought how great the day would be if my back holds out -- so I might possibly walk around seeing all the booths I missed in my abbreviated visit yesterday. I finished putting on my clothes with a black t-shirt and black ball cap, grabbed my keys, and we were off to the "circus."

As we were getting out of the car downtown, a half dozen college-aged girls waved frantically and, in unison, yelled, "Hey Earllll!" – dragging out his name like the cloud of smoke from his signature cigar. I looked over at him in amazement as he smiled broadly and waved his hat at them.

[180]

"Friends of yours?" I asked smiling. He looked at me bashfully as he placed his hat back on his head. He kept his eyes fixed on the lovely girls until they disappearing behind a large U-Haul truck.

Without comment, we walked to the crosswalk where we agreed we would separate for the day. While we stood there two more girls passed us just as the light turned green, and towards him, said, "Hi Earl, see you in the beer tent." Before he could step from the curb three other young ladies recognized him, smiled, and spoke to him warmly. Finally, between greetings from his fans, Earl turned to me and said:

"Girls are charming creatures. I shall have to be twice seventy years old before I change my mind as to that". ~MT 1906~

I stood there with an envious grin as he crossed the street and his hat bobbed through the large mass of festival goers.

Soft Water

Everyone who reads my *facebook* posts knows that occasionally Earl annoys me; probably because I'm over 50 and from time to time everything annoys me. Today I was more disappointed than annoyed. Regardless of his occasional lapse in social courtesies, his habitual smoking, ashes everywhere, his questionable habits in the kitchen or bath, and sometimes his unbending dogmatic commentary, I have never considered him a dope.

Earl was on the porch as the sky darkened and the breeze flipped leaves over to indicate imminent rain. From inside, I kept tabs on the weather, while emotionally reading the many kind *facebook* posts for my old friend Richard Mudd who had passed away the day before.

There was a large dead branch about the diameter of my thigh that hangs just a few feet from the power line that runs from a pole by the street to the house. Every time I look at it I fear a strong wind will knock it onto that wire. Should that happen, it will surely peel the wire off the house and not only cut off our power, but will leave a live wire snaking and sparking on the ground. I reassure myself by supposing that staring and worrying I would greatly change its direction of fall, thereby causing no problems whatsoever.

As I glanced outside and then back to the computer screen and back again to the outside I notice that rain has started and is increasing rapidly. I could hear the water rushing through the downspouts and pounding on the garage roof only a few feet from the window near my chair.

Just as I was about to take a better look from the porch, Earl came rushing into the house, walked right past me and made a bee line into the kitchen. I heard lots of noise and I went to see what he was doing. I found him cradling two stacks of various-sized pans and pots in both arms. "What **are** you doing?" I asked excitedly.

"I'm going to catch rainwater," he said pushing past me and heading for the door. I followed him onto the porch just as he lost his grip on the armload of cookware and it came crashing down all around him, miraculously missing the toes of his bare feet. Before I could say a word, he stripped to his undershirt and pants.

"Back in the 1800s there were rain barrels to catch the water or at least a cistern to hold it. There is nothing better than rain water to wash your hair," he spoke quickly as he gathered the pans tightly back into his arms. I opened the door for him and he walked out into the driving rain. Before he could take five steps he was completely soaked and I could see blue-striped underwear through his now transparent white pants.

"I'm going to wash my hair in rain water tonight," he said loudly enough to be heard over the pounding vertical sheets of rain and banging thunder. I smiled as I watched him place the pans all over the driveway. The first saucepan was full before he could set the second one down. The musical staccato of the rain hitting all the different-sized pans was a weird but fitting soundtrack of the ballet of Earl strategically placing pans as if one spot was better than another. Watching his carefully placed pans fill up with rain water he stood there, hands on hips, looking as satisfied as if he had just completed construction of the Hoover Dam and was changing the course of a mighty river.

I laughed and then yelled loud enough to be heard above the deluge, "So you wanna wash your hair in rain water?"

He turned to me with his dripping hair plastered flat all over his head and covering his face all the way to the tip of his nose and said, "It is the best feeling in the world, Tom, to wash your hair in rain water."

I ducked inside the house to get the only product he uses for his body's hygiene and opened the storm door and threw him his bar of Ivory soap. He caught it with both hands and as he looked at it, he suddenly realized just how foolish his enterprise was. He turned his back to me, stood perfectly still for several seconds and then began rubbing the bar of soap slowly onto his head making watery suds in his sopping hair.

I watched for a minute wondering if he would let the rain rinse off the soap or if he actually would use one of the pans full of water. I decided to not watch as his image was already tainted enough by his performance in the pouring rain. I walked into the house to retrieve a couple of large, dry, bath towels, which I brought out and left in easy reach just inside the storm door.

A half-hour later, I heard the pans again. They were empty and Earl was slowly stacking them on the porch floor. Soon, after I heard the door latch for the final time as if to say, "I'm home".

Shortly after that, Earl came into the foyer with one towel wrapped around him and the other like a huge swirled turban perched on top of his head.

"So, you got your hair washed with rain water did ya?" I asked sarcastically smirking at him.

He looked at me with complete embarrassment and said, "I am sure glad I thought to gather all those pans and just in the nick of time". He had no sooner finished that sentence when he began to loudly laugh, which of course solicited my outburst as well. Once we stopped cackling and he was bending forward drying his hair with both hands, he said sheepishly,

"Old fools is the biggest fool there is." ~MT 1876~

"Yes, but they sometimes sport a very clean coiffure," I thought.

What did I say?

After reading the newspaper about the recent long-overdue awarding of the Medal of Honor to a World War II veteran, I shared my view about the value of life especially when serving in the military.

"In my opinion heroes never set a course to become a hero, it just happens in the heat of battle, within the confusion of the noise and chaos, or maybe the feeling of helplessness that pushes one to try and gain some control."

I added that at the exact moment a soldier does something that later proves to be heroic; I don't think he even considers the possibility of death. The danger doesn't even occur to him, and he instantaneously responds with a 'somebody needs to do something' attitude.

Earl softly said, almost tearfully, "At times I am sure that some heroic people consciously choose to give their life for their country, their family, or close comrades."

After a short pause Earl looked up with a drawn, solemn expression I had never seen before, indicating that he possibly was reflecting about a past connection in his own life. He opened his mouth to speak and then closed again. A few seconds later when the words tried to emerge they nervously skipped and stuttered clumsily from his mouth.

"The t-t-trouble is n...n..not in dying for a f...f...friend, b..b..but finding a f...f...friend worth dying f...f...for." ~MT~

I continued to look at him sensing I might be seeing someone entirely different than Samuel Clemens for the first time. He had sunk in his chair and his expression was a foreign one to me. What seemed like one of our typical conversations had sparked something very troubling for him. I knew there was nothing left to do but sit quietly and hope for a more pleasant mood to surface.

The room was completely silent as I pretended to read a magazine, but all the while I closely watched from the corner of my eye to see if he was okay. Eventually he got up, cleared his throat, and once again, back in perfect Mark Twain character said, "I'm going for a smoke", and left presumably for the porch.

The Convert

Earl stood at the window this morning overlooking the porch and its lonely, empty furniture, he asked, "Is summer over?"

"No, not really over, just winding down," I answered from the kitchen, "We'll have a few more very hot days before it's over".

[184]

He walked back into the kitchen to finish his coffee without his usual cigar, which I know is frustrating for him. "So tell me again why I had to swear an oath to not smoke in the house if I'm careful and neat," he asked changing his tone from the last time he asked me this question -- thinking perhaps my answer might also change

.   "Well, let's just say that since I don't smoke anymore, I prefer not to breathe it", I answered slowly so as not to be misunderstood.

"Oh, so when you're not here, it's **okay** that I smoke in the house?" he asked hopefully. I paused then explained that even when I did smoke I hated the smell of cigars and their foul residual odor that lingers for days.

There was no reason to rub salt into an already open wound, but this conversation evoked a memory from my hitchhiking days -- back when that was a cheap and safe way to move about the country. After standing in the rain for hours, a car finally stopped to give me a ride. When I opened the door to get into the car, the foul stench of stale cigar smoke hit me like the thwack of a coal shovel across my face. I closed the door and stepped back into the rain. I will not insult Earl or his habit of smoking up to ten cigars a day with the telling of that story, but I'll not be a party to his practice either. Having been a smoker, I know that there is nothing worse than a convert. A person who once smoked like a steam engine and quit successfully, has nothing but horrible things to say about the effects of smoking, the cost, the putrid smell, and the brainless people who still engage in the "filthy habit."

We sat there for a bit while Earl continued to read some newspapers from yesterday when I offered a suggestion, "I could make up a little area out in the shop where the paint-booth used to be. There's an exhaust fan in the wall, lots of light, and the furnace out there keeps it really cozy all winter long."

He lowered his paper and said, "Will you come out there and sit with me while I smoke?"

I smiled and said, "We really don't talk that much while you are smoking on the porch. It is usually me doing the talking and you reading and puffing". I could see by the look on his face that my answer isn't what he wanted to hear so I added, "Well if the fan is on to move the smoke, I'll keep you company." He smiled and started reading again.

From behind the paper tent, he asked, "Can we bring a porch chair to where I am smoking?"

[185]

"Sure you can, and a table too if you want," I answered. Feeling like I'd just given whaling rights to Japan, I got up from the table and cleaned up the evidence of our breakfast.

I went into the living room to get comfortable in a spot I have arranged on the couch. I have a small pillow to sit on, a towel that drapes over the back of the couch, a two-foot piece of a swimming noodle that serves as a lumbar support, and another throw pillow in front of that to cushion the small of my back. It isn't the most attractive ensemble but it allows me to sit for a few hours pain free. As I was fluffing my pillows and straightening things I heard the front door open and close. I no sooner got nestled into my seat when I thought I smelled cigar smoke. As I opened my book and looked for my place on the page, the smell of smoke grew ever stronger. I assumed that the large front window to the porch had been left open and the smoke was invading the house from there.

I got up to check and found the window closed. However, from the corner of my eye, I saw a cloud of white smoke swirling around in the computer room. Earl was sitting in a wicker porch chair in the center of the room and the ceiling fan whirred at high speed directly above him. He could clearly see my jaw-dropping shock and sense my immediate anger. He quickly but nervously pushed out the first words, probably assuming that an initial assault might insure success, "I have the chair here and the fan going just like you said!"

I loudly slapped the switch on the wall shutting the fan off, my hands found and gripped my hips tightly instead of his throat, and I said sternly, "Earl you know this is not what I meant; now put the chair where it belongs, and find a place to smoke other than in this house."

He stood up from his chair; lit cigar still clenched in his teeth, and started gathering the newspapers. "Get that burning cigar out of here first...right NOW!" I bellowed. "You lied to me when you promised that you wouldn't smoke in this house, now get that damn thing outta here". Earl took the cigar outside and quickly returned to turn his would-be smoking lounge back into my computer room.

I was spraying Vanilla Fabreze around as if chasing a rabid fly with Raid while Earl picked up the last of The New York Times scattered on the floor. If he had a tail, I thought, it should have been curled up under him like any self-respecting and embarrassed creature caught in such a foolhardy scheme.

As he struggled to move the wicker chair towards the front door, he mumbled under his breath, just loud enough for me to hear:

[186]

"It is often the case that the man who can't tell a lie thinks he is the best judge of one." ~MT 1894~

Jungle Jurisprudence

I took the dog out this morning and she looked off in the woods as if she heard something or wished she'd heard something. You never know with dogs. She had to sniff every blade of grass, stop, look around some more and sniff some more -- until she finds a spot that is to her liking. I try to not be annoyed, but it can take an infuriating amount of time for her to find the perfect place to deposit a thimble full of liquid.

On the way back to the house she saw a squirrel and for a moment I thought the next scene might be her running off barking while dragging a full grown man's arm and severed shoulder bouncing along through the leaf covered woods with his hand still clutching the leash. I pulled her back to me and told her "no," which means about as much to her as saying "microwave." She is a great dog when she wants to mind me, but when she is on her own or spies another living creature she is a wild beast with one speed..."full tilt."

As soon as we re-entered the house and I unhooked her, she made a beeline for her water dish to refuel her urine pump. As I took off my jacket Earl asked me if she had a good run. I explained that taking her off of the leash would be like opening the starting gate at Churchill Downs.

"How is she to get any exercise if you just walk her around the back yard?" he asked. I explained that the long brisk walk she takes every night is all the exercise she needs to be healthy.

"Maybe, but all of God's creatures need to get out and run, to breathe deep, to stretch themselves, that is the rule of the jungle," he said grabbing his lapels, which sometimes indicates his impending comment is a load of manure.

"Law of the jungle or no I'm not prepared to do much more unless I could hold a long rope out the window and drive with her running alongside the car," I answered.

"Speaking of exercise, when was the last time you got out and observed God's law of the jungle? When was it you went for a long brisk walk stretching your leg muscles and pushing yourself to raise your heart rate?" I asked glaring at him. Earl stood there for a second obviously considering "God's Law of the Jungle," and how it couldn't be stretched wide enough to vaguely pertain to him. I continued, "Well, you are all fired up that I should observe some law I've never heard of -- and most likely one you made up -- but since you have, please tell me how that law applies to you.", I said.

Earl shifted his weight from foot to foot like a boy caught doing wrong. He looked out the window, down at the floor, and then back up in my direction. Finally I could tell that the words were formed, the rationalization was complete, and he was about to etch his response in some imaginary stone tablet somewhere. From his uneasiness I knew that his answer would not satisfy my question, but my curiosity was sufficiently piqued as I waited for his crafted answer.

He again grasped both lapels, cleared his throat, and said: "Contrary to God's Law of the Jungle regarding exercise...

"...I have never taken any exercise, except sleeping and resting, and I never intend to take any. Exercise is loathsome. And it cannot be any benefit when you are tired; and I am always tired." ~MT 1905~

"So, Earl, you think that **all** of God's creatures should obey the "law of the jungle?"

"Absolutely so!" He quickly answered.

"You are one of God's creatures? Why do you get a pass from exercise?" I asked.

A fast moment passed and then he said, "When God made all the creatures he had something particular in mind. When he made me he was thinking of something entirely unique and exclusively different from all the other creatures he had thrown together. If that were not the case a Giraffe would have written Tom Sawyer. My job, while the rest of the world is frolicking and running about in their divinely ordained exercise, is to inspire them with clever wit and whimsy."

A Peek behind the Curtain

This morning after breakfast, Earl and I were sitting in the living room. He had just returned from smoking and I was finishing the last of my coffee and the

[188]

small Sunday paper. I asked what he had planned for the day. He said that he really didn't have any plans, which of course means that he will do what he does every day: read and smoke, and read.

I have tried to convince him to write and even offered to get out the typewriter for him, but he always has an excuse. His usual response is that he has written all that was in his head and there is nothing left to share with a world that wouldn't appreciate his abandonment of retirement for their entertainment. Of course it is easier to dress the part and quote the man than it is to actually duplicate the writing genius of Mark Twain. It would be most interesting to see how far their similarities extend. It is intriguing that someone would dedicate much of his life to someone he must admire deeply. Behind the man I know as Earl, there has to be a very interesting story.

What would cause a person to abandon his entire existence and morph into someone else completely in both appearance and style? Who is Earl, where is he from, does he have a family somewhere, and what prompted him to become Mark Twain so completely that his own history and persona have disappeared? I look at him and wonder what's going on in his mind. Perhaps he had some of the same troubles that plagued Mark Twain, struggles that few people knew about that were only hinted at in some of his darker writings.

As we sat there, in the calm, I was more tempted than usual to stare at him -- as if I might suddenly get a glimpse as to who he really is. After a few minutes I gathered up my coffee cup and spoon and took them into the kitchen. While I was standing at the sink for some reason I turned knowing I was no longer alone. There was Earl, down on one knee petting a happily squirming cat on the floor in front of him. He loves the cats and usually, if you can't find one, you needn't look further than Earl's bed. The cats, too, enjoy the guest who showed up one day and became a fellow member of the house.

As he stood up slowly with the help of a ladder-back chair I asked, "So Earl, where is it you are from?" Without as much as a twitch he said, "Florida, Missouri of course, well more Hannibal than Florida, but I was born in Florida because there was Cholera at the time in Hannibal." Waiting a few seconds before firing a full broadside, I added, "Is it coincidental that you and Sam Clemens are **both** from Florida, Missouri? Is that where you first became fascinated with him and his work?" As I posed these questions, I casually wiped the counter that didn't need wiping, hoping to create a sense of casual conversation rather than a pointed interrogation.

"Whatever do you mean, **both**, Tom? You know full well my history. While you certainly are not a Twain scholar you know more about me than most," he said obviously annoyed. I thought carefully about what I would say next, seeing as how Twain wasn't standing there in the room with me and Earl had slipped behind him becoming his thin faint shadow in the dim kitchen light.

After what seemed like a very long, expectant pause, I said, "So your life today is good. If you had to choose, it would be a good fit for you?" I was hoping he'd slip back into Earl as quickly as he left, perhaps exposing the mystery.

"It couldn't be better," he said, again returning to pet the black cat that was rubbing around his ankles begging for more attention. "I have been on the road lecturing most of my adult life and being here right now is good. It is actually more than good; it is fun", he said. "Isn't that right big boy?" He said giving Lalo a few firm pats that caused the cat to rise on his back tiptoes to meet Earl's hand.

"I am glad that you have found comfort and enjoyment here and your life is good. You certainly have brought much interest and excitement to my life, that's for sure," I said hoping he'd forget my prying inquiry and allow it to become a welcome compliment. "There is much more we can find to do if you are game?" I added quickly, hoping I hadn't caused a lasting rift between us.

Earl stood there rolling an unlit cigar in his lips with his right hand before removing it, turning to me, grasping his left lapel with his left hand he found a summarizing phrase that I assumed must be one of his favorites:

"Let us endeavor to live that when we come to die even the undertaker will be sorry." ~MT 1894~

Another query avoided. Earl has certainly cloistered himself deeply enough that my simple questions weren't going to easily allow a long penetrating look into his actual life.

A Flash from the Past

Frequently, and for no apparent reason, memories rush into my mind while it should otherwise be engaged. I might be reading a very interesting book, watching the last 20 minutes of a captivating movie, writing an email, or doing just about anything, when some vivid recollection stops everything and insists on my complete attention. Usually I am taken by complete surprise, as those

[190]

intruding random thoughts have no relevance to the current thought or activity. They are seldom unpleasant and easily entice me to immerse myself totally into them and enjoy the ride back in time. Living with someone whose entire life is based completely on history and memories, might have something to do with the frequency that I experience these trips to the past.

I was sitting at the computer this morning reading about the troubling situation continuing in the Middle East when a memory from childhood pushed everything else aside in my mind and started running from the beginning just like a movie.

I was a young boy digging a 'fort' in our back yard. I recalled Everything: the digging, the shaping of the hole, creating a roof with boards, dirt, and leaves. I gathered the supplies to make it a safe hideaway. I can clearly remember getting the rag rug for the dirt floor that we saved from when I was in kindergarten, a kerosene lantern, matches, a hunting knife, a can of pork and beans, a can opener, a spoon, and a comic book. It was in the late fall of the year and the kerosene lantern not only made it bright enough to read, but also cozy warm. The dirt room was only about three feet high and maybe five feet square. I remember that it had a hatch cover made of a couple of boards nailed together with roofing nails that hazardously stuck through the underside. It was crude but it helped to hide the entire fort from view. I remembered the first day that I built it and furnished it with all the comforts a young boy might ever need. Once inside I had the feeling of complete safety hidden just a few feet from any threat that lurked outside. Thinking back to the kerosene burning in a nearly airtight would-be tomb I am very lucky I didn't suffocate.

It was great hiding in there bundled up in my wool coat, reading the comic book, and eating Van Camp beans out of the can -- all in the safety of my underground fort.

"Mom sent me out looking for you and I couldn't find you. Where were you, anyhow?" My brother asked at the supper table. Knowing those steps I heard above me were my brother's and he didn't know I was huddled inches beneath his feet made me smirk to myself. Finding out I fooled my older brother made the whole experience even more successful.

Why these thoughts randomly return intrigues me, and I am always surprised at how real they feel so many years later. Being able to vividly think about something you once did is most pleasant. Recalling the actual feelings precisely as you did then is physically warming. Wrapping them around you like a quilt stitched together with heirloom reminiscences provides more comfort than all the possibilities of a vague future. The past holds title to everything that I am, and I am thankful for that. My selective memory allows only the beauty of those moments to be recalled. The ugly news of those days never accompanies the rose colored pictures my mind ratchets up when I least suspect. It's during those times that I obviously need a break from the bleak reality of the day. It is amazing the way my mind protects me by taking me back to the naive fantasies only a childhood can provide.

Having this memory still smiling fresh in my mind I looked for Earl so I might share it with him. He was fully dressed, sitting in bed with many pillows behind him, his legs crossed at the ankle, and he held a book open on his chest. I asked if he had a minute; putting his book down, he invited me in. I stood in the doorway and told him about my little recollection and how it fascinates me that such obscure, but wonderful moments rush back sometimes. He listened, paused politely for a moment, and answered in his sometimes unpredictable cynical fashion:

"Certainly memory is a curious machine and strangely capricious. It has no order, it has no system, it has no notion of values, it is always throwing away gold and hoarding rubbish." ~MT 1905~

Earl picked up his book and opened it. I didn't bother with a reply as I know by now that a Twain quote means that; "The case is closed" and nothing else needs to be said, and is usually unwelcomed. In truth, it didn't really bother me that Earl didn't fully grasp my point. My mental picture of that childhood event 60 years ago cannot be minimized or erased even by Mark Twain himself.

It's pronounced the way it sounds

Looking out the front window last night Earl stood perfectly still and unblinking as if he were watching something that might disappear in an instant. I was walking through the foyer when I stopped a few feet behind him to look around him hoping to see what had his complete attention. After several seconds, I realized that he wasn't focused on something outside, but was lost in thought. I moved on to the living room and picked up the dwarf sized evening paper. After several minutes I saw him turn and walk into the computer room towards the kitchen.

A bit later he appeared in the living room carrying a short glass half-filled with bourbon and sat down in the black leather chair. "It sure is getting dark earlier," he said drawing the glass to his lips.

"Yes it is...sad really. The summer flew by so quickly and not because I was so busy doing so many fun things," I lamented. "Everything seems to go by so much faster these days." He didn't answer and out of the corner of my eye I could see that he was again staring straight ahead. I lowered the paper, looked at him and asked, "Are you okay Earl? You look like something's bothering you."

Earl sighed deeply like an overwhelmed mother at the end of her day, "I am just lonely for the road. Well not the road exactly; but the crowds, the performances, and applause one hears when he stands before an audience reading and reciting his own remarkable work."

I thought for a moment wondering if perhaps my attempt to dig into his past has caused him to want to leave.

He added, "Do not misunderstand; I love it here, Tom one could not find a better host. Maybe you could relax the military rules about smoking a smidgen, but a finer host I have never had anywhere in my thousands of miles of travel. Don't think that my longing for the roar of the crowd has anything to do with your hospitality; I would feel this way right now regardless of where I might be. I could be in a row boat on my favorite lake in the world...Lake Lucerne and these feelings would still be plaguing me."

After several minutes and with my paper now flat in my lap I asked, "So what are you going to do?" He shrugged and said he didn't know, but was seriously thinking of booking some shows. Once his statement was complete and the silence returned, I could see that his trance-like state had returned. At that moment there was nothing more to be said; I turned my attention back to the paper.

We sat like that for the better part of an hour until he drained his glass, stood up, and left the room. A short while later he returned, sat down, crossed his right leg over his left, and with his forefinger and thumb of his right hand he began to twirl the end of his mustache. Again he stared straight ahead.

His comments got me thinking about booking a speaking performance right here in Bowling Green. The university has guest lecturers and poets come in periodically; maybe they would be interested. I was almost immediately stopped in the development of my idea, as I wondered how I could present the notion to the University and, of course, to Earl. I certainly couldn't tell them that I have THE real Mark Twain available for a speaking engagement! And I definitely couldn't tell my friend that he would be billed as a Mark Twain impersonator. Perhaps, I thought, I just call it, "An Evening with Mark Twain." That would satisfy everyone, wouldn't it? Perhaps that title too close to Hal Holbrook's "Mark Twain Tonight", I thought. Obviously, there is a lot to ponder carefully before going any further.

In the midst of this idea, I thought of something that had escaped me until this moment. I always call Earl, Earl. I mean I never refer to him as "Mark" or "Mr. Twain." How is it that he allows that? Does it sound like a mockery to him, as it sometimes does to me? When he first introduced himself to me, he referred to himself as the "Earl of Prose." Does he not feel a subtle sarcastic dig each time I shorten his preferred alias simply to "Earl?"

I turned to him and asked, "So, Earl does it bother you that I call you 'Earl'?"

He blinked rapidly a couple of times as if being abruptly awakened from a deep sleep.

"Does it bother me that you call me 'EARL'?" he repeated slowly as if to be certain he heard me correctly. "Does it bother you that I call you Tom when your real name is Thomas?"

"Of course not, that is **my** name", I said smiling. He looked over at me, took his hand away from his moustache, grasped his lapel, thought quietly for a moment, and said... "Tom if you want to have a pet nickname for me, I am not going to feel anything but endearment. Not many people are afforded such affection as to be awarded a nickname from a good friend." A short pause allowed me sit there thinking over that last exchange carefully. Then breaking through the silence he added with a small grin:

"Names are not always what they seem. The common Welsh name Bzjxxllwcp is pronounced Jackson". ~MT 1897~

Happy Birthday Seth Robert Lambert b. 9-17-90

My son's birthday is today and thinking back to the day he was born and all the time we have spent together promotes a smile.

[194]

Since his earliest days, he has always kept to himself, with little effort; he could remain inconspicuous in the shadows of his older brothers. If something went wrong and I had all three boys in front of me trying to discover the culprit, it was never Seth. Even when his older brothers made a strong case against him, I rarely believed that mild-mannered Seth could have done what they said. He would never argue his case he would just stand there calmly and smile innocently. No father in his right mind would suspect Seth of doing wrong.

Flying under the radar as he did for so many years, he did not have the routine interactions with me that his two brothers did. What he didn't understand at the time was that some of their frequent face-time with me was of the negative sort. His method of being obscure allowed him to engage with his parents mostly on his terms and timetable. Looking back I think the consequences of being too visible were crystal clear, and his way – while not apparent to him at the time -- was probably the much safer way.

Today he is a gregarious man with a contagious smile and thinks nothing of taking the stage with his guitar, using the speaker stack we built together, and playing music he   has written or covering someone else's. The first time I saw him standing in the bright lights on stage and singing into a microphone was a jaw-dropping experience. "That's Seth up there," I would say to myself -- almost in disbelief and smiling ear-to-ear. He prefers a different style of music than what I enjoy, but I'm so proud of how he immerses himself into it to the point of playing it as well as it can be played. The times when he has performed music more to my liking, he has usually played the lead guitar parts better than the original artists. His rendition of the lead guitar parts in "Running down a Dream" by Tom Petty, or "House of the Rising Sun" by The Animals are pure, sweet, and more imaginative than the recordings that made them famous. I love his "House of the Rising Sun" lead so much that I have it as the ringtone on my phone. The times when I could sit behind the mixing board and listen to the band that Seth and my son Chris was in were the best a father could hope for.

I have spent hours listening to all of my boys playing music and those are the absolute best memories. I'm sure I have not heard the last of Seth's music. I am looking forward to one day seeing him comfortably standing on a stage again and blowing the doors off the place with his awesome guitar work and infectious smile

I was sharing my joy with Earl this morning and said that that I am very pleased with the man Seth has become and that his choices, (while not always what his parents envisioned), were good solid ones for him. He has grown into a

[195]

low-maintenance man with high ideals with intense loyalty to his family and friends. He was raised with lots of love and direction in spite of his erroneous perception that he was sometimes the forgotten third child.

Earl sat there quietly allowing me to share my pride for a moment and then said, "You are so lucky, Tom. You have children who have taken charge of the road that lies before them. You sir are lucky, damn lucky," he said pursing his lips and slowly nodding up and down.

"I am a fortunate father that is for sure," I said humbly knowing that most of the credit for my boys' ethics should be credited to their mother. I sat there smiling, recalling when Seth was a baby and would fall asleep in my arms every night as we rocked together. I then quickly fast-forwarded to the man he is today. Earl, lowered his paper, looked at me fondly, and said,

"The very best thing in all this world that can befall a man is to be born lucky." ~MT 1892~

"Know when to hold 'em...know when to fold 'em"

Earl sought me out last night and shared an interesting bit of his history with me.

I sat down at the kitchen table prepared to enjoy a cold can of Pepsi. Earl was seated across from me swirling a single ice cube in a small glass of scotch. He took a sip from his glass and began to tell a story.

Before he came to Ohio he had been staying with a family in Oak Park, a suburb outside of Chicago. While he was there, he also wore his welcome thin by repeatedly sneaking a smoke inside of their house. The people he was staying with had a small child; and shielding children from second-hand smoke has become as habitual as protecting them from strangers, people with the flu, colds, etc. I knew that there had to be more to the story than the cigar smoking issue or he wouldn't have brought it up. He cleared his throat.

"When I arrived by train in Chicago for a speaking engagement at the Oak Park Library, during "Oak Park History Month". I was greeted at the train by a very nice young woman who was the chairperson of that event. She was responsible for escorting me to my hotel, to the library that evening, paying me when I was finished, and transporting me back to my Chicago hotel." He said.

"She was an effervescent sort and clearly very excited to have Mark Twain there for 'History Month'." As they stood outside the train station trying to get a cab during rush hour, her pocket phone rang. It was the hotel informing her that because of a large convention in town, his room had been double booked and they had been unable to find him another room anywhere in Chicago. With the weather threatening to dump rain at any minute, she asked in exasperation if he might consider staying with her and her family. She assured him that his accommodations in their newly renovated garage apartment would be considerably larger and more private than any hotel. He agreed and they walked quickly back to the train station and headed off to Oak Park -- about a half-hour ride from downtown.

The speaking engagement went well, of course, and everyone was thrilled with him. His hosts who insisted, since he had no immediate plans, he should stay on a few days as their guest. His stay was warmly extended at the end of each week, and he was treated to many mini tours into Chicago, including several museums, Navy Pier, and nice restaurants. The highlight of his time in Chicago was their warm hospitality in their turn-of-the-century home in a very affluent section of Oak Park.

He made friends with all of the neighbors quickly, and after he was invited to her husband's weekly poker game, he became a regular. All of the players were novices and their main purpose was to have a night out away from their wives to drink, smoke cigars, tell lies, and play a little poker. Earl couldn't have been happier with their choices or priorities.

According to his tales, Twain had played lots of poker in his day on the Mississippi stern-wheelers and telling lies was proudly second nature. He was amazed by the amount of money that was nonchalantly squandered each week by these men. They cared little about poker or the money they wagered. But their competitive egos pushed them in amateurish and inexperienced efforts to end up with everyone else's money. Earl learned to read every player at the table extremely well and by the third week of his stay, he had increased his bankroll by more than $5,000.00. He appeared to drink as much as his new friends, when most often he merely lifted his glass to his lips without swallowing a drop.

In the coming weeks, he won a lot more money and decided that he should move on because there was no way he could stop himself from 'shooting fish in a barrel', or from coveting the money so easily available from such rookies. He explained that he never cheated these fellows, but also never looked away if one of them flashed his hand in Earl's direction. I listened carefully to his story and

[197]

his marginally ethical gamesmanship for a reason that might alter my trust of him.

When he eventually left Oak Park and headed east, his suitcase was 'much heavier', (that was his vague depiction of his winnings), than when he arrived three months earlier. I was beginning to wonder nervously if there was a suitcase full of cash in my house when he quickly added that upon arrival in Toledo, he opened a bank account. I breathed easier.

"So what is your point of bringing this all up to me now?" I asked curiously.

"Well, I want you to know that I am not a scoundrel, but I am a man who's capable of taking advantage of an attractive situation for financial gain if all of the participants ignorantly tolerate it," he said before draining the last drop of melted ice and scotch from his glass.

I thought for a minute and asked, "So, if you did nothing dishonest why did you ever leave Illinois and the barrel of golden fish?"

He twirled his mustache a bit and then said in a matter-of-fact tone a quote that I remembered from the discovery of his overnight guest. I suspect that this is a phrase he is forced to use frequently.

"A sin takes on new and real terrors when there seems a chance that it is going to be found out". ~MT 1899~

I'm Getting Used to This

When I got up this morning and walked into the kitchen I could see Earl through the partially open door of the laundry room shuffling about. He had taken the clothes from the dryer, and was refilling it with wet clothes from the washer. He makes me nervous when he does laundry because sometimes he "helps" by washing my things. I now have several pink t-shirts and a sweater that might fit my smallest cat. I think he grasps the general concept of sorting whites from colors, but almost everything he owns is white so it is easiest for him to assume everything you wear goes into hot water and washed together.

I said good morning to him as I turned on the brewing machine and then asked, "Would you like a cup of coffee"?

[198]

"No thank you Tom, I have had two already," he said over noise of the dryer.

I swallowed my vitamins with a large glass of water and dropped a bagel into the toaster just as the coffee was finishing. I stood at the window looking out over a bright sunny morning and considered what I might do with the day. The grass looked high enough to mow, and there were several other things that needed attended to before winter sets in. It is difficult to do needed projects with my nagging back issue, but there are several other things I can do if I can muster a smidgen of ambition.

I was finishing my breakfast and contemplating my day's activities when Earl emerged from the laundry room. He was carrying most of his freshly laundered outer clothes on hangers hooked on his forefinger. He was wearing a pair of wrinkled black Adidas running pants and a Wal-Mart t-shirt that said: "Thank You for Supporting Special Olympics". There was a large puddle-looking blotch of gray paint on the belly, appearing more like a drink spill. His outfit commanded a picture, even a facebook post, but I simply could not do it.

"What are you going to do today?" he asked.

I shrugged and said I wasn't sure, and asked quickly, "Why is there something you want to do or need to get done today?"

"Not really, but thought I should check with you before I made any plans of my own" he said.

"If there is something specifically you want to do, let me know. I was thinking about mowing the grass, but cannot do that until this afternoon when the dew has dried. If you're planning to go downtown sometime today, I can give you a ride," I added looking for any distraction or excuse to scratch mowing from my 'to do' list.

"I might head up to Grounds for Thought after lunch and read for awhile," he answered. "Let me know when you are ready and I'll give you a ride," I said heading to the sink.

After finishing in the kitchen, I brushed my teeth, got dressed, and walked into the living room. Earl was already completely dressed in his usual attire, save his hat. He had a cat curled in his lap and a book open and was reading by the warm radiance of the table lamp. He didn't look up as I sat down on the couch and scanned through yesterday's newspaper for something I could possibly have missed in its miserly eight narrow pages. I did find something I hadn't already

[199]

read, but it still didn't interest me enough to do any more than read the headline again.

I put the paper down and looked over at Earl who was deep into his book. He looked like a compilation of several pictures I have seen of Mark Twain over the years. Sitting in this subtle light my imagination easily projected me back 100 years to his study in Hartford -- possibly having a comfortable chat together in the soft glow of gas lights. His presence here allows my mind to occasionally flee to a simpler place and time to talk with Twain during his finest moments. I wonder sometimes if I am accepting and enjoying his charade into the past just as much as he is. No matter which century we happen to be in at that moment or what we talk about, it always brings a satisfied smile to my face. I sat there five feet away from him. He was oblivious to my gaze, silent but conspicuous, and I could clearly imagine him turning to me and quoting:

"A good memory, and a tongue hung in the middle. This is a combination which gives immortality to conversation." ~MT 1872~

Preemptory Strike

It is Sunday, a day that by Christian convention should be used to reflect and give thanks. Earl of course has never been governed by convention of any sort. Anything related to Christianity is merely fodder for his atheistic writing or rants. I typically refrain from engaging him in theological talk as it usually riles him so completely. His points are certainly worth hearing, but sometimes his sourness makes it difficult to focus on much beyond his bristled tone.

The warm morning was welcomed today as we sat comfortably outside in our usual chairs. Many of the cars that passed had passengers who looked to be dressed for church. Any notice by him of where they were possibly heading could cause a long diatribe about the evils of worship, or more exactly CHURCH.

I usually don't mention anything about church or religion around him unless I haven't seen the veins in his forehead for awhile. Today I felt like they needed inspection so I said, "Would you be interested in going to church sometime?"

After a very long pause his head swiveled towards me like the turret on an Abrams Tank. I could sense the shell being rammed into the breach and careful aim being taken directly at me. Finally and explosively he said, "I have no need

[200]

of any future self preservation or any feeble guarantee that it even exists. Give me this warm porch, a friendly cat on my lap each Sunday morning, and I will hold an appropriate and effective worship service right here."

I smiled inwardly knowing that I had succeeded in firing the first shot. "You don't seem to care about the direction your soul is headed, Earl, haven't you any worry of where you might be for all of eternity?" I said fanning the flames.

Again the slow turn of his head, the scowl on his face, and the fast and noisy folding of the newspaper meant that I was in for a full broadside. I leaned away feigning fear as his eyes grew wide and he thundered:

"I have long ago lost my belief in immortality--also my interest in it....I have sampled this life and it is sufficient....Annihilation has no terrors for me, because I have already tried it before I was born---a hundred million years---and I have suffered more in an hour, in this life, than I remember to have suffered in the whole hundred million years put together." ~MT 1907~

Hearing his humorous answer sponsored a satisfied smile that subtlety stretched my face. My conscience surfaced quickly and I realized it was rude of me to use Twain's predictable response for my own amusement.

Somewhere in the midst of Earl's portrayal of Twain his own personal pain seemed to fleetingly appear. He was of course quoting Clemens perfectly including Twain's perceived emotions within the words, but there was something deeply accurate that seemed to briefly emerge from beneath and then vanished just as quickly.

The Graduation Present

Monday's day trip into Indiana to visit the Auburn - Cord - Duesenberg Museum was especially enjoyable. The air was cool, the sun was warm, and there wasn't a cloud in the Robin-egg blue sky all day. Though the drive was about two hours long and I was on my feet for most of the day, my back didn't hurt too much. Perhaps the excitement of seeing so many beautiful cars in such a true to the period presentation dulled the pain enough to completely enjoy the experience.

[201]

Maybe that is the secret to pain management. Perhaps if people busy themselves with lovely things and positive outlooks, the ills of their lives can be kept at bay. "How profound", I said to myself with a laugh.

Earl and I waited patiently on the porch for my good friend Tom Sockman, who graciously volunteered to drive. I was dressed comfortably in jeans, a long sleeved polo shirt, and comfortable deck shoes. Earl of course wore what he always wears; a white suit, white vest, white shirt, black tie, and shoes that look more like slippers than shoes. He had his hat with him, but only wore it when we walked from the car to the museum and again at lunchtime. He was excited to get away and museums are one of his favorite destinations -- after concert hall stages and some libraries. After only a few minutes of waiting Tom pulled into the driveway and we were on our way.

Both Tom and I had wanted to see the museum for a long time, but this would be our first visit. Tom is retired from his own auto repair shop so his interest was more technical in nature than mine. My primary interest was directly tied to the night of my high school graduation, when my mother's cousin Andy Adler drove to our house in creamy beige 1936 Cord convertible coupe. After some playful debate he allowed me to drive that magnificent car around the block, (with him sitting right next to me of course). To me it was the most amazing car in the world. It had a very distinctive 'coffin' hood and grill design, stainless steel flex tubes that came out of the sides of the hood and through the fender to the exhaust pipes under the car. It had flip-up headlights built into the fenders and its power steering allowed it to corner as effortlessly as a bicycle. What a thrill it was to drive such an incredible machine if only for a few minutes. I loved that car and saw it only a couple more times before Andy died in 2004. I told that story to my companions on the way to Indiana to the very place Andy's car was designed and built. I wondered what had happened to that car and his vast collection of vintage cars after he passed away.

The museum is in the original building that housed the showroom, design offices, and company headquarters. The larger section of the building looks newer and I assumed it was added later to accommodate the huge amount of exhibition space. It all blends so well together that the minute you walk in the door you feel that you are transported back to the 1930's. It is completely styled in Art Deco -- from the large silver concentric circle ceiling light fixtures to the geometric designs in the terrazzo floor.

Judging by his expression Earl was also impressed. He was walking slowly several feet behind us, looking at the sharply defined outline of the square columns and the bold Art Deco gold and green wallpaper frieze around the top of the room. It was obvious that bringing him here was a first-rate idea.

We walked around looking at the amazing cars and at the turn of each corner there were always more surprises. But the surprise that nearly took my breath away occurred when I almost walked backwards into a roped-off car. As I felt the rope tighten against my calf, I whirled around to face a 1936 Cord convertible coupe. It was parked right by the front window of the showroom and the presentation card on the pedestal told its story. "Mr. Andy Adler from Millbury, Ohio having been an avid charter member of the Cord-Auburn-Duesenberg Owners Club donated this car and two others to the museum upon his death..........." As I stood there reading silently I could feel my face widen into a smile that would last the entire day. I excitedly waved Tom over, and in his usual subdued manner he was also impressed with the irony.

I looked around to tell Earl or someone else, anyone else, but there was nobody around except a guy in a starched gray uniform sweeping with a wide green dust mop. I told him, (while pointing), that I had driven that car once. Looking up briefly he dryly said, "That's cool", but unfortunately quickly moved along before I could launch into my story. With my day feeling complete I took many pictures before reluctantly turning away. I felt like I was leaving a lover waving from the rail of a departing ship and couldn't bear to look any longer.

I moved my feet trying to redirect my eyes and attention to a very long black Duesenberg sedan sitting close by with its chrome gleaming in the spectacular focused lighting. We finally left the showroom and walked into another exhibition space through a corridor lined with more lovely cars. I briefly looked over my shoulder back to the hard-to-believe surprise and continued to smile.

When we were in the part of the museum that houses the very early motorcars from around the turn of the century, Earl was approached by a couple that saw him standing close to a French electric car from 1889 who started asking him questions as if he was a museum guide in period dress. In complete character he told of the times he had "piloted" motor cars, and of a time while driving a car almost like 'this one' in France he had scared many chickens and a farmer off a dusty road as he rocketed by them at 5-8 mph squeezing the bulb of the horn loudly. The only thing missing from Earl's presentation was a long white duster coat, goggles, and a white driving hat. They laughed and he laughed and eventually they went away perhaps just as impressed with their surprise 'find' as I was with mine.

The day at the museum was filled with many pleasant surprises in the design and technical innovation present in the 1930s.The ambiance of the entire facility eased us all back into time in a way that not only made it feel familiar, but also very comfortable.

During lunch and a couple other times during the day I was drawn to remark again and again about my surprise at finding that wonderful car in the place of its birth. After mentioning it for what I thought, (and probably my friend's hope), would be the last time, Earl quoted Twain and accurately captured the moment.

"Repetition may be bad, but surely inexactness is worse." ~MT 1880~

The Never Forgotten Lesson

My friend Deke Leuke nominated me on facebook to compete in the "Grateful Challenge". Today I am writing my entry for day six.

On each of the seven days I am required to list three things that I am grateful for and then nominate three friends to do the same for the next week. Once completed, I sometimes worry that my responses are self-serving. Am I listing them for the world to see how appreciative and humble I am, or to remind myself how many truly wonderful things I have in my life?

I have purposely left some items out and forgot to include other very obvious things. The list is always accurate and sincere, but mostly is just what I feel or can recall at the very moment I'm writing them down.

It feels like being asked to name my favorite person. I don't have a favorite person per se, but if pressed I would try to think of one. Most likely the first name out of my mouth would be what everyone would remember. Once you have said it you cannot go back and change your choice without diminishing the importance of the person you named. My point is that I have listed things that are important to me, but the number next to them or on what day they were listed doesn't mean that is the definite order of their importance in my life.

The things I am grateful for and I have written over the last six days causes specific recollections to surface when seeing them in print. When I wrote "pool" down this morning one particular event came to mind. This one sliver of time does not define my entire love affair with pool, but for some reason it cast me back to a time when perhaps the word 'pool' can only be loosely associated with a very memorable event.

At about fourteen, I was a frequent fixture at DeWalt's pool hall. It was **the** hang-out for many boys and while smoking, swearing, and tobacco spitting was commonplace it was actually run fairly tightly by Keith DeWalt AKA: 'Keeter', the owner.

[204]

On a typical day when the payphone on the wall in the front of the long room would ring after school at least ten voices would yell, "I'm not here!" For reasons I didn't understand at the time whenever there was a call for me Keeter would insist that I answer the phone. I could never just dodge the parental search like the other boys. On mornings in the summer Keeter allowed me to sweep up, help him stock the pop cooler, and help him clean the tables. We would do this pretty early in the morning before anyone came in for a shoeshine or a game. It would take about three hours and for helping he would let me shoot pool until the place filled up and he needed the table for paying customers. If he got really busy he would let me rack balls and even shine shoes with a reward of more table time or a bottle of pop and sometimes the added bonus of a bag of Cain's Marcelle potato chips.

He was a kind man, even though he appeared tough to maintain control. Otherwise, it could have been chaos. He was quiet most of the time and a bit hard to read, but deep down he really loved kids. He had to, as the cavernous room was so loud that the echo of the balls being banged around the tables paled in comparison to the din created by dozens of cocky young boys all trying to out-talk each other.

I was never a really bad boy, but I had an affinity for finding myself in trouble -- usually because of my poor choices in comrades. I was a great follower back in those early years.

On one particular night a group of 'friends', (I use that term very loosely), loudly came in the back door of the pool room joking and pushing like typical boys. I was sitting in the long row of yellow wood theater seats on the south wall watching games on two separate tables, imagining I was the one shooting. I did that frequently when I didn't have money to actually play. While watching a game, I would select the next shot in my head and then telepathically try to influence the player into shooting that shot. If he selected a different shot and missed I would say to myself, "You should have listened to me". It was cheap entertainment; it taught me to look closely at the table layout and concentrate on each shot and to play position by planning ahead all the way to the last ball.

One of the boys came over to me -- a tough kid who was no stranger to trouble -- and asked me if I wanted to go for a ride. I said sure and the three of us went out the back door. Parked in the dirt lot right behind the pool hall was a very nice and very new turquoise and cream -- two-door -- Nash Rambler. We piled into it and off we went down Court Street. After driving around for about an hour I asked who owned the car and the boys in the front seat looked at each other and laughed. The driver answered, "It's a friend's," and they laughed very

[205]

hard which pulled me into the inexplicable glee, too. As we were busting with laughter the driver manically cut through the corner of a lawn at a four-way intersection. We laughed even harder as he continued to drive through lawns and over curbs, causing us to bump our heads on the roof. Soon after, he came to an abrupt stop in the parking lot of the 7-Up building on Maple Street and everyone else bolted in different directions. I leaned over the seat and opened the door, crawled out of the backseat, closed the door, walked around and through the open window turned off the ignition and headlights, and casually walked the four blocks back uptown. Looking back I wonder why, at the time, I didn't think it was odd to pull up there, leaving the engine running, the lights on, and run away.

I no sooner came into the poolroom through the front door and took a seat watching the older men playing snooker when two policemen came in the backdoor. They looked around and made a bee-line toward me. They flanked me and asked me, "Where have **you** been tonight?" and before I could answer, Keeter walked up between them and said, "He has been here all night giving me a hand. Why?" They said that someone had stolen an unlocked car from a man's garage and went joy riding in it causing lots of damage to lawns all over town. Apparently some observant citizen saw the car driving crazily and recognized, or thought they recognized the kids inside, and reported it. The cops stared at me a little, looked around the room again, and left after saying, "Well if he has been here all night".

As soon as the screen door slammed, Keeter looked at me sternly, bent down close, squeezed my shoulder enough to get my complete attention, and in a very strong but whispered tone he said, "If you ever get into a car with those kinds of knuckle heads again I will kick your ass up and down Main Street! Do you understand me?" I nodded as his grip intensified and said, "I promise Keeter, I'll never hang out with them again". As I rubbed my shoulder and he walked away I could hear him say, "That's all your poor mother needs is for you to get arrested for stealing a car. Goddamn stupid kids don't have the sense God gave a goose. Getting in a car with those idiots, what could you have been thinking?" I didn't say a word, but I knew that he was right and I would steer clear of them in the future avoiding the police and his vice-like grip.

Since that time, pool means so much more than just a game that is played on a green cloth-covered table. For me it means being in a safe place, where I felt cared about by a man who risked a lot for me when I was so hungry for companionship I choose the wrong friends. From that event on, I had a new admiration for Keeter and understood why he wouldn't let me get away with things that some other kids did. He was a subtle father figure for me all the way through high school offering unsolicited advice or scolding me when I found myself in some stupid situation that seemed like a good idea at the time. Nobody else ever knew what he did for me that one particular night and we never spoke of it again. Looking back now I have a feeling that I wasn't the only boy he discreetly tried to get on the right path.

The single word 'pool' this morning in my list of things I am grateful for sponsored the telling of this story; and after Earl sat patiently and listened he paused for a moment, smiled, and said:

"Pool is not a matter of life and death....it is much more important than that."
~Earl (AKA) Mark Twain~

The Vivid Past

A great thing about living with someone whose life is totally consumed by the past is that you are often thrust back into your memories to recall your own particular history. Earl, (whether he's actually Mark Twain or not), by his mere depiction and presence forces me to view life at an earlier time. His appearance into my world has caused me to recall and relive some special events that have been obscured by the never ending torrent of current, less appealing events.

Once retrieved, I examine each memory carefully as if I was opening a fragile antique parchment letter. Only small glimpses can be seen before it is completely unfolded. Once revealed I become Indiana Jones holding the illusive crystal skull and am mesmerized by its beauty and clarity.

Traveling back to relive these fine memories in real-time has become a tour I happily welcome. The amazement I feel by "being there" again is an uncomplicated sensation. Perhaps that is my goal, my self-preservation mode to be childlike again. I think a safely constructed memory is always more enjoyable than the actual experience ever could have been.

The best part of fond recollections is they never hold dire world news, a skinned knee, angry parents, or anything I wouldn't want to revisit. Enough unpleasantness will surface in my life that my mind doesn't need to build an easily accessible place for them. I reject taking precious time away from the present to slowly waltz through the past only to be sad. My preference for entertaining old memories is that they are extremely pleasant or at least they ended well.

What a warm and welcoming fire good memories have become, and having Earl here has been the spark that rekindled them.

"Live each day like it is a cherished memory and one day it will become one."
~TL 2014~

Tap-Dancing Willie Suttons

Earl was sleeping and I had been sitting on the couch thumbing through a billiard catalog imagining having a room to put a table and all of the accouterments.

I was wide-awake and not able to slow my mind enough for sleep. Laying the catalog aside I rested my feet on the footstool, crossed my arms on my chest, settled back into my nest of pillows, and closed my eyes. I had no intention of sleeping, but I never-the-less folded up into the same position that works well for thinking, reflecting, and/ or sleeping.

It was quiet except for the occasional sound of a car driving by. With my eyes closed, I sat there, and allowed my mind to empty itself of all thoughts and worries. That's not always easy, but today my mind was as blank as a freshly washed schoolhouse blackboard. Knowing my capacity for relaxation, it wouldn't be long before some inexplicable notion would abruptly slide into my mind like Kramer on "Seinfeld" and command my full attention. I smile imagining that image, and within minutes I had successfully evacuated my awareness, and waited.

I hadn't been sitting there five minutes when another childhood memory swiftly appeared and started flickering in my mind like an old newsreel. Just like the pool-hall recollection this one involved breaking the law. The whole incident raced through my head from start to finish and then slowly started again from the beginning.

Four of us eighth-grade boys were slowly wandering down South Main Street on a rather cool night in October of 1959. It was a school night and we all should have been home by then. We scuffed along the sidewalk very close to the windows of all of the buildings and looked in at whatever the faint glow from the street lights revealed. We crossed Clough Street and peered into the grocery store around the huge painted ads on the windows at the shiny carts lined up on the other side of the glass, past the converted street car that housed The Giant Hamburg, a barber shop with its single brown leather and porcelain chair that had an apron folded over one arm waiting to cover a customer, the paint store with pyramids of gallon cans close to the front of each window, and the shoe shop next to the alley. We halted in front of the shoe shop and I stepped forward to peek in. I had a pair of shoes being repaired there that I had dropped off a few days earlier. Stanley, the Russian immigrant owner, always put the repaired shoes on the shelves on the north wall of the shop. I put my hands around my face and pressed against the glass of the door to see if mine were on that shelf. Just as I rested my weight against my hands, one of the boys twisted the knob of the door and it swung open, with me nearly falling onto the floor inside. The bell attached to the top of the door pierced the silence. "Holy shit!" I said. "It's unlocked!" Looking like Meerkats standing as tall as we could, we looked up and down the street with our collective attention coming back to the open door.

"Let's check it out", said the boldest of the group.

"I'm not going in there," I said, my fear pounding in my throat and ears.

"Aw c'mon". "There's nobody around", he said baiting us on.

Again we all looked left and then right and then in unison we rushed the door clumsily. In Three Stooges style, we got stuck in the opening. (Thinking back, I wish someone had said a very appropriate 'spread out'). Once separated and inside, with great care and silence, I closed the door holding the knob with the corner of my coat. ('I don't want to leave any fingerprints', I thought).

The inside of the shop was bathed in the beam of light from the streetlight and I could see the very long machine against the wall. It ran on these very wide leather belts and big pulleys with several different sized wheels that did grinding, smoothing, or polishing. In the center of that long shaft of the machine was a waist high switchbox that was mounted to a piece of pipe that went down to the floor and connected to the huge motor. On the front of a gray box were red and green buttons that operated the machine and also triggered a vacuum somewhere hidden in the shop. Two of the boys were behind the counter picking up hammers, fingering the small nails in the iron carousel on the workbench, rifling through drawers, and examining the various heel and toe plates kept in a small rounded-front glass display case. Just about then one of my brain-surgeon friends pushed the green button of the machine and it slowly started to come to life and hum loudly. "Turn it off...turn it off!" I yelled. He quickly reached over and pushed the red button and the machine slowly stopped whirring, the loose belts slapping, and came to a stop with a loud squeak. The rest of us were staring at him with disgust written on our faces, "What?? I just wanted to see what that button was for," he whispered loudly looking back at us with a smirk. (He was the same genius who thought I should take my repaired shoes 'while I was there').

[209]

I was still near the front door keeping my eyes "peeled for the cops" as any good robber in the 1950's would do while the others continued to fumble around looking at stuff. One of them opened a box of unique steel plates that only one person in town wore. At that time all of my friends wanted to wear heel plates, the bigger the better and many of us did when we could afford them or talk our parents into buying them. Some boys who had more money available had heel and toe plates. I don't know how other boys rationalized wearing them to their parents, but I told my mother that if I had the 35 cent size plates, (the biggest available), the heels would last longer. It was true but that certainly wasn't my reason. Most of us had them to look cool as we clicked down the street sounding like horses in the movies as the tough hombre rode slowly into town.

While riding our bikes we would drag them on the street to make an impressive shower of sparks. All around, heel plates were just as important as cuffed jeans and white t-shirts and they were a very convincing part of the tough-guy uniform.

We stood there all marveling at the huge plates worn by the bookkeeper at Kaufman's. His name was Fito and he had polio as a child that caused him to shuffle both feet as he swung himself from side to side when he walked. These plates were formed to arch up over the toe about a half of inch. It took six nails to hold them on instead of the three in standard heel plates. As we stood there looking at the Holy Grail of heel plates one boy said, "I'm taking a pair". He took off his shoes and quickly put a shoe on the foot-shaped iron post. He took a pair of big end-nipping pliers and yanked off his old worn plate. None of us were a bit surprised by his ability to do this, as we had each seen the procedure countless times with our own shoes. He nailed a plate on the back and another on the front and then reached inside of each shoe checking to be certain that the iron shoe rest had caused the nails to bend over properly.

"That is so cool", I thought. In turn each of us did the same thing, but the last boy, -- the audacious one of the group -- put one on the heel and three more on the sole covering almost the entire bottom of his shoes with steel. After about an hour of banging loudly inside the shop we resumed our spy-like stealth and left the shop as quietly as a troop of mafia tap dancers.

Unfortunately, we left five empty boxes of these highly identifiable heel plates in the top of Stanley's trashcan.

We each carefully walked home stepping onto a lawn when any cars approached as to not make a sound. All was well until the next day at school when out of the blue we were all summoned to the principal's office at the same time. It seemed that our antics of sliding across the hardwood floors and loud

[210]

tapping on the marble steps before school was observed as a "conspicuously suspicious activity", and coincided with a call later that morning from the police department alerting the school officials to the recent theft at a local shoe repair shop. When we walked into the office, there sat Stanley and a police officer. Standing with his arms folded tightly across his chest was the principal, Mr. Littleton. Judging by the scowl on his twisted face he looked like at any moment he would angrily produce the feared and fabled electric paddle.

Stanley wanted only to be paid and not press charges against us. He was such a nice man and I felt really bad about my part in stealing from him. He had always been so kind to my mother by extending her credit and even sometimes doing extra things at no charge knowing she was a widow with little money. As he sat there in his soiled leather apron looking sullen and betrayed, I felt a tear run down my cheek as I told him, "I am so sorry".

We were told by the policeman that we had exactly one week to pay for the plates, and were also ordered by the principal to have Stanley remove and dispose of those annoying heel plates immediately because they made huge gouges in the school's wooden floors, not to mention the annoying noise. As we filed out of the office, the Einstein of the group turned to me and asked, "How'd they know it was us?" I just looked at him, shook my head, and rolled my eyes.

Thinking back over that futile exercise in thievery I came upon a quote by Mark Twain that was custom-made exactly for the mentality of the four boys who happened by the shoe shop that night:

"It is better to take what does not belong to you than to let it lie around neglected." ~MT~

Bloody Murder

Earl occupied the big leather chair and I was in my usual spot on the couch. He was reading a hardbound book, after finishing the newspaper in typical fashion as evidenced by the pile at his feet. He takes each part of the paper apart and reads or looks at every single page. He sometimes folds the pages into quarters so he can hold them like a document using one hand, and when he has completed them they slide onto the floor as if he were a old-time radio announcer. That's why reading after him can be infuriating, depending on my mood and willingness to hunt and reassemble the whole newspaper.

He is holding the book like a hymnal in the palm of his left hand, and with his right forefinger resting on the top of the right corner poised to turn to the next page. Squeezed in next to him in the chair, lying with all four legs straight up, is Lalo the black cat who regularly seeks Earl out as he reads. Every so often after he has turned a page he'll reach over and give the cat a scratch on his belly or pat on the head, which causes Lalo to stir a little and sometimes emit a little squeak of appreciation. Earl's comfort level is easy to see in moments like these. Making himself 'comfortable' as I instructed when he first arrived has never been any trouble for him. He roams about, and gets cozy in all the rooms of the house.

He closes the book over his worn leather bookmark and lays it in his lap. "I enjoyed reading your story yesterday about the shoe shop caper. It shows me that you were a typical trouble-seeking boy, but had a conscience too. That is a terrible combination to have, Tom. It often leads to seclusion and extreme boredom."

I looked over at his smile peeking through his salt and pepper mustache and immediately suspected that he had a story of his own waiting to emerge. "What's that adage that says: 'It's better to beg for forgiveness than ask for permission'", I said. He nodded approvingly.

On more than one occasion he has shared with me some of his escapades as a young boy. Of course I never really know if the stories are actually his, Mark Twain's, or what he thinks Twain would have come up with if given the opportunity. My own exploits are very different from his, but they all were generated in the inventive, albeit mischievous, minds of boys always looking for something 'different' to do. Girls never seem to get into the same kind of trouble unless of course they are hanging around with boys. Trouble seems to impose a strong gravitational pull on pubescent males in a way that they never can completely avoid or outgrow. There is always more to a boy's devious idea; you always need another boy to validate your plan with a emphatic "YEAH!!" You need to be able to count on him to compound your idea by adding his own touch, i.e., "more gasoline", "more gunpowder", or how fast we will need to run from the scene to not get hurt or caught.

Earl sat up, pulled his vest down, cleared his throat, and then launched into what had been poised on his tongue for several minutes.

"When I was about twelve or thirteen I had a favorite trick I frequently played on people. I had to do it in different parts of town than just my own neighborhood so people wouldn't get wise to who was doing it. First I needed the largest tin can I can find a number 10 I think; about four feet of jute bailing twine, and a big chunk of rosin." He intentionally paused for me to ponder the ingredients. (Boys do that so the excitement builds with all the imagined possibilities).

"Okay, you got that; a can, twine, and rosin?" You first make a hole in the bottom of the can the size of the twine to fit through. Then you take the twine and push it through the bottom of the can from the outside. Then you make knots in the string in the inside so it can't slip through the hole. Late at night, you sneak up to someone's bedroom window while they are sleeping and hold the can against the center of the glass window. Then you take the chunk of rosin with your other hand and start pulling it along the stretched string from the can down the full length of the twine. In about five pulls when the string gets coated with rosin it starts making a howling sound and after a couple more very fast pulls the room fills with the sound of a woman screaming as if being murdered."

He now is laughing out loud and having trouble talking. "One time...........we..........did this at the school teacher's house......... and she......... came running out the front door in her nightgown yelling for... help". She looked up and down the street hoping someone would come and rescue her from the banshee in her bedroom," he could hardly contain himself now and laughed so hard he woke the cat who disappeared in a black blur. After a pause to regain his composure he continued. "We used to do that a lot especially around Halloween." Once you have the technique down you can duplicate the sound of a cat yowling, a baby crying, or a woman screaming in about any key. It is all determined by how fast or slow you pull that rosin down the string," he said. His devilish laugh and great idea would be appreciated by boys of any age and certainly had the boy in me eager to try it.

"That sounds like a great idea and it doesn't take a lot to it make it either," I said excitedly as if I was making plans to do this myself and soon. Just entertaining the thought and living through the anticipation of doing this to someone proves that the boy is never too far from the man when mischief becomes an accessible option.

He sat there with a wide smile -- most likely thinking of the many times he scared the wits out of the people of Hannibal, Missouri (if, indeed this was a prank he actually played or one that Twain himself might have used during his youth). Shifting in his chair and changing his expression to a more serious and stern look he said, "If I was a responsible adult, perhaps a father trying to impart good values on my children, or live the life as a better person I might write something to address the "practical joker", something perhaps like this":

"He is a pitiful creature indeed who will degrade the dignity of his humanity to the contriving of the witless inventions that go by that name." ~MT 1870~

"...But since I am not...I didn't!"

A Study in Red

I had a doctor appointment today in Toledo and Earl asked to ride along to keep me company. We both got into the car, each carrying travel mugs of breakfast blend coffee. Earl hasn't quite got the knack of turning the cover on the lid with his thumb in order to dispense the coffee. Frequently I would see him tip the mug up to his mouth only to pull it away, look at it for a second realizing that it is closed, and then open it and drink. The first few times were understandable, but forgetting it almost every time after that became a comedy to watch. Finally I said, "Why don't you just unscrew the whole lid and drink it normally?" He looked at me and said in an annoyed tone, "Tom, I am trying to adapt to the new ways of the world, please allow me to learn?" I mumbled "whatever" in his direction and started looking for my exit.

When we arrived at the huge medical complex I looked for a parking place close to the door as it had been spitting rain all the way there. After we got inside it was quite a long trek to the office. We were a bit early which is my practice, (I hate being late for anything), and upon entering the doctor's office took a seat in the waiting room. There was a very short round lady sitting a couple of seats away on my left wearing jeans and a top that probably once fit her properly but now had its buttons screaming. On the other side of Earl, (who was sitting on my right), was a couple in their mid-thirties. The woman had a tall boy about four or five on her lap; his feet dangled and almost touched the floor. Earl was thumbing through Psychology Today, and I looked for email on my phone.

We sat there for about ten minutes when the door opened and a tall shapely woman in her late 20s walked in. She was impossible to not notice and the whole room turned to look as she entered. She was dressed very conspicuously and out-of-place for what you generally see in a doctor's waiting room. She was wearing very high red spike heels, an extremely short, skin-tight black skirt, a wide shiny red belt, a very low-cut crisp white sheer blouse with ruffles around the neck and puffy sleeves. A thin strapped red bra showed through the blouse. The outfit was completed with a large bead red necklace, a large red patent-leather purse that hung on her forearm, and a wide-brimmed red straw hat. The man with the wife and son was more than glancing; he was staring. About the same time I noticed he was looking, his wife gave him an elbow to the ribs. That was pretty harsh, the woman had only been in the room for thirty seconds and already he was in trouble? Earl makes no bones about staring or sometimes even pointing; but today he was being less obvious. He pretended to only glance at her as she entered, walked by him to the reception desk, and then to her seat.

She had shoulder length wavy raven hair, not much make-up except for lipstick that matched all of the other reds and made her skin look even paler. Her nails were of course the same shade of red and were longer than practical for anything other than appearances. After checking in at the desk, she picked a seat right across from Earl and me. She stood in front of her chair as if to make sure everyone in the room was paying attention, and then she very slowly sat down as if the chair could be very hot. She settled into her seat with her knees locked together. She leaned over to sit her purse on the floor while simultaneously protecting any perceived glimpse of any under garments by pushing the palm of her left hand into the triangle void of her legs and skirt. The glaring reality that she purposely neglected was that while she was bent over searching deeply in her purse her large breasts were almost completely exposed. Her bra, (what there was of it), was the most abbreviated and sheer that I had ever seen and left nothing to anyone's imagination as the ruffles of her blouse draped out providing the unavoidable and orchestrated spectacle.

After a full minute of this detailed display Earl and I, at nearly the same time, looked toward the other people sitting around us. The lady to my left was obviously appalled. Her mouth was agape and her spread palm was against her chest as if to still her heart. The mother to our right had turned herself in her chair blocking her son from the blatant flaunt, which allowed the husband to stare without discovery. He took full advantage of the opportunity and judging by the size of his eyes, he completely enjoyed the unhindered view.

Earl turned to me and whispered, "I don't know what she is looking for in that purse, but I hope she doesn't find it anytime soon." I looked at him and his face was covered with a huge boyish smile and his eyebrows were arched as high as they could stretch. Not looking directly at her was like trying to not look directly at a solar eclipse, but for different reasons. She finally pulled her hand out of her purse folding the straps over the top and sat back up. She was holding a cell phone in a Rhinestone covered case that I suspected would have been much easier to find in a room full of women. Sitting there very straight in her chair, she used the phone to slowly ease her legs apart in order to wedge the bottom edges of the phone between her thighs, and casually started texting. Earl and I looked at each other at the same time knowing that we could no longer deliberately look in her direction. Her veil of modesty had not only been lifted but her open legs were now holding her sparkling phone more or less as a twinkling invitation to look. As if it was not already abundantly clear, we both discovered that her favorite color was indeed red. Sometimes the color was transparently sheer faint red, but red just the same.

As I sat there trying in vain to concentrate on the carpet, the ceiling, anything other than the display 'spread' before for Earl and me, my name was called. I went into the office leaving Earl alone with 'Scarlet', and wondering if somehow

[215]

that whole scene wasn't simply a prank staged for a hidden camera later to be seen on TV or the internet. My appointment was longer than I expected; when I came out Earl was the only one in the waiting room.

On the drive home, he described the entire event to me in a way he might have had I not been there and actually seen "things" myself. Reliving it was certainly not boring, and the new details of what occurred while I was having my examination was depressing knowing that there was more to the 'show', and I had missed it. I sat quietly and allowed his eye for details and his flair for physical description to carry our raging hormones — without the 'r'-- through it again. After he was finished he paused for a few seconds and then said:

"There are no grades of vanity, there are only grades of ability in concealing it." ~MT 1899~

Could've Fooled Me

It was October 1st and the morning air was fittingly cool as I stepped outside. Today was the day I set aside to replace the storm door. I bought a new one months ago, but circumstances and procrastination have not permitted me to get it done. Standing there and looking at the old door that fits perfectly and from the outside appears fine I wondered if there was any part of this project, (if I am not careful), that might cause pain. I decided I should wait until I have some additional educated hands to help set the new door into the opening. The doctor did say, "No bending, twisting, or lifting more than ten pounds". I have followed his advice so far, and there was no urgent need to do this today and risk further complications. My procrastination intellectually embraced my new caution, and the door project was shelved

As I opened the house door Earl was standing with a second cup of coffee in his hand, a newspaper tucked under one arm, about to step out on the porch. I smiled and asked him if he was warm enough in just his summer suit. He replied that he should be fine. I stood aside allowing him to pass and then said over his shoulder, "There is that heavy Cancun throw on the love-seat if you need it." He raised the paper in the air as if to say, "thanks" and turned the corner of the 'L' to his regular chair.

I tried to remember the other things on my list that I might get done. I try to get something done each day no matter how small. It makes me feel useful if I can accomplish even the smallest of tasks. Yesterday I replaced a defective socket in the bathroom light bar. Earlier in the week I sorted through all the junk mail and various things that accumulate on the end table next to my living room roost. As I walked into the computer room I noticed balls of white cat fur and I instantly knew that this would be vacuum day. I love the cats but the two female Maine Coon Cats have very long hair that comes out in small clumps leaving bothersome little tufts of cotton candy-looking deposits all around the house and on everything I wear. Their fur is very fine and the tail hair on the white cat can be four inches long. So on days that I vacuum I also have to occasionally flip the sweeper over and with pliers remove the long white hair wound around the rotary brush. Getting that 'project' done will be enough for one day. With my agenda decided I went to change clothes and get started.

After dressing in my jeans and a well-worn Bryan Adams t-shirt I was ready. Just as I was about to head to the backroom to get the vacuum, I saw a familiar large dark square slowly move past the front window. A UPS truck had stopped in front of my driveway.

I waited to see if he was dropping something off here or across the street. Sure enough he stepped out of the truck and headed up our short drive. My usual driver is a very friendly, bubbly young man, not too tall, and until the snow flies he will be wearing his brown shorts every day. I walked onto the porch just as Earl was about to open the door for him.

The driver was holding a large box. He stared up at Earl with a very astonished look as he handed the box off to him and said, "You **do** know that you look like Mark Twain, right?" "He is my favorite author and his picture is on every book of his that I have," he added with a very large grin. "I'll bet you get that a lot since you dress like him, and with the hair and everything." Earl sat the box down on the porch carpet and smiled at him. "Son, I am so glad that you enjoy my books and that my presence here has obviously made your day. If you would bring one of those books by sometime I would be happy to autograph it for you."

Turning towards me the smiling driver laughed and said, "Your friend is a real hoot Mr. Lambert and if he was a little younger and Mark Twain was still alive, he could have fooled me. See you later...have a great day, Mr. Twain!" he said still smiling as he bounded up the driveway and into the truck.

After he pulled away and disappeared down the street Earl turned to me holding both lapels and with a pronounced scowl on his face said:

"Twenty-four years ago, I was strangely handsome. The remains of it are still visible through the rifts of time. I was so handsome that human activities ceased as if spellbound when I came in view, & even inanimate things stopped to look--- like locomotives & district messenger boys & so-on. ~MT 1887~

[217]

Living with Tom

This morning while seated at the table, Earl was unusually pensive and appeared to be distressed while he waited for his breakfast. After studying him sitting at the table slowly stirring his black coffee, I decided to risk an intrusion and asked, "You don't seem like yourself this morning; is something on your mind? Anything you want to talk about?" He didn't look up and kept slowly stirring his cup.

Several seconds of silence ensued and I was tempted to ask again, thinking he hadn't heard me the first time when he suddenly broke the silence, "Have you ever felt like there is something you need to be doing but just can't get yourself motivated to do it?" He said glancing over at me.

I was standing at the stove frying our eggs when I laughed and answered. "If you are talking about procrastinating, you have asked the perfect guy." I chuckled hoping to soften his seriousness then added, "Just yesterday, I looked at the storm door and wondered when I was going to get around to replacing it, considering the new one has been in the shop for almost a year".

He again turned in my direction with an expression I had never seen before. "I'm not talking about household tasks, Tom. I am talking about something that drives you, but for one reason or another you cannot get yourself up for it," he said.

I thought for a moment realizing that I should not continue to try to draw parallels to ease his lack of impetus. "Why don't you just tell me what's on your mind, maybe I can help," I said while gently plating the steaming eggs.

He looked back toward the table and kept stirring as if by looking deep into the cup his answer might float to the surface like the magic 8-ball. I put our breakfast on the table and a moment later returned with four slices of buttered wheat toast, (his favorite), and sat down across from him. I stirred some sugar into my coffee and waited.

We ate more quietly than usual. I was chewing more softly than ever while hoping he would reveal what was troubling him. His mysterious dilemma hung in the room more noticeably than the light fixture above the table. The silence dragged on for several more minutes.

After he had eaten all of his bacon and about half of his eggs he said, "When I left Oak Park and headed east I had this plan that when I got to someplace that was comfortable and unencumbered, I would write another book. Well, here I am, in a perfect place to do that and for six months I haven't done a thing but sit, read, drink bourbon and scotch whisky, and smoke cigars!" His failure to resume

[218]

writing had welded itself to his attitude of leisure living. "How long can I expect the public to hold out for another literary masterpiece from me while I fool around taking it easy?" He added rhetorically.

I decided to remain silent and not disrupt the anticipated flow. He dropped his fork onto the plate loudly and said, "Tom, they aren't going to wait forever are they?" I shrugged uneasily not knowing for sure who, at that moment, I was listening to. He continued, "They have been so loyal to me for so many years. Their adulation and praise belongs to me, not some Johnny-come-lately with a typewriter or computer," he said rising from the table and dropping his napkin on his plate.

He left the room and headed outside for the nicotine comfort of a cheap cheroot.

After I finished cleaning up the kitchen I joined him on the porch. He had only the nub of his cigar left clenched tightly in the right corner of his mouth. He was staring off through the screen appearing to look at nothing and everything.

I decided to suspend either Earl's or Twain's solitude, sat down in my usual seat, and I asked," If you were to start writing, what would you write about?"

After a few seconds he said emphatically, "That has been what has stopped me from even beginning. I have no idea what I could pen now that would satisfy the anticipation of my readers. Everything I have written was so long ago, and even though it is timeless in its immense popularity, I don't think more sequels seem appropriate," he answered in an unusually bewildered tone, but drenched in his notoriously predictable modesty.

I thought for a moment, considering 'his' readers and wondered if he was referring to the people of the 1800s that loved Twain's writing and stage readings. Or was he perhaps speaking of the millions who have read his work since Samuel Clemens has...uh...died. Maybe the many folks he has met since he resurrected Mark Twain as a living, breathing character are the readers he has in mind. Confused by the complex timeline, I decided to wait for him to clarify the audience that he feels has been short-changed.

We continued to sit there in the warm and empty quiet of the Indian summer morning when suddenly an attention-grabbing idea broke through my short lived hush. "I have an idea Earl!" I said excitedly. "Why don't you write about the time you have spent in the 21st century? You could make humorous assessments, evaluations, and comparisons to life now versus life in the 1800s. It would be the reverse of "A Connecticut Yankee in King Arthur's Court.".

His face seemed to light up as he turned towards me and removed the button of a cigar from his mouth. Obviously stirred by the notion he said, "That, my friend is a great idea!" With his smile growing bigger and broader he quickly added, "And I could call it (*he paused*),..."Living With Tom"." I returned his appreciative smile and nodded approvingly, thinking that is was indeed an excellent title choice. After a moment of self-inflation my smile slowly drifted as I considered whether he was referring to 'Tom Sawyer'.

His customary color and passion returned to his face and I felt that I had possibly motivated him with something more than just another great breakfast. I rose from my chair preparing to leave, he gave me a soft appreciative smile and said:

"A great soul, with a great purpose, can make a weak body strong and keep it so..." ~MT 1896~

How do you Really Feel?

This morning I was reading writings from a different sort poet I have admired since the 1960's. His name is Richard Braughtigan and his peculiar slant on things, have always provoked my thoughts and frequently amused me as well. I am so glad that I stumbled on this book recently, as I assumed I had lent out and it was never returned.

Walking into the living room Earl leaned down and looking at the title, ("The Pill Versus the Springhill Mine Disaster"), asked me, "What in the world are reading"? I cheerfully explained that Braughtigan was a favorite of mine for a long time and how thrilled I was to rediscover this book. As he settled into the leather chair I proceeded to read him a couple of poems ending with my all-time favorite Braughtigan poem "Milk for the Duck". I knew I was smiling broadly when I finished and looked over at him. His brow was deeply furrowed and his mouth was tightly pursed into a tight line barely visible under his frowning mustache. I asked him what was wrong, and he told me that he was never too keen on poets or poetry. Immediately I set out to defend Braughtigan because he is obviously so far above what comes to mind when one merely says the word, 'poet'. Earl's scowl deepened with every word.

"Okay, have you ever heard a better metaphor in your entire life describing loneliness than this one?, I asked quickly as I re-read the end of the poem "...and I feel like a sewing machine that just finished sewing a turd to a garbage can lid".

"That pretty much nails how low this guy feels, don't you think?" I asked not really wanting anything but concurrence. Looking over at Earl sitting stoically in his chair with his arms folded firmly across his chest defensively it was apparent that he doesn't share my admiration for the metaphor, nor the poet in the slightest.

"Okay what about this one?" I emphatically read three more poems in rapid succession getting louder and more expressive with each one, thinking that he would have to like them if I just read with more urgency and excitement. Again his face or his body language showed no hint of appreciation or approval. After a lingering glance at him I noticed that his intensity, anger, or possible annoyance hadn't allowed him to even blink.

"I thought of all the authors in the world, Mark Twain would be the one most likely to embrace the radical approach Braughtigan's imagery brings to his poetry. I consider both of you to be rebels in the way you paint pictures for the reader with words arranged in a way that few others would."

Earl sat there for a full minute, then finally blinking a couple of times, he uncrossed his arms, crossed his legs, grabbed both lapels, and with his faced still screwed into a frown he turned slightly in my direction and said:

"There are things which some people never attempt during their whole lives, but one of these is not poetry. Poetry attacks all human beings sooner or later, and, like the measles, is mild or violent according to the age of the sufferer." ~MT 1869~

"Further", he said raising his eyebrows:

"What a lumbering poor vehicle prose is for the conveying of great thought!....Prose wanders around with a lantern & laboriously schedules & verifies the details & particulars of a valley & its frame of crags & peaks, then poetry comes & lays bare the whole landscape with a single splendid flash. ~MT 1906~

A Great wit...and more

Today is another day that is too damp and cool to sit on the porch. Those days of comfortably chatting or reading outside are rapidly and sadly coming to an end as winter looms larger with each passing day. Of course Earl will still be out there relentlessly puffing on his cigars regardless until the temperature eventually pushes him to find a warmer spot. Our daily talks with each of us sitting in our favorite wicker chairs will have to wait until late next spring to resume. In the meantime it seems that we have reasonably adapted to the more-confining trappings of the living room.

This morning after breakfast we both shared the room with each of us lost in our own focus. Earl was engrossed in reading the "Times Picayune" from last week, which arrives by mail from New Orleans several days after it's printed. I had my feet up with a black and white cat stretched out and sleeping on my legs. I, too, had been reading but had laid the book aside and was sitting there quietly with my eyes closed, my head leaned back, and thinking about the pleasant evening I spent last night.

My sister, whom I don't see very often, is in town for a few days so we went out to dinner together as the only allotment of time available for just the two of us to meet. After the few customary encounters with our waitress, we settled into catching up on things of familiar interest to us both. It really isn't important what we talk about just as long as we are together and sharing. Her natural excitement about things is infectious which makes it easy to get caught up in whatever topic surfaces. She talked about some of our colorful relatives as I intently listened to details that I couldn't remember ever hearing before. It is always a joy to listen to her particular view on people or events. Her sense of humor and attitude towards so many things runs a very close parallel to my own, which makes most everything feel easy and familiar.

I always walk away from our brief times together feeling like I just enjoyed a great therapy session with someone who is fond of me and knows my innermost feelings not because I have told her, but because she just knows.

She and I were very close when I was growing up. My mother was so consumed with trying to keep a family in food, clothes, and a home that frequently my sister, (Pat), had to step in and be the 'mother' for me. Some of my earliest recollections are things that happened with her or while I was in her care. Her willingness to be there has never wavered even though the last 50 years have kept her far away from me on one coast or another.

Last night she shared something that put her in a completely different light than ever before. The day our father died she went into his room to kiss him goodbye before she left for school. As my sister, (who was ten years old at the time), got up to leave, he told her that if anything ever happened to him, he knew she was strong enough to take good care of the family. Hearing this for the first time I instantly rationalized that all that she had ever done for me was because of the last words she heard from our father. It all added up now. The reason she cared for me so thoroughly when I was growing up was simply because she was mandated by a dying request from my dad. Just as fast as that notion entered my mind, it disappeared and contrary evidence flooded my head.

Her lifestyle frequently has been interrupted by her willingness to be there for others whether across the street or across the country. The common denominator in every tragic or troublesome family event in my memory is that my sister was always there to assist without ever ripping the reins from anyone's hands. She does what she does in a sensitive and welcoming manner and always without a feeling of intrusion. I don't need to look any deeper than her general demeanor to see the genuineness of why she is always there whenever she is needed. At her own husband's funeral she saw me crying, walked over, and threw her comforting arm around me as if I was the one that was hurting the most.

This morning as I sit and reflect on several slivers of events that have helped forge our love for each other I am so grateful to have HER as my sister. It's a warming feeling to have so much more than just DNA in common.

I was reminded of a particular Twain quote that I thought summerized my thoughts. I looked it up to make sure I had remembered it correctly.

"This kind of love is not a product of reasoning and statistics. It just comes---none knows whence---and cannot explain itself. And doesn't need to." ~MT 1906~

A Ludicrous Opinion

The blood moon came and went without the end of the world prophesized in the Bible's book of Revelations. I got out of bed to see it for myself, but the trees were too close and extend too high in front of my house. Of course, I certainly wasn't getting dressed to drive anywhere to see it. So I crawled back into my toasty bed saying, ("Oh well" to myself), having seen one before. Also, I know that there will be thousands of pictures from around the world that will record the entire event, (in time lapse high-definition photography), plastered all over television and the Internet.

Earl was in the bathtub when I got up and made my coffee. He hums loudly while he bathes which always makes me smile even though I know that his soaking will monopolize the bathroom for at least an hour. I have tried to gently persuade him to take quick showers as he has in the past, but when he tries he sometimes forgets the proper sequence. He turns the showerhead on, and then the water, which of course rudely soaks his hair with cold water while still standing outside the tub. He knows how to do it, but taking a bath must just seem easier and certainly more familiar if he is trying to remain authentic to the 'period'. In any case he does get himself clean taking a bath, which is the point

[223]

even though it ties up the bathroom considerably longer and uses more water than a fast shower.

I was rinsing my breakfast dishes when I heard the faint squeak of the bathroom door, and he walked into the kitchen.

Leaning in the doorway he asked, "What are your plans today?" This question has been repeated so often that it has become more of a morning greeting than a query, so I have stopped searching for a specific answer every day.

"I have no immediate plans, but sometime today I need to go to the grocery store. He asked if he might go with me and I said, "of course you can."

He went out onto the front porch to replace the pleasant scent of a fresh bath with enticing aroma of wet moldy trash burning on a manure pile. I shook my head in disgust as I saw the thick white cloud of smoke drift past the front window while I made my way into the living room. My opinion about smoking is typical of a "convert". I smoked for 40 years and now I cringe *almost* every time I get a whiff of tobacco smoke. I say almost every time, because sometimes when someone first lights a cigarette and I get the smell of that initial plume of smoke wafting from the end, I want to rip that cigarette out of their mouth and suck every bit of smoke left in it. My addiction and my distaste for the filthy habit are different sides of the same coin. With cigars, however, my feelings have always been constant. I abhor the smell of the smoke itself, and the lingering odor of stale pungent smoke is worse than anything I have ever scraped off of my shoes.

As I settled into my arrangement of pillows Earl came in and sat down in the big wing-back leather chair, which I have mentally dubbed, 'The Throne of Earl', and opened a book. We both sat there for a few minutes before I asked, "Do you see any irony in taking a fresh bath to rid yourself of dirt and odor and then immediately following such a successful effort, go out and saturate your clothes with cigar smoke?" He sat there for a moment, cleared his voice, and grasping his lapel with his right hand, he looked directly at me as if standing high above me in an ornate pulpit and said,

"He [Satan] said that unpleasant smells were an invention of Civilization---like modesty, and indecency.... To the pure all smells were sweet, to the decent all things were decent." ~MT 1900~

Without another word or gesture toward me he re-opened his book and began reading like my question wasn't "pure" enough to justify a "decent" answer.

More Accurate than some

I completed another one of those ten-question online surveys this morning on my phone; this one was, "what city is best suited for you to live in?" By other people's results I saw some of the possible matches for me. The questions themselves hint to where I should be living, but until you actually "click for results" it is usually a surprise. I assumed I wouldn't get Paris, London, or Istanbul, and I was right. The result from the ten obviously very scientifically formulated questions was New York. I put little stock in any of those surveys that supposedly will determine what occupation you should be, your creative level, the best color for you to wear, etc., but when the results are consistent with what you would have chosen yourself then suddenly you look at the survey as having uncanny accuracy and credibility.

I put my smart phone aside and reached for the book I have been reading. It's a trashy novel, (a trilogy), but I have so much time invested in it, I feel I must finish it. If nothing else, it is teaching me a wider variety of adjectives to use. This author has a couple of favorites and freely uses them sometimes three or four times on one page. In any case I slowly pick up the book and open it to the $ .51 grocery store receipt fittingly marking my place. The story is set in Seattle and while trying to envision the sun setting on Puget Sound described at the top of the page my mind is drawn back to the survey saying I should be living in New York. My imagination instantly shifts to Manhattan and the incredible sunsets I enjoyed looking west over New Jersey.

Several years ago I actually did live in New York for a short time and my stay there, while desperately lonely at times, was exciting. I was thrust into City life having grown up in a small Ohio college town, and everything about New York was thrilling and often scary. In the summer of 1964 there were riots in central Harlem. From the roof of my twelve-story building at the corner of 116th Street and Riverside Drive I could see the glow of fires behind the skyline a hundred blocks north. I never felt threatened by them at the time, as my comfort zone would not allow me to focus on anything much above my stop on the subway at the end of my street. My life in New York was filled with so much naïve exploration and discovery. At that time if you were 18 you could drink 'hard' liquor, and I always had a fifth of Old Crow bourbon in my room. At the time I thought it was the really 'good stuff', but years later when I became a bartender I found that it was as close to good bourbon as water is to coffee.

While working at Time magazine I would frequently ask people about certain places I wanted to see. My co-workers, who were seasoned city dwellers, would advise me if those proposed places were indeed safe to visit, and what time of day or night was best to go.

I once went to a club on 7th Avenue and 48th Street called the "Metropole Cafe". After entering under its brightly lit sign I found to my complete surprise Gene Krupa playing drums with a high-energy jazz band. He was sweating so much that the sweat was literally running off his face and onto the snare drum. His talent, which I had first seen in black and white movies of the 30s and 40s mesmerized me. Seeing him there in person in the bright spotlights of the otherwise dim stage while I drank my bourbon and ginger ale was thrilling. The small round tables with tiny electric lamps, (with white satin shades), completed the surreal experience of possibly being thrust back in time at any moment to double breasted suits, hand painted ties, and Fedoras. It was just one of the many impressive things I found in my exploits around the city in search of intriguing places.

I sat there thinking fondly of those days long ago and looked over at Earl. I imagined that the authentic Mark Twain once lived in large American and European cities and now he is here in the form of Earl living in the same small town I left at 18 for New York. He seems quite satisfied with this place, but remembering that he/ Twain once traveled the globe frequently makes me wonder how long his character can appear vaguely authentic sitting in the living room of an ailing cabinet maker in small-town Ohio.

Suddenly I heard myself say "So, Earl, do you ever find yourself longing for the bigger cities, the excitement of Broadway openings, the Can-Can girls of Paris, the Mediterranean beaches, the big halls of Australia, the canals of Venice? You have lived abroad or in sophisticated cities for many years. I find it odd that you can be content here in my small hometown that has so little to offer such a world traveler such as yourself."

I knew full well that Twain would have had an accurate and truthful answer, and I was very curious as to what Earl would have to conjure up to make his response remotely believable.

He lowered his paper into his lap and paused. "Those places are fine places, but a cozy home and hearth is the refuge a weary traveler is seeking after so many years on the run", he said while stroking the sleeping companion nestled next to him with his one hand and his mustache with the other. "Also Tom, this town has more below the surface that you have merely scratched. You've lived on top of the mine so long that you no longer see the shine of the gold."

'Nice dodge' I thought, when he added:

"Unquestionably, the popular thing in this world is novelty." ~MT 1889~

You're Welcome

There is much to do to prepare for winter, and being a lot less limber than last year makes some things difficult. I will wait to ask my son to clean out the gutters until all of the leaves are down so they will be totally leaf free until this time next year. I have already replaced the furnace filter and taking the screens off the windows is something I am certain that I can easily do. I have decided to put up a vinyl snow fence around my ailing Yew bushes in the hope that the deer don't eat them to the nub again this year. The herd has grown in the last few years and their destruction has boldly expanded closer to my house. I know I will need manpower to drive steel fence posts etc., but I think that I can do everything else by just taking it slow and easy. I wish that my houseguest would lend a hand, but that idea brings to mind some scary possibilities so I quickly dismiss the notion.

The leaves are changing colors faster as each day passes, and the rain has caused them to become too heavy for the trees to hold. They now coat my entire front yard in a yellow and orange blanket. The porch furniture remains uncovered or stacked, as doing so will officially close the door on the summer of 2014. Earl is determined to squeeze every last moment of comfort from the porch by sitting out there and smoking several times a day. I can imagine him in the dead of winter wearing his Karakul Lamb collared brown wool coat sitting in that same chair, his plaid scarf wrapped around his head with just his lips exposed enough between the folds to be reached with his cheroot, and all the while the stinging winds swirl around him while he puffs his indispensable cigar.

I was getting the trash and recycling together when Earl exited the bathroom. Seeing me bending down to tie a bag, he said, "Here let me get that for you." He took that trash bag from my hand and continued to tie it in a tight knot. When he finished he asked it that was all, and I said that it was, and smiling he quickly and without hesitation turned and took it out to the container that I had moved next to the street last night. I met him entering the front door as I was carrying the small bag of cans and huge pile of newspapers to the recycling bin. "Here, give those to me," he said. Squeezing the papers top and bottom tightly together he took them from me, and with the bag of cans hooked on his thumb, he headed out the door. ("I could get used to this", I said to myself) He returned shortly and asked if that was all there was and I said that it was and I thanked him. "No problem", he answered causing me to almost fall down as I snapped around to stare at him in disbelief. "I mean, you're welcome", he said sheepishly knowing how much I detest that response. "You are getting **way** too familiar with this

[227]

century, my friend", I said with a half smile. He chuckled a little and said, "In my haste to acclimate and blend into the citizenry I am sure I have picked up things that most likely would offend sticklers with long standing attitudes about over-rated social courtesy."

I was walking into the kitchen to replace the liner in the wastebasket when I answered him with, "True dat!" I was closing the door of the trash cabinet when I felt him behind me and as I turned around to face him we both broke into laughter at each other's out of character retorts.

I finished up quickly and went to the living room to read. I had not been more than a few minutes behind him and already his four-legged friend was on his afghan-covered lap, purring loudly and fast asleep in a black furry ball.

Following my glance and sensing my surprise he said with his cockiest of smiles, "I have the same effect on women...five minutes in my company and I have them purring." I automatically assumed he was going to say 'asleep', but just like the help he extended moments ago, he surprised me.

Sitting down on my nest of pillows I realized there was a chill in the house. As I got up to check the thermostat, I noticed we had left the front door wide open. I closed it with a quick shiver and walked over to adjust the thermostat. Returning to the living room Earl quietly said:

"Shut the door. Not that it lets in the cold, but that it lets out the coziness."

~MT 1889~

A Whiff of Bravery

Skunks! Do they have any redeeming purpose on this planet? Having had a recent issue with Skunks I did some research on them. They are strange animals and one of the few creatures that have no natural predators. The information I was reading at a Zoology site said that the reason so many die on the roadways is that they naturally are not afraid of anything, cars and trucks included. After centuries of trials they know to stand their ground because they have a very effective defensive weapon that sends predators running with their eyes burning and permeated with a smell so strong that it totally interrupts those animals ability to hunt. A scared and confused predator is no longer a threat; he becomes a unwary and confused victim.

My backyard abuts a woods separated by a small fence that only reaches part of the way across of my lawn. The deer, rabbits, squirrels, possums, -- and now the skunks -- use this open area as the on-ramp to my yard. Living in harmony with nature works better when watching wildlife shows on TV than it does in real life. The deer have destroyed many of my bushes, the moles have built the equivalent of the Los Angeles freeway system, (completely underground of course), in my side and backyard, the squirrels chew the cedar trim around all of the doors and posts of my shed and shop, and now the skunks are burrowing next to the foundation of the garage.

In my attempts to curb the destruction I have found a few remedies that discourage my little forest neighbors -- or maybe just pisses them off -- which in any case suits me just fine.

I have become wearily familiar with the level of frustration expressed by Bill Murray's character in Caddy Shack. I have not resorted to dynamite, although the idea of using explosives is always in the back of my mind. Hot pepper sauce mixed with water and sprayed on the wood surprises the squirrels and keeps them away until they acquire a taste. Granulated bobcat urine worked to scare the deer until they discovered that there are no bobcats anywhere around here and giggling they continue to wreak havoc on my shrubs like an eye-level banquet I planted with their winter appetite in mind. Rabbits are annoying, hopping eating machines that cut flowers right down to the dirt; they single out the exotic imported varieties like Impatiens and Begonias. I have seen snobbish ones appearing to eat with a furry 'pinkie' in the air. You cannot ever completely get rid of those little bastards with any of the store-bought deterrents. Fencing works but then you have all of your flowers in prison, so what's the point?

I take the dog out every night before bed with one of those fishing reel type leashes. I always take a very bright flashlight so I don't stumble and die walking through the mole's subterranean expressway system or trip on a deer rolling on the ground and laughing after discovering more bobcat urine. One particular night a few weeks ago, I scoured the yard as usual with my flashlight before venturing off the concrete guardedly looking for any critters, particularly skunks. A neighbor had her dog 'skunked' a while ago and using all of the remedies and cures found on the internet still didn't get rid of the odor. Keeping that in mind I have become more careful before stepping into the clearing of Wild Kingdom.

Another serious concern is the presence of any animal, (regardless of size), that could cause my dog to separate my arm from my shoulder by launching like a cheetah after a gazelle on the Serengeti. Everything looked to be clear of wildlife as the dog started her sniffing ritual. Out of the corner of my eye, I saw something moving. As I turned I could see a skunk casually meandering along the edge of the garage. The dog was occupied trying to determine her urine smell from that of the wild bobcats and didn't notice it several feet away. We escaped unscathed. After that I discovered that skunks were coming closer to the house. I have of course smelled them, but seeing them casually walking right up to the house was more of a concern than ever.

The Animal Control officer with the city came the same day I called and set a trap. Each morning, I gingerly peeked around the corner of the garage to check the trap. Sure enough on the second day there was black and white stink machine walking in circles in the wire cage.

I brought Earl out into the backyard on the pretext of showing him something "interesting". When we got close to the corner at the back of the garage, I held back as he continued to walk forward. When he got to the end and could see around the corner he jumped back quickly yelling, "Whoa!" We both were pressed up against the back of the garage about five feet from the corner when I whispered, "Why don't you go pick up that trap and take it into the woods and let "Pepe Le Pew" go free?" He backed up further pushing us both further from the corner. His eyes were as wide as an owl when he said -- while pushing past me -- and headed to the house:

"The human race is a race of cowards; and I am not only marching in that procession but carrying a banner." ~MT 1907~

There is no Free Ride

During the last several months since Earl first appeared here I have not known how Bowling Green became his eventual destination. Until this morning, that is. I was talking about my plans to go into Toledo tonight to a play at the Valentine Theater, and during a lull in my telling, he shifted the conversation to how he came to be in Bowling Green. In Earl's typical Twain style he sat back in his leather chair, crossed his right leg over his left and twirled his mustache with his right hand. He grasped his lapel with his left hand and proceeded to tell the tale as if he were standing on a brightly lit stage before an eager crowd. (Did I mention the accompanying Missouri drawl?)

"My train arrived in Toledo at the ungodly hour of 4:30 am on a Monday morning. There was only one other passenger that departed the train, -- a homely young woman --, who was met by what I assumed were her mother and father. After several cheek-to-cheek hugs and smiles, they left for the exit leaving me, a disinterested custodian who was marginally cleaning the waiting area, and a bored lady reading at the counter of a newsstand/ ticket window. Still hearing the echoing footsteps of the departing trio, I settled into a seat in a row of connected chairs against a wall allowing me to see the entire room. I noticed as I looked around that from my vantage point I could see all of the walkways and stairs leading to the trains, the restrooms, and the long wide window-lined exit ramp that leads to the street." He cleared his throat and continued to detail the room.

"There was evidence that at one time this had been a bustling station, certainly with more life than it currently represented. There were areas that appeared to have been locked up for years, their windows covered with paper or painted over, and some with chairs or vending machines pushed in front of their onetime busy entrances as if to say, "Have a seat until we open up again or 'till you die, whichever occurs first." About half of the ceiling lights were lit and only a few of the wall sconces worked or were perhaps turned off to save cost. In the dim of the depressing station and without too much effort I could easily imagine people coming and going, all of the various shops busy selling twaddle to travelers, the garbled echo of so-called 'announcements' blathered by some station master that always added the same confusion to every train traveler in the world. Knowing that I was the only traveler there to appreciate the unusual quiet that hung in the cold cavernous room lonely for company caused a smile".

He related that he snoozed for what must have been a long time, because when he awoke there were small crowds of people moving about in all directions. The unintelligible announcements that were conspicuously absent only hours before filled the room loudly and briefly muffled the sound of footsteps on the uneven and patched terrazzo floor. Looking at the clock, he was surprised that it was past nine. He had slept much longer than he had imagined.

He yawned, buttoned the top two buttons on his wool coat, adjusted his hat, grabbed his suitcase that had been safely tucked behind his legs, and stood up. He looked left and right and then decided that it was time to make his way outside and walked toward the exit. The dark night before was a bit foreboding with so few people around, but in the safety of daylight he comfortably ventured down the long hallway that arched up high above the tracks that he could see extending in each direction from the neglected dirty windows on both sides of the exit way.

When he reached the street, where there were a few taxis parked along the curb, he walked to the one in front and got into the backseat. He asked the driver to take him to the biggest and safest bank in Toledo. They roared off and minutes later stopped in front of Fifth Third Bank in the heart of downtown Toledo. He paid the driver and stepped out of the cab into the cold, but bright March morning. Looking around briefly he walked into the bank carrying his tattered cloth suitcase. After filling out forms that stated that the cash he was depositing was not from illicit drug deals, (which is required for deposits over $10,000.00), he was on his way with a checkbook and a few hundred dollars in his pocket.

Back on the street he looked up and down searching for an indication of which direction might take him to the university. As he stood there a lovely young lady seemingly appeared out of nowhere and asked if he was looking for a good time. He turned to her and exclaimed that he was always looking for a good time. She flashed him a smile, linked her arm in his, and off they walked down the street, he in his brown wool coat; she in long high-heeled black boots, a very short red skirt, and tight pink vinyl jacket. They hailed a cab and as they got in she asked where he was staying. He paused, and then answered, "The State University". They drove off with the cab driver saying, "A trip to Bowling Green will cost you a hundred bucks." The girl who had unzipped her coat revealing her low-cut black t-shirt chimed in with a giggle, "The further you go the more it costs you sweetie." Earl smiled and shrugged and then sat back as the girl nonchalantly rubbed his thigh and chattered on about nothing of substance stopping only to occasionally pop her bubblegum. Earl was thankful that she had come along as he had no clue how to get to Toledo's campus and certainly had no idea that it would be so far from the train station.

In less than an hour they were on Wooster Street in Bowling Green turning into a motel parking lot next to a McDonald's. Earl looked out the window of the taxi and could see the beige brick buildings of the campus across the street in front of him and became excited.

He turned to the girl, grabbed her hand, and while gently squeezing it he said, "I want to thank you for the 'good time' and for getting me to the university."

"Wait a minute buster. I think you are forgetting something", she said yanking his hand towards her.

"Oh yeah, what was I thinking...I am so sorry", he reached into his pocket and removed his wad of money that was folded in half with a rubber band around it. Pulling out two fifty-dollar bills he handed them over the seat to the driver.

He was about to put his cash back into his pocket when the girl loudly said, "I don't care if you want to go inside or not, this was not a free ride, Pal!"

Earl said he understood and that is why he gave the driver a hundred dollars. "I'm not talking about the driver. I am talking about me, your "tour guide" for the last hour."

Earl was confused and more dumbfounded as she pulled six fifty dollar bills from his hands, "For the ride", and then reached and pulled two more for, "Cab fare". He got out of the car, and holding the remaining few bills he watched as the black and white taxi with the cute, helpful, but expensive guide disappear into traffic.

"So that is how I ended up in Bowling Green", he said smiling at me.

I thought for a minute and then said, "For five hundred dollars you could have hired a helicopter."

He looked at me and then said with a smug smirk, "But, does that come with a personal tour guide?"

I went on to explain what I thought was painfully evident to anyone with an ounce of sense from any century that this type of 'tour guide' generally won't take you anywhere in the geographical sense. I flippantly told him that he had been screwed and not in a good way. I shook my head in disbelief as he sat there scowling at me in the appropriate manner I am sure he thought Twain himself would. I was still shaking my head as he said,

"There is no character, howsoever good and fine, but it can be destroyed by ridicule, howsoever poor and witless." ~MT 1894~

A Port in a Storm

Yesterday while I tried to digest Earl's account of how he arrived in Bowling Green, I felt compelled to clarify a part of his story that didn't make sense to me. When I returned from the play "Pass it On" in Toledo, (a historical and humorous trek through the founding of Alcoholics Anonymous), I immediately looked for him when I entered the house.

He was still up reading in the living room when I approached him.

"Say, can you explain something for me?"

"Sure what's on your mind?" he said, lowering his book.

"Well, when you told your colorful story about your taxi trip to Bowling Green it seemed that you were really looking to go to the University of Toledo. You ended up in Bowling Green instead, but you never mentioned why you stayed", I queried.

With a relaxed grin he said, "I meant to say the word 'university' in a generic way, as I knew there was a university in Toledo, but this one in Bowling Green is fine too."

[233]

More confused I asked, "So you weren't trying to get to the University of Toledo?"

"Oh yes, I was, but that is because I knew there was one there. I wasn't aware that there was one here too."

Getting mired further and also becoming frustrated I moved forward to the edge of the couch as if being closer to him would allow any measureable logic to easily reach me.

"Earl, I am more confused than before I asked. Either you wanted to go to UT or you didn't, which was it?" I said impatiently.

He brushed his hair back over his head with his right hand, sighed, and then said, "I was looking for a university and I knew Toledo had one. But when I ended up here at Bowling Green State, that was also a satisfactory destination. You see Tom, one thing I have discovered while traveling across this great country is that when I walk into any campus union and am recognized I will automatically have a place to stay and, while it isn't my direct goal, also plenty to drink. Usually I can pick from several options before my final choice is made. I sometimes conduct my preference like a lottery, which of course makes all but one student feel like he has lost out on the most unimaginable and incredible thrill of actually having Mark Twain as his houseguest. Does that answer your question, Tom?"

I envisioned his well-executed scheme, and suddenly it dawned on me that I had "inherited" him from a student while sitting in 'Grounds for Thought' coffee shop downtown. I too was mesmerized by the presence of a "Mark Twain" looking character and apparently enough to take him home, where he is sitting right now.

"How did I come to fit into your free-loading plan? Did my interest in Twain catapult me to the head of the line?" I said with indignation spawned also by my embarrassment of having been duped like so many before me.

"You Tom were different. You had a probing interest that transcended my celebrity status. You wanted to know so much more about me than those young university students. Their over-riding motive was to have a famous ornament in their house; with you, it feels more like friendship."

As he spoke I wondered if I was being manipulated or had I just been genuinely complimented for my depth and integrity. I opted for the latter, giving him the benefit of the doubt. Even if he was using me I am getting more out of this and in ways that he cannot possibly imagine. Having Mark Twain in your house would certainly be a once in a lifetime experience, but having someone who thinks he is Mark Twain gives you all of Twain and an entire other person as well. More for my money, and far more fascinating I thought.

Satisfied with his reasoning for being in Bowling Green and here in my house, I got up from my seat to leave. He turned to me and said in Twain's most sincere tone, "I could easily stay in any hotel in the land. I have the means you know, but that would deprive people of seeing the everyday comings and goings of a true national treasure. I would feel terribly guilty if I were to become so selfish."

I stopped next to his chair, looked through Twain's earnestness etched on his face and said, "Humility is a suit you sport proudly my friend".

As I was walking away feeling like I had finally gotten the last word I heard from over my shoulder:

"There's a breed of humility which is itself a species of showing off..." ~MT 1893~

Every Tear is a Tear

I got up in the middle of the night to go to the bathroom and noticed a dim light burning in the living room. I remember turning everything off before bed, or so I thought. When I rounded the corner from the computer room I could see Earl's disheveled hair like a white ball of cotton extending above the leather chair. I walked into the room delicately in case he was sleeping and as I turned in front of his chair he looked up at me with red-rimmed eyes. His glasses were in his lap lying on a manila folder and he was holding a handkerchief in his right hand. He obviously had been crying. I gingerly asked if he was okay.

"I'm fine Tom, just thinking about my family", he said with a rasp in his voice.

"Anything you want to share?" I asked softly.

"No, not really...I just need a minute," he said wiping his eyes and then his nose.

Sensing that I had embarrassed him with my intrusion I got up and walked out of the room briefly squeezing his shoulder as I passed. "I'm here if you want to talk," I said softly.

I felt helpless and confused. Of course I had no way of knowing if at that moment he was "in character", reflecting on Mark Twain's family, or if he was thinking about his own "real" family. Some of Earl's family is probably still living, and caring about him. I decided not to press for more information, but would just simply be readily available should he need me to talk to. I thought about the folder in his lap and my curiosity almost persuaded me to go back and probe for answers, but I didn't. I assumed that whatever it contained was the cause of his sorrow, but it was his business and not mine.

I went back to bed and after a few minutes of speculation about what was making my friend sad, I fell asleep. I woke up, not immediately remembering my night-time interruption until I found Earl sitting in the kitchen having his coffee. He was sitting there pretty much like he does every morning now that it is too chilly to enjoy our coffee on the porch. But today, I looked at him differently. I saw a man who looked sad and bothered by something that I was unable to help shoulder.

"Hello!" he said cheerfully, taking me by surprise

"Hi", I replied cautiously. I looked at him carefully to see if in fact his attitude was without any sarcasm.

"Great day today!" He exclaimed excitedly.

I carefully looked at him again before answering slowly, "Well I guess it is. Are you okay?"

"I couldn't be better. I got some things out of my system and now I am ready to take on the world...one imbecile at time", he said with a loud laugh.

Looking at him now and comfortably seeing the Earl I'm used to, I pushed aside the sight of him crying in the middle of the night. I felt a sigh of relief and focused on making my coffee.

As I was finishing my bagel, Earl headed outside somewhere to smoke. I finished drinking my coffee and put my mug in the dishwasher, and turned it on. While it filled with hot water I took a soapy dishrag and washed the glass-topped table. As I reached the side where Earl had been sitting I saw the manila folder on the chair next to his. I thought about opening it, but instead decided to put it up on the table where it would be easy for him to find.

I went back to the sink and rinsed out the dishrag and then walked back over to dry the table with a clean towel. I was rubbing quickly in circles when I looked down again at the inviting folder. My drying movements slowed and then came to a stop as my curiosity peaked. After looking both ways and without any further pause, I picked up the folder and opened it. Inside was a single piece of paper, which after, having already abandoned my integrity, I read. While I stood there invading his privacy, I was struck with the depth of Earl's commitment to his embodiment of Mark Twain. Earl's feelings for the man, his life, and all the things that troubled him seemed to vicariously recreate Twain in the most complete ovation one could ever assemble.

[236]

Reading the single typewritten page of Samuel Clemens's own thoughts he wrote after reflecting on his daughter Susy Clements' death at age 24, I had to remove my glasses and pat my eyes dry imagining his grief. Feeling the weight of the words I was seeing, I read through it again more reverently and slowly the second time. As I saw the words "Susy Clemens dead at age twenty-four August 18, 1896", they struck me with such sheer sadness that I surprisingly felt myself start to well up with tears.

"It is one of the mysteries of our nature that a man, all unprepared, can receive a thunder-stroke like that and live. There is but one reasonable explanation of it. The intellect is stunned by the shock, and but gropingly gathers the meaning of the words. The power to realize their full import is mercifully wanting. The mind has a dumb sense of vast loss--that is all. It will take mind and memory months, and possibly years, to gather together the details, and thus learn and know the whole extent of the loss".

"A rare creature; the rarest that has been reared in Hartford in this generation. And Livy, (Twain's wife/ Susie's mother), knew it, and you knew it...And I also was of the number, but not in the same degree--for she was above my duller comprehension. I merely knew that she was my superior in fineness of mind, in the delicacy and subtlety of her intellect, but to fully measure her I was not competent."

"It kills me to think of the books that Susy would have written, and that I shall never read now. This family has lost its prodigy.... only we have seen the flash and the play of that imperial intellect at its best."

"She was a poet--a poet who [se] song died unsung." ~MT 1896~

I finished reading and put the paper back into the folder carefully and slowly as if by showing some tender respect now, I could somehow undo my prying assault. I felt bad for reading it and sad for what it revealed and could not separate the two. Within his own words I felt the devastation of Mark Twain after losing his second child. Earl's late night tears were undoubtedly not merely part of maintaining his "role". Beneath it all, Earl must have his own sorrow like all of us. I may never know if he cried purely for his own sadness or for the pain of Samuel Clemens.

The Regal Pairing

Thinking over our recent chats I am drawn back to the story of how Earl came to Bowling Green and more importantly, how he came to live with me. He stopped short of actually telling that part of the story, but my take on it has to be close to his, although it would be interesting to hear his version once it travels through his creative imagination and into the person of Samuel Clemens.

It was a day in mid-March; the entire town was being covered with what appeared to be at least a 3-4 inch snowfall. It was dusk when I headed uptown. The streetlights generated a glitter-like shimmer on the falling snow, and even though it appeared beautiful it was very slippery. I took my time making my way to the coffee shop to meet a musician who was interested in playing for our annual fundraiser in June. Parking the car in the icy parking lot was challenging. We had so much snow all winter long and it was never totally removed before another storm came along and dumped more on top. Under this fresh layer there were chunks of older snow that had turned to ice, making getting out of your car one leg at a time and finding level footing a precarious maneuver. The paradox of snow's beauty is only obvious once you step onto it.

The back of the building was lovely to look at. The way the snow coated and softens the edges and rounded the sharp angles of the roof made the rear entrance of the coffee shop look like a warm inviting enchanted cottage in the woods instead of a gray concrete downtown building. Slipping and sliding my way up to the door I walked in and down the long hallway to the huge library-style room lined with books and cream- colored yellow wood tables. The strong but welcome smell of coffee filling my nose was pungent and friendly.

When we spoke several hours earlier my prospective musician said he might be late depending on the weather. I walked up to the counter and ordered a Mocha Latte. Standing at the counter I scanned the room focusing on nothing while I waited. Once I had my coffee I looked around more thoroughly for my six o'clock appointment. He had said he would be wearing a black hoodie and an orange BGSU beanie. Near the back of the room my inspection was halted by an oddly dressed figure standing at the end of a table, talking to three very attentive college-aged people seated in front of him, (a girl and two boys), as if he was giving a lecture. At first glance he looked like Colonel Sanders of Kentucky Fried Chicken fame.

Momentarily forgetting my reason for being there, I slowly walked toward them as if being drawn by a friendly and warming campfire. I sat down at an adjacent table where I could hear them clearly and also see the entire room.

From where I was seated, I would not miss the arrival of my guitar-playing contact.

I was captivated by this man's dress, which seemed vaguely familiar but also completely out of place. A frothy sip jolted my memory and I quickly turned my head toward him. "That is Mark Twain", I said to myself in amazement. I must have looked pretty unusual right then as I had my coffee mug lifted to my face, but my head, (with my mouth agape), was turned towards the man at the other table, away from my coffee. I unconsciously made a first-rate decision not to tip the mug, and sat my coffee down. I continued to stare at the visitor, with my mouth open in amazement.

Moments later one of the two boys got up and eagerly shook the stranger's hand while gathering his coat and preparing to leave. The strikingly pretty girl got up reluctantly as if she didn't really want to leave. She embraced him with a long hug, rubbed his back with both of her wide-open hands, and kissed him gently on the cheek. The man smiled as the two left the table -- with the girl blowing a kiss over her shoulder -- and walked toward the frosted-over door in the front of the shop.

Just as the door closed, I caught the glance of the man and tried unsuccessfully to look away.

"I notice that you have been watching me," he said with a smile as he grasped one of his lapels and started toward my table.

"I am sorry if I was starring, it is just that you...well you're...you know you're," I stammered.

Before I could finish he stopped in front of me and said, "My clothes? Well yes they are a bit different from what you see around today to be sure, but very commonly worn by the best dressed men of my era."

'Era?' I thought. What does that mean? He must have read my brittle smile as confusion because he then quickly added.

"Let me introduce myself, I am Mark Twain, the 'Earl of Prose,'" he said with a warm smile.

I slowly took his proffered hand and said, "Glad to meet you, 'Earl of Prose.' My name is Tom Lambert, 'Duke of Woodworking', mocking him with my own faux title.

I smiled at my clever admission and asked him to join me. (Of course he had no idea that I was familiar with Twain's writing and was what one might call a dedicated fan, but what American boy wasn't at some time or another). He pulled out a chair and while still standing asked me my vocation. I told him that I was primarily a cabinetmaker, which launched us into a mutually enjoyable conversation about the calming effect of working with wood. I don't specifically remember that part of our talk as I was more mesmerized by the accuracy of his dress, his manner, and his uncanny resemblance to every published image I had ever seen of Mark Twain. I never gave much thought to reincarnation, but mathematically it worked. Twain died in 1910 and this man must have been born around 1938-1948. Assuming that, reincarnation could be an actual possibility that would easily explain his presence here and now in the 21st century. I had a more plausible explanation; he was just riding on Twain's reputation and popularity by assuming his identity. Regardless of the reason he was fascinating to listen to, and a total living compilation of every picture I have ever seen of Samuel Clements.

The remaining fellow at the other table got up and, while buttoning his coat, said good-bye to the "Earl of Prose", "Don't forget your bag behind the table, Mr. Twain. It was really awesome having you with us this week." He then looked at me pointing first at my new friend and then at me and said, "You cool with this?"

"Ah...sure. I am cool with about anything", I said, somewhat puzzled by the question.

"That's cool because this man, (putting a hand on Twain's shoulder), is a very good guy and I wouldn't leave him with just anybody!" he said. With that, he shook Earl's hand and disappeared out the front door. After watching the door close my interesting friend sat down and joined me.

"Where were we?" he said flashing a broad smile.

Before we could either say a word my phone vibrated in my pocket and (holding one finger aloft as if to say "just a minute"), I pulled it out to discover a text message from the musician I was waiting for. 'Cannot make it... Snow too deep and coat too thin... I'll catch you later with the CD of my music...sorry! Jake'. I looked up at Twain's apparent clone and asked him what his plans were for the evening.

"I actually don't have any plans", he answered. It seems as though I will have to find a place to stay as that young man who just left here has been my host for the last several nights."

"I'll tell you what," I said, I have a huge pot of spaghetti sauce simmering on the stove at my place. Why don't you come over and have a nice meal, visit for a while, and then we'll figure out finding you a place to stay."

He looked up at me with a huge Twain smile and said, "That would be lovely, Mr. Lambert."

"Tom, please," I replied, and off went the parade of royalty towards the back door with the 'Earl of Prose' totting his old cloth suitcase and the 'Duke of Woodworking' leading the way.

When we pulled into the driveway, which was covered with snow again, I turned to him and said, "It is not every day that I have a famous guest for dinner."

He turned to me with a very serious look upon his face and said,

"What is fame! Fame is an accident. Sir Isaac Newton discovered an apple falling to the ground--a trivial discovery, truly, and one which a million men had made before him--but his parents were influential and so they tortured that small circumstance into something wonderful, and, lo! the simple world took up the shout, and, in almost the twinkling of an eye, that man was famous." ~MT 1868~

Looking back to his initial night here, I have to smile that his response that first night was a 'Twain' quote. It, ironically, established the format of all our conversations to come.

Writer's Block?

When I came out of the bathroom this morning I found Earl hunched over the kitchen table writing feverishly on a legal pad. There were several crumpled balls of yellow paper which must not have made the cut and five ball-point pens lying to the right of his elbow. I stopped next to him causing him to look suspiciously toward me and shield the page from my view. "I'm not trying to read what you're writing; I just am wondering why you have all of these pens?" He calmly said, "I grabbed them all from that cup on your desk trying to find one that worked. I wish the world still used pencils it would make it a lot easier than these things!"

Looking down, I noticed the two of the five pens were yellow highlighters which of course wouldn't show up on a yellow legal pad and the another was a sentimental pen that belonged to my father and hasn't written a word in over 65 years.

I didn't look at him again while I made my breakfast even though I was brimming with curiosity about his writing. He could be trying to finish one of Twain's books, or perhaps a letter to some of his, (Earl's), family I thought.

Whatever he was writing, it certainly wasn't a shopping list given the speed and intensity of his scribbling. When my coffee finished brewing, I walked past him quickly with my eyes straight ahead so as not to exhibit my building nosiness. I sat down in front of the computer and looked over my shoulder at his back, which shuddered with each quick movement of the pen. I could sense his intensity from there. He was anchored firmly, and obviously consumed in thought. His right elbow rapidly jerked away from his body while he wrote. Watching him I imagined how back in Twain's day if a person was writing with a pen instead of a pencil they would have to stop to dip their point frequently. How many words did they get written before being interrupted by that maneuver I wondered? The flow of fast-moving thoughts might have to stop and wait for the pen to catch up. If I were trying to write with that equipment, I would lose half of a mentally-composed sentence when forced to pause to re-fill the pen point. Thank God for the ease of the computer keyboard to write everything as you think of it.

I opened and read my email, and answered the few that required a response, and occasionally looked over to see if there was any change in Earl's position. Once or twice he reached up with his left hand and ran his fingers through his white hair, but resumed his pose and kept writing as if on a deadline.

It was now an hour later, my bagel finished, my coffee cup empty, and I was about to venture into facebook to see what kind of interesting puppy pictures, funny videos, or world issues were posted in my absence. Before indulging in what could be a lengthy expedition, I rolled my chair back and gathered up my cup and plate and turned towards the kitchen. Earl heard me moving behind him and again stopped writing and shielded his paper. I walked past him briskly hoping to assure him with my quick passage behind him that I wasn't trying to steal the smallest glimpse. As I rinsed my plate, I smiled thinking about how ridiculous we were reacting. I have seen his handwriting before. I would have to stand for several minutes at close range, maybe with a magnifying glass, to decipher even a single word. I turned to him smiling and told him so. He laughed a small laugh and said, "You know, you're right I can hardly make out the chicken scratching myself."

I pulled up a chair on the other side of the round table and sat down. "What are you working on?" He thought for a second and then said, "Just something I wanted to get finished."

That was not what I wanted to hear. In my mind, I said, "Earl, I need details here...this is no time for secrecy or subterfuge. Come clean, tell me what you are working on. You are a writer so you owe it to me to tell me. You gave up your writing privacy when you assumed the role of Twain. He was a public figure so whatever you do in his name or while in his image should also be public, at least to me."

Hearing those ludicrous words in my mind caused me to smile knowing that I was becoming desperate to find out what he was working on. So desperate in fact, that I was throwing most of my logic and all of his liberty to the wind. "Oh, so you have been working on this for a long time?" I asked casting the bait.

"Yep, I have," he answered still looking down at his work.

"Dammit Earl", I thought – but said, "So this is part of a larger piece...an ongoing body of work?" (moving the line carefully with the rod tip and causing the fly to dance on the surface).

A long pause ensued before he looked up, removed his glasses, and said, "I guess you could say I have been thinking about it for awhile now".

"Crap, crap, double crap" I thought, and then asked, "You started writing this a long time ago then? And you are now just getting around to finishing it?" (Whipping the line like a fly fisherman), "Anything you want to share? I mean if you would like to run it by someone I'm right here. Right now would be good since it's fresh in your head and I am familiar with Twain's...uh your style".

"Thanks but I think I am fine with where I am so far," he said with a polite smile as he started to open up and flatten the discarded papers.

I abandoned my quest and reeled in my line knowing that today's elusive catch had escaped my best bait.

He got up from his chair, turned the pad face down, and went to the shredder to   destroy my last hope of uncovering the mystery.

"What is it you are writing?" I blurted out. Following quickly I said, "I can only assume that since you said you had started this some time ago that it might be one of the several books that you started before you died...I mean that Twain started before...those books, you know the ones that still need finishing. If that is what you are working on I won't tell anyone, Earl, but please tell me 'cause I am going crazy seeing you writing so eagerly and not having a clue as to what you are writing."

Standing at the back of his chair, he picked up the pad holding it tight to his chest and with his brow locked into a long flat furrow he said,

"I shall never finish my five or six unfinished books, for the reason that by forty years of slavery to the pen I have earned my freedom. I detest the pen and I wouldn't use it again to sign the death warrant of my dearest enemy". ~MT 1906~

"Alrighty then," I said to myself. After a couple of seconds I sighed and then said, "If you should ever want to share what enticed you back into your temporary servitude today, I am here to listen."

Without a change in his expression as if my words never reached him he turned and walked towards his room. As he disappeared through the doorway I thought, "So, Twain did use a pen...I knew it!"

Why, the Nerve!

I heard the door knob quickly release the latch from the jamb and then the bang of the fast swinging front door against the marble table behind it. There was a shuffling commotion and the sound of what I assumed were bags being slid on the hardwood floor right inside the door. The door quietly closed and latched as if to weave an apology for the abrupt entrance. I heard a loud cough, and the gravelly clearing of a throat. Earl was home.

I got up from my seat to greet him. As I walked toward the door I caught his glance and he smiled warmly at me. "How are you good sir?"

I felt a smile of my own and I replied, "Just fine, thank you. Did you have a good time?"

"I cannot remember such a wonderful time spent anywhere, which is saying a lot considering it is only 150 miles from the simmering cesspool called Washington." He said shaking his head. I decided that I wouldn't respond to that directly as I wasn't in the mood to begin what most likely would evolve into a long political diatribe.

"The weather was very nice wasn't it? I followed it on the news while you were gone. I couldn't see where it rained at all anywhere close to Williamsburg," I said enlisting a subject change.

"The weather was certainly grand Tom, you are right. There wasn't a cloud in the sky until the bus rolled into Columbus about three hours ago to pick up more passengers," he said smiling as he picked up his two bags and walked toward his room. "Do you want this bag too?" I asked as I reached down to pick up a small flat white paper bag from the chair by the door. "No, just leave that there", he called from over his shoulder.

I went into the kitchen and made us each a cup of tea which sounded good on a cool and somewhat dark afternoon. Shortly after, Earl walked into the kitchen holding the small white bag. "I was in the gift shop after my speech and I found something that I know you will enjoy, assuming you haven't seen it before," he said. With that he handed me the bag, and I looked in the end of the and discovered a book. I pulled it out and turned it over. "The Diaries of Adam and Eve", (Translated by Mark Twain)," was the title. I opened it and on the backside of the cover was written: "To my good friend Tom who has made his house my home. Best Regards, Mark Twain AKA Earl.'"

"Thank you for thinking of me Earl", I said looking fondly at the inscription.

"I found it quite by accident in the back of the store. Someone obviously put it there in error between a book of poetry by Walt Whitman's and Stevenson's 'Treasure Island'." He said with a gruffly frown. I imagined him in a gift shop and finding, (in obvious and complete shock), Twain's works anywhere except stacked high all around the entrance with posters and portraits of America's greatest author. 'Wait a minute', I thought..."after my speech". What speech? He was going there to see Colonial Williamsburg as a tourist not to give any speeches.

"Earl you said, 'after my speech' is when you found this book. What speech?

"Tom, as you know wherever I go I am always found to be the most recognizable face in the crowd", he began. "So, as I was walking in the vicinity of the desk to purchase my ticket to tour the village, a lady quickly walked up to me from my right wearing a maroon jacket, blue skirt, an official looking gold name badge, and asked me if I was looking for the Historical Preservation Society luncheon. I thought for a moment if I was hungry enough to eat lunch so soon after breakfast and decided that I could eat a little something, so I said, 'yes'. She grasped my elbow and off we went towards a tall set of white double doors that were standing wide open, -- flanked by two men dressed in long red coats with gold piping, white ruffled shirts, tight black knickers, white stockings, black shoes with big silver buckles, -- and posed smartly on their stoic heads were white wigs complete with a little black bow at the back on the end of a short braid. It was impossible not to note the exact details, they were very period correct Tom like I was going in to visit the Queen of England herself in the 1700s. Inside, the high-ceilinged walnut paneled room was filled with large round tables covered in white linen, and encircled with loudly talking people. My guide ushered me to the front of the room to a long table and pulled out a chair for me next to a large walnut lectern with a microphone attached. She stood at the podium and looking down at me she announced to the crowd with a proud smile that she had finally found today's speaker wandering in the foyer and now lunch was going to be served."

"So why did she think you were the speaker for this luncheon?" I asked impatiently. "I'll get to that in all good time Tom," he said with a devilish grin. "Anyhow, so we all ate while being served by an entire black wait staff. That disturbed me some, but I knew that this event was trying to resemble something historical so I let it pass."

"We finished eating a very nice meal of Cornish game hens and wild rice. Following our generous meal my hostess made several comments about the annual fundraising campaign, which had produced over a million dollars in donations. She assiduously thanked by name the members of several committees who were successful in garnering those contributions."

"After the polite applause subsided she again affectionately looked down towards me and said, 'I didn't know if he was going to actually make it here today after his text message about his flight arriving late into Richmond, but nonetheless, here he is. Ladies and gentlemen can we give a warm Friend's of Williamsburg welcome to Mr. Mark Twain?'

"I stood and shook her hand not knowing what I was going to say, but rest assured I am always prepared for an audience. I thanked them all for coming and for killing such a little chicken just for me. When the laughter subsided I proceeded to entertain them with stories of my own history growing up in Hannibal, Missouri, my life along the Mississippi, and curiously interesting anecdotes from my many trips abroad. About 20 minutes into my entertaining talk, there was a ruckus at the double doors that caught my glance. When one of the men cracked open one door to investigate the noise I could see that there was a man outside that was dressed a bit like me who was most agitated. Before the entire room was bothered by the distraction one of the men stepped outside and before closing the door I could clearly see this figure dressed in white flailing his arms about and pointing towards me with anger in his eyes. I continued for a hour, of course finishing to a standing round of applause from everyone including the wait staff that came back into the room from the kitchen where they must have been listening.

"The hostess hugged me gratefully and with a big smile said that I was so much more authentic than what she saw on Youtube. I greeted the several people who had gathered around the front table and was looking to make my way out toward the village when the kitchen door burst open and a very excited and cheap imitation of myself ran up to me screaming, 'You impostor, what do you think you are doing?' He looked as though he was about to punch me with his fist that was clenched tightly alongside his hip when I reached out and pulled his frightfully ugly white wig off of his head exposing his bald head and two pieces of double faced tape.

"'Who is the impostor here you scoundrel? It appears to be you.' I said to him as the two doormen escorted him to the exit with his feet barely touching the floor, still arguing his case, and with his false hair in his hand and one side of his poor excuse for a mustache flopping about.

"As I was exiting the lovely dining room my hostess's assistant handed me a white envelope with the name 'Mark Twain' on the front which later I discovered contained a small stack of hundred-dollar bills. Shortly afterward I made my way towards the restored village with a complimentary pass for a private guided tour by carriage, given to me by my very apologetic hostess who was so embarrassed by the 'intruder'."

"So you took someone else's place as the speaker, got him thrown out, and after a free meal, you got a carriage ride through the village with his money in your pocket?" I asked. I was not actually surprised, but still somewhat shocked by the depth of his contempt towards the *other* 'actor'.

"Tom, the man was an impostor, a cheap imitation, a rogue wearing a wig and a fake mustache trying to steal my soul to make a few dollars on my good name", he said with his eyes narrowing and his lips pursed. I decided that this was an argument that I could not possibly win since he is after-all the 'real' Mark Twain so I remained silent.

Earl was clearly unsettled by my judgmental tone, but also very amused with himself for the way he had handled the outcome. He looked past me for a moment as if to re-play the entire event, fixed on me again with a twinkle in his eyes, said:

"I love to hear myself talk, because I get so much instructive and moral upheaval out of it, but I lose the bulk of this joy when I charge for it." ~MT 1906~

An Act of Redemption

I was spending my rainy autumn morning doing laundry when Earl poked his head into the backroom asking if there was room for some of his things. I nodded then said, "I 'm doing whites right now. Do you have your stuff sorted and ready to go?" He said he did and went to retrieve them. I would rather do his laundry any time than have him surprise me by washing mine. His idea of washing clothes is to cram everything in the washing machine and push start.

He returned with a pretty large pile of whites, which now meant that I had enough for two loads. It's no big deal to wash his clothes in **my** century. I sure

[247]

wouldn't be volunteering if it was the 1800s and I was scrubbing everything on a wash board, rinsing, and wringing by hand. If that were the case he would be on his own. I winced imagining being huddled over a grueling washboard for hours. I would never be able to straighten up. Sounds like a good reason to live in the present I thought. I closed the washing machine, added the detergent, and set the temperature to hot.

Back in the kitchen Earl was having a light breakfast of coffee and toast. I reheated my lukewarm breakfast coffee and joined him while I waited for the wash to finish. I broke the silence by asking more about his trip. Of course he was not bashful and directly rejoined his escapade in Colonial Williamsburg as if he had only paused to take a breath. He didn't have as much to say about the village as I thought he would, but he was very impressed with the Governor's Mansion. We spent some time comparing notes on what we both liked about that grand house. I was taken by the craftsmanship in creating such a fine home with simple tools and he was impressed by the palatial feel of the furnishings and the lovely garden. I shared some pictures on my phone from my trip there two years ago, which we both enjoyed seeing.

I got up to check on the laundry and when I returned his cheerful mood seemed to have changed; he was sitting quietly. I sat down silently so as not to disturb his contemplation. After a few minutes he looked up at me and said, "The part of the trip that had the biggest impact on me was my bus-ride home". "Really, how so?" I asked. He went on slowly to tell me a wonderful story.

When he took his seat near the front of the bus in Richmond he immediately noticed a lady sitting by the window he found difficult to ignore. She was dressed in a very modest printed blue dress with a navy blue sweater wrapped tightly around her. She had a black purse with the straps over her wrists that she held tightly in her lap. She was staring blankly out the window. He could tell by the look on her face that she was not a joyful traveler and seemed to be deeply troubled. As the bus lumbered along through winding roads of Virginia and the beautiful vibrant fall colors, Earl occasionally looked across the aisle to note that her expression was unaffected by nature's grandeur passing outside of her window just a few feet away.

The bus made a half hour stop at Waynesboro, Virginia to pick up passengers. Earl got off the bus to get soft drinks and a snack. While he was standing in line to re-board the bus he looked up to see the lady still sitting close to the window with the same blank look as before. Now that he could see her entire expressionless face she appeared more troubled from this side of the glass. When he finally re-boarded, his original seat and the one next to it were now occupied by a college age couple. There were other seats further back but he opted for the seat next to the lady. When he settled into the seat beside her she pushed herself tightly towards the window. After the bus started moving Earl spoke to her with a smile acknowledging the wonderful fall colors along the road.

After several minutes of hanging silence she turned slightly and said, "I have always loved the fall colors, but this year not so much." After a respectful pause Earl offered her a bottle of iced tea and asked her what made this fall different from any other. After her own brief hush she looked at him with red-rimmed light blue eyes and thanked him for the tea, and said, "I am on my way to visit my dying son, and it is just really hard to see any beauty in the world right now."

All suitable words escaped him, so Earl opened the package of Lance cheese crackers with peanut butter and held them in front of her. She looked into his eyes as she carefully took one from the package and said, "Thank you sir. You are so kind."

They sat quietly for a bit, and then he asked where her son was. She told him that her son was seriously wounded in Afghanistan last year and has been in a V.A. hospital since. His health had deteriorated over the last few months from several stubborn infections and she was notified last week that they had done all that they could and he had only a few days to live. She was so worried that she wouldn't get to Ann Arbor before he died. She hadn't seen him in over four years and while he was deployed overseas, his father had died from cancer due to exposure to Agent Orange in Viet Nam. Her story was more than sad; it was heart wrenching. Their family had lost everything paying medical bills, trying to save her husband with medicines that the VA would not or could not provide. Now her only son lies dying alone in a hospital a thousand miles from their small town in South Carolina.

She sat there looking down, sparingly taking small sips from her bottle of tea as if she was on a desert and needed to conserve the remainder for the long trip ahead. As they rode and finished the crackers, she eventually shared that she had pawned her husband's Viet Nam medals, some other household items, and her wedding ring to get enough money for the bus ticket. She had no more family anymore and considered the pawnshop a last resort. She was a very simple woman indicated by her dress and demeanor, but Earl sensed that she was also strong and proud. She had deeply affected Earl with her sad story, and, at one point in his retelling, I could see tears in the corners of his eyes.

As the day started to fade and the bus wound through the beautiful country of West Virginia, Earl did his best to lighten her mood. He told his favorite stories that always brought laughter to even the most somber of people, and managed to get a giggle or two from her as their time together became more familiar and comfortable.

She told him how she ended up in Georgia when her husband was drafted during the Viet Nam war in 1966. She talked about living on post at Fort Gordon with hundreds of other wives who worried together but hid their fears with nightly games of cards and cheap beer. Her life from the time she was first married to the present was regularly filled with worry and pain. It ripped at Earl and he tried his best to lift her depressed mood with his normally contagious humor. Knowing that this lady was about to suffer another intolerable loss made his quest for a smile from her so much more important than any audience he had stood before.

When the bus pulled into Bowling Green he looked at her and softly said, "Well this is as far as I go." She reached over and took his hand as the bus door opened a few feet in front of them. "You are a good man, Mark," she said.

Sitting there holding her hand with both of his the driver interrupted, 'Bowling Green...all out for Bowling Green.' Earl slowly pulled himself free, and reached into his breast pocket, pulled out the envelope from Williamsburg with 'Mark Twain' written on the front, put it into her hand, and said. "I want you to have this; I'm wealthy beyond my needs. Get yourself a nice meal and a place to stay." She looked up at him as her tears began to gush and spill down her weathered cheeks and said, "I cannot take this. You don't need to..." He held his finger to his lips and shook his head. Still looking thankfully into his eyes she said, "God bless you Sir!" Their hands slipped apart as he rose from his seat. As he got off the bus and looked back he could see one hand spread wide against the window as if to say "good-bye," and the other trying to muffle her sobs. Earl walked away feeling better about where the $2500.00 ended up and how it came to be in his pocket in the first place.

I gazed intently at him as he dried his eyes with the corner of the breakfast napkin. I felt guilty for my indictment of him yesterday. His face solemnly indicated that he had more invested in her pain than he was willing to express.

"That was a wonderful thing to do, Earl," I said with my voice quaking a bit. He sat there looking for a way to rein in his emotion. After a short pause he cleared his throat, and quoted something that fit perfectly.

"A dignified and respectworthy thing, and there is small merit about it and less grace when it don't cost anything." ~MT 1873~

A Narrow Miss

The weather has been unsteady for the last two weeks. The temperature has fluctuated between warm fall to early winter. Upon rising one doesn't know what task to take on for the day or what is the appropriate attire. It reminds me of my days spend at Fort Jackson in Columbia, South Carolina.

Earl and I were finishing our morning coffee as I launched into one of my many military memories. He sat there with a newspaper in his hand politely listening to me as my memory gathered clarity and steam and the words began to flow.

"I was drafted in the biggest draft in American history. It was November of 1965 and while at Fort Hayes in Columbus, Ohio I witnessed something I had no hint was even possible. We were instructed to 'count off' to three. All of the 'ones' went to the Army, the 'twos' to the Navy, and the 'threes' to the Marines. I didn't want to be a part of any of them, but I was a 'one' so I went and stood under the sign that said ARMY with the other scared young men. It was a very uncertain time in America if you were between the ages of 19 and 25. Only a few years before, the Bay of Pigs incident and the subsequent Cuban Missile Crisis threatened to draw the whole world into a nuclear war which scared everyone I knew into thinking our last days on earth possibly were drawing closer. Standing there in that crowd of boys knowing that some of us were headed to war, I again had that same frightened feeling. Looking around I was reminded of the cattle in the movie 'Hud' being crowded together not knowing what was coming next, but ominously sensing it was not going to be anything pleasant. My suspicions did not fail me.

"Once we arrived at Fort Jackson in the red clay and scrub pines world that defines most of the South, we were issued our ill-fitting uniforms. Soon after, we were hustled into our barracks, which hadn't been used since WW I, but because of our large numbers had been hastily reopened. Being the biggest draft ever, some recruits who otherwise would have been medically deferred, were pressed into service along with the all the able-bodied boys. Washington had a plan to have so many American troops on the ground in Viet Nam that the North Vietnamese would quickly give up the fight. It ended up having the opposite effect on that enemy.

"In any case I was there to receive my basic training and become an American fighting machine alongside guys with asthma, night blindness, and even a guy from Massachusetts that had little five-inch club feet. He wore specially constructed brown shoes. He would eventually be sent home but not before he was forced to train and complete the 25-mile forced march with a full field pack. Those of us who were physically able were never fully prepared for war and because of the 'hurry up' training we never would be. However, we followed our orders and did what we were told.

"The barracks' boilers were coal fired and if we were lucky they got stoked at least once a night giving the first few of us into the latrine in the morning tepid water to shave and shower with. There were large red painted tin cans hanging throughout the big room that housed our bunks that we used for our discarded cigarettes, which was odd because we were not allowed to smoke inside the barracks. There was an inch of water in the cans that froze during the night. The room was always cold because of more 'military wisdom' that dictated every other window should be opened exactly two inches, and that we all should sleep head to toe – to prevent infection and illness. The plan didn't work and many got very ill, particularly the boys from the warm climes. There were four young men from Puerto Rico who had to sleep on the floor of the Orderly Room next to the pot-bellied stove because they simply could not keep warm with the two thin blankets we were issued. They too disappeared before training was complete.

"South Carolina had an extremely odd temperature range. It was unlike any place I had ever been to, heard of, or imagined, but the surreal atmosphere fit perfectly with everything else I had been surprised by since leaving my comfortable home in Bowling Green, Ohio.

Waking in the morning to freezing temperatures and then rapidly getting dressed in long johns, two pairs of socks, and zipping the wool lining into my field jacket wasn't that unusual the first time I did it. I had lived in the northern winters so it was no big deal to me to bundle up for the cold. We rushed to the mess hall for morning chow in a crowd of young men with white clouds from our breath hanging above us. We had to stop before each meal to do the required exercises before entering the mess hall. The ten inclined sit-ups were difficult, but the brutal horizontal ladder was extremely tough in the mornings. The ice-cold, steel pipe against your bare skin, (no gloves allowed), made your hands numb by the time you reached the end 20 feet away. If you were unsuccessful, you had to go to the back of the line and try again. Sometimes guys would miss chow altogether because they couldn't get through it, and, of course, it got tougher and seemed colder each time they tried."

I looked over at Earl and he was intently listening to every word and seemed not to have moved since I started talking.

I continued, "The mess hall was always at least a very humid 80 degrees and there was no time to take your coat off. You had fifteen minutes to clear your stainless steel tray of eggs, sausage, toast, oatmeal, coffee, milk, and a mystery substance to me called 'grit's. Sitting there eating as quickly as we could after the fast exercises outside, and in a room that felt like an oven caused everyone to become sweat-soaked. Then back outside we rushed to the barracks to grab our gear for the day to train in the field and freeze all morning from being wet with sweat. Did I mention that this entire time we had at least three drill sergeants literally yelling in our faces? 'Hurry up lard ass. My grandmother can run faster than you and she's 85!' 'Why are you shivering Martha, it ain't cold?' 'Get moving before I put a boot in your ass!' "These were just the nice things they yelled at us." (I said with a insincere laugh).

"By ten o'clock in the morning the temperature would be 60 degrees, and by one o'clock it would be over 75 degrees and we would be miserable in all that clothing. There was no way to properly prepare for the day when getting dressed each morning. We couldn't walk into the weeds and remove our long johns, and there was no place to carry them or the lining from our field jacket even if we somehow had the time of place to remove them. It was the worst weather extremes I ever experienced and if I were dead and in hell I would expect it to resemble South Carolina in the winter," I concluded.

Back in the present, I said, "I'm sorry for assuming you would actually like to hear about all of that, but the weather the last few days reminded me of that time so long ago. Once my memory gets rolling, sometimes it's hard to stop."

Glancing towards Earl I knew that his mind was searching for an appropriate exclamation point to put at the end of my lecture. His paper was folded and in his lap since his reading had been postponed, and he twirled his mustache with his right forefinger and thumb like he was more in tune with my rambling than I thought. After a few minutes of staring blankly, he slightly turned to face me and said:

"I find that, as a rule, when a thing is a wonder to us it is not because of what we see in it, but because of what others have seen in it. We get almost all our wonders second hand". ~MT 1897~

I had the distinct feeling that Twain's quote didn't exactly say what he was thinking. He does that sometimes because I guess he thinks he has to say something I will think is profound.

The Signal

Yesterday Earl and I went out for dinner to a restaurant in downtown Bowling Green that I rarely frequent, but thoroughly enjoy every time I think to go there. The food is always good and the atmosphere is warm and comforting.

Actually, the building once housed, Isaly's Dairy Store years ago and at one time I worked there as a soda jerk. I had to dress entirely in white complete with the white paper hat that said Isaly's on the side in green script. The entire south side of the store from front to back was one long counter. The cafeteria line was at the far end of the tall room. It had a long steam table with a stainless steel tray glide in front of the angled glass. I remember many working people from the downtown area came in for the lunch special. Isaly's served many good things all day long until they closed at ten o'clock. The food was typical cafeteria fare, but the biggest draw was the soda fountain area, which was in the very center of the store. There they had a great assortment of ice cream including their signature Klondike bar. Instead of a standard round scoop of ice cream, (which you could get if you wanted), the ice cream in the cake cone was a four inch elongated spoon shape that came to a point. If you had a real hunger for ice cream they had another, (in the same shape), about ten inches tall called the Skyscraper. If you weren't careful or ate too slowly your ice cream could easily run down your arm or end up on the sidewalk.

In the front of the store was a case where you could get the usual deli meats and cheeses. But Isaly's specialized in chipped ham that was extremely popular. Right behind the deli case was a huge car-engine-sized red and chrome slicer that could slice the ham so thin you could practically read through it.

There was a lady who lived about three blocks away next to the Post Office – Mrs. Lichty -- who came into the store frequently, always to buy two pounds of ham. She always had her big German Sheppard with her who walked without a leash and was always at her left heel. When she stopped walking, so did the dog. If she stood longer than a couple of seconds, the dog patiently sat and did not move until the woman told him it was okay. When she came for ham at Isaly's the dog would sit outside the door until she came out. I had seen them walking downtown for many years when I was young, and long before I worked at Isaly's. There were a few years during my high school days when a gray squirrel occasionally rode on the dog's back all the way downtown and all the way back home.

I was working one summer evening and about seven o'clock I looked towards the door and saw her big German Sheppard with a brown bag in its mouth. The lady was nowhere to be seen. The dog stood in front of the two glass doors staring at me. I slowly walked to the doors and opened one a crack. The dog didn't move. I reached out and petted him. He still did not move. Finally something told me to take the bag from his mouth. As I grasped the bag, he opened his mouth gently allowing me to take it. Inside the bag was a note, 'Please cut me two pounds of ham shaved very thin. Here is the money. When you have the package of meat and the change from my $5 dollar bill please put them back in the bag and tell my dog to go home'. I stood there completely amazed, but slowly closed the door and sliced the ham as instructed. When I was done I put the ham and change in the bag, and tightly rolled the end of the bag, and opened the door. When I reached towards the dog with the bag he slowly opened his mouth and gingerly closed his teeth over the rolled end. He looked up at me as I said, "Go home boy". He immediately turned and walked the 15 feet to the curb and stopped. He looked up towards the traffic light and it was red so he sat down. A few seconds later it turned green and he got up and trotted on down the street toward the Lichty house. This was repeated occasionally while I worked there; her dog never once became distracted by the many people who would pet him as he waited patiently for his 'order', or as he walked down the street toward home.

I told Earl the story as we sat and waited for our entree. We both laughed as I continued to look around recalling other childhood memories that were triggered by things in this lovely room. When the waitress brought our steaks she looked at Earl and slowly pointed to her lips and smiled. A second later she left and I asked if he knew her. Looking down at his plate and cutting his meat, he shook his head. I was not very good dinner company as I was sidetracked by the ever-flowing thoughts of days gone by in Isaly's. We were both very hungry and ate with great focus as we made quick work of the delicious New York Strip steaks.

When the waitress came to bring us the check she again brought her fingers up to her lips while she offered a small smile to Earl. I looked at him, shrugged, and slid my chair out from the table and walked to the front to pay followed by Earl only a few steps behind. When we reached the cashier she looked up and smiled, "Was everything okay?" I said "yes" almost mechanically, noticing that she was looking past me and smiling at Earl. She placed her finger softly against her lips in a similar fashion as the waitress and coyly smiled. From behind me I heard Earl say, "Oh what the hell," as he pushed by me and kissed the girl right on her mouth. She snapped back holding one hand flat against her forehead quite exasperated and said loudly, "What do you think you are doing?" I was now standing behind Earl as he answered her quickly, "You cast the bait and I took it". "Sir, I was trying to let you know that you have a piece of lettuce stuck in your front teeth," She said. There was a long silence that seemed to last an eternity when finally Earl said very matter-of-factly, "Well thanks for the great meal, the clue to my hidden garden snack, and the after-dinner kiss." He then pressed his way quickly through the waiting crowd and went out the door. I sheepishly smiled and hastily followed pushing my credit card receipt into my pocket.

Once we were standing on the sidewalk I sensed that there was little I should add to what just transpired. To embarrass him further would serve no purpose. We turned and walked towards the parked car. When we reached the car he turned suddenly, grasped a lapel -- and perhaps thinking his behavior needed further exaggeration to be clear – said in a theatrical voice:

"Affection and devotion are qualities that are able to adorn and render beautiful a character that is otherwise unattractive, and even repulsive." ~MT 1874~

On the silent ride home I tried in vain to merge his confusing words to the scene I had just witnessed. "Earl, my friend, you sometimes leave me speechless", I said to myself as we pulled into the driveway.

A Well Balanced Meal

Although I was still reeling from my night out to dinner with Earl I could not help but recount many memories of things that happened at that same location. I think the reason I went there after school instead of Roger's Drugs or Woolworth's was because Sarge, who managed Isaly's, let us smoke. I never had enough money to be a big spender and have a coke or ice cream after school, but as long as someone at the table bought something, we could sit there and smoke and laugh for as long as we wanted. I did not go to Isaly's every day because I usually had an after-school job, or more likely, because I fell into step with other boys on their way to DeWalt's pool hall. When I had my paper route, I would sometimes hang out there with my pals until the last minute and then race down to get my papers. I was routinely late and got chewed-out by Cap, the Blade manager. Always promising to be on time from then on, and, of course, it wouldn't be long and I was late again. Ironically the Blade office was in the alley at the rear of Howard's bar, where I would end up working years later.

During my telling the dog and ham story, Earl said he noticed that I appeared pre-occupied and that I curiously looked around the restaurant randomly smiling. "You did regain your focus once I kissed that girl at the register," he said with a deep belly laugh. "Boy that sure got everyone's attention, well at least hers."

[256]

"You're lucky she didn't call the police and file charges against you for assault," I said. "Assault?" He asked. How many girls can say that they were kissed by Mark Twain? She now has something extremely exciting to tell her grandkids. I'll bet when she got up that morning she had no idea that when she went to bed that night she would have such a memory to lull her to sleep". He said while grabbing his lapel. ("Or wake up screaming in the middle of the night?"), I said to myself.

As we sat there I recalled what I thought might have been one of my last times in Isaly's, or at least the most noteworthy.

"Do you want to hear another story?" I asked of my captive house guest. "Sure, I am a lover of stories even if they are true," he said, folding his paper.

"I was working full-time as a bartender at Howard's in the fall of 1967. Howard's had the oldest liquor permit in Bowling Green issued in 1933, right after prohibition. It was a very old bar. Back in my mother's day it had been a Chinese restaurant. Now it was just a dark bar that locals patronized during the day. At night the college crowd took it over. It was almost like two different places. The people who worked during the day had little contact with the people who worked nights. I was the exception as I worked a split shift on Saturdays. I would come in at noon -- relieving the morning bartender--, work until six, and then return again at eight and work until we closed at 1:00 am. On Saturdays one of our local beer truck drivers would tend bar from 6:00 am until noon. The Saturday crowd was usually farmers who had brought grain into town or shift workers from the Heinz Ketchup factory a few blocks away. George, the bartender, would drink almost a whole fifth of Kessler's whisky in that six hour period. He always had a snoot-full when I came in at noon. George had a weak stomach and if there was anything nasty in the restrooms etc. he would beg me to please clean it up. He nearly gagged just asking me."

"Are you following me so far Earl?" I asked. He was still intently listening and answered, "I'm hanging on your every word Tom."

"One Friday night after work I had an after-hours party at my apartment above Hutchinson's optometrist shop on East Wooster Street. One of the new waiters, Nick Porter, passed out on my couch. When I got up around ten in the morning I woke him and asked if he wanted to get something to eat. He agreed and after I showered and dressed for work we headed off to Isaly's, which was less than a block away. We went down the cafeteria line, which was set up for lunch, and I selected something I hadn't had in years but always liked: A scoop of mashed potatoes and a scoop of dressing covered with beef gravy that cost all of 50 cents. Nick opted for the 99 cent meatloaf dinner and we took a seat in a booth and picked at our lunch. Neither of us knew until we faced all that food that we were more hung-over and thirsty than hungry. I stirred the potatoes, dressing and gravy around with my fork and made it into something that I surely didn't want to eat. Isaly's was one of the few places that served milk in a full pint container, which that morning I was more interested in than anything solid and I drank the better part of two cartons."

"While stirring that concoction, we hatched a fiendish prank. I put my gravy combination with the lumps of dressing carefully into the carton with the remaining milk. Nick added all of his peas into the mixture. Then we were ready."

"It was a quarter till twelve when Nick walked into the bar and took a seat far from the morning regulars that were sitting at the bar by the front door. George was standing in front of them with his usual glass of Kessler's in hand and with one foot on a beer case. He slowly walked down and asked the college-aged stranger what he wanted and Nick ordered a beer. When George turned to go to the cooler, Nick pulled out the milk container and with a loud retching sound, squeezed it all over the bar making a huge puddle of very convincing faux vomit. George quickly turned to see Nick wiping his mouth and saw the bar-top defiled with his worst nightmare. I was outside peeking through a gap in the curtains and quickly made my entrance. George was holding a hand over his mouth and pointing, his wide eyes were filled with terror, and pleading for help. I quickly reached into the mélange and said excitedly, "Cool.... PEAS!" I picked one up and popped it into my mouth. Instantly, George had his head in the waste can donating his morning whiskey back to Mr. Howard. The old fellows at the other end of the bar rapidly shuffled out as if tied together at the waist."

Earl was laughing hysterically, literally holding his stomach, and half bent over in the leather chair. We were both laughing so hard that all the startled cats left the room quicker than the farmers from the bar.

"So what.....happened.....then," he asked barely being able to get the words out between his deep laughs. "Nick and I laughed and cleaned up the mess while George made a hasty exit out the front door, without his coat, and still wearing his white apron. I didn't tell George the whole story until a few weeks later and he wouldn't talk to me for almost six months after that. Eventually that prank became his favorite story and he told it often while I stood next to him with an irrepressible Cheshire grin. It made us good friends, but it took a while to happen," I said still smiling.

Earl wasted no time punctuating my story.

"Always acknowledge a fault frankly. This will throw those in authority off their guard and give you an opportunity to commit more." ~MT~

Different Guy same Job

I was startled awake this morning by an unfamiliar sound. I opened my eyes, slowly sat up in the bed, swung my legs out, rose to my feet, and pulled back the lacy curtains to peer outside. About two hundred yards away were three big, white stern-wheel riverboats. There was much activity in the area and the boat on the right had a thick white plume of steam shooting into the morning sky with a loud penetrating whistle indicating that it was about to cast off out onto the water.

Standing at the window, still not quite awake, I looked out across the wide expanse of water to the trees lining the bank on the other side, and saw nothing that was vaguely familiar. Bringing my attention back into the room and looking at the frilly curtain in my hand I realized that I surely could not be where I went to sleep. I tentatively turned around to discover that the room was completely furnished in wonderful antiques complete with a pitcher and bowl setting on a beautiful quarter-sawn Oak Commode. I looked into the pitcher and was surprised to find that it wasn't a decoration; it was full of water. I walked back to the edge of the bed and unsteadily sat down on the white chenille bedspread and took another slow look around the room trying to uncover a clue to where I was. In front of the window and on the stand next to the iron bed was a brass lamp with a painted shade and a tall glass chimney. It had no cord. There were no electrical outlets or switches anywhere in the room. "Where am I? What is this place," I thought anxiously. There is a river outside with stern wheel boats moored, a bedroom that looks like it came straight out of a western movie, and nothing that looks correct to me except my iPhone on the bedside table lying on a starched crocheted doily. I picked up my only link to all that was familiar and pushed the power button...'No Service' flashed on the screen. That somehow didn't surprise me.

I quickly got dressed, slid my phone into my pocket, opened the door quietly, and hesitantly walked down the dark wooden stairs towards a frosted glass front door and into a very bright foyer. Just to the right of the entryway was a parlor. A maroon velvet rope blocked the doorway. I looked in and examined the room. The floral printed wallpaper went from the floor almost to the ceiling where it met a small wood molding that continued around the room. There were two gold-satin-covered, Walnut framed round backed chairs in front of the big

[259]

window, and an oval, white-marble-topped Walnut table between them, which held a large brass oil lamp with dangling crystals around the painted shade. The lace curtains were drawn back at each side and a sheer panel covered the window, -- which did little to prevent the bright sun from bathing the entire room in yellow morning light. There was an Oak pump organ trimmed in Walnut burl on one wall that appeared to be brand new and a large hearth fireplace on the opposite wall with its white-painted mantle adorned with several framed pictures. The remaining wall was a large archway leading into what I assumed was a dining room, judging by the big table surrounded by a number of chairs. A large oil chandelier hung low over the center of the table.

Just as my eyes were about to finish panning the room I heard a voice from behind me, "I'll bet you are hungry". I turned to see a large, round-faced, black lady smiling broadly and wiping both of her hands on her floor length apron.

I think I smiled back and said, ".... Ah yes, I guess I am hungry. Can you tell me what town this is?" I asked uneasily.

"Where are you?" She said with a laugh. "Why you're in Hannibal, Missouri, the same place you were last night I 'spect. C'mon let's get some breakfast into you before you expire." she said turning towards what I assumed was the kitchen.

I blindly followed her down the dim hall and into the bright white room at the end with 'Hannibal' echoing in my head while still trying to figure out how that could possibly be true.

The kitchen was also perfectly assembled with the same museum quality period furniture I had seen everywhere else in the house. She pulled a chair out for me from the table and motioned for me to sit. She went over to a black-iron cook stove trimmed in shiny nickel and rattled a spatula in a big iron skillet. She raised her left elbow and with a ringing sound she tapped against the skillet and then sat it back down. She turned towards me with a steaming plate in her hand and placed it in front of me. There was a big slice of ham, three eggs, some fried tomatoes, and a big mound of grits. As I laid my white napkin across my lap she poured me a large cup of coffee from a blue speckled enamel pot and put a large dollop of butter into the center of the grits. "Eat now son, before it gets cold," she said pushing a basket of biscuits towards me.

I picked up my fork slowly and put some egg into my mouth. It was delicious and as I chewed I heard my muffled voice ask, "What year is it?"

She looked at me with her head cocked a bit to the side in obvious disbelief and answered, "Why, its 1850".

I dropped my fork and said in complete astonishment, "What, 1850? It cannot be 1850...it was 2014 yesterday."

"Well I don't know what you et before bed but it has been 1850 since last January," she said with a loud laugh.

I slowly put a piece of savory ham into my mouth and chewed it. It was so good that even though I was completely confused, I also felt comforted by the wonderful food that was prepared just for me. I finished eating everything on my plate, even the grits and wiped my mouth with the white napkin. The whole meal seemed to be gone in less than a minute.

"That was one of the best breakfasts I have ever eaten", I said patting my full belly and placing the folded napkin on my plate. I had no sooner gotten those words out of my mouth when a loud ring came from down the hall behind me. The lady quickly went and opened the front door. I couldn't hear what was said, but moments later the lady and a young man about fourteen entered the room.

"You have company," she said. I looked at this chap standing in front of me. He was dressed completely in white, except for black suspenders, and tilted back on his head was a straw hat. He was barefoot, which I didn't notice at first because his feet were so black with dirt I thought they were shoes. Standing in front of me was someone I felt I should know, but I couldn't for the life of me figure out who he was. Suddenly he said, "Well, are you ready?"

(Ready? Ready for what I thought?) "You have me at a loss my friend. I have no idea what you are talking about", I said nervously.

"We have unfinished work to do and you promised me that you would help", he said in a presuming tone.

"I did?" I stammered. "Well if I made a promise to help you then I will. What is it that you need help with?" I asked prepared to keep my word.

Without a reply he turned towards the front door and I automatically followed him forgetting to thank my hostess who seemed to instantly vanish from the room.

We stepped out through the front door, across a wide front porch, down five worn wooden steps, and into the blinding morning sun glaring off of the river in the distance. We continued on down a short flower-lined, dirt path and through a gated opening in a large planked wooden fence. He stopped and turned towards me and again I asked what we were going to do. He pointed behind me. As I turned I saw a big wide brush lying across a bucket filled with white paint.

[261]

"We are going to whitewash this fence. You are going to get the pleasure of applying the whitewash while I sweat in the shade watching you", he said.

I thought for moment and then quickly recalled reading a story identical to this when I was a young boy. I picked up the brush and smiled, remembering how that tale turned out I turned back towards my young friend and told him that I wasn't being suckered into his trick. He insistently blurted out,

"You must. If you don't it will alter the space/ time continuum!"

His pressing words reminded me of Doc in "Back to the Future", and as I looked at my new friend he suddenly started to morph into an old man. His height increased and he was rapidly aging before my eyes. As his hat slipped from his head I could see his hair getting longer, becoming full, wildly disheveled, and turn from dark-brown to pure white. A thin burning cigar appeared to sprout in the corner of his mouth under a huge rapidly growing and curling white and silver mustache. He looked vaguely familiar now, but scary at the same time. Frozen in terror I dropped the brush into the bucket, splashing paint over both of us. And as I tried to run I felt him grab me and hold me back. He said, "HEY...HEY...HEY!" loudly, and then at once with a harsh flinch I opened my eyes.

I was sitting in my nest of pillows in my own house and Earl was leaning over me with his hands on my shoulders. "Hey, are you alright?" he asked, his face twisted with concern. "You must have been having a bad dream. You were dozing when all of a sudden at the top of your voice you said, 'I'm not falling for that again'. I didn't want to scare you, but thought I better wake you before you knocked over the lamp or something."

I sat there for a second wondering who would paint the fence since Earl woke me up. Then I chuckled a bit and said, "It wasn't the worse dream I ever had, but it certainly ranks as a bizarre one. I don't think I would have had that dream if my name wasn't 'Tom'", I said with a relieved laugh. Earl flashed me a confused look and promptly shrugged and turned to sit back down into his chair. After a time he said, without looking up:

"While you are in a dream it isn't a dream---it is reality, and the bear-bite hurts; hurts in a perfectly real way." ~MT 1897~

Red, White, and Blues

Earl remembered it was Veteran's Day before I did and set forth to clear his throat and tell me about his brief time in the Confederate Militia (The Marion

Rangers). He was with them for only two weeks thrashing about in the mud and avoiding a little known colonel at the time -- Ulysses S. Grant. He only joined the confederate forces so he wouldn't have to pilot Union troop boats on the Mississippi. He deserted and went west. His reason for leaving, he said, was because when he joined he was unaware of the politics of the South. I didn't press him on his reasons or express any opinion that would appear as disapproving of his refusal to serve. Whatever happens in a boy's mind during the dark time of war is between his conscience and him. I cannot even imagine being forced into fighting against other Americans in the way that the Civil War dictated. War is always an ugly affair but fighting your own countrymen is unimaginably barbaric.

Earl expressed the climate surrounding the time of his (Twain's) joining. He heard nothing of the slave issue specifically, but was very aware of the hatred felt towards the leaders in Washington who had crossed the line and snatched the rights of the states to govern themselves.

"Had I known that I was signing up to fight so one man could maintain his ownership and control of another man through slavery, I would never have put my name to such a cause. Once I discovered those motives I quickly left that rag-tag group of would-be soldiers and set out for California, which I heard had no soldiers fighting for either side," he said. He went on to describe the attitude of those southern recruits as being so ready to fight that some of them showed up for war carrying nothing more than pitchforks and hunting knives. Most didn't have guns, because they couldn't leave their family without the only rifle needed to provide food. They didn't know if weapons would be provided to them before being sent into battle, so they showed up with what little they had.

He looked sad when he talked about seeing those boys for the last time, almost as if he had really been there. He had the same expression on his face that I felt in my heart. I've heard it labeled 'survivor guilt' by professionals, but giving it a small title does not minimize or shorten its duration. Losing your comrades so savagely while you seemingly tap-danced through your military time leaves any man with a compassionate conscience pensive. He said he felt bad for not serving, but added that fighting for the southern cause was tantamount to buying and keeping a slave himself, which he could never possibly do. I understood Twain completely and admired his decision to simply quit which wasn't entirely different from my own contemplations during my time in the military.

I talked about how I felt when I arrived to my Advanced Individual Training, B-15-4, in tent city at Fort Jackson after basic training. How those first days were terrifying even though they were considerably more relaxed than basic training

[263]

had been. I expressed how I felt knowing that there was a war going on, a big war at that, and we were getting ready to go there. Fear gripped each of us even though we hid it the best that we could as any 'strong' man would in those circumstances.

The group that welcomed our class was class number two. The radio operator course was eight weeks long and we were class sixteen. All of the even numbers were in one camp and the odd numbers in another so we were eight weeks away from graduating. Class two was graduating the following weekend, and we got very close and friendly to them during that short time.

They were the first guys that had been in uniform longer than us who weren't screaming in our faces all the time. It was so easy to like those guys. They were helpful in telling us things that only veterans of the school could know. Some of them came into our tents and sat on our bunks. We laughed and talked like we might if we were all on a friendly camping trip instead of trapped in freezing Army tents in January far away from our loving and warm homes. We were guys from all over the country, all different races, cultures, some with distinctive accents, but all equal to one another in the brutal reality of a war that faced us.

We were not required to attend the graduation ceremony but nearly all of us went because of how those guys reached out to us with their help and friendship. We met the attending family members who lived close by and wished their loved-ones well before they returned home the next day. It was a nice day and memorable because by being there -- during what little free time we had -- showed them how important they had become to us. We actually hugged each other without retraint before saying goodbye to those guys we most likely would never see again.

The tedium passed slowly as we were in our classrooms being instructed to receive and send Morse code for seven hours each day. I equate learning Morse code to being in a dumpster and having ten people beat on the outside with hammers. It gets to the point, (and actually happened to some), that you just want to pull off your headsets and run outside and listen to anything other than more dots and dashes. It must have been a common occurrence because when some of our guys in fact left the classroom, the sergeants would quietly slip out of the room and follow them. Twenty minutes to a half hour later the soldier would return to his desk, put his headphones back on, and continue as if he had merely taken a latrine break. Sitting in those green-painted rooms in the drab gray cubicles for hours each day felt like some sort of secret torture tactic. Knowing that our friends in class two had endured it made it possible for us to tolerate it as well.

One week before we were to graduate we heard some horrible news that was casually blurted out at our morning formation. Twelve of the boys from Class Two that had orders for Viet Nam were all killed or severely wounded in a mortar barrage, as they exited a plane on the tarmac at Da Nang air base. Later we found out that they had no weapons and were carrying only their duffle bags when attacked. The remainder of our time at radio operator's school was deathly solemn. I was so affected that I could not concentrate at all in class that final week. All I could hear through the headset were their voices those last nights before they shipped out. The laughter, the carefree jokes about going to war, and their advice to us as to how to easily make it through the school echoed in my head.

I was failing in my daily sending and receiving tests and was accused by the staff of malingering, which is Army talk for goofing off. Nothing could have been further from the truth. I was trying so hard to concentrate and advance the way I easily had for the first seven weeks. I was a good soldier, which kept the bull's-eye off of me, and always looked perfect in my uniform. I had learned how to shine shoes in the barber shop while in high school and my brothers' who had both been in the military showed me how to spit shine my boots to avoid being hassled by the cadre. It made no difference how hard I tried or how good I looked to the instructors, it was clear I was not going to become a radio operator. I was told to pack my gear and they transferred me to cook school, which was considered one of the worse punishments available. What they didn't know was that when I was asked at the reception station what M.O.S., (job), I would like in the Army I told them I wanted to be a cook. Overnight I was where I wanted to be, even though the Army first had to turn my wish into a chastisement.

My thoughts of those guys from class two and the others I later found out didn't survive the war, frequently left me feeling like it should have been me that perished instead of them. So many great guys from my basic training class that were killed, kids from my hometown that I had known my whole life and one from my graduating class lost to a war that ultimately would not be won. "The loss of 58,000 American boys adding to the 3,200,000 total of people who died during that war was all that was achieved," I said grimly. I sat there quietly thinking back to those days during the war when every week I opened the paper to see several more names of young men who willingly gave their lives to what they thought was ensuring someone else's freedom. Names of guys I didn't know, but felt deeply connected to. It was such a sad time for America, a sad time to be a surviving veteran.

Earl was unusually quiet. After all, what could be said to change the bleak truth of either of those experiences? A few minutes later he turned to look at me.

[265]

His eyes were wet with the reality of the topic and his voice while gentle, stuttered to emit the words that came from a place more personally heartfelt than just in his role as Mr. Clemens:

"Man is ...ttthe only animal....ttthat deals in...ttthat atrocity of atrocities, War."

~MT 1909~

I got up and silently moved from the room to give him some space as he was more shaken than I have ever seen before.

Esther's Delight

When I walked into the kitchen this morning and looked out the window, I was surprised by the endowment the night had brought. I almost hate to say the word out loud. It is the equivalent to inviting catastrophe by saying, "I hope we don't have a flat tire while driving across a lonely desert." My superstitions are few, but seeing **snow** for the first time makes me want to make a circle of salt on the kitchen floor and sit in the center of it wearing a necklace of garlic.

Earl came in and sat down at the table as if waiting for a show to begin. I looked over at him, swept my hand toward the window, and said, "Did you order this?" He held both hands up with his palms facing me and said "Don't look at me, I think it might have come from your cousin Esther Shroyer." I smiled and nodded knowingly, as Esther starts in the summer wishing for huge snowfalls and isn't bashful with her excitement or anticipation. I finished making my coffee and joined Earl at the table.

"I can remember the first time I saw snow in Hannibal. I was about seven, but it didn't stick around long enough for me to put my hands into it to truly experience what it felt like. There was just enough of it to cause me to wonder what it would be like to live in Canada or Alaska. How would the people move about, travel, or just walk? The small measure we received in Hannibal looked like wheat flour dusted across the ground resembling our kitchen table when mother made pies. It was beautiful but certainly very troublesome in great amounts I thought, but since there was so little of it I forgot about it quicker than it could melt or blow away," he said.

I wondered if Hannibal ever actually received any snow or was this more of Earl's poetic license. His very thorough research of Samuel Clemens, while not always completely factual through his portrayal, usually had an element of truth.

"When there was sufficient snow we used to go sledding on every little hill we could find", I replied. In Bowling Green it was tough finding anything tall enough to give us much of a thrill. When I was growing up the reservoir hill everyone uses now on (Conneaut Avenue) was either off limits to me or too far away. I cannot remember even hearing of it back then or I certainly would have been there, rules or not. I never went there until I took my own boys when they were young.

"I first experienced the fun of sledding by tagging along with a family that had a car and drove to the big hills of Fort Meigs on the Maumee River. Usually my friends and I just pulled our sleds around Bowling Green looking for some huge hill to magically appear. I envied families that had a toboggan that could seat four or five people, but then they also had a car to take them to where the big hills were", I said longingly. I added that as I grew up the excitement of sledding was sometimes annulled by the thought of repeatedly having to climb back up a hill caked with frozen slippery snow. The effort sometimes seemed futile unless of course the ride was a long exciting one.

Earl sat back in his chair, grabbed a lapel, and said, "Why I remember the first time I saw snow that was deep enough to fully enjoy. One Christmas we went to visit some distant relatives who lived in Illinois west of Chicago in a little town called Capron. The older kids took the younger ones out to sled down the long smooth hills and out onto the frozen Piscasaw River using coal shovels. We sat on the shovel with the handle sticking out in front of us. When we were getting on we would grab that handle and pull it up as far as we could to keep the shovel from sliding away, and then once we were settled in and ready, we would lower the handle and off we would go. We used to take an old candle and rub it on the bottom of the shovel to make it go even faster. If we were headed towards a tree or needed to stop we would lean one way or the other and pull up on the handle, which acted as a brake of sorts. It wasn't foolproof, though, and more than once an unsuspecting nose was bloodied by the handle flipping up against someone's face because they could not stop before hitting a tree or a rock hidden under the snow. We were lucky none of us was killed, but we had such fun that winter up in Illinois," he said with a wide grin.

When Earl and I talk it might seem like each one of our stories is trying to over-shadow the other's. That isn't the case, at least not from me. When one of us says something, it triggers a thought in the other that sometimes immediately follows without much of a pause. To the casual observer our exchanges might appear to be a duel of tall tales. Actually Earl and I play off each other so well because we both have lived a long time, and there are many hidden memories that need prompting, -- as only a good story from the other can provide.

There was a brief silence, and I jumped in. "I can remember once when my older brother Jim and I took an old wooden Vernor's Ginger Ale pop case that was made for quart bottles and nailed barrel staves on the bottom for runners. We sanded them and coated the 'skis' with paraffin. We hooked our dog, 'Bootsie' to the box with a piece of clothesline rope. With a piece of baloney in my hand I ran out in front of him as fast as I could run on the hard packed snow in the street in front of our house as my brother rode in the box yelling "Mush...Mush" while snapping a makeshift clothesline rope whip attached to a stick. It was a great invention and much fun. However each time I remember that story there is never any part of it where I am the one riding in the box. I can remember bending over gasping for breath with the cold winter air ripping into my throat and panting lungs and hearing my brother yell, "c'mon...mush mush we need to get back on the trail" as he waved the whip in the air. Being the younger brother allowed me hang around with older brothers, but it also meant that I was forced to do everything they didn't want to do", I said smiling and remembering how gullible and obedient I was.

"I hope that this winter isn't like last", I said with a sigh. Earl turned to me and said that living in Oak Park last year was exactly like northern Canada must have been when he first imagined it 60 years before. "We had so much snow that even the kids grew to hate it," he said. "As a matter of fact they were crying to go back to school"

"Once it gets up to the roof I am going to call Esther and tell her what I think of her snow", I said with a laugh. "I'll dial the telephone for you", he said with a chuckle.

We sat there both smiling when he added:

"Albeit snow is very beautiful when falling, its loveliness passes away very shortly afterward. The grand unpoetical result is merely chilblains & slush" ~MT 1870~

"Well, then there are the warm memories that last long after the spring thaw." I thought.

Today Earl told me that he is thinking of heading south for the warmer weather. I haven't had time to digest that news, but suffice it to say that it will surely change my life if he goes. I certainly cannot blame him and if he does leave, he'll take my best wishes with him.

I have enough written material compiled from his time spent here to put into an organized printing, but I always thought that when he eventually left that I would be completely prepared with a 'final chapter' of sorts. The more I think of it now the more I realize that perhaps a final chapter isn't as possible as I might want it to be. He will be here, and then he will be somewhere else. Wherever he lands, his saga will continue but with someone new. The end to his stay with me should not have the feel of an epitaph, but more like the anticipation that follows when the circus pulls up stakes and moves on to entertain in another town.

So, is there a final chapter? I am sure that a day with come after Earl has gone when there will seem to be less to write about, but as long as his memory is with me I'll have enough to chronicle our conversations and exploits every day for the rest of my life. As I sit here trying to focus on all of the positives of having my house back, even the absence of his rancid stale cigar smoke doesn't appeal to me.

Another Face in the Crowd?

After breakfast Earl and I spent some time talking about the possibility of him leaving. He was sitting in the leather recliner with both hands behind his head looking blindly towards the ceiling as if he could clearly see paradise. "There will be no more snow to shovel, lots of girls in bikinis, white sand beaches, and lazy palm trees swaying in the warm breezes," he said with a big smile, his face almost shining.

I also smiled and nodded in agreement when the pessimist that lives inside of me piped up, "Well then you have the Palmetto bugs, the humidity that is so thick you can hardly breathe, the occasional hurricane that destroys everything but the sand, and it inconveniently rains nearly every day."

"Leave it to you to make a grand idea even more attractive", he said sarcastically putting his hands into his lap.

"I'm sorry Earl, I am just telling it like it is. If you want to live there I think you should, but personally I'd rather shovel snow than live in harmony with two inch bugs that look like cockroaches on steroids," I said in my best cynical tone. "Besides that Earl, you are going to a place where many of the men wear white year round, have chalk-colored hair, big mustaches, and smoke cigars. You could live there for ten years before anyone recognized you," I said with a laugh.

After a few minutes of silence he spoke. "I never gave that a thought Tom. I do so enjoy it when people see me and become excited that they are in the presence of a great author and national icon". You could hear doubts mounting in his voice.

"You are living in a college town in Ohio where everyone or nearly everyone looks at you and sees Mark Twain and no one else. Are you willing to give up your celebrity status for warmer weather and become just another person with white hair in Florida?" I asked glossing over his 'greatness' comment and sounding as if I am trying to convince him to stay.

He sat there twisting his mustache with his right forefinger and thumb as he does when he is in serious contemplation. "Hmmmmm. You have given me something to seriously consider Tom. I'm not sure that I am prepared to be just another mature man in a sea of white suits engaging in the boredom of croquet or shuffleboard?" he said with his eyes wide. "Can I selfishly deprive people of knowing me or at least recognizing me because I blend so easily into their sea of mediocrity?"

"Earl I know it sounds like I am trying to convince you to stay here. In a way I guess maybe I am, but if you want to go to Florida please know what to expect there. I mean we both hate the snow to some degree, but you never shoveled any of it yourself last year even though you got here at the tail end of winter. You really aren't expected to do much around here at all. You are allowed, even welcomed to be Mark Twain and the only iron-clad rule is that you don't smoke in the house. If you go to Florida you won't be able to smoke anywhere, because everyone there is on Oxygen." I said with a chuckle. "Do whatever suits you, but I know from being around you for nearly nine months that a lot of what satisfies you is being accepted as Mark Twain not merely a person pretending to be him.

"You went to Detroit and were recognized. You went to Williamsburg and were asked to speak to a historical group. Earl there isn't a day that goes by when you are out at the library or Grounds for Thought that someone doesn't ask you if you are Mark Twain. Even the UPS man knew who you were. Are you willing to trade your distinction here for possible obscurity in sunny Florida?"

He sat there for a moment still twirling his mustache when he looked up and said, "You have proposed a question that deserves some serious thought, and I am going to consider all of my options before deciding. My leaving here has to be a crushing prospect to you, and before I do irreparable damage to you, I will think things through completely."

"Irreparable damage", really? Missing our chats will disrupt my comfortable daily ritual for awhile, but it's not likely to push me to a point of absolute desolation, I said to myself. His presumption of my dependence on him as my sole intellectual stimulation can be incredible at times, but it fits perfectly with the ego that Twain himself would disclose in those circumstances, and in some ways he is, of course, right.

I told him that I was going downtown later and asked if he would like to join me. He said that he would and asked if we might stop by the drug store while we were out. I said, "Sure" and reminded him of the Arctic blast that has pushed the temperature below freezing and suggested he wear his wool coat and scarf.

As he got up and stood next to his chair he looked at me in a way that I instantly knew he was prepared to add a footnote to our earlier exchange. "Tom I appreciate your insight into my pending decision, but understand that whatever I eventually do will be based entirely on my need for a nurturing environment that will fuel my artistic expression, and also satisfy my adoring fans." Another well executed Earlism that is convincingly appropriate for his role. While sliding his coat over his shoulders and looking out toward the door I was holding open for him, he said:

"Imagination labors best in distant fields." ~MT 1869~

And, we were off.

Someone's Surprise

During those last couple of weeks I had been required to consider the likelihood of not living with Earl for much longer. The reality of his possible departure for warmer weather conjured the apprehension that I might have to get used to a less exciting world. If he does move south, my life will no longer be the rich stimulating daily smile-fest that I have grown to appreciate for the nine months of his stay.

When he first appeared our dialogue was more abbreviated and somewhat guarded until we settled into the certainty of living with another person who appeared so much different than ourselves. The quirks and habits exhibited as we circled and sniffed before becoming certain of each other have now become the traits we are the fondest of. Knowing that all that has matured between us might disappear very soon is replaced with the hollow feeling only the possible separation of good friends regrettably provides.

Accepting that he is not actually Mark Twain, but treating him as if he is has become so natural that I no longer spend as much time thinking about Earl's true identity, where he's from, or why he's chosen this path. His fantasy has spilled into my life to the point that when I have a question that I would have liked to ask Mark Twain, I just automatically ask Earl. I have accepted his role; I have embraced it to the point that I, too, can live simultaneously in two different eras.

[271]

The idea that my reality would return to living in one single century seems pretty dreary after my frequent jaunts back to the 1800s with Earl. Who would have thought that an incessant cigar-smoking curmudgeon from the past could have such an infectious and affectionate grasp on someone from the 'future'? These last months have been a habitual escape from the passing of time for me. Perhaps that is what guided Earl into his disguise in the first place: The idea that becoming someone from the past allows one to stand in a single spot in history forever while the rest of the world goes on, advances, grows old, and eventually dies. Assuming the persona of a revered and famous, long-dead writer is certainly much more enjoyable than contemplating one's own less-than-luminous life or mortality.

For the enjoyable banter we shared in the shade of the porch or comfort of the living room I have him to thank for providing me with nearly a year of vacation. It undeniably has been a vacation. A vacation, by definition, is to relinquish or to depart from the usual and customary. His presence unquestionably has caused me to deviate from my conventional world, not from some sort of horrible existence, but by transporting me through stories to an enticing atmosphere Mark Twain could easily and routinely supply. Being taken away, but still connected to all things I love, has to be the best time travel imaginable. I will sincerely miss those excursions if he leaves. Returning to my pre-Earl life will be different to say the least, but my memories, and written journals (like picture postcards), will serve to remind me of the time Mark Twain came to visit.

Sitting here this morning contemplating the intrinsic solitude his absence will most assuredly bring I cannot help but smile. Just knowing that somewhere in Florida at this particular moment there is a person who is living, what he is certain, is a happy and full life and who is in for one huge surprise. One cannot ever completely return to 'normal' once 'The Earl of Prose' enters his life as subtlety as a lost kitten. I envy them, (whoever they are), because they are in for one unforgettable post-Christmas gift.

"The Christmas holidays have this high value: that they remind Forgetters of the Forgotten, & repair damaged relationships." ~MT 1907~

Lonesome?

The smell of fresh coffee and frying bacon filled the kitchen this morning like all mornings and apparently enough of that enticing aroma had crept under Earl's door to cause him to promptly seek its source. Just as I was taking the bacon from the skillet he came and stood in the doorway wrapped in his thin

Japanese robe and rubbing his eyes. "What time is it?" He asked with his raspy morning voice.

"It's a little before ten. Why, do you need to be somewhere?" I answered

"Nope just wondered what meal I should plan on eating next. That bacon smells wonderful...got enough for two?" He asked raising an eyebrow wishfully.

"There is plenty, would you like some eggs to go with it?" I asked.

"That'd be great Tom. I'll be back in a minute." He went off toward the bathroom as I started frying three eggs sunny side up in the fresh hot grease. Moments later he reappeared and sat down at the kitchen table in front of the big cup of coffee I had filled for him. He took a noisy sip and asked me how long I had been up. I answered that I woke up before eight, but the sound of the rain on the skylight put me right back to sleep until nine-fifteen. I plated his eggs, put five pieces of bacon next to them, and added four halves of whole grain wheat toast. When I got to the table he was poised like a cartoon character or a maybe a Viking with his fork held tightly in one fist and his knife in the other. I smiled knowing there was no image intended, and his posture was just his hunger's anticipation. His fork got busy immediately almost finishing one egg before I turned back to the stove. He really enjoys his food, especially breakfast. If he does leave all someone needs to do to attract him is to cook breakfast with a window open. The thought of Earl walking through a sunlit neighborhood somewhere in Florida with his nose in the air sniffing like a hound brought a smile to my face.

I finished cleaning the kitchen, and polished off my coffee. The day was the typical shade of gray that follows a November morning rain. I thought about what I might do today and my possibilities and excitement matched the lifelessness of the weather outside. Besides doing laundry, I guess it will be a day of football or National Geographic specials on Netflix. The relaxed mood is certainly not well suited for reading as that endeavor would most certainly turn into a nap.

I put a load of white clothes into the washer and the contents of the dryer in a laundry basket and headed towards the living room stopping long enough to check the thermostat in the foyer. I always get cold after I eat and this morning I felt colder than usual. I was right, I had not adjusted the temperature yet this morning and it was still set to the 62 degrees from last night. With a shudder I kicked it up to 68 and went in to sit down.

I was folding towels when Earl came in and announced if I needed him he would be in the shop for his morning smoke. I smiled as the door clicked shut. I never have thought about needing him until our recent conversations about his possible move. He doesn't contribute much around the house in the usual sense. He does do a few things, but most of that is because I have made something into a rule of the house. Like putting the paper back together so I can read it without spending an hour looking for all of the pages. Other than a couple of housekeeping chores his requirements are few. I have treated him more as a guest than someone who needs to earn his keep. Anything he adds by helping out I consider a bonus. I guess that having raised kids automatically engages the concept of communal responsibilities of those who stay for extended periods. So needing him in the sense of him shouldering his share of the household tasks has never been a real concern. I have discovered over time that I have grown accustomed to his company, his peculiar slant on life, and our deepening friendship.

I know I haven't asked too much of him, at least I hope I haven't. I have confidence that his decision to leave was not caused by what he might consider unreasonable demands. Sitting here and thinking of Earl out in the shop smoking alone makes me feel a bit guilty. Am I being too strict about where he must smoke? I dismissed that possibility immediately. No matter who might be staying here, cigar smoking in the house would be off limits. I mentally went through a quick list of people I would love to 'hang' with -- JFK, Jesus, Rod Stieger, Lincoln, Will Rodgers, Churchill, Willie Hoppe, Gandhi, Paul Newman,-- and none of those on that list would be smoking cigars in my house. Smiling, I thought I might make an exception for a young Sophia Loren.

There has to be a point where the comfort you want in your home supersedes that of ANY other person, (living or dead). Isn't that the point of having your own house? You make it fit your particular solace. People who twist their faces into a knot when they find out I have four cats miss that concept. They assume that somehow my extended family is an inconvenience to their capacity to visit me. I certainly will not herd the cats in their direction, but at the same time I will not apologize for their place in my home...our home. I concluded that I have been a good host to Earl. I have afforded him even more considerations and hospitality than I would extend to most guests. Having a clear conscience, however, will not fill the void when he leaves.

He came into the house, hung up his wool coat, and walked into the living room heading to his favorite chair. "How will he ever find another chair that will fit him so completely", I thought as I watched him preparing to lower himself into the waiting dimple of what has become his leather throne. He sat down in polite silence, as if my mindless magazine page-flipping required absolute quiet. I looked up as I tossed the magazine aside and said, "You know Earl I am going to really miss you when you leave." He crossed his legs and smiled back. "You'll always have my books to remember me by, or the smell of cigar smoke in your workshop," he said with his patented smirk. "I had Twain's books long before you came, but having Samuel Clemens of sorts here in the flesh was so much more than just reading his writings. I want you to know that seeing you leave will be tough. I just hope that your stay has been a comfortable one. I would hate to think that your leaving has anything to do with a lack of hospitality from me."

"On the contrary, Tom, I want to leave while we still are such good friends. I don't want to leave quickly like I did from Oak Park," he said with a devilish chuckle. "You have been a good friend and I want to keep it that way. Now, that isn't to say that if I were to stay another few months that we would be rolling around in the street tugging at each other's hair like pubescent boys, but I need to move occasionally and now that the weather is getting frightfully cold, it seems like a good time to do that", he said trailing off a bit on his last few words. "And, he quickly added," I sure ain't gonna spend another winter anywhere that is like last year's in Chicago. If hell is cold instead of hot you can bet that Lucifer himself built a house on the east side of Chicago right next to Lake Michigan."

I was feeling better that I was not part of his decision to leave Ohio for Florida when he said, "In one way you are a bit responsible for my leaving." I looked up quickly locking my eyes to his. "Really, what did I do?" I asked in complete shock. "You have gotten to know me to the point that you are no longer in awe of my status or celebrity. You know me now as a friend and while you always treat me with respect you rarely become slack-jawed by any of my utterances like you did when I first arrived". I sat there for a second deciding how much guilt I deserve to digest from his admonishment when he continued; "As you pointed out the other day I live for the limelight. Not that it brings that much joy to me directly, but because people need to meet me. To reach out and touch the hem of my notoriety might be the only real thrill they ever will have in their modest lifetime. My talent should not be shared with just one man in Ohio no matter how nice or engaging he might be. I owe myself to the world. Like the Bible says, 'don't hide your light under a basket'. To keep all of my humor and insight between just you and me would be so selfish, don't you agree?"

I was able to stammer out a, "ah well....of course!"

"So you see Tom it isn't so much about leaving here as it is about continuing on," he added. "I must travel to where people are anxiously waiting to meet someone of my standing, to relish greatness in person. To experience first-hand why Mark Twain is the greatest author who ever lived is something no person should be deprived of. My duty to these people sits high above my own desires. After considering what you said previously I am firmly convinced that being recognized will never be a problem for 'The Earl of Prose'.

I wondered for a moment if Earl's portrayal had not far exceeded Mark Twain's infamous ego and self-importance. Who is he convincing here, me or him? Surprised by Earl's over-the-top grandiosity I sarcastically said, "I can only assume that inside your head it has to be a quiet and desolate place sometimes with no equal to talk to." Obviously missing my meaning or perhaps ignoring it he pursed his lips and shook his head side to side slowly and said in complete Twain believability and seriousness:

"Be good & you will be lonesome." ~MT 1897~

This was another time when his quoted response did not exactly fit the subject discussed. He seemed to hurriedly pull something out of the air in order to stop the conversation. He is going to leave, of that I am sure, but the impending weather or those pretentious reasons he so easily spouted is not the whole story. There is much more than he is telling.

Tougher than an Oyster Shell

My Thanksgivings have started and ended the same way for years. First I enjoy my morning coffee watching the Macy's Parade from New York, then a fine meal with my family, a few hands of Hearts or Euchre during the Detroit Lions football game and then some overloaded sugary desert and the return back home to uncontrollably fall asleep before ten. Of course Earl has no clue that my ritual is iron-clad, but as soon as he has breakfast I instruct him on what to expect for the remainder of the day. He didn't react one way or the other, so I assumed all my plans were acceptable or at least endurable.

He said he actually has seen the Thanksgiving Day Parade several times and would enjoy watching it as long as he could also read during the broadcast. He was also affable about the exodus to my son's house for the family meal. The only thing that agitated him was that there was also no inside smoking area at my boy's house. To enjoy his cigar, he had to stand on the open porch in the cold. Needless-to-say he didn't smoke much. He enjoyed the home-brewed beer, surprisingly was helpful when it came time to clear the table, and joined right in the annual card game ritual. He seemed to be right at home with all of us and even a couple of times paused to watch football on TV. There were a few times however, when his familiar accent was less apparent and his normally bold speaking tone was prominently subdued. Perhaps he was dropping his guard, or feeling lonely about leaving. In either case it was conspicuous, but not so much that that it required more than a briefly raised eyebrow, and only by me.

[276]

When we finally arrived home around nine we were both tired but not ready to call it a day. As I found places in the refrigerator for the leftover goodies I brought home, Earl settled into his usual seat in the living room. When I came back into the foyer and with a shiver I turned the thermostat back up to 68. I opened the door for my anxious dog and went out with her to make sure she didn't get distracted from her bodily function and run into the woods. The air was brisk and had a hint of winter in its smell. I am not mentally prepared for another winter, but what choice do I have but to embrace it. Cali ran in circles looking for that perfect spot as I lied to myself about how many fun things there are do while trapped inside for four months. Now that I have this long journal detailing Earl's stay maybe I can organize it into something readable. Standing there at the edge of the backyard, with the trees bare of leaves, and seeing my breath didn't allow me to get too excited about any winter prospect. The dog trotted back and we walked back into the cozy warmth of the house, one of us relieved, the other obsessing over the impending cold.

Earl had the newspaper open in his lap with all of the Black Friday sales ads scattered around his feet when I stepped over them and took my seat. I have learned that if I want to know something that he isn't exactly ready to tell me, I should ask while he's reading. He is more apt to let something out while concentrating on something he is engrossed in. It's similar to when I was young and asking my mother for something while she was talking or better yet laughing on the telephone. It usually works with Earl, but I don't use the ploy so frequently as to make it too easy to recognize.

Today was different. Earl would be leaving soon and I had enough questions that I could put him in a room with a single bulb hanging from the ceiling and grill him for hours slapping a rubber hose against my palm. My time to find out the truth was running short and if I was going to solve his mystery I better get busy.

"Earl, I noticed a few times today when you appeared a little less like Mark Twain than usual. You know...I mean less like yourself... but him too. Do you know what I am trying to say?" I asked.

He slowly put his paper down and without smiling he turned towards me and said. "I know what you are trying to say Tom, but I think you just haven't ascertained my many moods. You rarely have seen me in family situations and my behavior is certainly different when surrounded by a man and his children. Were you expecting me to swear and incite some sort of mayhem? I can be a thoughtful guest on occasion you know." He said with a small sarcastic smile.

Oh great, now I've done it. I have upset him and he is perturbed with me, but I carefully push on. "I am not talking so much about your behavior as I am your personality. There were a few times when I thought I saw someone else besides Mark Twain in front of me. When we were all watching football right after halftime it seemed that there was someone else in the room with us. I don't know, I probably shouldn't have brought it up, but I had a definite feeling that Twain went away for awhile."

There was a short pause and then he said in voice I seldom have heard, "You know I am not Mark Twain and surely the real me slipping to the surface to take a breath like a breaching whale at times should not surprise you or cause you to comment about it. Please know that there will be a time and a place when this all adds up for you, but for now can we please just drop it. It has been a great day with you and your family...Tom let's not spoil it."

Having heard his every word I sat there feeling at fault that my curiosity possibly jeopardized an otherwise perfect day with my friend, but his admonishment revealed again evidence of the pain that he's carrying somewhere under Twain's convincing façade.

I added, "You know Earl, you are right. Please forget that I asked, but know that I ask for all the right reasons. I know there is someone there that I never see except for a few fleeting moments and I can't stop myself from responding when it looks like who I am seeing is hurting somehow. I have learned several times in my life that a problem shared is easier to bear." (*I paused a moment to allow my words to sink in*) "My curiosity isn't just me being nosey. It is just when I see pain in someone that I care about I cannot stop myself from trying to help. Perhaps I dig too deeply at times, and while my questions possibly appear as just more annoying probes, there is a caring friend behind it all." Not wanting to be scolded a second time, I stood up to leave the room.

Earl sat there very still looking straight ahead as if lost in my sentiments or searching for his own. Finally he looked up and slowly turned to face me. "You know that Twain had words at the ready for every situation. No matter how solemn or joyous the occasion he never was without a snappy comeback. Living in his life for so long I have realized that there were times when he, too, wasn't himself. When losing his businesses, his fortune, his children, and his lovely wife, he didn't always have the proper words to express the depth of his despair or sorrow at those exact moments. Only later could he revisit his feelings and put into words exactly how he felt. So today was a day when reflecting on times with family caused us both to react differently than what each of us are used to. I know that you care, and I also know that you fancy yourself as someone who can

[278]

always find the truth no matter how well it is hidden, but I humbly ask you to be patient with me."

I felt like I had hurt him. I knew what he is saying was right; I do pride myself in discovering the truth even when everyone else gives up. He is a friend and I have used that closeness at times to try to push into his past. I felt awful and while I stood there feeling sorry for being found out and being so insensitive, he looked back towards me with a softened look.

"You know if Twain himself were here he would obviously have something to say to finalize this moment. He would look you in the eye much the way I am doing now and say something to put an end to this conversation and move on to the next. Imagine that Earl has lost something to cause his mood to become dark and reflective and then Twain breaks the silence talking mostly for Earl's benefit."

"Don't part with your illusions. When they are gone you may still exist, but you have ceased to live." ~MT 1897~

When he finished his mouth curled into a small friendly and familiar Twain smile and he picked up the paper, opened it, and resumed reading as if none of that conversation had ever taken place.

Green Umbrellas

I have been so busy with my new job, preparing for Christmas, etc. that I haven't had much time to focus on Earl's comings and goings. Maybe that is a good thing. He is obviously researching a trip, but he hasn't made any attention-grabbing preparations to actually leave. I assume he will not simply slip out while I am sleeping. A farewell with some degree of fanfare and sadness most likely is what he wants and expects. A long ceremonious goodbye fits perfectly with everything I know about Twain's flair for the dramatic. It will indeed be sad when he finally leaves, but in our talks he promises to write frequently or sometimes call. It won't be the same as having him sitting there in the leather 'throne' or in the wicker chair he fits so well on the porch, but at least we will still connect occasionally. The idea of his eventual migration feels like when each of my sons moved out. They were staying in Bowling Green, at least, so their leaving wasn't that difficult to accept. When Earl leaves I know it will feel like goodbye regardless of any promises of continued contact by either of us.

While we finished our coffee in the kitchen I recalled the few times I had been to Florida and the things I most enjoyed there. While it is a piece of the United States, there are parts that look so foreign to me. Walking along the beach in some areas has a feel I would expect on the French Riviera, Spain or Brazil. Since I have lived much of my life in the farmlands of Ohio, Florida feels too exotic to actually be American.

I sounded like I was channelling Rick Steves when I said:

"The one thing about Florida that fascinates me most is the Palm trees, especially the Royal Palm which grows really tall. The dead fronds need to be trimmed at least once a year and the trees that are very tall need a professional in a lift truck to do it. It is an expensive to have perfectly manicured Royal Palm trees." I continued, "The first time I visited Florida and pulled into the drive of the people I was staying with I assumed they were rich because they had three small palm trees in their front yard. It took me only a few minutes to realize that they were not rich and that every part of town, even the slums, had palm trees planted everywhere. Their height or their grooming might indicate wealth, but just having a palm tree in your yard isn't the same as having a Mercedes in your garage," I said. Earl laughed and said, "Seeing any palm tree regardless of its grooming would be a welcome sight after seeing the gray trees here looking like wretched skeletons with broken arms. The idea of leaning against a palm tree and, tipping my shoes up, and watching white sand pour out is tantalizing after walking through freezing snow for six months last year in Illinois," he said with his eyes wide and a smile emblazoned on his face.

I asked him where he might be going in Florida, and he answered, "It is a toss-up between The Keys or someplace on the Gulf side. The Keys might be better for a freer thinking citizenry, but seeing the sunset over the Gulf really appeals to me, too. I might just take the train as far as Jacksonville and then decide which way to go."

Only having spent time on the gulf side I can attest to its beauty, but I know Earl well enough to know that the atmosphere in Key West would suit his character and need for attention better than the laid-back west coast of the Gulf.

"I personally can see you fitting in better in Key West than with the retirees on the Gulf side. Also, being at the very tip of Florida you WILL see the sun set over the Gulf. The carnival atmosphere, the drinking, the parties, and the endless supply of admiring ladies from the north would suit you. Not to mention that Earnest Hemingway made Key West his home so it is writer friendly," I said. He slowly turned toward me and raising his right eyebrow he said, "Do you actually think Hemingway and I are alike? Over the years I have read his sad little books, and while I find them somewhat interesting I surely wouldn't put the writings of the two of us on the same side of the library. So, do not think that walking

[280]

through his haunts in Florida is somehow going to give me great comfort as if I am in the company of some imagined contemporary."

I sat there for a minute realizing that I had thrown down some imagined gauntlet before adding, "Maybe Hemingway's notoriety occurred because there was no one else there to contest his worth. He **WAS** the only resident celebrity of Key West at the time. Wouldn't it be intriguing to see how the people there today would receive the great Mark Twain?"

He thought for a moment twirling the end of Mark Twain's mustache with his right forefinger and thumb. "I certainly owe it to the good people there to find out. You have helped me to make up my mind, Tom. I had been leaning towards Key West but needed a nudge, thank you!" He said with a relieved smile.

"Well you can bet that there will be plenty of palm trees blowing in the breezes there", I said.

After a moment of percolating silence he said: "A palm tree....

"Nature's imitation of an umbrella that has been out to see what a cyclone is like and is trying not to look disappointed." ~MT 1897~

It's Official

This morning I received the news. Earl is leaving on December 26. He prefaced his announcement by saying that he wanted to be with my family for Christmas. Knowing how he feels about religion and church affairs this is both a personal sacrifice as well as a pleasant time spent with those he has grown to care about.

The reality of him being here for Christmas day gives me a chance to buy him a meaningful gift to take with him on his journey. I thought of something I saw at the store the other day that I think might suit him. There is retro looking luggage that is made of heavy aged canvas with two leather straps that buckle across the sides. It has a heavy duty, rounded arched leather handle on the top and an inconspicuous slide-out leather-wrapped handle that telescopes from inside and allows you to pull it along on wheels. It is discreetly modern in function but old-looking with its leather-reinforced corners and aged-looking brass hardware. The suitcase he struggles with now is falling apart, the hinges are broken, and the remaining stitching is coming undone. I'll have to think this over carefully as I know that the suitcase he uses now is period correct. Except for the wheels I think this new bag would blend into his character perfectly, but that is my 21st century opinion.

[281]

The morning is dim and the only light in the living room is vaguely streaming from the lamp in the foyer as I settled into my 'spot' on the couch. At first glance it is difficult to see the black cat stretched out next to Earl's leg in the black chair until Lalo blinks and those two yellow circles appear like the invisible Cheshire. "I am going to miss this cat." he said petting the purring body gently with his left hand. "Any chance I could sneak him into my bag when I leave?" he said with a wry smile.

"You can try but I'll bet he wouldn't be a very good traveler, and I would hate to see what he might leave in there for you to find when you open it." He laughed and said, "You are probably right, but I sure am going to miss this guy. Even with my occasional torture of cigar smoke he has proven his loyalty by comforting me each day with his sleek warm body. I have a hunch he will miss me too, probably as much as any human he has ever known."

Without becoming dreary I told him that he is always welcome to visit and stay as long as he might wish. I added, "That is assuming F. Scott Fitzgerald or Walt Whitman isn't staying here at the time," I said with a bit of sarcasm and a laugh. Earl turned his attention from the kitty and scowled at me and then curled his mouth into a submissive embarrassed smile. "That was good Tom...that **was** good".

After both of our chuckles faded I said casually, "It really will be different around here without you. I was hoping before you left, you know… to find out more about who you were before you became Mark Twain." A long silence ensued. The room seemed to get even darker and the air somewhat colder. It felt a bit like a thriller movie the moment before something bad was about to happen.

"Earl turned slowly towards me as he always does for emphasis, and with his face tightened into a scowl he said firmly, "This **again**? Is that so damned important to you? The fact that I am completely Mark Twain in every respect isn't enough for you? I am Mark Twain, Tom. That's who I am today and who I'll be tomorrow whether I am here, in Florida, or Timbuktu. Who I might have been in another life isn't important anymore. Your occasional inquiries, while normal I guess, are, quite frankly, irritating."

I reeled back and thought about what possessed me to ask in the first place, but as usual I mentally lowered my shoulder and pressed on. "Just know that you are a living anachronism. You are a buckboard traveling down a road with modern day cars and trucks. If you think you will quietly slip into Florida without anyone noticing that you are from the 19th century and are 180-years old, you are sadly mistaken. Then that is the whole point, isn't it? To be noticed and adored for the person Mark Twain was during his lifetime? (*I paused briefly*)... I did not intend to irritate you or to dig deeper than you think I should, but please put yourself in my position for a moment. Here I am living in 2014 and suddenly while at a coffee shop there appears a man claiming to be from the 1800s. That isn't something that happens frequently to someone and to not be curious to the point of asking questions to make sense out of it would make me a complete idiot. If a meteor in the shape of George Washington fell through your roof back in Hannibal, Missouri would you just whistle and walk past it? You created this mystery here Earl, not me. If you were just an average guy I might meet on the street I wouldn't be wondering about your past life, at least until we became friends. I would wait for you to share what you felt you wanted to share. I would naturally be more patient if this was a typical circumstance, but it isn't normal. My God man, you are Mark Twain!"

He sat there without moving or looking at me. "He is still annoyed with me," I thought. After a couple very tension-filled minutes he said quietly, "I guess you are right. The attention I bring on myself induces this intrigue. Maybe that is part of why I try to be so real to everyone. So I will never stop being Samuel Clemens long enough for anyone else to emerge. Tom, I have to be who I have become; it is all that I have. Perhaps that is why I keep moving around the country so I can find new people who will be satisfied with just having Mark Twain in their lives. I know that you mean well and that your questions are not wholly out of curiosity. We have become friends and friends always want to know more about each other. Just know one thing. Who I am today has brought more joy and comfort to so many, including myself, that I could never be anyone other than who I have become. Can we just leave it at that?" Sinking back into the black leather silently resembled what a deep sigh might look like if it collapsed into a chair.

Watching him while he spoke I could see some pain revealed in a way he has not shown before. Even his voice sounded a different. For a moment I think he was not talking to me as Mark Twain, but the person he has deserted so deeply inside of that famous character. It was more of the small shard I suspected I saw on Thanksgiving. On one hand I felt ashamed for pushing him to this point, but also felt somewhat privileged that he let me in more than ever before.

I paused a minute before softly saying, "I just care about whoever you are Earl. I have shared so much of who I am with you and was hoping that maybe one day you might let me see more of who YOU are as well. I know much about Mark Twain by reading his works, other people's accounts, and now 'his' long stay with me. Someday maybe you will trust me enough to open the curtain wide enough for me to see the real you. Neither of us is perfect, we each have led lives that we sometimes regret, but for now I'll drop the whole thing. You are my guest, Mark Twain, and until you leave later this month, we are going to have some fun. If you ever want to reveal anything to me, just know that I care and can be trusted with whatever you care to share."

His kind eyes were thoughtfully focused on mine as he spoke. "If I ever decide to open the Pandora's Box that holds my past, I will find you, Tom, and I'll share its contents with you. I know that there is nothing in your curiosity that is mean-spirited. You care about me...the real me and that means more than you know. I'll keep a tight lid on that for the moment and just keep doing what has become so familiar and comfortable. Thank you my friend."

As he got up from the chair with one final pat for Lalo with his left hand he faced me, grabbed his lapel with his right hand, and returning to his best Mark Twain voice and stance he said:

"Truth is the most valuable thing we have. Let us economize it." ~MT 1897~

A Circle of Warmth

Now that Earl's leaving is definitely a reality I have being thinking more about how we should spend the time that is left. Our last conversation was tense in the beginning, but by the end of our exchange I felt better for having the talk that I had been pushing for. That isn't to say that I am any less curious about what preceded his conversion into Twain, I am just not going to ask him anymore about it. The couple of weeks that are left here in Ohio will be mostly about whatever he wants to do. I want his send-off to appropriately illustrate that he is going to be sincerely missed no matter who he really is.

Having my own Children and looking forward to the Christmas season with them is so much a part of my life. When I was young and growing up with my mother, two brothers, and my sister all of my holiday activities were centered on family and home. That was of course true throughout the year, but especially during holiday celebrations when everyone was so much more affectionate to each other. Looking back on my childhood, Thanksgiving and Christmas were the two times of the year when I felt equal to every other kid that I knew. I did envy the amount of toys the richer children my age received, but I was also very thankful for the gifts that I opened excitedly on Christmas morning and the open expression of love I felt from my siblings even if it would only last for that one day.

Later on, when I started to raise a family of my own and shopped for Christmas gifts for my children I felt the hardship that my widowed mother must have endured when adding up costs of being an effective Santa Claus. Christmas to her was expenditures that she could barely afford, but through her savvy spending we never went without a proper celebration. Christmas was especially hard for her emotionally as well. My parents were married on Christmas day and doing all the things alone to prepare for what should have been a doubly great holiday for her always brought some sadness. She was able to hide it very well from us children, but as we grew up we would sometimes catch her standing at the sink wiping her eyes on Christmas day. Even though things were tough for her she made Christmas the same special day that every child starts to dream of once the days get shorter and the air gets chilly. There were several Christmases that I remember when we had someone come and share the day with us as they were going to be alone and without family. Those were special days that bring to mind the true meaning of Christmas and sharing with others.

Thinking about the day I accidentally saw the box of pictures Earl quickly tried to shuffle from view, reminded me that Earl has or had a family, too. His being here as Mark Twain obscures that sometimes, but it is very evident from little hints he has given that somewhere, at one point in time, he had a loving family, and maybe a wife. Knowing how I feel about my own family made me ache thinking what he might be feeling during Christmas without those he loves surrounding him. With that in mind I am determined to have a great family holiday and send him into the land of coconuts and palm trees with a smile on his face and maybe a new suitcase rolling at his heels.

He was sitting in his usual spot with his "friend" sprawled on his lap when I walked into the living room. I told him that my son Chris has graciously offered his home to have Christmas again this year and wanted me to make sure Earl knew he was invited to join us. "Well, that is mighty nice of him", he said. "I like that boy Tom. Actually I like all of your boys; they all are so damn intelligent. Where do they get that?" he said with a chuckle.

"From their mother to be sure. My gift to them was brown eyes and bad habits", I said.

"No doubt...no doubt." He said with a chuckle. "Please let him know that I would not miss spending Christmas day with all of you for the world and thanks so much for including me."

"You know, Chris has really been trying to make that house into a nice home since he bought it from my mother in law's estate." I said. "I don't think it was the house he would have necessarily picked out for himself, but he has adapted to it well knowing that it made a great investment, and of course holds so many memories of his time with his grandmother. It has been a few years since my mother in law moved into a assisted living facility, but Chris has been able to keep the warm family feeling there that we all have enjoyed over the years. Christmas there will feel good and natural even though we sadly will not have Grandma hosting like she always did. We are, however, excited that you will be there to share the day with us. It'll be a lot of fun for sure."

Earl was looking at me when I finished my sentence and he lowered his head towards Lalo lying across his legs and as he was petting him slowly, he said, "Love these times you are having Tom. Embrace them. Wrap your arms around each moment and each person you love and put them into your heart forever. There is nothing, and I mean nothing on this planet that is worth more than hearth and home". (*After a pause*) He slowly raised his head and looking blankly toward the curtained window and he quoted in true theatrical fashion the following statement. I could tell that it was memorized, rehearsed, and undoubtedly spoken many times before, but the tear at the corner of his eye was most likely a new addition, but unquestionably just as genuine as the meaning of Twain's words.

"There is a trick about an American house that is like the deep-lying untranslatable idioms of a foreign language—a trick uncatchable by the stranger, a trick incommunicable and indescribable; whatever it is, is just the something that gives the home look and home feeling to an American house and makes it the most satisfying refuge yet invented by men—and women, mainly women." ~MT 1892~

Impending Joy

I was working in the shop yesterday on a Christmas gift I am making for the wife of a good friend when out of the corner of my eye I saw the door open. Earl was standing there in his wool coat, cigar in his mouth, and wearing a red and black plaid Elmer Fudd fleece lined hat. I turned off the saw, muted the sound on the MP3 player with a remote control, and while smiling at him I asked what he needed. He asked if I was planning to go downtown, or was I going to work in the shop all day. I answered that I hadn't planned on it, but if he needed a ride I would gladly take him. He nodded and then said, "I would really appreciate that, I have some things I need to get." He said he would be outside smoking his cigar when I was ready to leave. "No hurry Tom. I just want to have a few hours to look around and with a bit of luck find some things. I'll catch a ride home, or maybe walk, so don't worry about that."

I completed cutting the final strip of Walnut that I needed to edge-glue to an exotic African wood to make the two-tone sides of the gift. I readied the clamps spread the glue on the edges of the pieces and clamped them tightly. It was a perfect time to stop. As I stepped into a sunny Sunday, Earl was just finishing his smoke. He looked up with a quick smile and said, "I really appreciate this, Tom." I said that I was glad to oblige, started the car with the remote start to warm up and told him I just needed to wash my hands and grab a Pepsi. I brushed the sawdust off the knees of my jeans and headed into the house.

I dropped Earl at the back door of "Grounds for Thought" knowing that all 'downtown' things for him start from there. He got out, thanked me, and disappeared into the rear door of the coffee shop.

Driving back home, I mused about him shopping. Does he mentally stay in character all of the time? When he sees something that undoubtedly would be "new-fangled" for Mark Twain, does he act surprised and/ or confused to maintain his charade? It must be exhausting to assess and react to everything based on the year it was produced. If a clerk were to be nearby when he discovered something 'new' would he feel it necessary to jump back in amazement, perhaps even grasping his chest with surprise? Does he react with astonishment to modern things even without any spectators just to stay 'true' to the character, and in practice? He has obviously seen many new things during his travels portraying Mark Twain. So where does he draw the line for the casual observer? Does he need to be stunned by everything new? When does he need to act surprised, and how does he explain his comfort with modern things to people who don't know that he has been living in the present for decades?

Whatever caused him to completely plunge himself into the character of Mark Twain had to be pretty remarkable for him to consistently go to such trouble. Portraying a person for a role in a movie or a play would be much easier I imagine. At the end of the day you could go back to being yourself or at least until the end of the play or movie. Earl can only be himself in his mind or when he is entirely alone. The rest of the time he must be someone else convincing in his look, speech, and every slight nuance of behavior that Twain undoubtedly would possess. One minute he is in his room being himself and then by the mere turning of the doorknob and the latching of the door he emerges as another man. It is dizzying trying to imagine what that must be like for him. Whatever the reason, he clearly feels that Mark Twain is who he wants to be.

I returned to the shop to check on my glued pieces that were clamped and drying. I was still thinking of Earl doing his Christmas shopping as Mark Twain. Since he's wearing that coat and ridiculous hat, he might not be recognized. He certainly doesn't look like any picture I have ever seen of Samuel Clemens. His hair is almost completely hidden making his face look much rounder than it actually is and his coat covers his white uniform, both of which would make him instantly recognizable. While shopping, perhaps he can escape from what presumably is an energy-draining practice and just be himself for a couple of hours. But what is the point of becoming someone else if you disguise that identity? As each day passes, my curiosity increases as to why he **has** to be Mark Twain with me. I wouldn't know his true identity if he was Arthur McGillacutty, John Smith, or Harvey Fartz. He could make up any name, but still be himself. Hiding in Twain's ego-laden limelight doesn't seem logical, but then what about this whole thing is logical? Will I ever know who the 'Earl of Prose' actually is and why he chose the path of deception that he did? *sigh*

Hours later, I had regained my full working momentum when the door opened. There stood Earl wearing everything from before, but with a huge added grin. "Can I come in? Are you in the middle of something or can you take a minute to see what I bought?" He eagerly asked. I motioned him in and he walked over carrying a few bags and set them on a small bare spot on the bench. He began opening them with great excitement. "I got this for Seth. It is a tablature book of Eric Clapton's most famous songs. See here, (pointing), here is Layla, Bell Bottom Blues, Cocaine, and all of his material from when he was in Cream." He said, turning the pages faster than I could focus on them. "And here is what I got for Daniel...(pulling from another bag a book with a black and white cover with a picture of the Golden Gate Bridge), the collected works of the 'beat' poets of the 50's Kerouac, Ferlingghetti, Ginsberg, Corso, and Orlovsky." Wrestling with yet another bag he produced a large book with a magician's flair. "Check this out, Tom". He said with his eyes wide. Holding a coffee table book entitled 'Modern Warfare' up to his shoulder like a TV model. "This is what I bought for Chris. Do you think he'll like it?"

Still trying to imagine Mark Twain actually saying "Check this out," or ..."when he was in Cream," I nodded and said, "You really found some great gifts. Where is mine?" I said with an exaggerated pout. "All in good time Tom...all in good time". He answered with a sly grin that he tried unsuccessfully to hide behind his mustache.

"So you think I have done okay for each of them?" I told him that he without a doubt hit upon something they each would really enjoy. He added that he would write something to each of them on the inside. I said that they would enjoy having that nice touch as well. In the few times he has spent with them, he certainly has a deep understanding of what interests each of them. They all eventually embraced him even though, in the beginning, they were somewhat suspicious of his motives for hiding himself behind a long-dead famous writer. They are young so everything old is somewhat odd of course, but if he's a friend of mine he must be okay. His gifts for them, however, will be received graciously and without distrust. They each assume that he is a good person whoever he is, and buying them gifts is unquestionably a heartfelt gesture of kindness and affection.

"So you didn't make it past the bookstore?" I asked. "I had no intention of going anywhere else. A book is the best gift in the world. It'll take you to places only the Wright Brothers could dream of." He said putting the gifts back into their bags.

"I get it, you love books, but do you have any favorites?" I asked innocently. He sat the bags down carefully and with his eyes full of the usual glimmer when he is about to say something that will delight himself and probably everyone else within earshot he said:

"My favorites are; Joan of Arc; The Prince and Pauper; Huck Finn; Tom Sawyer."
~MT 1908~

He left the shop and as the door closed and he disappeared from the window I thought of how wonderful this Christmas is going to be. This will be another time that the Lamberts will again share a holiday with someone who otherwise might be alone.

Christmas Indeed

Christmas morning arrived without snow, a cookie plate left with crumbs, or an unfinished glass of milk sitting near the Christmas tree. Actually it was a slow start compared to the Christmas mornings when there were three young boys living in the house. Earl was the first one up and was making coffee when I

[289]

entered the kitchen around 7:15. We didn't need to be at my son's until ten-thirty so there was plenty of time to have a leisurely cup of coffee before we needed to leave.

It was the day before he leaves for Florida, but that fact would be temporarily overshadowed since it was Christmas morning and my emotions needed to center elsewhere. The keenness of seeing everyone's reactions to the gifts bought and given would leave little room for melancholy or pensive reflection. This is one day when nothing should interfere with or snatch away the feelings that took a year to plan, anticipate, and finally experience. I will deal with a myriad of emotions that tomorrow will inevitably bring when I leave him at the train station in Toledo.

Earl and I quietly shared a bagel knowing that we would be having a fine brunch in a couple of hours. As we sat enjoying our coffee he broke the stillness, "So, are you going to miss me when I'm gone?" I sat there quietly for a long time before launching into something I had written and rehearsed. "Earl, have you ever had a toothache?" I finally asked.

"Well of course I have…why?" He said surprised.

I secretly smiled seeing the annoyance etched on his face, no doubt assuming I was equating his departure to a toothache finally going away.

"Well, Earl, when one first encounters tooth pain it seems that it will last forever. And sometimes when the intensity subsides slightly you still have that nagging sensation that it will be around for a long time with its lingering ache. My entire life hasn't been a toothache exactly, but there has been a part of it that hasn't overflowed with creative delight until you showed-up. For many years I had this twinge to rub elbows with writers or artists. I hoped that through sheer osmosis, it might inspire me to return to something I once truly loved. So when you came along I felt a strong compulsion to start writing again -- and with more dedication and excitement than ever before. Your leaving tomorrow doesn't imply that the pain will return, quite the contrary. By being here as Mark Twain you have stretched me to a point that I can never go back to where I was before. I will continue to write regardless of the quality or quantity because it satisfies a need in me to create in a way that nothing else ever has. Not even working with wood, which you know I love, gives me the thrill of pulling something out of thin air and giving it life. So you weren't the toothache Earl, you were the medicine."

Living With Earl

He sat there looking at me while slowly wiping his mouth with his napkin. Laying it carefully over his plate he looked up with that rare yielding gaze that I feel emanates from the person inside and said, "You have given me inspiration, too, my friend. You have taught me to laugh at myself and to move forward when, occasionally, I am wrong. Your ability to swallow hard and admit your transgressions has given me more humility than I already had and certainly more than I needed." He said with a hearty Mark Twain laugh. Pausing for a minute allowing some seriousness to return along with a sensitive glance toward me he added. "Actually though being here with you for all of these months have given me perception into things I frankly didn't feel I needed to examine. At some point even Mark Twain, or perhaps a person being Mark Twain, may need to look at things pointed out by someone who is more objective than that person might be able to be, since he is all wrapped up in his own affairs. My ability to be a convincing Mark Twain doesn't totally stop me from thinking about who I was before. You have shown me that being exactly who you are is not a terrible thing. You are not exactly a simple man, Tom, but you do your best to keep life uncomplicated. You are always yourself regardless of what you might be feeling inside. I probably never will totally master that approach to living, but I have picked up enough of it from you to look forward to a day that maybe I can be myself both privately and publicly."

I was touched and surprised by his candor. Of course he would feel obliged to say something complimentary or at least pleasant before leaving after all this time enjoying my space and hospitality. His sliver of self-disclosure was so much more revealing than any before and certainly more than I expected or was trolling for. I presume that within my sometimes rigid, but always accommodating generosity and my probing questions, I have touched his heart to the point that he has lowered his guard a smidgen. Although he always assumes an intellectual level far above mine when in character, there are other times when I feel that we are totally equal and on the same emotional level. Through my gentle advice and objective counsel I may have successfully reached a besieged soul eager to be more than another man's shadow.

While I cleaned up the kitchen and readied the food I was taking for our Christmas meal, I couldn't help but ponder his reasons for leaving. I was not prepared to imagine how I will feel when I sit down to coffee in an empty house. I was not concerned about *who* he wants to portray; that's his business. And, being Mark Twain is how he ended up at my house in the first place. He clearly isn't a famous person, although he is incredibly talented and compellingly plays one. I doubt he's a criminal avoiding detection, or merely a Clemens wannabe searching for fame by playing the part. Rather I see a tormented man haunted by something that eight months of living in close proximity with me didn't reveal. I cannot imagine anything so agonizing that could force me to become another person so entirely that I would willingly give up ties to my family, my friends, and everything that has taken me a lifetime to become. To live in a self-imposed and sometimes emotionally land-locked exile of a long dead and sometimes troubled writer is disconcerting to imagine.

When we talk I always experience Earl's Twain in the words he uses or the phrases he quotes, but underneath there is a glint of someone else who has become more apparent with each passing day. The mid-west winter weather gives him a great excuse, but clearly there are other reasons why tomorrow will be his last day in my house.

I have been trying to convey to him subliminally during these last few months that he, (the person behind the white suit), deserves to be happy. Twain had his life, now Earl, (whoever he is), has his and it should be a happy one. At least it should be authentic. Vicariously living through Samuel Clements might afford a safe haven temporarily, but at the end of the day -- when he is all alone in his room with no one to convince or entertain; -- Earl's happiness should reside in his own heart and mind. When the day comes to shovel the dirt back into the ground, Earl needs to know that he will be the only person in the box. It will just be him and his headstone will not read "Samuel Clemens."

Looking at him now I wonder about all of the Christmases Earl spent before becoming Twain. What were they like? When did he abandon his 'real' life and adopt another that was more attractive to him than his own? I imagine that his memory is a crowded and likely a tortured place to visit. Trying to juggle all the details in order to be two people would be such an exhausting endeavor. Isolating one from the other would be like picking the fly specks out of pepper.

I look at Earl and I always see Twain first, but that is the outside, the costume, the performance. As I packed the food and got dressed, my mind filled with thoughts of him, his reasons for doing this and that, and of course his leaving. I eventually returned my focus on enjoying a lovely Christmas day with my family and my first and last one with Mark Twain.

We gathered up the gifts and food, and loaded the warming car almost to the roof with Christmas goodies, and eagerly headed out to see my family. There were very few cars on the road giving pause to note that everyone was probably either with relatives or friends or on their way. I think about people who have no one and instantly become more thankful for what I have. I felt joyful that Earl would be surrounded by my family today, and not alone somewhere feeling who knows what.

I pulled into the drive and the boys came out to give us a hand. Earl emphatically declined help with the gifts he had carried on his lap as if by being held their contents could easily be exposed. Once into the inviting warm house, complete with the smell of fresh evergreen, each of my sons gave me a huge hug. There is never any bashfulness about showing how much we love each other. Open display of affection is one thing that we have shared since they were small boys. I love it. Earl received several warm two-hand handshakes as we hung our coats and hats, put the gifts near the tree, and took the food into the kitchen. Almost immediately we all took a place at the table as the steaming food was being set out. There was a din of talking and laughter, when without direction, we all became silent at exactly the same time. We stood around the table holding hands and said a prayer together. I stole a glance at Earl to see his reaction knowing how Twain felt about praying, but he looked unaffected. We had a great breakfast casserole with sausage, potatoes, eggs, and covered with lots of cheddar cheese. Fresh fruit, cinnamon rolls, and gourmet coffee rounded out the meal as we laughed and ate quickly anticipating what was to come, but not so fast as to not savor the delicious meal and the warmth of the moment. We abandoned the dishes and the food on the table and exited to the living room where the huge eight-foot Christmas tree nearly reached the ceiling. Finding comfortable spots we all decided that Christopher as our host, and as such, should play Santa and hand out the gifts. There was much mayhem with gifts being opened here, there, and just seconds apart. It was impossible to fully see everything each person was receiving. In other words, it was typical.

When all the gifts from the family had been exchanged and the air in the room relaxed Earl stood, grabbed a lapel with his left hand and said, "I have something for each of you, but before I give them to you I want to say a few words."

"Well of course you do", I said smiling.

He affectionately shot a mock sneer at me, and then continued in his best Missouri drawl. "When I came here last March I didn't know anyone, but that quickly changed. I met some great college students who took me in and almost killed me with their kindness and their endless supply of alcohol. Then I came to stay with Tom and I slowly got to know each of you and that has been a most wonderful experience." With this he cleared his throat and dabbed at his right

[293]

eye discreetly with his right forefinger. "What I am trying to say with a bit of difficulty is that knowing Tom and all of you has been great and…(his voice now quaking), I will miss all of you fine young men. I hope you enjoy the gifts and Merry Christmas…and…well uh, Merry Christmas." He sat down quickly with his head lowered discreetly hiding his moist eyes. I could tell that his abbreviated remarks were less than what he intended, but that is all that he was able say.

As the boys each opened their books they were sincerely enthusiastic with Earl's careful and specific selections. Once they had said their thanks, Daniel, (after reading Earl's inscription in his book), got up, crossed the room, and gave a surprised Earl a warm hug. Earl regained his poise and handed me a small package. I carefully opened the Christmas wrapping and there in a royal blue binding lying in neatly folded layers of white tissue paper was a immaculate first edition of "Tom Sawyer". Knowing a little about original works of Samuel Clemens I was certain that this book was easily a $ 10,000.00 gift. I held it with my mouth agape for several seconds before finally saying, "I cannot believe this Earl. This is so amazing. Thank you so very much?" I looked over at him as he sat in a complete Mark Twain pose; legs crossed, leaning back in his chair, and fingering his mustache. He looked at me grinning, and said, "I thought I would buy you something that I knew you would enjoy and remember me by… Open it up…read what is written on the inside." I carefully lifted the cover being so cautious. "It's not a baby Tom…just open it up". He said smiling broadly.

Inside of the cover were these words written in ink:

"From one Tom to another. One of dubious character and one with a deep understanding of what true character is. I'll leave it up to you to decide which accurately pertains to you." It was signed Mark Twain AKA: "The 'Earl' of Prose".

I got up walked over to him, and without hesitation he rose to his feet and I gave him a huge hug. I whispered, "Thank you my friend." As I pulled away and giving him a grateful smile I looked into the warmth of his eyes and seeing his delight knowing that he had truly touched me with 'his' book.

We sat back down and the room got very quiet…eerily quiet in fact until Seth suddenly pierced the silence.

"Dad, don't we have something for Earl?"

I feigned my wide-eyed surprise with my hand melodramatically over my mouth and I said, "Oh my God I almost forgot."

I got up and went into the dining room and returned sliding a big box across the carpet. It was wrapped in parchment colored paper covered with famous Mark Twain quotes we each had written on the outside with different colored markers. Earl smiled fondly at the home-made amateurish wrapping and then, looking at each of us, immediately started pulling the paper off the package. Once revealing the cardboard box underneath, Daniel handed him a knife and he cut the heavy tape on the flaps. As he peeked in the end of the box his eyes got big and then he looked up. "It's not a baby, Earl, open it up", I said with a smile so wide I could feel my face stretching.

He reached into the box and pulled out a canvas and leather suitcase. He had a look on his face that I had never seen before. He ran his hands over the brown leather handle, leather corners, and the two belt straps that buckled around the outside. A few moments later Chris said, "You better look inside." Earl carefully clicked each latch open, unbuckled both belts and opened it up slowly. Inside, (each item was wrapped in a different Hawaiian print shirt), was a box of cigars, a triple flame butane cigar lighter, a leather-covered hip flask, and a quart of Elijah Craig 21-year-old bourbon.

He was visibly moved by it. The bourbon alone was $150.00 and you could tell he knew the value by the way he carefully handled the bottle. Earl suggested we share one drink together and Chris rapidly produced tall shot glasses for everyone, except me, of course, who received an ice cold Pepsi. We proposed a 'to your health and safe passage' toast and they all drained their glasses quickly except for Earl who closed his eyes and swirled it in his mouth savoring it completely before swallowing. The consensus was that it was the smoothest bourbon any had ever tasted, and Earl added with his lower lip quivering and in a voice unknown to the character of Mark Twain, "This bottle will only be enjoyed on special occasions and while thinking of all of you". He cautiously wrapped each gift back into its respective shirt, and carefully latched the suitcase, setting it close to his chair and gave it one final tender rub over the smooth brown leather corner. I caught his glance as he looked up with a sigh, and I knew he was overwhelmed.

We finished up a wonderful day indulging in several games of poker, euchre, and hearts, which Earl played and thoroughly enjoyed interspersed with a few breaks for a cigar and one more small taste of his "special" bourbon. After an early evening snack of barbecue sandwiches and homemade cheesecake, we decided it was time to get back home. Earl was going to have to repack everything using his new suitcase. We all said our goodbyes with each of my sons saying they would miss him and they all hoped he would return one day. Earl announced that once he got established in Florida, they could each come down there to see him in the tropical weather. Everyone shared genuine hugs before the front door finally closed, leaving a very special Christmas firmly in our hearts.

I parked in the driveway and without any words we unloaded the car. I was putting things away in the kitchen when Earl walked in, leaned against the doorway, and said. "I just want you to know that your family made me feel like one of them today, and I will not soon forget their generous feelings. Every gift I received means more that I can tell you Tom. Thank you for this day of family; it was so very special. He paused as if he wanted to try and add something, but instead he said with a small quake in his voice, "I am bushed and need to get some sleep. I think I'll take a smoke and then turn in."

I looked at him also wanting to say something significant to cap such a meaningful day, but all I could muster was a meager, "Okay. Well I'm glad you enjoyed everything…I'll say goodnight then".

He turned to leave the kitchen and said, "Please make sure I am up by 7:30?" As he disappeared out of the doorway I said behind him, "I will…Merry Christmas Earl". I could hear him say quietly as he closed the front door heading out for his last smoke of the day, "A Merry Christmas indeed".

December 26, 2014

I woke up early having slept better than I had in weeks. A very unique Christmas was unfortunately over and I exhaled a deep sigh knowing that it'll be 364 long days before another arrives again, and without Mark Twain to share in its happiness. It is rather appropriate that Earl is leaving on a day that feels so dreary compared to all of the ones leading up to yesterday's climax of good times, love, and unusual friendship.

The day is dawning slowly but judging by the first peek of morning light it will be a nice day for travel. I looked at my watch and saw that is was 7:20. I hurried into the kitchen and started breakfast. I put Chris's breakfast casserole from yesterday onto a plate and put it into the microwave waiting to start it until the toast was finished. The coffee was brewing when I went to Earl's door and quietly knocked. "Time to get up, breakfast will be ready in about five minutes." Returning to the kitchen I heard the toaster so I started the microwave. Stirring a bit of cream into his coffee I sat it down on the table in front of the spot that had become his for the last eight months. I no sooner got the steaming mug of his favorite 'Grounds for Thought' blend on the table when Earl entered the kitchen completely dressed.

"I didn't know you were up already", I said surprised to see him.

"I couldn't sleep so I have been up finishing some writing since about three a.m. Everything smells great, anything I can do to help?"

"Nope, just have a seat and enjoy…it's all ready."

I sliced his toast and put a bagel into the toaster for me before taking his plate to the table. He thanked me and I returned to retrieve the bowls of fruit from the counter and put them on the table. I am going to miss seeing him sitting at the table with a fork in one hand and a knife in the other both pointing up in anxious anticipation. I have never seen anyone outside of cartoons actually posture like that waiting for their food to be served. Possibly that was typical in Twain's time, but, in any case, it was amusing to see him looking towards the stove with his eating weapons cocked and at the ready. I smiled.

As we peacefully ate our breakfast he mentioned again how much he appreciated and enjoyed spending Christmas day with my family and me. "It felt so natural, sincere, and…..." He trailed off without finishing. I could tell by his condensed disposition that he was in fact quite stirred and couldn't finish his statement or elaborate more without being pushed to tears. I smiled to myself knowing that a our relaxed, family-style Christmas, combined with a farewell party of sorts, was without a doubt a great success and exactly what we needed to do to properly send someone of Earl's earned importance on his way.

Although he is leaving the warmth and comfort of my home I feel that I am sending him on his journey knowing that he is fondly cared about and will be sincerely missed. I assume his likable and exaggerated curmudgeonly nature will garner him friends just as rapidly in Florida as it has everywhere. I shouldn't fret about his welfare. It's not like I am sending a child off to college five states away.

This isn't his first train-ride to a strange place, he'll do fine. "He better do fine", I said to myself.

I rose from the table as he went out to have one last smoke before leaving. I looked behind him as the door closed. His new suitcase was setting in the foyer, his wool coat draped over it, and his signature white Panama hat balanced on top. His old valise sat next to it looking tired and weary, wrapped with a worn leather belt. Staring at his bags by the door they appeared like the shoes of a runner poised in the starting blocks, and that representation instantly solidified that he **is** leaving…and soon.

He came back into the house and said that we should probably get on the road shortly. I nodded and turned to go brush my teeth as he nervously paced in the foyer, either because he was worried of being late or the longer he remained here the harder it would be to leave. I hurried from the bathroom knowing that he was anxious to get on the road. When I came back into the room he was gone. I heard his quiet voice delicately drifting from the living room. I took a step closer rising up on my tiptoes to see over the high back of the leather chair. He was down on his knees talking to his faithful friend Lalo who was squirming on the carpet under Earl's soft caresses. "You better be a good boy while I'm gone. You hear me? I am really going to miss you, little buddy. You take good care of Tom, he loves you too you know. He is a good man and knows how to treat a good friend." As he started to stand up I quickly slid back into the foyer looking the other way as not to be discovered eavesdropping on his private farewell to his favorite cat.

We silently put on our coats and each of us picked up a bag, walked out of the house door, slowly moving across the porch that had hosted many fine talks, and stepped out into a sunny winter day. We put the bags into the back or the car being very careful with Earl's new suitcase. As the hatch closed and latched, we each opened our doors and unhurriedly got in. The trip from the house and into the car seemed to scroll in slow motion as if every moment was worth noting in its entirety. Leaving any movement, no matter how small out of his departure might diminish its impact. Once the doors were closed, the long journey to the car was final. I looked at him sitting there gazing straight ahead and asked, "Well, are you ready?" Without turning he wordlessly nodded. I backed out of the driveway slowly and we were off to the train station 25 miles away.

We arrived in Toledo after what seemed like an incredibly short ride. The trip yielded little conversation other than small talk about the weather and the traffic before we left Bowling Green. It was so uncomfortably quiet that I put a CD in the player and absently listened to the music the last few miles. There were several cars in the dismal parking lot, which I assumed translated into many travelers as well. I was not wrong; the run-down Amtrak station was bustling

[298]

with people coming and going. There were a few groups standing in small circles laughing, touching, and exchanging hugs and kisses until they dispersed and went their separate ways. Earl and I were unduly somber and still as we both stood against the discolored wall as if we were waiting for the coffin of a dear friend to arrive.

Finally I couldn't stand the sour gloom any longer and I said, "You do know that life will not be the same with you gone. Who am I going to scold for smoking in the house or tearing the paper into a million pieces?" I said with a laugh. "Who is going to sit on my porch and agree with my political rants? Or aggravate my kitties just for the fun of it?"

He turned to me with a child-sized shy smile and said, "It did get familiar didn't it?" I returned a satisfied grin as I looked up at the clock noticing it was nine-forty. His train was scheduled to leave and 9:55 so I suggested that we should head downstairs to the platform. It was unseasonably warm so it wouldn't be too uncomfortable standing in the unheated, but covered boarding area. I looked for the stairway leading to tracks 5, 6 and 7, and we walked down joining the assembled crowd saying their goodbyes amid the strong smell of diesel exhaust.

We stood there silently waiting for the boarding of passengers on the Jacksonville, train. Earl was looking down past the side of the idling train cars following the shadowy tracks that extended out of the darkness of the soot covered terminal turning into two shining silver arcs in the morning sun. He looked up at the superstructure supporting the rusted corrugated steel roof with the scrutiny of a building inspector. He tied his right shoe…twice. Only once after we reached the lower level did he look toward me, and then only to nervously flash a very brief smile before looking away.

Once people started to move towards the train Earl started to fidget nervously so I suggested that I should get going. We stood there looking at each other not knowing what to say when out of my mouth I heard myself utter, "I never had a friend like you before." He looked me right in the eyes and warmly replied in a voice different from his preferred character, "That goes for me too. I have known a lot of people, but you are the only one who dug deep enough to try and find the guy hiding beneath Twain's costume." I was about to reply when he bent down and from behind the leather strap holding his old suitcase together he pulled a manila envelope. Handing it to me he said again in that same unfamiliar voice, "Maybe this will help you better understand. Thank you for everything Tom, I will never forget the time I spent here or all the great talks we shared." He

[299]

reached out, grabbed me, and after a swift awkward hug he gathered up his bags. Without saying another word he stepped up and into the train. I stood there watching his white hat bobbing in the yellow light of the car as he walked down the aisle and sat in a seat on the other side of the train. After standing there a moment wondering if he would look back or wave I slowly turned, walked up the stairs, and through the depressing lobby leading to the exit and onto the street. I left feeling like I had just been filmed in a typical farewell scene from a 1940's movie.

———

The Final Scene:

'Supporting actor says a quick goodbye on the train platform to his brother, (the lead actor), who is going off to war. He stops at the stairs leading up to the terminal and lights a cigarette. He blows out the match with an exhale of smoke and looking back toward his brother in uniform who is walking quickly to catch the moving train carrying his leather and canvas officer's bag. As his brother disappears into a cloud of steam and as the train chugs out of the station he tips his hat to the departing train affectionately and disappears up the stairs.'

--Fade to black...THE END...Run credits—

———

I vaguely remember making my way back to my car while clutching the envelope tightly under my arm. Inside the car I opened the flap just enough to see that there was more than one handwritten page, and while closing it I, too, hoped that its contents would indeed allow me to 'understand'. I laid it carefully on the seat where the previous passenger, its famous author, had sat not long before.

I left the rough, cracked, and pothole-riddled parking lot with Eric Clapton singing "Goodnight Irene" straining sorrowfully from the CD player. The odd but fitting accompaniment of the lonesome wail of a train whistle ferrying escaping people away from this dreary station blended perfectly into the sad waves of the melody as I drove back home alone.

December 30, 2014

Several days have come and gone since I returned from the train station and Earl's envelope is still lying on the kitchen table where I left it. Resting by the very spot where he always sat, it summons me to look inside. It seems to have been waiting for some ceremonious opening since it was laid there. It is so ironic that for nine months I have casually asked, kindly poked, stealthily hinted, and finally badgered him to explain some things to me, and now that the answer probably lies only a few feet away and I am hesitant to open and read it.

"You were in such an all-fired hurry to dig into his life because somehow it was so important for him to reveal it to you". I said to myself. "You, who are you anyhow? You are just one person who has crossed his path, but you had to be the one to run him off with all of your prying questions under the pretext that it would be good for him to open up. Why couldn't you just be content having someone live here who was fun and entertaining without sticking your meddling nose into business that didn't concern you?"

I stood by the table feeling guilty and looking sadly at an envelope that I

[301]

certainly wanted, but was embarrassed to have. Why couldn't I have simply settled for playing along? Having a famous writer from the 1800s live in my house and share experiences with me in a way that I couldn't possibly get from anyone else should have been enough. I had to push for more when he clearly didn't want to provide more. The longer I looked at the envelope the more disgusted I got with myself. I had simply become an ordinary nosey guy, who behind the guise of friendship and concern had successfully forced a nice person away with my intrusive need to know his 'whole story'.

The envelope was curled slightly from being held so tightly under my arm as I left the station and the partially open flap was curled upward resembling a smile. While I stood there looking for a reason or a sign to open and read it, I quickly rationalized that a smiling envelope could only be taken to mean one thing. I picked it up and without delay pulled the pages onto the kitchen table, and I slowly slid down into my chair and began to read.

Christmas night 2014

Dear Tom,

I have known for a long time that somewhere along my journey I would probably have to explain to someone why I assumed Mark Twain's identity with such unwavering devotion. I think I knew after our many talks early on that it would most likely be with you that I would eventually share my story.

From the beginning you balked at calling me Mark, Sam, or Mr. Twain. You insisted on calling me 'Earl' after my presumptuous introduction as "The Earl of Prose". Your childlike imagination allowed you to play along much better sometimes than I think you realized, but you never for one minute accepted my character without also noting that there was someone else hidden beneath. In all of the years I have been living this "act" on the road, you were the only one who consistently cared enough to not just blindly accept it. All my quick quotes and mannerisms entertained and satisfied you for the moment, but you frequently listened with an eyebrow-raised curiosity, and with sincere affection, to take a deeper look.

I can only guess that you feel like you might have helped to push me on my way with your occasional probing questions, etc., but the truth is I am not ready to become Jon Marshall again anytime soon. I will continue to live as Mark Twain for as long as I live, because that is the only way I __can__ live.

So here is my story. This will cover what I want to say and any details I did not think of probably shouldn't have been written anyhow.

As I have disclosed already, my given name is Jon Marshall, and I am a 66 year-old Viet Nam veteran, a Mark Twain impersonator, a lover of all kinds of music, a long-time, devoted appreciator of women, a onetime owner (if one can say owner) of three wonderful cats, a writer of sorts, and a widower of a wonderful woman who breathed new life into me when I thought mine was over.

When I returned from the war some of my wounds were not as visible as others, as you well know being a veteran yourself. I was suffering from post traumatic symptoms that were unfamiliar to most V.A. doctors at that time, but manifested into serious issues making acclimating back into civilian life impossible. My drug addiction that raged while deployed in Viet Nam subsided once I returned to Walter Reed and began a 12-step program. But, the grip of addiction paled in comparison to the next battle that lay ahead.

Upon my return I was unable to talk, and when I say talk, I mean that literally. From the time of that attack in Viet Nam until I was sent home, I never spoke or felt that I would utter a single word ever again. It took months of therapy to learn how to make the simplest guttural sounds and then several more months to actually attempt words.

The dilemma was that when I finally learned to speak again, I stuttered so badly that talking clearly was virtually impossible. During those many months of working with a therapist, she was able to slowly get me to read aloud from childhood books that I enjoyed and was familiar with. After about a year and a half of dedicated daily sessions, I could occasionally read without a constant stutter.

Tom Sawyer and Huckleberry Finn were the two books that we used that allowed me to sometimes read without severely stuttering. I could never speak in a normal conversation without being overcome with frustration trying to force the first single word out. I wrote things down hoping that I might read them aloud as I had the portions of those books, but that trial had little lasting results. Reading passages aloud was still my only success. Conversational speaking using just the words formed in my head was still impossible.

[303]

I ultimately got a job in a very noisy plant where the workers consistently needed to write notes to communicate with each other, and that was a perfect fit for me. I was able to hide my condition for a long time, avoiding the break room or other situations where I might have to talk to someone. It is amazing how long you can go without ever saying a word if you have to.

I eventually married my therapist, and for years she worked patiently with me each night at home trying to develop my speaking skills. We found quite accidentally one night when I was showing off while reading from Mark Twain, I didn't stutter. And, if I took on his character complete with accent, perceived mannerisms, etc. I could speak just as clearly as anyone while using my own words. I experimented with impersonating different people and actors and the result was confusingly depressing. My ability to carry on a normal conversation clearly when I mentally assumed the person of Samuel Clemens was astonishing. All I had to do to avoid those terrifying moments of not being able to speak intelligibly was to envision that I was Mark Twain reading or quoting something he wrote.

I bought every Twain book ever written and read them doggedly over and over. I found many pictures of his clothes, studied the way he stood, his mannerisms, and closely duplicated every detail as best I could. The more I studied him the better I became at speaking. After a couple of years portraying him at parties, social gatherings, and in the company of a few close friends, I was asked to perform my impersonation for a theater group's annual banquet. I nervously practiced for weeks and for the first time since that mortar attack in Viet Nam stole my young voice, and I was on that stage with my cigar in my right hand, my lapel in my left, I actually felt closest to the person I once had been. At that moment I was most confident and the applause confirmed I was apparently also pretty amusing. The night was not only a success because I hadn't stuttered, but also showed me a path to being happy while doing something I enjoyed.

I don't know if the comfort I felt being Mark Twain simply came from the early lessons of learning to speak by reading his books out loud, or if it was just easier to be him than it was to be me. I really don't care much about the "chicken or the egg" question that lingers behind how I finally returned. The important thing is that I finally came home from Viet Nam. I was just so happy to have some type of outwardly normal life again. My existence today might not be typical by anyone else's standards, but it is as full as it needs to be for me and a whole lot better than it was in 1970, so I simply accept it.

When my wife died in 1996, I was able to talk to the many people who attended her funeral by merely using the same tools she and I discovered together. I imagined that I was Mark Twain and she was my lovely bride Olivia. That day and the many evenings I have performed in character before and since, have given me the courage to keep moving forward.

[304]

Living With Earl

She is the one who patiently walked me forward from that trembling young war veteran who couldn't utter one understandable word to a man who now can speak in front of hundreds. I have a life today, even though it might appear to partially belong to someone else, and I owe it all to her and to Samuel Clemens fascinating and assumable character.

I have occasionally attempted to wear other conventional clothes, but it felt incredibly un-natural and was too stressful. It is just much easier and I am so much more at ease being a complete Mark Twain in manner and dress. Since there are no direct surviving relatives to Samuel Clemens, my assumption of his personage hurts no one and allows both him and me to live on spreading his words and philosophy happily to eager people wherever we roam. Being such a conspicuous character has forced me to communicate more often than the average person, which of course helps keep my speaking skills and confidence sharpened.

So now you know the whole story, and why I had to leave. When I feel people are getting too close or I feel poised to lower the screen that keeps me comfortably hidden, I need to go somewhere new. Besides, sympathy doesn't rest too well on me, it never has, and I know you well enough that you couldn't help extending it to me. I am fearful of what might happen if I am forced to deal with things differently than what has worked so well for over 40 years. Could I revert back into that speechless, shell-shocked boy again struggling to get a word out? I don't know, but I do know that I cannot risk the possible trauma of being someone other than my rescuer, Mark Twain. For years he has allowed me to contentedly dwell within him giving us both a new life. If I am hiding from myself, it is only to survive, and I can easily accept that without any guilt. Together we make a pretty convincing portrayal and one that has paid me handsomely with a sometimes lucrative living and the freedom to speak.

I have allowed you to get closer than anyone ever, and because of that it makes you a lasting friend. Please know that our talks were always between Tom and Jon. Even though I had to always return to character doesn't mean that you weren't talking to or reaching ME. When you talked, Jon heard you, and he answered you sincerely as himself even though at times he was playing the outward role of Twain to the hilt. Once we were well acquainted you were wholly in Jon Marshall's company in all of our conversations. My views on politics; women, or racism, while sometimes resembling Twain's, are completely my own. I simply used an appropriate MT quote to finalize our exchange and still appear in character. Just know one thing; Twain's inability to be humble is absolutely the most enjoyable part of being 'him'.

Do not blame yourself for my leaving as it was bound to happen. Your concern and recurrent questions finally pushed me to a point that I had to tell someone who I knew would truly understand the pain and also the triumph that my wounds from the war eventually spawned.

We will stay in touch Tom.

Warmest Regards,

Jon Marshall…AKA Earl/ Mark Twain

p.s. I hope to one day return for a visit. Bowling Green, Ohio feels more like home than anywhere I have ever lived.

I slid the papers back into the envelope, wiped my eyes with the sleeve of my t-shirt, and went to find my 'first edition' of Tom Sawyer given to me by Mark Twain himself.

Acknowledgements

To my Wife Beth, by allowing to be excluded from all parts of this writing it forced me to keep my entire concentration on Earl and Mr. Twain.

To Sue Ann Ladd, for a cover drawing that brought Earl to life.

To my sister Pat Newman, your tireless editing was incredible. I hope I got it mostly right.

To Bill Newsted, for his friendship and expert assistance with design.

To Judy Fitzwater and *Jennifer Marsh*, your instruction, character, and help were more than inspiring.

To Sally Ortiz and Renee Cristen, my partners in a class that nurtured me beyond words.

To Pat Szymanowski, my enthusiastic "test reader".

And finally, to all of the loyal facebook friends who encouraged me to put my daily reflections of 'Earl' into something more durable.

Tom Lambert